SCAR THE SKY

SCAR THE SKY

A NOVEL

J. TODD SCOTT

CROOKED LANE

NEW YORK

Books should be disposed of and recycled according to local requirements.
All paper materials used are FSC compliant.

Published in the United States by Crooked Lane Books, an imprint of
The Quick Brown Fox & Company LLC.

Crooked Lane Books and its logo are trademarks of The Quick Brown Fox & Company LLC.

Library of Congress Catalog-in-Publication data available upon request.

ISBN (hardcover): 979-8-89242-309-0
ISBN (paperback): 979-8-89242-316-8
ISBN (ebook): 979-8-89242-310-6

Cover design by Emily Mahar

Printed in the United States.

www.crookedlanebooks.com

Crooked Lane Books
34 West 27th St., 10th Floor
New York, NY 10001

First Edition: September 2025

The authorized representative in the EU for product safety and compliance is eucomply OÜPärnu mnt 139b-14, 11317 Tallinn, Estonia,
hello@eucompliancepartner.com, +33757690241

10 9 8 7 6 5 4 3 2 1

For Delcia

Welcome home . . .

Contrary to the common expression, lightning can and often does strike the same place twice.

NATIONAL GEOGRAPHIC

Bolt From the Blue

THERE ISN'T A cloud in the sky when Andi Ellis is struck and killed by lightning.

Ten miles away, over in Barrenton, light rain falls beneath a leaden ceiling of westward drifting nimbostratus, amorphous gray sheets barely glowing from within. But in Dupont, out by the field hockey pitch where Andi stands, the heavens are clear, the late summer sun high and hot and so bright you gotta wear shades.

Andi's blue eyes are hidden behind a fancy new pair of tortoiseshell glasses with bottle green lenses, and she's smiling, laughing, still more than a little hungover from an impromptu birthday bar crawl the night before. She's just turned twenty-six.

She's making jokes, and not kindly ones, with best friend and fellow teacher Joyce Madras about *another* teacher, that weird new substitute hire Max Conroy, when the one-inch-wide bolt, traveling at 186,000 miles per second, superheated more than 55,000 degrees—hotter than the sun itself overhead—pierces her heart.

Joyce will say later that for a few moments, surely no more than two or three heartbeats, Audrey Ann Ellis seemed to almost shine *inside out* with a horrible, black light.

She *burned*.

Joyce herself flies back four feet, hair smoking, skin tingling, ears ringing.

Most of Andi's clothes—a Halestorm T-shirt and khaki shorts—blast off her body, and the iPhone in her back pocket fuses into a knotted fist of plastic, silica, and ionized glass.

Those brand-new glasses splinter and snap and fly from her head, the lenses spiderwebbing. And the crystal face of her grandaddy's old watch, the one he wore in the skies over Hanoi, cracks, and the hands turn black and stop at exactly 2:29 PM.

Tossed and tumbled like rolled dice, Andi lands several feet away, where she lies face down and very, very still until the crowd watching the W. T. Dupont High Cavaliers junior varsity girls field hockey team starts screaming and yelling and running in every direction away from the impact.

Only Max, that weird new math substitute in his first semester at Dupont, runs toward Andi.

Max allegedly knows CPR from a storied stint in the military, yet his hands are shaking as he hammers at Andi's bare, ashy skin, where Lichtenberg figures—the branching burn pattern with feathery limbs, like a tree—radiate across her chest in ruddy lines.

He tries for two minutes and twenty-nine seconds to bring Andi back from the dead.

At last she coughs out a thick, bloody gout of ash and smoke, her heart reluctantly starting up again like an old car engine turning over, just as a Cooke County ambulance appears, rumbling across the manicured playing fields, big wheels chewing up abandoned drink cups, folding chairs, and sunglasses.

By the time it rolls to a stop next to them, Max has taken off his T-shirt to cover Andi's naked body and is holding her trembling hand.

* * *

In the immediate aftermath of the event—that's all anyone will ever call it—Andi can't remember much and doesn't want to talk about what little she does.

A black light . . . a black burning light like a dark, dying sun inside her heart.

She experiences all the expected symptoms, pain and dizziness, muscle weakness and seizures, a persistent ringing in her ears, so much so that when she turns the latest Halestorm album as loud as it will go, the sound still seems subdued, muffled, as if wrapped in gauze. She finds she can barely sleep or even concentrate for more than a few moments at a time and even when she closes her eyes, white and black flickers spark against her shut lids, like the constant flashes of old cameras or distant heat lightning hidden by clouds.

That black light.

Her skin feels slick and shiny and taut to the touch, like it doesn't fit her right, as if she's borrowed it from someone or something else. And her heart feels weird too, as if out of rhythm from the world around her.

In the quiet dark and solitude of her apartment, she picks through her blackened and ruined clothes, gently touching again those melted things that used to be her iPhone and her grandaddy's watch, perpetually stopped now at 3:32.

She often also finds herself standing naked before her bathroom mirror, tracing the burn scars radiating like lacy spiderwebs over the gentle curve of her left breast down the rest of her body. Runs hands across those alien petroglyphs, those Lichtenberg figures, the so-called *lightning trees.* Even days later, long after they were supposed to disappear, they still feel too hot to touch. Dozens of pinprick holes on the soles of her small feet still bleed, as well as a couple of bigger indentions, round as quarters and tender to the touch, deep enough to measure with the tip of her finger.

When she turns off the bathroom lights and stares at her bare body in the dark, she swears that she *glows*, those lightning trees blooming on her skin flickering with their own dark, innate light.

The open, empty sky scares her now. Forecasts calling for rain make her cry uncontrollably. She fears she's going crazy.

She researches online about other lightning strike survivors like herself, the *Lazarus syndrome*, those who died yet were somehow spontaneously revived, and she re-ups a lapsed script for Luvox to steady her nerves.

But not before she starts seeing ephemeral glowing motes out of the corners of her eyes—ghosts, haunts, luminous will-'o-the-wisps—call them what you want. Constant companions she can't avoid, tiny black lightning bolts she can't blink away.

The immediate aftermath turns into several weeks, then six months. Andi's father had run out when she was nine, and she's long been estranged from her mother, making it all too easy to ignore her handful of increasingly sporadic entreaties. But soon enough, the generous gifts and concerned calls from friends and associates dwindle, even from Joyce Madras. And although the administration at W. T. Dupont is more than solicitous, insisting her position will still be there whenever she's ready to return to the classroom, the truth is the world is moving on without Andi Ellis, and she knows it.

She knows the stories about her are already circulating, changing with each breathless retelling, branching further and further from the truth like the Lichtenberg figures on her skin. Empathy turning into pity and fascination, fact into fiction, until she's little more than an urban legend, a myth. Until even Andi isn't sure what to believe anymore.

The only person who persists in trying to reach out is Max Conroy, although she avoids his calls too, until late one night in a moment of exhausted weakness, even his voice is better than the ringing in her ears, the flashes of light in her eyes, the thoughts in her head. And maybe she owes him that much. He brought her back to life, after all.

He speaks only briefly about what he saw the day she was struck and died, as unwilling to revisit it as she is. But he tells her how her skin was on *fire* when he first touched her, leaving them both wreathed in the steam smoking off her body. How in that one moment he thought or imagined or dreamed of a tiny, liminal jolt, like a last spike of the sky coursing through her, jumping to him. How it closed some mystical circuit, somehow changed him too, *merged* them, his heart beating for hers. Swears to her that it granted him the strength to save her.

And he tells her how she looked so beautiful lying there on the ground, surrounded by all that fiery light. Like a burning angel falling from the sky. He claims not to be a religious person, doesn't believe in God or any higher power, at all, but quotes her a Bible verse—

His appearance is as bright as lightning and his skin as white as snow.

Max starts calling her his *lightning angel* and although the two of them have almost nothing in common—don't like the same music or movies or TV shows; have no interest in the same politics or religion or art or literature; aren't even close to the same age—they share one undeniable bond.

He held her life in his hands.

* * *

Andi doesn't return to W. T. Dupont and neither does Max.

She can't or won't shake the trauma of that day in September, all the lingering aftereffects, real or imagined. And Max is the one constant who doesn't ask her or push her to, even if most days she feels less like his beautiful lightning angel and more like a lightning bug trapped in a Mason jar, her life nothing more than constant, flickering motion, although she isn't going anywhere at all. She needs true, clinical help, but Max reminds her that what she's experienced, what she is *still* experiencing, is nothing short of a miracle, a life-altering stroke of fate most people will never be able to grasp, much less appreciate.

But eventually, Andi discovers there *are* others out there like her too, tiny groups and communities who've accepted the limits of what modern medicine or science can explain, who've somehow come to terms with their inability to simply heal or move on.

Survivors.

And although Max is troubled by the flurry of personal emails and messages she shares online and worries about her meeting a group of strangers in person, more than a year after the event, she sells her car and dumps her apartment—Max is living with her by then—and the two of them leave Virginia in Max's white Jeep Grand Cherokee.

And once they're gone, much as Andi predicted, the stories about her—her *and* Max—take on a life of their own. They grow roots and branches, spreading like a great tree, like creeping kudzu, like more Lichtenberg figures. Allegedly, the grassy spot where she was struck stays perpetually barren, and no clock or TV ever works quite right again in her old apartment. It becomes a rite of passage for some freshman to come to school every year on Halloween dressed like the pretty, lightning-struck teacher, hair teased out in a grotesque, mad scientist display, clothes strategically torn and blackened. Rumors circulate that she and Max went all "Bonnie and Clyde," or joined a cult out west, if not started one of their own.

That's why it's such a surprise to Joyce Madras when seven years later Andi calls her.

* * *

The call comes out of the blue too, from a number Joyce doesn't recognize, to a number she had gotten after Andi last lived in the area.

But Joyce knows immediately it's her, that it's *Andi*, despite how her voice has changed, roughened, aged, over the years.

Joyce finds herself crying just to hear her old friend, who she remembers as being a vibrant young woman, fearless and fun. There was a light around Andi even then, where she could hold court in a bar and sing along with all the latest songs, a barely smoked cigarette floating in one hand and a never-empty beer in the other. Dark hair messy, makeup perfect, a smile on her lips. Andi was everyone's favorite teacher, but more than that, she was Joyce's best friend and hearing her again after so much time lost is bittersweet, amazing, heartbreaking.

Like hearing a ghost whisper your name.

Joyce has so many questions, a million of them, but most of all, she wants to apologize, to beg forgiveness. For not understanding, for not being more supportive or more mature, for not pushing harder to help. For not having done enough, all those years ago, whatever enough needed to be. For not being a better best friend.

Andi wants to apologize too, for the way she left, for all the things she was afraid she couldn't explain, for fear that no one would understand or believe her anyway.

But even now, after all this time, Joyce senses there are things Andi can't or won't say. Maybe Andi only called to hear an old friend, to *remember*, so they talk about everything and nothing, mostly about the past, Andi carefully avoiding much of what's happened to her during the intervening years, until Joyce finally asks about Max Conroy.

Andi tells Joyce she left him, that it didn't end well—bad enough he may come around looking for her. And when Andi confesses that it was risky to them both to reach out like this but worried it might prove riskier if she didn't, Joyce realizes Max was the main reason for this call all along. At least by calling, Andi hoped she could warn Joyce, so Joyce would know to be careful, to be alert . . . to keep her eyes open.

Because he will come looking, JoJo. He's going to come looking for me, now that I've finally gone.

Andi tells her not to bother writing down Andi's number, because it'll be changed by tomorrow. But before Joyce can ask Andi what the hell all this is about, and more importantly, why the hell she should be worried about Max Conroy, the line suddenly buzzes and zips and crackles.

Hums with static so vibrant, so loud, so *violent*, it almost makes Joyce drop her phone.

Oh my God, she thinks. *It's just like that day in September all over again . . .*

. . . the lightning . . .

. . . the lightning . . .

Despite all the weird distortion, she yells out for Andi, calls out to her, begs her, but can't hear a reply, can't make out Andi's last words or warnings . . . but does catch or imagine *another* voice on the line, faint, faraway, frightened.

A voice . . . just as panicked as Joyce.

And although Joyce Madras will never know for sure, or ever hear from Andi Ellis again, she'll forever swear that second ghostly voice was a *child* calling out again, again, again—

Momma . . . Momma . . . Momma . . .

A little girl crying.

Until the line goes dead for good.

Contrails

Part I

CHAPTER

1

Ajo, Arizona

Andi left before sunrise, the desert sky just catching dawn fire, making the three-hundred-mile round trip to Tucson in one day, and now sits on an old Phelps Dodge mine road east of New Cornelia, watching the road behind her swim in watery late afternoon light.

Cloudless sky above. Bright infinite blue beyond.

Empty.

She doesn't always go to Tucson, sometimes Gila Bend instead. That's only about ninety miles round trip, give or take—far shorter—but Gila Bend feels so much smaller too, leaving *her* feeling so much more visible, traceable, exposed. Her friend Stephen heads south of the border for supplies every now and then, but despite the two years she's holed up in New Cornelia, Andi still isn't comfortable making that crossing.

Stephen once said it's possible their whole little wayward community is already south of the border, but no one in New Cornelia has ever bothered to check a map—certainly not Bella or the others who've been here for a decade or more—and no one who might care about such legal or official things has ever come out to a look. Out here, the sun and the mountains and the low desert constantly blur the horizon, erasing all kinds of lines, hazing away every boundary.

The reason you hide out in the Sonoran Desert on the farthest edge of Arizona within the shadows of the Little Ajo Mountains and the Organ Pipe National Monument and the Tohono O'odham Nation Reservation is because it's the sort of place people don't come looking for anything.

Not only do the other New Cornelia residents almost never make the trek to Tucson or Gila Bend anymore, most also won't even hazard the much shorter trips to the rez or Ajo. True, there are only a couple of shops on the rez, mostly just a dusty, desperate casino next to a gas station off Highway Mile Marker 55. And Ajo is little more than one Circle K, an Olsen's Market, and old mine company housing that's been scooped up by snowbirds and retirees fleeing California. But even that's too much contact for some, allowing Andi to earn her keep in New Cornelia—and a few spare dollars as well—by running into the city for those things that can't be otherwise delivered or traded for.

Ajo does get its surprising share of visitors, artist types drawn to its raw, rugged, desert beauty and unique history; the grandly named Sonoran Desert Inn and Conference Center, built out of the bones of an old school; and the abandoned open pit copper mine that gave rise to the town.

Native Americans were digging hematite out of the low mountains circling Ajo for hundreds of years before Spanish explorers arrived on horseback. Ajo copper was once transported by ox cart across the desert, loaded up on steamers in San Diego, sent as far away as Wales. The veins were exploited in one way or another almost constantly—with varying degrees of success—for decades, and the land still bears the scars of those endless efforts and operations, all those dashed hopes and dreams, now just meaningless roads and crushed rock and rusting equipment.

The open tailings pit is a raw wound in the earth more than a mile across, more than a thousand feet deep, bottomed out by a bright blue pool of chloride water. To Andi, it looks like a great, glaring eye, staring up from below.

Watching, judging, waiting.

Once the mine shut down for good and most of the land and equipment was sold off, a company came in and put in a solar farm—21,000 photovoltaic panels—following the desert contours on the flanks of the pit. Andi has a clear view of them from her and Ruby's old single-wide trailer, and although the dark panels are designed to capture light, not reflect it, she still likes to imagine she can trace the sun's rise and fall across sky in all that shiny, black silicon.

Those panels don't keep the rain away; even the barren Sonoran desert gets some hellacious storms now and then. That's why she keeps the bright yellow StrikeAlert HD detector close on the carabineer at her hip, and another much larger one back at the trailer. But she still finds comfort in the thought of all that sunlight and heat held so close, so tight, like a closed fist. Like holding daylight, like holding summer, in your hand.

She checks the time on her cellphone, knowing Bella is already anxiously waiting for her. Visiting Bella is always a process—a lengthy, complicated, miserable process for both of them—after Andi's been to the city. But Bella bears it because of the Biscoff cookies packed in the cooler in Andi's backseat.

Andi bears it because she doesn't trust anyone else to look after Ruby.

Andi checks the time again, then the cracked digital on the truck's dash, still set for Central time. Neither her burner cell nor the dash clock are the same, or right, not even within an hour of each other. But she long got accustomed to doing this sort of math in her head, on the fly. She's been parked here for a good twenty minutes—and it's still twenty minutes more to New Cornelia's first trailer—with no sign of a car behind her.

Out here, with all the long sight lines and empty scrub, that's usually enough.

The old F-150's AC gave out last year, so she has the windows rolled down, a bare breath of breeze moving through the cab. The wind isn't doing much to cool her, but she's fine with it. She's gotten used to the constant calefaction, even loves it in a way—that perfect, blue, cloudless sky, marred only by the occasional circling turkey buzzard. Ajo gets about eight inches of rain a year, with three hundred sunny days. Temperatures soar well past one hundred in the summer, a parched heat so unforgiving that it sucks all the moisture out of the air, turns the sweat on your skin to salt and dries the tears in your eyes before they have a chance to fall.

Incalescence so immense and powerful it's like a great, fiery hand squeezing your lungs and heart.

Waylen likes to joke that your oven is a dry heat too, and you sure in hell don't want to live inside there. But for all his complaining, he doesn't leave. Not Bella or Stephen either, or Erwin and Leah or any of the others. None of them. *Not me*, Andi thinks. For many of those who've made their way to New Cornelia, there's nowhere left to go.

Andi plays with the pendant at her neck, a jagged pearlescent mineral that holds a greenish glow, a deep spark, deep within.

She, too, knows it's nearly impossible to outrun every storm, every cloud in the sky. But she keeps trying, and all the way *out here* . . . at the edge of the goddamn world . . . is close as she's ever come.

Finally satisfied that the road's still clear, she slips the heavy, loaded Smith & Wesson she's been holding in her lap back beneath her seat and aims the truck toward home.

CHAPTER

2

New Cornelia, Arizona

Bella's created a kind of outdoor shower out of bee-hauling tarp and parchment paper and three five-gallon Home Depot buckets, two filled with hard water, one with hydrogen peroxide. A wooden plank, once part of an old Ikea dresser, holds a bar of canola oil soap and a well-used aluminum-free deodorant, as well as a folded set of Bella's old clothes.

Bella's scared of odors—well, that's one of her fears—including the outgassing of chemicals and solvents from clothes and even skin, scented hair products, gels, and lotions. The sort of stuff Andi herself hasn't worn or worried about in months. Like she isn't worried about stripping naked—everything but her pendant, never that—casually peeling off her own clothes out in the open, revealing her long-suffering body to the grit and heat and ferocious desert sun. There are few prying eyes out here anyway.

Andi doesn't hate her body anymore, not so much. Neither the wounds and stigmata she still carries nor the way she's been both hollowed out yet somehow tightened too, taut like a guitar string, like fucking steel wire. Her skin is ruddy now, almost dark, bronze and burned by the sun.

Andi only has to go through Bella's "decontamination" process when she returns from town. Bella's self-diagnosis is *neurasthenia*, a weakness of the nerves, a sensitivity to modernity. More than that now, Bella is allergic to everyone and everything beyond her beloved New Cornelia and the desert.

Everything seemingly except Biscoff cookies—a bittersweet hint, reminder, or simply a taste of Bella's life before she fled here.

Bella doesn't talk much about BNC—Before New Cornelia—and no one's sure Bella is her real name. But she is beautiful, stunning, and they can all agree on that, with her piercing green eyes and clouds of windblown, naturally gray hair.

If Andi is bronzed, Bella is *gold*. The years of sun and sand have cleansed her, permanently stripped her down to her essential elements, laid everything bare, leaving nothing superficial or artificial. Whoever she was before—BNC—is gone now, and there's only those green eyes and gray hair and warm husky laugh.

Even as sick as she is, even on those mornings when she's so pale that she's almost translucent, almost too weak to stand—mornings that have become more frequent, no doubt—Bella is a force of nature. She claims she can still smell smoke that lingers from the old, abandoned mine, sense distant desert rain two days before it falls, even hear the hum of Waylen's electronics—his damn electric *toothbrush*—more than two miles away.

But nothing about Bella's past or eccentricities matter to Andi. Bella might be afraid of the world outside of New Cornelia, a world of modern conveniences and lights and electricity, plastics and metal, gluten and MSG, doctors and diagnoses and in-patient hospital stays, but she is patient and sweet and gentle with Ruby, willing to watch her when Andi goes to town.

And Andi sympathizes. After all, Bella isn't wrong.

The world *is* a dangerous fucking place.

Andi finishes scrubbing off, making sure she thoroughly wipes down the cooler stuffed full of cookies with the hydrogen peroxide. She slips into Bella's clothes, an old T-shirt so threadbare it's like smoke on her skin, like faint fingertips grazing the back of her neck. When she arrived at New Cornelia, she wouldn't have been able to fit into it, but it billows off her now, ruffling in the light breeze, threatening to lift her skyward like a sail.

God, this place changes us, whether we want it to or not.

She grabs up the cookies and heads to the porch where Bella and Ruby are waiting.

* * *

If Bella is a pane of glass, transparent, seven-year-old Ruby is a little matryoshka doll, an infinite set of diminutive fairy tale princesses—painted, lacquered, intricate—each more mysterious and impossible to decipher than the next.

Once you think you have figured her out, there's another lurking beneath her pale blue eyes.

Andi loves her little girl but doesn't understand her, not at all. Not even close. They couldn't be more different in temperament or design, and though Andi attributes some—*okay, most*—of that to their self-imposed itinerant and nomadic lifestyle, to Andi's projected fears and her failures, it's still fair to say that Ruby's always been an enigma and likely always will be. A puzzle with both too many and too few pieces.

There's also those two other things: the secret Ruby carries that Andi's tried hard to deny, and the awful truth Andi still refuses to admit to herself, but that Bella (far more perceptive and sensitive in every way) seemed to intuit right away but has never voiced—

Andi never, *ever*, wanted to be a mother. And her beautiful daughter is a living, breathing, painful reminder of Andi's past life, as powerful and life-altering as the lightning bolt that struck her.

But Andi's love for her daughter is a nesting doll too, another always ready to reveal itself, infinite layers all the way down to what's left of her heart.

Now Ruby races by her with barely a look, heading toward the truck, full of the other treasures from Andi's trip. Andi watches her go, shaking her head.

"It's the dog thing, again," Bella offers.

"There's no dog in that truck."

Bella laughs. "I know that. *You* know that. But *she* doesn't. And that's the fun of being a kid, of still being so young."

"What? Constant disappointment?"

Bella smiles again, gentle, patient. "Surprise, *mija*. Hope." Bella waits as Andi wrestles the cookies out of the cooler and hands them to her. Bella doesn't want to touch the Igloo plastic, despite Andi's repeated scrubbing. "You were a kid once too." She eases herself down on the wooden porch, gently, slowly, unwrapping her treat. She's wearing a bottle-green sari skirt and a T-shirt, Fleetwood Mac 2009 Unleashed Tour. "And I promise you, there *will* be a dog one of these days. There should be."

"You going to let a dog stay here with her when I'm out running around?"

Bella thoughtfully chews a cookie and offers one to Andi. "I generally do find animals so much more agreeable than people. Had a collie once, if you can believe that. Just like Lassie. Oh my, what a pretty dog. Called her Stevie, in honor of our very own Ms. Nicks here." Bella plucks at her tee. "But no. I couldn't manage the dander now, the fur would ruin what's left of my lungs. And this place is so hard on dogs. Too hot, too many cacti, too many scorpions and snakes." Bella waves at the rusty landscape around them framed by the Little Ajo mountains. "Holes and washes everywhere. Remember Joanna and Drew Barbour?"

Andi had met them when she and Ruby first arrived, carrying everything they owned in her truck, both younger than her by a handful of years. He was into tech or finance, had large brown analytical eyes that were often sad or downcast, his whole face a frown. She suffered from fibromyalgia and anemia and axial spondyloarthritis and electro sensitivity, always wore big smoked sunglasses, inside and out. They'd read about New Cornelia, and Joanna was the impetus for their relocation from Seattle to the desert. But it never grew on Drew, who missed green trees and cool weather and rain, his friends and the life they were building there, BNC. They argued all the time. Only three or four weeks after Andi met them, ten months into their stay, they woke up and left one morning, abandoning their small plot and their expensive Airstream.

Suddenly *up and leaving* wasn't unusual. New Cornelia could be hard on people too.

"They went through two dogs," Bella says. "Little ones, dachshunds, I think. I know for certain Jo liked each one of those dogs more than she did Drew. Honestly, he didn't like *her* any better, not by the end. And he absolutely hated this place from the start." Bella closes her eyes and savors her cookie.

Andi says, "Well, I like it here."

"Sure, you're busy making a life. But Ruby, she's just marking time." Bella squints at something in the distance, where the sky meets scrub. "Drew never believed Jo, not *really*. He thought her illnesses were, well, all just up in her head. He wondered if she was *weak*. He loved her enough to come out to New Cornelia before finally resenting her too much to stay." Bella follows her first cookie with another, like a chain smoker. "So, like I said, you're going to get that girl a dog, and then you're going to get out of here. Because you can't keep her here or she's going to resent you too. She's special and beautiful, Andi, and you can't deny that. It's too lonely for her . . . and we're all just a little too crazy."

Now it's Andi's turn to laugh. "Don't say that. You're not crazy."

"Tell *that* to Drew Barbour."

Andi doesn't even bother nodding, as Ruby, who's finally accepted—again—there isn't a dog with a big red bow for a collar in the car, picks desultorily through the items Andi did bring back. Waylen's Irish booze and American beer. Stephen's plant magazines and books. Tabby's new CorningWare. Erwin and Leah's groceries, from their long and very detailed list, written out in Leah's precise and very beautiful script.

A sudden laugh carries up to Andi and Bella as Ruby finally finds the two presents Andi brought for her, a copy of *Luminous Living Things That Light Up the Night* by Julia Kuo—and a one-pound bag of peanut M&Ms.

Ruby's laughter is a living thing too, fierce and vital. *Alive.* A fleeting thing that Andi doesn't hear often enough. She keeps Ruby's hair cut boy-short, easier to take care of out here, dresses her in boy's clothes and hand-me-downs too, whatever Andi can pick up on her trips to town. There are lots of reasons and rationalizations Andi makes for these things, but there are times now when she doesn't recognize her own daughter or who she's becoming. A little girl living like a fugitive, who hasn't committed any crime at all.

Bella is right, Ruby isn't truly thriving out here. She's merely surviving, marking time, serving out a sentence she doesn't deserve. And even if that is good enough for Andi, it won't be good for Ruby, not for much longer.

"How do you feel?" Andi asks Bella.

"Oh, I'm going to feel all this later." Bella sees the apology in Andi's eyes and heads it off. "No, not your fault. It's just getting harder and harder to scrub the world off. There's just so . . . *much* . . . of it. But spending time with Ruby is worth it, and you too, just like these damn, silly cookies." Bella folds up the bag with reluctant finality. "And the others need you to make these trips. I'll be fine."

But *fine* means Bella might spend the rest of the day curled up on the worn couch in her trailer, shaking, dry heaving. A piercing headache turning screws behind her eyes, making her nauseous to even breathe, her thin walls closing in tighter and tighter, leaving her drenched in sweat, both hot and cold to the touch, head full of static. That's Bella's *fine,* but Andi has also seen Bella when it gets bad, truly bad, and that is so, so much worse. Andi hopes those cookies and Ruby are worth it.

"It's going to rain," Bella says, standing, stretching, sniffing the wind.

Andi looks at the cloudless sky, bright, blue, and smooth enough to throw a handful of sand off. "It's called *petrichor*, that earthy smell. Caused by ozone, and plant oils, this thing called geosmin, the very rain itself. The droplets carry ozone sparked by lightning."

"You know that because . . . ?" Bella gestures vaguely to Andi's bare, scarred arms.

"Sure, yeah." Andi stands too, whistling to Ruby that she's on her way. "Every rain droplet is like a tiny thunderstorm. Each one holds a lightning spark."

"A pretty thought. But you know, *mija*, I smell the rain *before* it falls. Before the storm comes."

Andi loves it that Bella calls her the affectionate *mija—my daughter*—so doesn't have the heart to tell her friend she's just catching the scent of a squall a few miles away, one just over the mountains and still unseen, parched earth opening wide like dusty arms to the humid air, releasing a cloud of decaying actinobacteria to the sky. With a good wind, that musky, rustic smell might carry for miles. Every minute of every day, rain falls over the world. There is always a storm somewhere.

Andi reaches over and hugs her. Bella squeezes back, her thin arms still surprisingly strong. Andi tugs at Bella's T-shirt. "Hey, did you really know Stevie Nicks?"

But Bella only winks and smiles, whistling a song that sounds familiar, like that smell of rain, before retreating inside her trailer.

CHAPTER

3

Lorman, Mississippi

LINNEA WREN HATES the rain, and it sure is raining like an angry son of a bitch right now.

The rain followed her and Rio out of New York, down to Charlotte, then to Atlanta, and eventually Nashville, where the trail went cold for two days before Rio made some calls, called in some favors, worked his special kind of magic, before they were up running again.

All because Abby Walden wanted to be a singer . . . wanted to be a *star*.

Linnea listened to William Walden's recordings of his daughter through the years, and she was no doubt good, far better than backyard karaoke. Had a sweet voice in the earliest ones, somehow shy and earnest, before turning sad in the later tapes. No, she was never going to be Nashville talented, but you couldn't tell that to a nineteen-year-old kid with stars in her eyes. And Senator Walden surely didn't, not after all those voice and guitar lessons, all the years of tears and drama, all of Abby's failures and setbacks.

A lifetime's worth for someone still so young.

She and Rio should've just started right off in Nashville, and Linnea guesses that they will argue about it later. Or *she'll* argue about it, maybe even get angry and a little loud about it—she's gotten better but at times is still a long, long way from good—while he'll just nod along quietly until her temper finally blows itself it out like a summer storm, like it usually does.

But not this biblical spring storm, which has dumped inches of cold water in their wake, flooding the nearby Mississippi River, swamping homes and freeways, causing power outages up and down the Eastern Seaboard.

God, she hates the rain, and what it sometimes uncovers.

* * *

She glances up from playing a game on her cellphone to see that Rio is finally waving her over.

He's standing beneath the awning of the Jefferson County morgue, finishing another cigarette with the county coroner, Jerry Lee. Adan Rio doesn't smoke, has *never* smoked as far as Linnea knows, but today he's suddenly a two-pack-a-day smoker, even if that isn't who he'll be tomorrow. Rio is a chameleon that way, speaks three languages fluently, maybe more, but his even better skill is *reading* people, having the knack of getting to know someone simply by putting them at ease. It isn't as much an act or a charade or mimicry as it is an effortless, uncanny ability to be *real*, somehow both genuine and studied, but also somehow never truly false. He's been smoking outside with the coroner for the last twenty minutes as if he's been smoking his whole life, protected from the deluge by the morgue's weirdly cheerful striped awning, patiently explaining what's brought a former federal agent and former cop both turned private investigators all the way from New York down to Lorman, Mississippi.

Explaining who they're looking for—and why.

And it's worked, because Jerry Lee is evidently agreeing to help them now, despite their lack of jurisdictional authority, despite the very real legal limits of their state PI licenses—and the very real trouble the coroner is risking for granting them this kind of access, given what they're here to see.

It isn't that Linnea can't be charming too, in her own way. She just brings other talents and abilities to her and Rio's partnership . . . or once did.

As Linnea opens the Explorer's door and catches a face full of icy rain, she spies Rio dropping his last cigarette to the damp pavement and stepping it out, before retrieving it and all the others and slipping them into his coat pocket.

He shakes his head and doesn't smile, and she knows what that does and doesn't mean.

After two weeks and almost two thousand miles, they've finally found Abby Walden.

* * *

She is somehow still pretty despite the days gone by and the things done to her.

Five-eight in her bare feet (unpolished toes). Shoulder-length blonde hair. Freckled skin that holds the faded remnants of last summer's tan, that somehow still seems alive, aglow, even beneath the morgue's harsh lights.

Found face up, blue eyes open, but closed peacefully now.

Linnea doesn't linger, just respectfully flips through the coroner's typed report and handwritten notes. Despite Jerry Lee's omissions, the questionable quality of some of his work and its hurried and perfunctory nature, she can't disagree with the man's conclusions, and that's what she'll tell Senator Walden when the time comes.

She takes her horrible pictures quietly and efficiently, without reverence, without much emotion.

It isn't that she isn't emotional. Words such as *difficult* and *volatile* and *explosive* used to be thrown around about her; there was a time when a scene like this would've provoked a whole kaleidoscope of . . . *volatile* . . . emotions. But that was all before those long, quiet months she spent recovering after Rio rescued her from that barn in Ruther Glen, first at NYU Langone, then Gracie Square, before finally returning from that enforced medical sabbatical with a newfound ability to fold her emotions down tight at the corners, keep herself perfectly smooth and squared away as a freshly made bed.

Like her Marine dad once said, you can bounce a quarter off her now. Her new talent, her own Adan Rio magic trick, is to outwardly *compartmentalize.*

The sight of a brutalized and abandoned Abby Walden infuriates her, and without a doubt later tonight she'll turn the hotel shower as hot as it'll go and stand underneath the scalding water to loosen tears that will likely never come, to dull the ever-present ache of wounds and scars that never goes away. But she's better equipped in the intimate immediacy of moments like these to hold on to her rising frustration and fury, to harness it, to focus it, to aim it. Her anger is a goddamn *laser* now, instead of a bomb.

Most of the time.

But even she finds it hard not to be shocked, not to gasp out loud, at the marks on Abby's hands. A kind of thermal burn pattern, a delicate feathering, running from the tips of the girl's ten fingers up her wrists, to the elbows. It takes a heartbeat or two before Linnea understands the image traces the very blood vessels themselves beneath the girl's skin, subcutaneous, as if the lifeblood inside Abby caught fire, blazing, burning free, an extravasation of red blood cells from the dermal vessels. Linnea has no idea about the type of pathophysiology at work here, can't even begin to explain *how* these markings were first made or are still present now, since there's no blood at all inside Abby Walden. Not anymore.

"I know," Jerry Lee says, noticing that Linnea's focused her iPhone on Abby's hands, firing off a series of close-ups. "Or guess I gotta say, I *don't* know." Jerry Lee is heavyset and deeply tanned, with small, dark eyes, and long, wavy, way-too-blond hair, both weirdly and wildly out of fashion. He looks like a badly aging guitarist in a southern rock band. Linnea knows he doesn't have a medical degree, that before his election to county coroner he worked as a funeral director for two decades, and still does when he isn't actively conducting death determinations for Mississippi. Jerry Lee doesn't have anything close to formal or even appropriate forensic training, but like Linnea, he's seen and touched lots of dead bodies. Too many. "Don't know how that girl got all those marks," he continues, "don't even know what to call them." He hesitates, shrugs, looks at his own thick, well-calloused hands. "Till just before the two of you showed up, didn't even know a name to call her by."

"Postmortem?" Rio asks from a corner of the room, where until that moment, he's been standing silently, arms folded, Carhartt jacket hiding tattoos inked all the way to both wrists. Abby Walden has tattoos too. A butterfly with giant wings on her shoulder, a tiny, laughing skull on her left hip, a rearing unicorn wearing a cowboy hat on her right.

Gently, Linnea pulls down Abby's lower lip, revealing *Dare Me* scripted there.

Her father told them she got it just before she left home and made no attempts to hide it from him.

Jerry Lee glances back and forth between Rio and Linnea, uncertain if Rio's question is directed at him. "Um, yeah, I'm guessing she got all burned up like that when she died. They brought her in as a suspected overdose, but that doesn't seem right."

No, Linnea thinks, *it doesn't.*

"But there wasn't nothing on fire where they found her," Jerry Lee adds. "Nothing scorched, least nothing I saw out there or read about later in the police report."

She was found a week ago at the North Fork Cole's Creek rest area, about forty miles away. Linnea and Rio were still in Nashville then, following the girl's ever fainter tracks.

Now Linnea can't take her eyes off those weirdly beautiful impossible marks, tattoos in their own way, or old photos, snapshots of a single furious moment in time. She can't begin to imagine the amount or type of heat or energy or pressure it would take to permanently imprint Abby's skin like that.

But she does know what they remind her of, images she is long familiar with, the sort of pictures it seems like she's been cataloging forever. Even her own. "Defensive marks," Linnea says aloud, as she slips her iPhone away and pulls the shroud back over Abby. "Defensive wounds, from when she fought off her killer."

* * *

Ten minutes later she and Rio sit in their rented Explorer, watching Jerry Lee lock up the morgue again as the rain sheets down. The coroner already has another cigarette tight in his lips.

"You pay him?" she asks.

Senator Walden doesn't have his seat anymore, or the same stature, but he still has a lot of money. And he told his two investigators to spend whatever it took to find his daughter.

"Yes. And well." Rio smells like smoke. It hangs on him, hangs between them. "I'll make the call to Walden tonight, after we get back to the hotel."

"No, wait till tomorrow. Let me get my thoughts down. Then we'll make the call. Together."

Rio nods and leaves it that. He can be warm, charming, and talkative, when necessary, but that isn't his normal temperature. Tends to revert three degrees cooler—quiet, a natural introvert—when it's just the two of them, when they're alone. He once told her it's because she makes him comfortable, at ease, and doesn't mind his silence, and he doesn't feel any pressure to fill it. But it's partly because she's always talked enough for them both. Rio enjoys an economy of expression, where she likes to overspend, overshare with him, all the damn time. He is stillness where she's constant motion, constantly *in* motion. Even now, even though her latest meds dial down so many of the images and voices clamoring for her attention, she likes to keep her hands busy, always messing with a pen or twiddling something. Needs to keep her brain busy too, so she doesn't dwell on or obsess over certain things.

"Do you want to talk about this?" he asks.

She had wondered when he was going to ask that, broach the possibility that lays before them beneath the shroud in the morgue. "No, not so much" is all she says. She sighs, her fingers gently grazing her eyelids, her temples, an unconscious gesture—a worrisome new habit that she can't seem to break. "But fine, what's your take on those marks?"

Rio studies the rain with his own dark eyes, finally says, "World Tree."

"And what's that?"

"Yggdrasil. The World Tree. It's from Norse mythology . . . cosmology. A kind of symbol. An immense, sacred tree, which connects . . . well, everything." He shrugs. "That's what it reminds me of, anyway."

A symbol. A totem. A message.

She shakes her head. "How do you even know something like that?"

He shares a subtle smile, one she knows all too well. "I read. A lot." He searches through his phone, texts her, her phone dinging gently a moment later. They each carry two phones, one for the world at large, one for each other. That was their system when they worked at the FBI and neither saw a need to change it, even when Linnea was healing. Even before either of them knew if she would ever work again. "Just sent you something about it."

She ignores it. "I'll check it out later. I need a shower. I need a drink. I need to call Dan and the kids."

Rio slips his phone away. Looks like he's going to say something and then changes his mind, says something else instead. "We're done here then." It isn't a question.

"We found what we were looking for." She starts up their Explorer. "It's time to go home."

CHAPTER 4

New Cornelia, Arizona

"THEY DIDN'T HAVE everything you'd ordered in yet, but hope these will tide you over," Andi tells Stephen, handing over a stack of gardening and horticulture magazines and books she picked up for him in Tucson. She watches as he dumps them on the table in his front trailer, fanning them out like playing cards.

After Stephen Chao had been struck by lightning, his world turned to colored lines.

He once told Andi it was like looking at everything through a weird, superimposed hologram, the very building blocks of the fictional Matrix. Before that, he claimed he never had much of a natural aptitude for math or computers other than video games, but after the bolt blasted a hole over his left eye, leaving him in a medically induced coma for two months, he woke to find his brain rewired, his thinking reduced to geometric figures and complex formulas.

He tackled the Riemann hypothesis, the Collatz conjecture. Music theory is math in a way too, and he suddenly found that he could play the piano, all that eye-hand coordination from gaming transferred to a Steinway's black and white keys. For a while, he also experienced a form of grapheme-color synesthesia, where certain numerals evoked colors. Four was green, five was red, seven was purple. Glowing lines and numbers, mysterious music, math in his head. It was like living inside a technicolor video game, trapped in the Matrix, all the time.

The amazed doctors in Chicago and then New York called it *savant syndrome*, a miracle, one of the most improbable, amazing cases they'd ever studied; maybe the most incredible case that anyone, anywhere, had ever observed or studied.

Stephen told Andi it was hell.

"This is great, so great," he says now, thumbing through one of the volumes, where brightly colored, impossible plants leap off the pages.

Andi glances at the pictures over his shoulder. "You really think you can get plants like that to survive out here?"

Out here is not only New Cornelia but also Stephen's second trailer, the one he's been converting into a tropical greenhouse the last few months. Cultivating carnivorous pitcher plants is his latest obsession, and he wears through his obsessions the way others change clothes, a by-product of a brain he doesn't understand anymore, supercharged by the lightning strike that nearly killed him. It blew out a hundred fuses in his brain, only to switch on a thousand more that no one knew existed, but that's something Andi knows about as well as anyone.

She and Stephen also have connections that no one else has, a friendship that existed before New Cornelia, another time, another place, far from here.

Texas. The Black Light Club.

"Not going to be easy, no doubt. But I'm making some progress." He shakes his head at her dubiously raised eyebrows, her glance out the window to the other mysterious trailer. "And no, I'm not ready to show anything off yet. But I will. Soon. Very soon."

She smiles, accustomed to his unveilings. "Speaking of soon, I already went by Erwin and Leah's, and they're talking about doing another potluck soon. You in?"

"Sure." He sweeps up his new books and magazines, making room for her to stay. "How was it? The trip?"

"Same. Good. Quiet." She doesn't elaborate and she doesn't have to, not to Stephen. "I gotta run though. Ruby's still in the truck, eating as many M&Ms as she can before they melt, and flipping through that book you recommended. She loves it."

The Kuo picture book is all about bioluminescence, the light of living things—fireflies, deep sea fish and squids, even fungi. Some in the Texas club used to swear they were bioluminescent too, that the lightning that nearly killed them not only left them physically scarred but also permanently *alight*, constantly aglow, forever bathed in a black foxfire only they could see, no different than the weird electricity-affecting auras that permeated them.

Andi believed that too—experienced it herself once upon a time—but not so much anymore.

Stephen once sat in a darkened room for five days straight, searching for that kind of light.

"I thought she would," he says

"Bella told me it's going to rain soon. That should be good for your plants, right?"

"Can be," he answers. He's got five 55-gallon rain barrels outside and somehow wired a whole autonomous sprinkler and light system for his greenhouse powered by a 12,000-watt Westinghouse propane generator. Andi has a small solar rig of her own to charge her constantly depleted phones and lighting strike detectors. Even Ruby's simple emergency cellphone can't hold a charge for more than five hours. "The water we get trucked in from Gila Bend is full of chemicals, salts, whatever. That's bad, and that's why we boil it. But rainwater tends to be acidic, has all kinds of bacteria and stuff also, so it's not great either. My plants need a carefully controlled indoor environment, so distilled or RO water is best."

"Then I guess you're going to have start trucking that in too," she says.

"I'll figure it out."

She smiles again. "You always do." She then touches his arm, gentle, lingering, discretely taking in his single-wide's stuffy front room and kitchenette, every available surface covered in stained books or notes or an abandoned or half-finished project. Old aquariums and computers and analog synthesizers. A hundred red fairy lights strung here and there. A massive chalkboard covered in equations and even a disassembled Peloton, reconfigured into a weird, druidic totem.

Dusty windows covered in aluminum foil or hand-me-down drapes.

She sees all his clutter, chaos, disorder, a mind laid bare or falling apart. That's also why she's *not* so discreetly searching his face and wrists for those telltale clues that he's about to lock himself away in the dark again, like he did before, when he got lost searching for the light inside him, trying to escape the Matrix. It was Andi who found him, who called the ambulance, who brought him back. Fortunately, he hasn't tried to *escape* like that since. Instead, after everything fell apart for them both in Texas, for the whole club, he followed her to New Cornelia, the only person in the world who knew where to find her, just as she's the only person in the world who knows where to look for him, when he gets lost inside his head.

She knows he probably loves her and hates that she can never love him back that way.

But she says, "I can't wait to see them, Stephen. I know they'll be amazing, beautiful."

CHAPTER 5

New Cornelia, Arizona

NIGHTFALL IS THE softest part of the desert.

The sky goes dark at the edges first, like a picotee flower, cerulean turning cobalt, then azure, then indigo. Then a handful of stars pop here and there against a deepening velvet background, flickering and wavering, like headlights on a mountain overpass.

But before even all that, the whole sky is a bouquet of wildflowers, rhododendron pink, lilium orange, gaillardia red and yellow. Bella once told Andi that desert dusk reminded her of a dancer's makeup, blush and brilliant; the heavens overhead powdery, hazy, colorful but muted too, gentle, even that furnace heat itself, even the hot, salted wind.

In the high hot of summer, New Cornelia routinely gets fourteen hours of raw, unforgiving sun a day. But even then, for the last hour and a half, just before the sun sinks for good below the mountains, the desert is almost tender, ephemeral, luminous, unlike anywhere else on earth.

Peaceful. Quiet. Amazing.

For that hour, Andi can almost forget where she is and why she's here.

* * *

Even after the long day at Bella's, the excitement of getting the new book and all that candy—or maybe *because* of those damn M&Ms—Ruby is a frenetic flare of energy getting into bed tonight, a cranky starburst.

Ruby's bedroom is at one far end of the trailer, Andi's at the other, balanced like a seesaw around the fulcrum of a tiny kitchen and living room, the whole thing about a thousand square feet and as long and straight as a bowling alley. There's a third bedroom for storage, although Andi doesn't have much, just some boxes and luggage. Andi and Ruby arrived with little, and nearly three years later haven't accumulated much. Few decorations, hardly any personal effects, no family pictures.

But Andi's done her best to liven up Ruby's room, even if only to hide the small Wyze camera in the corner or the Mr. Goodbar swing-away security bar covering the lone window. She painted the metal bar the same cake-frosted pink as the walls, let Ruby decorate it with butterfly stickers—dotting the popcorn ceiling with even more luminescent star and nebulae and constellation stickers—and stuffed her two tiny shelves with used books and a battered terrarium that Stephen's promised to fill with one of his pitcher plants. Despite the threadbare carpet, the gently used things, the worn and faded stuffed animals that Ruby already seems to have outgrown—all the bits and pieces of other families' lives Andi made their own—her daughter's room is homey, even if Andi has a hard time considering this trailer a home.

More like a refuge, a retreat, a stronghold.

Ruby's dark hair is damp from her bath, despite Andi's best attempts to dry it and the chilled air from the chugging box fan in the corner. Curled on her bed, she refuses to settle down, whipping through the pages in her new Kuo book, showing them to Andi.

"Careful with that, Ruby Tuesday, we don't want to the tear the pages."

Ruby holds up a free hand, small, tanned fingers spread open, peering at Andi through them. She bites her nails, although Andi's tried about everything to get her to stop. "I don't like that name. It's silly." She wiggles her fingers, as if trying to magic Andi away.

Andi laughs. "It's silly and sweet and that's the whole point." For so long, Andi refused to use it at all, because of the man who gave it to her and the memories it conjured. But even she slips up now and then, mostly when she's tired or irritated with Ruby.

"I want to glow too, like the fishes," Ruby says, suddenly changing subjects, waving her new book around again. She kicks off the covers Andi is trying to tuck over her legs, and after two back and forth stanzas of tucking and kicking, Andi finally lets her be. She'll just throw them off in the middle of the night anyway. Andi often lays awake in her own bed and watches her daughter sleep through the grainy camera eye of the Wyze, waiting for that very moment, when Ruby ends up on her back, head turned to one side, softly breathing, arms spread wide as if wanting a hug. Coverless, open, exposed. Andi can't imagine sleeping like that, so free, so unfettered, so . . . *unprotected*. Andi sleeps in a tight ball, hugging herself, covers pulled up tight, as if avoiding the night and the things in it.

"Maybe you will when you're older. We'll see." Andi slips the book free from Ruby's grasp and tosses it on the bookshelf. Then sighs and stands and straightens it, giving it a place of prominence. She doesn't want to teach Ruby to be careless, thoughtless, with things that matter.

Ruby drops her hand. "Like you, Momma?"

Andi is about to turn off Ruby's light, but her daughter's words stop her. She sometimes says odd things like that, and Andi has no idea where the ideas come from, what her daughter means, if anything. Any attempt at prying an explanation out of her is met only with a shrug or Ruby's piercing blue gaze.

I hate that her eyes aren't mine . . . I hate it.

But those eyes aren't Ruby's fault. Nor Andi's scars nor this shabby trailer, nor the desert dust that gets into everything, no matter how much Andi scrubs or washes. Like living at the beach without the benefit of the ocean, all sun and sand and not a drop of water, waking up day after day salted in your own sweat. Those eyes alone can't be blamed for this whole marginal existence, the hanging on, the constant looking over her shoulder, stealing moments here and there, as another day or week or month slips through her fingers like all that sand.

No, none of this is Ruby's fault, but that doesn't mean that besides blaming herself, Andi doesn't sometimes blame Ruby too.

Andi turns off the light and waits as all the stars and constellations on her ceiling glow green, filling the room with ghostly light. Ruby loves to stare at the real stars in the night sky, but these make her happy too. They settle her down in a way that Andi can't, no matter the infinite stories Andi reads to her or how long she sits and strokes her hair.

"Love you, bumblebee. Get some sleep."

Ruby doesn't answer, like most nights. Just takes in her tiny plastic stars overhead. Maybe in her own way, she's praying. For a moment, Andi looks down at her own slim arm, turning it this way and that in the loaming dark.

Like you, Momma?

If she still glows, she can't tell.

She isn't a lightning angel anymore. Somehow, in the last ten years, she's fallen from the sky and landed here and doesn't know when or if she'll ever take off again, and that scares the shit out of her. But at least her hands don't shake.

At least Ruby is safe.

And that must be worth a pair of wings.

* * *

A couple of hours later, Andi sits outside, smoking a fresh cigarette, one of the treats she bought for herself in Tucson.

Two soft packs of Marlboro Reds that she'll partition out one at a time.

The lingering smoke is one reason Bella will never come over for long—that and the interference from the additional Wyze cameras Stephen wired for her out here, one at each corner of the trailer. She has sightlines along all four cardinal directions, and motion-sensitive floodlights to turn on before she goes to sleep; there's an orange Post-it reminder hanging by the front door and a second one by her bed, but she's never needed them. It did take her a few weeks to dial in the lights' sensitivity so they wouldn't flick on with every pygmy owl winging by. Now only something bigger than a coyote sets her small corner of the Sonoran Desert ablaze in white light.

Otherwise, most nights, it's mostly dark. Dark for miles and miles, but not pitch black.

She and Ruby aren't totally alone.

Even from her ratty folding chair, she can make out the distant winking lights of Waylen Burrows's High Country. Waylen likes to remind everyone that he isn't electrosensitive, he isn't even *sick*, although he's still forced to park his fifth wheel at the absolute farthest edge of New Cornelia so his wi-fi and computer setup don't interfere with Bella and the others. Andi likes Waylen well enough, a big ruddy man with a perpetually sunburned bald head, and she appreciates how he keeps an eye out for everyone. But you talk to him too long, and you find yourself sucked into his mirror world, a funhouse of conspiracies and the End of Days predictions. Fortunately, Waylen spends most of *his* days in a folding chair in the thin shade thrown by his RV, baking in the heat as the ice melts in his fourth drink of the day, turning the tepid water to rust, content enough to work his way through another bottle of Malloye's and wait for the end of the world.

Closer now, she can pick out the jewel green miasma of Stephen's makeshift greenhouse. To the left of that, Erwin and Leah's all-year-round red and white Christmas lights, slung low over the four or five picnic tables they've collected out back. A handful of other tiny, wavering glows—like breath-blown candles or the cherry end of cigarettes—dot the desert, marking the trailers and RVs that make up New Cornelia. The latter have to dry-camp or boondock like Waylen since the community's few utility hookups are already taken by the singlewides, but portable solar panels and water and fuel deliveries now make even those almost permanent, or as permanent as anything can be out here.

The desert around her is as inky as the night sky, lit by fallen stars all its own.

People come and go from New Cornelia, some staying just long enough to die here; few ever living and thriving as long as Bella. Andi and Ruby's trailer had three previous owners in the seven years before they arrived, the last being a former petroleum engineer from Houston who shot himself in the desert after only three months.

Three years on and Andi and Ruby are practically lifers.

But the money she emptied out of Max's and her joint account is dwindling by the day, and no amount of bartering or trading or tips from making runs to Tucson or Gila Bend will make up the difference. She can't put a price on safety and sanity, but she can put a price on schooling and doctors and integration and the contours of something closer to a normal life.

She flicks ash into the dust at her feet, feels the night slide over her skin. Back in Virginia, before she was struck, she'd loved to run—three, four, five miles a few times a week—but only runs now at the desert's driest, at summer's zenith, and only as long as she's wearing her lightning detector. That's her life now, and Ruby's too, held together by equal measures of hope and fear, patched up and painted over again and again like their trailer.

Bella likes to joke that she and the other New Cornelians are outcasts, crazy, but none of them *truly* feel that way, certainly not Bella herself, even if the worst of their symptoms drove them from their families and friends and lives and nearly out of their minds. Instead, they've mostly felt shunned, misunderstood, battling skepticism and ridicule when the medical community decided their environmental illnesses were merely psychological disorders. Andi's experienced that all firsthand; she *lived* it after she died and was brought back to life.

For her it was sudden movements suddenly causing overhead lights to flicker and fade, like the static discharge beneath a heavy wool blanket. Her laptop and her TV remote refusing to hold a charge, and almost any digital clock in her presence seeming to constantly run minutes if not hours behind. The dread of watching the battery in her cellphone drain just by holding it in her hand.

As bad as Andi's manifestations had been, as debilitating and lingering and unknowable as their symptoms were for most of her former friends in Texas—outcasts too, in a way—it was something else that drove Andi to abandon them, flee Texas, find New Cornelia. Despite how careful she's been—is *still* trying to be—she knows she's running a risk that her precautions will grow less sure, less safe, less secure, because she's gotten so comfortable here, so friendly with Bella and the rest.

So exposed.

There are precious few perfect escapes from a dangerous world, and it can be dangerous to have friends.

Wynona. Minnie and Billy. Cole. Stephen. Tassa.

Ethan.

Even Max.

The Black Light Club. The lightning strike survivor group they once helped create.

Stephen keeps an eye on the internet for her, tracking and eavesdropping on that loose universe of other lightning strike survivors, and although he doesn't like to worry her, he can't hide his concerns from her either, all the things he's seeing and hearing.

He's still looking for you, Andi, right now, he's out there—

Bella's right, sooner or later Andi will need to get Ruby away from here, but for now, for tonight, she's content to sit a little longer and enjoy her extravagant cigarette, holding the hot cigarette smoke in her chest, near her heart, counting all those comforting, familiar lights flickering out over the desert. She can start making her plans in the morning to move on . . . *you're running again* . . . somewhere with more to offer Ruby, but still without a lot of rain. Even after all this time, Andi keeps a list in her head—Wendover, Utah; Winnemucca, Nevada; Bishop, California—just like everyone in the club used to. It was their constant conversation, their dream, finding a place truly free of storms, of lightning.

Ethan had made the decision to move to Reno in the weeks before he was attacked, begging her to go with him. But she should've remembered Max knew all their lists and dreams too by then, and hers most of all.

He always knew her dreams.

So maybe when she leaves New Cornelia, she goes right into the eye of the storm: the Pacific Northwest, the Cascade Mountains up to western Washington or Oregon. Or Hialeah, Florida. Or Thibodaux, Louisiana. The last place anyone might think to look for her. Andi doesn't know if she can live under the constant threat of grey clouds and rain, but she might have to try, *really* try, for Ruby's sake, if not her own.

She's just about to put out her cigarette in the bottle of beer she's been nursing when one of those desert lights catches her eye. A sudden change in shape or color, a wrinkle or ripple. With so much emptiness out here, the world a vast, blank canvas, you get pretty good quick at picking out any kind of difference, no matter how small.

The light sparkles, seems to rise and to fall with Andi's breath.

It's *moving*, right to left, east to west toward the mine and the mountains, not north to south along Highway 85, to Ajo or Gila Bend beyond.

Andi studies the glimmer as it flickers and fades before disappearing beyond Waylen's RV, wondering who the hell would be out here at this time of night. Even the Border Patrol doesn't bother much anymore, and if they do, it's by helicopter, high overhead, far above the grit, sand, and dust.

No, this is a *vehicle* of some kind, driving right through the heart of New Cornelia.

Going, going, gone.

Someone either truly lost or another new outcast.

Or someone who knows exactly what they are looking for.

CHAPTER 6

Lorman, Mississippi

LINNEA KNOWS RIO about as well as she knows anyone, and still doesn't know him at all.

He's ten years younger than her, and before his time in the FBI did a stint in the military he doesn't much talk about. He was married before too, the union having lasted less than two years, and he doesn't talk about that either. He has no kids and appears not to want any, although he's always been more than willing to play friendly uncle to hers. As far as she can pry out of him, he keeps no girlfriends or significant others around for longer than a couple of months.

Not for lack of interest on their part.

Adan Rio is what Linnea calls a real looker: dark-eyed, dark-haired, lithe, graceful. But he's one of those people uncomfortable with those kinds of looks, with being looked *at*, so he downplays them at every turn, hiding behind sunglasses or a baseball hat or a Carhartt jacket. He keeps his hair too long and tends to slouch, folding his six-foot-three frame in on itself. Yet across his back and shoulders she knows he has a full-color tattoo reproduction of the Aztec Sun Stone, the *Piedra del Sol*, although he doesn't share its significance other than that it's a nod to his heritage, a mother who spoke

Nahuatl and a father from Durango, Mexico. Both arms have mysterious sleeves: macaws, monkeys, crows, and tiny Aztec gods.

One whole arm has Quetzalcoatl, the serpent.

For someone who keeps imagery that obviously means so much to him inked so visibly onto his skin, he keeps it all mostly to himself too.

Honestly, he's a goddamn puzzle near impossible to figure out.

Any other man might be jealous of the time Linnea's spent with Rio, but even without fully understanding it, her husband's always accepted the unique nature of their relationship, the gravity—now the trauma—that will forever pull them together. Both still suffer scars from their last official case. While Linnea wears a lot of hers outside—along her back, her arms, her neck, her *eyes*—Rio bears his beneath those colorful tattoos, deep beneath his skin, closer to his heart.

Mostly invisible, but no less prominent, if you know where to look.

But even Dan Wren's forbearance has limits, and as Linnea sits on her hotel bed and listens to their daughters, Olivia and Lucy, argue loudly in the background of their phone call, she is glad to tell him she's coming home.

"Not what you hoped for?" he asks, gently eliding the rest of his question. He's driving the girls back from soccer in Rockland. The three of them have just gone though some drive-through, and Linnea can imagine how the whole van now smells like hot grease and French fries, onions, or tacos. Even catches the audible crinkle of takeout bags and foil. Both she and Dan are capable cooks when they have the time, when she isn't three states away and he isn't juggling care of their girls and his work teaching English and writing at SUNY New Paltz. "What did former Senator Walden say?"

Dan doesn't push, not with the girls sitting within earshot, but he doesn't need to. He likely knows by the weight in her voice alone. He knew all along the risks she was taking by working with Rio again and had been vocal about his concerns.

"Nothing yet. I am just working on my report now. I like to have these conversations face to face, but we'll call him tomorrow, break the news and then follow up in person once we're back upstate."

She can almost hear Dan nodding on the other end, gesturing over his shoulder at the girls to pipe down, "So, see you tomorrow then?"

"It's twenty hours on the road, Dan. But we'll do our best."

"No, it's good. It's fine. Just drive safe and all that."

Linnea is almost certain she hears Olivia call Lucy a *bitch*. "You want me to yell at them for you?" she asks.

He chuckles around a mouthful of food. Dan isn't a laugher, but his easy smile can light up a room. "Nah. I'll deal with it. Remember, darlin', these are the times we're gonna miss so, so much." He chews, swallows, suddenly silent. She knows that look on his face, can *see* it, the faded spot between his blue eyes, the rough lines at the corner of his mouth, hidden by the salt and pepper beard he favors in colder months, and hasn't shaved yet. She's been staring at that face for more than twenty years now, has watched it weather and age like a stone in the sun, and still loves every crack and line, can still feel them under her fingers, even when he isn't with her. "How are you holding up? You gonna be okay?"

"You need to stop asking me that. Both you and Rio."

"Fair enough, Lin. Fair enough." Softer now, says, "But, you know, it's not an *unfair* question. Not unreasonable." He pauses, apparently willing to wave the white flag. "How old was she again, this girl?"

Linnea closes her eyes, so she doesn't have to look at the hotel room ceiling. She's lying on her back, on the bed, laptop open next to her. The screen, filled with pictures of dead Abby Walden, is her only light.

Not just dead . . . *murdered*.

"Too young," she finally says. "Far too young."

* * *

She never meant to fall asleep and wakes minutes or hours later still wrapped in darkness, her work phone gently pinging, throwing pale light on the ceiling like a falling star chasing its own tail.

At least she doesn't startle awake choking back a scream, jolt upright, clawing at imaginary wood, clawing at her eyes. Even with her current combination of meds, it still happens now and then, although mercifully not as often.

"Wake you?" Rio asks as she fumbles the phone to her face.

"No," she lies, trying to check the time, to figure out how long she's been out. Her constantly lying about whether she's asleep or not is a now familiar punchline, both to Dan and to Rio, particularly since Rio never seems to sleep, at least never for very long.

"Dan and the girls?"

"Ready for me to be home. *I'm* ready for me to be home."

Silence ticks by on the other end, and she doesn't like the sound of that.

"What is it?"

More silence, until Rio finally says, "I got a call . . . but we don't have to talk about it." Then adds, "Or maybe we do. Or maybe we *shouldn't*."

It isn't like him to be this undecided; it's not like they never envisioned finding Abby Walden this way. When they worked together before, death was their constant companion, hovering overhead like a bird on black wings. Rio once told her about *psychopomps*, spirit guides to the dead, often taking the form of birds: crows, owls, sparrows—just a few of the animals tattooed on his skin. He wondered once if he and Linnea were psychopomps too, in their own way.

Maybe we find peace for them, Lin, a resting place. Maybe we guide them home.

They had taken on the case of a runaway daughter, a *missing* daughter, but daughters go missing for all sorts of horrible reasons. They both know it, like they both had known Linnea would eventually have to face a moment like the one back at the morgue. Like this one now. But there's something else at play here too, and whatever it is, she's tired of both her husband and her partner treating her like broken glass, too brittle and too sharp to handle.

"Go with it," she fires back at him, her cop lingo resurfacing. When she was still in uniform, before her stint in homicide and the detective shield that came with it—before she started working at the FBI—she barked that command over a patrol mic more times than she could ever hope to count. Some of the other officers used to call her *Three Star*, like a three-star general. It wasn't a compliment.

"Jefferson County Sheriff's Office was first responders to Abby," Rio says. "Small office, lots of auxiliary and part-time staff, not a lot else."

A lot of rural sheriff's offices and police departments suffer not only from staff shortages but poor training and education as well, despite the federal grants available. Linnea's former department in Poughkeepsie took advantage of those funding initiatives, one of which sent her to her first homicide school in Washington D.C., then to a ten-week-long FBI-led forensic pathology and profiling advanced academy block, and eventually to the FBI itself. But most small forces never deal with many murders or missing people, so they turn those cases over to the state police or the nearest large city department.

"But now," he continues, "we also know *why* they didn't put her prints in NCIC."

"Because there were no prints to run," she finishes for him. Those weird burns on Abby's arms *immolated* her prints, making them almost impossible to process, no matter who got around to it. Otherwise, Abby might've been identified days earlier. Instead, it was her car that got ID'd first, a late-model green Subaru that Senator Walden bought her when she was sixteen, discovered at the Ash Street Bar and Grill in Port Gibson, Mississippi, twenty miles from the rest stop where Abby was found. The car was abandoned, locked, empty.

A young Port Gibson PD patrol officer who frequented the Ash Street Bar and Grill ran the plates after noticing the Subaru sitting overnight—an abandoned car not so unusual for a bar, but its faraway New York tags were. Port Gibson was even smaller than JeffCo Sheriff's, but once he put Abby's plates in the system, the dominos started falling in their direction.

Although Rio's contacts and accesses used to make the work easier, their success often came down to luck, good and bad, often at the same time. Sure, it's getting harder to simply disappear nowadays. Not that people *can't*—at least half a million do every year—but most are found quickly, and more importantly, safe. That still means thousands gone missing, and almost five thousand unidentified *bodies* recovered a year, leaving yet a thousand more still unnamed, unclaimed, months, years, even decades later. Abby isn't going to be one of those statistics, but that will be cold comfort for Bill Walden.

Maybe we find peace for them, Lin, a resting place. Maybe we guide them home.

Senator Walden might have answers now, but nothing close to closure, now that Abby's case is no longer merely a missing person or runaway, not an overdose, but an open homicide.

The truth Linnea knows by heart is that neither Abby nor her father are going to find peace for a long, long time, maybe never if her killer isn't caught. The Mississippi Bureau of Investigation will take the homicide lead, and Walden might try to extend her and Rio's retainer to ride shotgun, but even his money and power and Rio's charm might not be able to pull that off. Most local law enforcement barely tolerate family-hired PIs, particularly in an active homicide investigation, even less so when those meddling PIs are far from home.

"So," Rio continues, "although her prints were never run, the NamUs car hit was still good."

NamUs—the National Missing and Unidentified Persons System—a network of investigative, forensic, and technological tools and support available to law enforcement, medical examiners, families, even meddling PIs. A searchable database of disappearances, a computer full of ghosts. Senator Walden didn't know anything about NamUs, and likely never would've thought of registering Abby, because to him his daughter wasn't missing, merely *lost*, and he'd hired experienced PIs to find her. But she and Rio knew better, knew all those awful possibilities, so they created a profile for Abby even before leaving New York.

Demographics, physical description, identifying marks, transportation—like the abandoned Subaru, which was the link that got them to Mississippi.

"And Jerry Lee, to his credit, used NamUs trying to ID his Jane Doe victim, cross-matching the few physical descriptors he had, the identifying marks he noted in his report: height, weight, eye color, apparent age, tattoos."

"Well, we didn't know about most of those tattoos, and I can guarantee that Senator Walden didn't either."

"*Yggdrasil,* Lin," Rio says patiently. "The World Tree."

Now that Linnea is fully up and awake, she slips over to the hotel's window and peers through the heavy drapes to the parking lot, holding her phone to her forehead, listening to Rio. *How many hotels like these? How many unfamiliar parking lots?* The rain has stopped but everything is still wet, slick, shiny, glowing unnaturally beneath the lot's big sodium lights, the dark outside ambient and liminal. She was once comfortable in this twilight world, spent more hours in its darkened folds then anyone should, but it makes her wary now. It makes her scared and sad, more than ever.

"That weird Viking tree?"

"Yes, the one that connects everything. Heaven, Earth, Underworld."

"But that wasn't a . . . oh, oh shit," she says, interrupting herself, angry with herself too, for only now getting it. Her great talent, *her* original magic trick, was being the one who made the impossible connections, saw the hidden patterns, was always several steps ahead.

Now she understands why Rio warned her they didn't have to talk about this, what he's been driving at from the start, even if a part of her had known all along, and didn't want to admit.

"Those fucking *marks*. Those flowery burn marks on her arms—"

"Yes," Rio says again. "Exactly."

And she's not the only one.

CHAPTER 7

Memphis, Tennessee

LINNEA AND RIO meet Rio's friend at Marlowe's Ribs off Elvis Presley Boulevard just a couple of miles from Graceland.

The friend—short hair, square hands, severe eyes—screams cop or spook or some other kind of Fed, even without the dark coat hiding the semi-auto in the small of his back; even though he's picking at a plate of fried green tomatoes and drinking a cold beer at 10:30 in the morning.

Marlowe's doesn't officially open until 4:00 PM, so they have the whole place, including the kitchen, to themselves.

They've been on the road for over four hours, before first light, driving through the mist of last night's rain. Technically, she's still heading home, at least going in the right direction, so Linnea hasn't yet called Dan to tell him about this unscheduled stop. But seeing the food and the beer and the empty restaurant suggests it isn't going to be a short one.

She asks Rio's friend if she can get a BBQ pork sandwich and one of those beers too.

* * *

Rio goes first, running down how they got involved with Senator Walden and Abby, how they tracked her down to Mississippi.

Halfway through Linnea's second beer, she shows Rio's friend, Devine, the photos she took of Abby in Jerry Lee's morgue.

"These keraunographic marks are known as Lichtenberg figures." She enhances Abby's markings—Rio's Yggdrasil, the World Tree—but in truth a *lightning tree.* "You generally only get them when you've been struck by lightning, real Wrath of God kind of stuff. It takes about three milliseconds for a bolt to rip through your body, bursting blood vessels the whole way. These kinds of marks would typically show the bolt's passage, like a ship's wake." Linnea pushes her beer away. She shouldn't drink with her psych meds, a bad combination, but she tries not to drink at home in front of Dan, who's struggled with the bottle in the past. The last few years have been one struggle after another for them both. "But they usually only last a few hours."

"These evidently don't," Devine says.

"No," she agrees. After talking with Rio last night, she stayed awake till dawn, researching lightning strike victims, learning that although hundreds a year suffer injuries, only about twenty die. One of the only rarer ways to die is a shark attack. "And I'm not saying these marks were *caused* by lightning, I'm just accepting that's the closest analogue. So, maybe it has something to do with proximity to time of death? Or another environmental factor at work? Honestly, I don't know."

And you don't want to know, Linnea, not really. But here you are, still sitting here, holding a beer so this stranger doesn't see your hands shake.

"If it makes you feel any better," Devine says, "they don't know either. And they've seen more examples than you."

Linnea catches that Devine doesn't include himself in that statement.

"How many?" she hears herself ask, although she really, really doesn't want to know the answer.

"Finish your breakfast first," he says.

Then he places two neatly prefolded fifties on the table and tells them to follow him outside.

* * *

Once they settle in his rented Tacoma, Devine pops open a laptop and shows them the pictures.

Pennsylvania. West Virginia. North Carolina. Georgia. Alabama.

Two white, two African American, one Asian.

All girls . . . *women* . . . ages eighteen to twenty-nine.

All slender, athletic, pretty.

All bearing those lightning trees twinning around their arms, neck, or chest.

All dead.

"Found more or less in the vicinity of remote rest stops," Devine says. The ultramarine light from his laptop, all those pictures of dead girls, fills the truck's small cab, enveloping them, washing over them in waves. It's like they're floating underwater, and Linnea can't escape those images, making it hard to breathe. "Every one of them. Strangled, but cause of death most often seems to be cardiac arrest."

"Like electrocution?" Linnea asks.

The laptop's aquarium light doesn't shine off Devine's dark eyes. "Like that, yes. Those are your marks."

"But how?"

"Taser," Rio suggests from the back seat. "Cardiac electric capture. Any kind of stun gun or electrical control device might do it."

"Sure, that's one theory," Devine adds. "Only takes two hundred microamps to stop the heart."

"But the heart is protected," Linnea counters, shaking her head. "All that soft tissue, and skin itself is notoriously resistant to electricity." She points at the Lichtenberg figure on the girl from West Virginia, twenty-five-year-old Allison Dufresne. "As you can see."

"And you'd expect any ECD dialed up that strong to leave lesions or severe puncture wounds," Rio says. "Something readily evident."

"There isn't," Devine said.

"But there *is*." Linnea leans over the laptop. "Not puncture wounds, like you might find with traditional stun gun prongs or leads. Just *these*." She traces Allison Dufresne's lightning tree, a roseate branching around the girl's throat, vines or stems gracing her skin. It's horrible, awful—unforgivable—even if there is preternatural beauty in it.

"I don't know what sort of device leaves marks like that," Rio says.

"And like I said, neither do they." Devine pops in a stick of gum and offers one to Linnea, then Rio. Both shake their heads no. "But that's the only theory they got. Electrocution either to incapacitate or kill straight off, then manual strangulation."

"That's overzealous . . . some kind of overkill," Rio says.

Devine shrugs. "Or just exceedingly thorough."

"Five women in thirteen months," Rio continues.

"Six," Linnea corrects him. "Abby Walden."

"Multiple states, multiple victims." Devine doesn't use the one word they all know, the one Linnea herself can't bring herself to say. "FBI has the bare beginnings of a task force looking into this. The Bureau, state police, a few other entities. It's still a jurisdictional mess although they did seed a handful of silent lookouts and triggers."

"Jerry Lee uploaded the Lichtenberg figures from Abby's autopsy," Linnea offers. "And they sent up a flare."

"One they couldn't miss," Devine says. "The marks were only noted publicly in the first two murders, before someone smart realized what they might be dealing with. They've since withheld the rest from the media, keeping them out of any official reporting. No sense revealing that only connection between the victims yet."

Linnea turns to Devine. "What's *your* connection then? I take it you're not on this task force *officially*."

Devine and Rio exchange a look, impossible for her to read. Devine says, "Let's just say I'm one of those *other* entities. Rio and I go way back, military time together."

She laughs grimly. "Rio's got friends like you all over."

Between Rio's time in the military and the FBI, Linnea's come to learn there's a shadowy world of organizations and groups, programs, and partnerships: secret eyes and ears everywhere, sometimes collaborating, other times at odds. Resources that most don't know exist, and that even fewer have access to. Rio's past is a skeleton key that unlocks a lot of secret doors, a past he steadfastly refuses to talk much about, even with her. It was that past that brought Senator Walden into their orbit when he first reached out to Rio for help.

Rio says, "I got a message from a Bureau friendly who gave me the heads-up, after seeing my name—*our* names—attached to the NamUs record." Rio looks almost embarrassed, ashamed, which is neither a common nor good look on him. "I made some calls, then Devine called me."

Linnea asks, "Has anyone called Senator Walden yet?"

"Not that I'm aware of," Devine says. "Again, a lot of concerns about media publicity, and some professional considerations given your parallel involvement."

"I'm not involved," Linnea says. "I don't work with the FBI anymore."

Devine flicks a glance from her to Rio. "Not you, *him*."

Rio says, "Neither do I. I'm retired."

Devine shrugs, suggesting that certain kind of men in certain kinds of professions don't ever retire. "Well, you at least *have* friends."

Linnea understands. Someone wants to figure out how they're going to handle her and Rio before they notify the very powerful man who hired them.

"Fine, whatever. But what about more victims, earlier?" she asks. "Going back even further?"

Devine nods. "Like I said, this is still early stage stuff, almost primordial." He gauges her reaction. "They're still pattern seeking, data and evidence collecting, figuring out who's going to do what, who gets to make the final investigative calls. On the Bureau side is an up-and-comer named Schweiger. He's nominally in charge, but that's no prize, particularly if no one listens to him. They're truly playing catch-up on this."

"And they're already far behind," Linnea says. "Big task forces are slow, unwieldy. They know better."

Devine shrugs again. "You know better than me."

"Multiple states," Rio says. "This one's smart."

"At the very least, mobile," Devine adds, before shutting down his computer, the sudden change in light unexpected but welcome, like surfacing from the sea. Linnea rolls down the window, thankful for the air, even though it's sticky and humid and chilly all at once. Back home, this time of year, you can still get late spring snow and crisp, cold air, like a bright line in the sky. She'll never acclimate to the south, which feels perpetually dank and dark, rain or shine.

"Southbound initially," she finally says, mostly talking to herself, still staring out her window. "Now westerly. So Arkansas, Missouri, maybe even Texas next. Has his own wheels, something nondescript, roomy. And a credible reason to be on the move so much for such long distances. Regional sales, maybe? Truck driver?"

"Makes sense," Devine concurs.

"Victim selection and access will be tougher to crack," she continues, "but with this many victims already, in such a comparatively short amount of time, there *will* be evidence." Thirteen months is an extremely short amount of time for this sort of predator, although most seem to ramp up when the shine of their work starts to wear off faster and faster, as they get closer and closer to their endgame. "Some kind of an identifiable pattern—eventually."

There's *always* an inevitable pattern to it all, as inescapable and final as gravity. If solving a serial crime is a math problem, then more deaths, more bodies, make all the subsequent horrible calculations easier.

Linnea fucking hates math now.

"I'll pass the word," Devine says, focusing his matter-of-fact stare on Rio, leaving her wondering again how these two know each other. "But Schweiger is still going to want to talk to you about your investigation and take whatever you got. Senator Walden's daughter is part of that pattern now—part of *his* case." He turns his flatline gaze to Linnea. "You know how it goes, right?" But he doesn't look at her square in the eyes, doesn't look at the tiny scars etched around her lids, barely hidden by her lashes.

"Fine," Rio interjects. "I've heard of Schweiger, he was rotating into BAU-5 just as I turned in my badge. He's competent."

BAU-5 was FBI's latest iteration of the infamous Behavioral Science Unit, at the National Center for Analysis of Violent Crime where Linnea and Rio worked together for five years.

"But we're going to share with our client first," she says pointedly. "All of it. Everything. So don't give me all this hush-hush, off the books, media-blackout bullshit. He paid us to find his daughter and needs to know what that means now." She pauses, taking in the pale spot on her hand where her wedding ring would normally sit—a white gold band with black sapphires, a replacement for the simple silver half-round Dan got her when they were first married, the only thing he could afford then.

She lost that cheap band she used to love so much, just before she quit the FBI. She only wears the new ring at home now, never while working, not anymore.

Devine nods at them both. "Got it."

"You have Rio's number then," Linnea says, popping open the door to the clammy chill. Tastes salt on the air, although they aren't anywhere near the ocean. "Good luck. And thanks for the beers."

CHAPTER

8

Brownsville, Tennessee

THEY ONLY GET as far as Brownsville, about sixty miles beyond Memphis, when Linnea can't take Rio's studied stare anymore and pulls over on the shoulder.

Big semis roll on by them, one after another, hauling harvesters and bailers and livestock. Each one rocks the rented SUV on its shocks, like towering, rusty waves against a smaller ship.

But nothing shakes Rio's gaze.

"I'm not asking, Lin. I *won't*," he says, nodding but not exactly agreeing with himself. "I'm just—apologizing. I never should've brought you into this. It was too much, too soon."

"Don't play the martyr, I wanted to get back to work, any kind of work."

And truth is she *was* going stir crazy, an awful thing to admit when you're sitting at home with your loving husband, your beautiful daughters, when you're resting and recovering and repairing relationships and yourself, finally *healing*. Finally whole. But even after everything that happened, all those terrible things, she was starting to feel like she was dying under Dan's watchful gaze and his cloying desire to care for her. Her therapy and meds might've sanded down and dulled most of the pain and the trauma and those ghostly voices and images in her head, but not her desire to feel something, anything, other than helpless, ever again.

"I know. But it was supposed to be divorces, insurance fraud, that sort of thing. That's what I promised. Not this. Never this."

Nothing like this, until Senator William Walden called.

"Just a runaway daughter," she says. "Simple."

"Simple," Rio echoes. "Once this breaks, Walden is going to bring to bear whatever leverage he's got. And he won't be quiet about it."

She and Rio worked so many cases togethers, racing to beat the devil—the next call, the next inevitable body, the next Abby, or Joanna, or Rosemary, or Shelly. She still remembers every name, every face.

Rio says, "Fortunately, a lot of good people are already on this thing, hopefully they're thorough and conscientious."

And there are a lot of good reasons why she and Rio are merely private investigators now, working fraud and child custody and infidelity cases. A hundred reasons—*all those old cases*—why once Devine started talking about all those other women, she suddenly wanted nothing more than to go home.

I'm not asking, Lin.

No, Rio won't ask, ever, because he understands what asking means, what it might take from her. But he also won't let this thing go, given what that might take from him, and she understands that too. He saved her life, once upon a time.

So she says it for him.

"No matter how many state or federal investigators they have, there's no one else who can look at something the way *I* can, who can make the kind of vital crime scene assessment they're going to need."

He nods, reluctantly. "But can you? Now? After all that's happened?" He shakes his head. "If we get in the middle of this it'll be tampering. We'll catch hell, lose our licenses, and the ink isn't even dry on yours yet."

But Rio isn't talking her out of it, and he's not truly thinking about the consequences.

It's that damn *car*—Abby's late-model green Subaru.

It's probably still just sitting in a police impound lot in Port Gibson, exposed, unprotected. It'll be as important as Abby herself to the newly formed task force, but it's in another jurisdiction, so who knows how long it'll take them to get a full team to it. She and Rio don't have any jurisdiction at all, or the forensic kits they'd normally use for blood or fiber sampling, but Rio isn't suggesting they go back and search for that kind of trace evidence anyway.

He wants to take a look at the car—wants *her* to *truly* look at it, the way only she can.

Abby Walden's part of the pattern now, she thinks, *and so are we.*

And, maybe, just maybe, a small part of her wants this now too. Maybe it was all she was waiting for back at home, slowly getting restless and frustrated. One more chance to try one small thing like this. Something easy, like the car.

Just *to look.*

To see what's truly been taken from them both.

"Damn," she says, as she waits for another hauler to blow by, eyeballing an opening into traffic, so they can turn around and head back, while still refusing to look at her partner because she doesn't want him to see the tears in her eyes. "Goddammit."

CHAPTER

9

New Cornelia, Arizona

It's Waylen who calls Andi and tells her about the stranger, last night's new arrival.

Lucas.

Luke.

He tells her what little he's already gathered about the man—although he assures her, he'll find out more, a lot more—in the coming days. He says Luke's Wolf Pup camper had Illinois plates, but he only got a quick glimpse. Once he can get a better look he plans to take a picture of the numbers and run the plates.

He tells her it only costs a hundred dollars a pop to run plates or a background check. But she knows just how meaningless a license plate or even a driver's license can be nowadays, how easy it is to change a name or an address, an age, a transcript. Numbers and details are superficially simple to alter or delete or erase. The devil is always in the details, hiding there.

No, she needs to know what Luke *looks* like.

Although she knows just how easy it is to rearrange a face too, hair and eye color as malleable as the weather. She's done it a half dozen times herself, Ruby's hair still cut short enough that from a distance or when it's covered with a natty baseball hat, she could be any kid anywhere. But it's almost impossible to change your *true* form. Some people hurt you so badly they leave scars in your head or on your heart that never quite heal or disappear either. Andi has her lightning scars and a Max-shaped hole inside her, and she can recognize it—him—anywhere.

That's why she needs to put eyes on this stranger herself.

But if it *is* Max, she and Ruby need to bolt immediately, not come back to the trailer, so she has Ruby ride over in the truck with her, tucked down in the cab.

Even a year ago Ruby wouldn't have complained. She's always understood the rules, the endless precautions, even if she didn't like them. But she grouses loudly today, making a face, staring back with defiant eyes as Andi fires up the truck and tells her to get her butt down before Andi swats it. It's an empty threat, Andi's never raised a hand to her and never will, so instead if Ruby will just please, *please* do what she's told without a fuss, Andi promises to run over to Ajo for those *paletas* from Olsen's Market she likes so much.

Her daughter agrees with a sly smile.

Andi now rolls through the morning light, windows down, the temperature already hitting seventy-five but still almost comfortable. She's wearing a long-sleeved, black tee faded to gray from too many washings to cover the smaller SIG semi-auto tucked in her jeans, and has the bigger S&W beneath her front seat where she usually keeps it. Ruby knows better than to go around touching Andi's guns, but she's shown her daughter how to hold one, about the trigger and safety, and even let her shoot the SIG a few months back.

Just in case.

They had blasted away at a soldier's line of Waylen's old whiskey and beer bottles out in the desert by the mine, sending scared road-runners scurrying from all the flying glass and loud, echoing reports. Most days, though, the surrounding desert is still and quiet, like now, like New Cornelia itself. If you need to do something outside, you do it early in the morning or well past sunset. The heat here has a way of turning the sky heavy and glassy, hammering the landscape flat, making even the mountains small and wavy and indistinct. It's like living inside a crystal ball or snow globe filled with grit and sand. The medical conditions that drove most of New Cornelia's residents out to the desert to begin with also keep them locked away, prisoners in their trailers or campers.

The desert is hot and clean and barren, free of a lot of environmental pollutants but not all. It has dangers all its own. The desert isn't *safe*—and although last night Andi had all but made up her mind to leave, now that the sun is up and she's facing that very real possibility she isn't sure she's ready to abandon New Cornelia or the few friends she has here.

Even if this man Luke isn't Max in disguise, a wolf in sheep's clothing, she prays he isn't just another grifter or opportunist or fugitive, because as resourceful as they all are in New Cornelia, there aren't any shepherds in this desert.

Their little flock is all alone.

* * *

He's standing outside with his back to her when she pulls up, tinkering with his RV.

Even before she sees his face she know it isn't Max.

It's in the set of his shoulders, the way he's standing, even how he bends down to peek at something under the camper, balancing himself on one hand. You can't live with someone, sleep with someone, breathe the same air, share the same *heartbeat*, and not know every inch of them.

Even if the very thought of him makes your skin crawl now.

Luke turns at the sound of her truck and waves, so she waves back, whispering beneath her breath to Ruby to hold tight, she'll be just a few minutes. When she gets out, she checks that her T-shirt is still covering her gun, assuming Waylen has binoculars focused on them both. But Luke either senses something in her posture or catches the look on her face as she glances back toward Waylen's RV, because just as he starts to walk forward, something makes him suddenly hesitate, stop.

Damn, he sees the gun tucked under my shirt.

"Hey," he says, pleasantly enough, although if he did just make out the contours of the gun beneath her shirt, his voice doesn't betray it. "Second visitor in as many hours. I sure didn't expect any kind of full-on welcome wagon. Kinda the opposite, honestly."

"We don't get many new arrivals, so it's less a welcome wagon and more pure nosiness."

He laughs, a warm and quiet sound. "I'm—"

"Luke, I know. Waylen, your neighbor over there, called me." She gestures to Waylen's mammoth High Country. "And you can bet our other little carrier pigeons are winging their way around right now. You'll learn we're something of an odd bunch out here, kind of our own tribe."

"I'm getting that vibe."

They stand awkwardly twenty feet apart, dust still hanging in the air from her truck's passage, dirtying and blurring the space between them. She can't begin to guess his real age, but he isn't bad looking, in a generic sort of way. Like he stepped out of a men's clothing catalog, Eddie Bauer or Marmot.

"Yeah, a tribe with some weird rules and customs, all of which Mr. Waylen Burrows likely broke, just to get a good look at you." She smiles. "I'm sorry, we really do try to be respectful around here, about personal matters, personal space—it's important. Kind of our core philosophy."

"But is that why you showed up, to get a good look, see me for yourself?"

"Sure, something like that." She gestures toward thick creosote with yellow flowers by his camper. "That's creosote over there, you'll be able to tell by the smell. When it rains, it'll turn so thick, so sour, you'll think the sky's dropped mothballs. It has special chemicals on its leaves to hold in water when it rains, a desert adaptation. Regular folks are usually only allergic to creosote, just run of the mill allergies, nothing dramatic, nothing fatal."

No, the desert isn't safe.

"Oh, I get it. I do. Kind of your own little wellness community. But I'm not sick, not in that way, if that's what you're asking."

She smiles again. "Let's just say we're all kind of like that creosote out here, adapting, surviving."

He shares her smile and finally takes a handful of steps forward. "I'm Luke Keats."

"I'm Andi."

Luke can't hide his surprise or embarrassment. "Oh, when Waylen mentioned someone named Andi, I thought—"

"That I'd be taller?"

He laughs loudly. "Honestly, I don't know. I'd read about this place, and wanted, no, *needed*, to see it for myself. I guess I'm just the nosy type too."

"What do you think, so far?"

He looks around, before settling back on her. "So far, even more interesting than I imagined."

"Well, you haven't really seen much yet."

"You been here long?" Luke asks.

"Are you a reporter?"

"I'm a cop . . . no, I mean . . . I *was* a cop." Something passes over his face, a flicker, a shadow, a trick of light. "I'm sorry, I'm still not used to saying that, and I forget sometimes. A *former* cop."

"Don't worry, we have a lot of *formers* here—former scientists, artists, teachers."

"You?"

She hesitates too, a heartbeat. "Like I said, I'm just Andi."

Before Luke can say more, a sudden, sharp bark and then a shriek behind her makes Andi turn to find Ruby standing outside their truck, a big dog circling her. Andi yells out, "Jesus, Ruby, *no*," and nearly reaches for her gun, before a hand falls on her shoulder, light, unthreatening.

"No, no, it's okay, that's just my dog, Chili." Luke whistles to her. "Chili girl, *sit*." After a long moment, Chili plops back on her haunches, tongue lolling, tail wagging.

The dog is the only one who doesn't seem surprised.

"Scared the—" but before Andi can finish, Ruby looks to her, eyes wide, not with terror, but wonder.

Joy.

Andi remembers what Bella said only yesterday—

I promise you, there will be a dog one of these days.

Ruby kneels by Chili, rubbing her hands in the dog's thick fur, laughing.

"Chili's harmless," Luke says, both hands now in his pockets. "A softie. She's like a million years old but good with kids."

"Great, that's really great," Andi says, trying to resurrect the smile on her face, but her heart is still up in her throat, hammering so loud she wonders if even Luke can hear it.

Oh shit, he's got a dog—a sweet, silly, stupid dog.

And she could have shot it right in front of him and her daughter.

* * *

"Really, don't mind Chili," Luke says a few minutes later, after things have settled down, as he and Andi watch Ruby chase her back and forth. "I'm sorry if she startled you. She's stubborn, but all bark and no bite."

"*You* should mind her, though," Andi says. "It's rough on dogs out here, with all the rattlesnakes. You need to keep your eyes sharp around dusk and dawn when those snakes go hunting. They'll hide right up under your camper there, where they can stay cool during the worst of the heat and then warm at night. Might want to get you a decent shovel to whack them away—or better yet, a gun."

"Sure, okay." Luke glances between his booted legs, as if a snake might be lurking there at that moment. But then he looks up at her and says evenly, "Is that why *you* carry one? For snakes?"

Andi lets slip an embarrassed smile and turns her attention instead to his camper. "That's a nice rig you got have. Fifty-five-amp converter, on-demand tankless water heater. Thermo-foil insulation and four hundred-watt solar panels. Two-inch lift kit and off-road tires. On the small side though."

"Oh, I don't need all that extra space," Luke says, "or the expense. Got a good used deal on this one." He grins. "You seem to know a lot about snakes and RVs."

"Well, as I'm sure Waylen told you, he used to sell them. He'll talk your ear off about them, if you let him." She and Max also lived in a camper of their own for about a year, one not much different than Luke's Wolf Pup. "He talks *everyone's* ear off."

"Thanks for the warning," Luke says. "Guessing I'll need to meet everyone else too, before long. There's like, a process, or something, right?"

Andi shrugs. "Something like that, if you plan on staying."

Luke looks around at the desert, at the day already getting hot and bright. Up close, he is older than thirty, probably. He finally says, "Hope to. For a while."

"Bella oversees the administration of New Cornelia such as it is, the rules and expectations. She's kind of our resident gatekeeper, keeps all our secrets, so to speak, so the rest of us can mostly keep to ourselves." Andi watches Ruby trying to get Chili to roll over or heel or do some other dog trick. But Chili only barks then chases after her tail, leaving Ruby laughing. They've kicked up a small cloud of dust, a dust devil that whirls away into the morning. "I mean, that's why we're all here," Andi continues. "And I assume that's why you're here too. Peace, quiet, privacy. No one looking for any trouble."

"Chili and I aren't trouble. I promise."

He sounds so sincere Andi almost believes him.

"Good. But—Bella's not much for visitors and less so for strangers. I'll help you get settled until you can meet her."

Luke doesn't do much to hide his smile at that. "Great, so we hang out a bit, and if you like me, there'll be like a meeting or a vote, then? What little I read about this place wasn't exactly clear."

"Oh, no vote, nothing serious like that," Andi says, laughing, before hollering after Ruby that they need to go, leaving Ruby pouting.

"We welcome everyone," Andi continues, as she walks over and shakes his hand, his bright eyes gray, like cool rain, like wet glass. But his hand is warm, his fingers strong, and she can make out faint scars on his knuckles, maybe old scratches. "It just won't take long to know if you can make it out here or not."

CHAPTER

10

Port Gibson, Mississippi

LINNEA AND RIO stand over Abby's car in the late afternoon sun.

Now joined by the PD officer who found it, Terrell Lomax, who's come in off duty, probably direct from working out at the gym, since he's still wearing a thread-bare Mississippi State T-shirt and dark gym pants and beat-up Converse high-tops.

He's young, good-looking, and worried.

"Y'all aren't getting me in trouble, are you?" He flicks a look back and forth between Linnea and Rio. "I mean, I thought this was just about some girl who ran off."

"No," Rio says. "You're not in trouble. And unfortunately, this is about more than a simple runaway now. Ms. Walden was a homicide victim—and likely not the first."

Lomax smiles nervously as if he's the butt-end of a joke, before silently mouthing the word *homicide*, as if he doesn't like the taste of it. "Y'all talking about a *murderer* running around Port Gibson?"

"Honestly, Officer Lomax, we don't know," Rio says, slipping off his dark sunglasses, his eyes serious and sad. "And in all truthfulness, we're not officially part of the investigation that will make that determination. The family only employed us to find Abby, and we've done that." Rio crosses his arms, nodding to the Subaru in front of them. "However, as representatives for the family, we still hold the power of attorney and the authority to tow this vehicle back to New York."

Rio almost makes that sound believable.

But Lomax shakes his head. "Terrell or Terry is just fine in these parts. And as polite as you two seem to be, if this car is *evidence*—which is what you're saying without coming out and saying it—then I think I'm going to have to ask the chief about that. Officially."

Rio nods and smiles. "No need for that, we don't *want* to take it back to New York, nor interfere more than we have. We would just appreciate being able to look it over. We drove back a long way to do that."

"But we are going to have to move it some," Linnea adds. She looks to Lomax, knows Rio admires the young man's unwillingness to get pushed around too much in his own backyard, and she does too. He's already checked their PI licenses twice, and even took pictures of them with his phone. "Not far though, maybe like . . . just into that garage over there." She points to the maintenance garage at the far end of the impound lot, likely where the Port Gibson police serviced their own vehicles, the way her own PD used to. "Just to get it out of the sun."

"Sun's going down soon," Lomax notes, slipping his hands in pockets, buying himself time as he appears to think it through, glancing back and forth between them again. Linnea guesses he's twenty-six, a shade older. Lanky, a basketball player's build. Finally, he says, "Just a look? That's all? Not taking anything?"

"No," Linnea says, raising her hand. "Scout's honor."

Lomax smiles nervously again. "Okay then, I think I can make that happen."

"Thank you," she says. Linnea *still* hasn't called Dan yet; hasn't told him she turned around and she's no closer to home than she was this morning. If anything, she's farther away. She knows what he'll say and won't blame him.

"What kind of clues y'all looking for?" Terrell Lomax asks.

Rio slips his glasses back on. “Not sure I’d even call them clues, Terrell.” He nods in Linnea’s direction, who’s already walking away. “But you can ask her.”

“Ms. Wren?” Terrell calls after her.

“Ghosts,” she says, over her shoulder. “I’m looking for ghosts.”

* * *

It began for Linnea when she was ten years old, when she realized she was unconsciously picking out and remembering background actors in scores of movies or TV shows, fleeting glimpses of passing faces that happened to reappear again and again, sometimes years apart.

A young man from both *ER* Season Five, and *Friends*, Seasons Four and Five.

A blonde-haired woman in the Denzel Washington movie *Fallen*, and Russell Crowe’s *A Beautiful Mind*, almost four years after that.

A boy who had a five-second walk-on in a Wendy’s Kids Meal World commercial in 1999 and then appeared—just as briefly—five years later in a Michelin ad.

She always called these faint traces of memories, these hints or echoes or recollections of people she never met, *ghosts*. And her ghosts were rarely quiet or cooperative.

At seventeen, when she worked at the local Maurices in her hometown in Corydon, Indiana, she caught her first ghost after reviewing hours and hours of grainy CCTV footage for the single, upturned face of a serial shoplifter. Three years later, for the campus PD at Ball State University in Muncie, where she was a sophomore, she ID’d a forty-two-year-old child predator from three weeks’ worth of mall parking lot security camera video.

The sudden unexpected and unwanted notoriety drove her to Vassar, in Poughkeepsie.

And Linnea’s ghosts were never just people. Beyond routinely, inadvertently, memorizing the faces of people she might have only seen for a moment—years or even decades apart—she lived with an innate ability to recall and recognize; to organize all kinds of imperceptible patterns; to see and remember hidden connections; discern and link together tiny accretions of detail. The world is full of patterns, *everywhere.* A necessary survival mechanism, human brains so inherently biased, so hardwired, to find them, even when they aren't there, there's even a name for it—*apophenia*—a bad tendency to make up patterns. One strand of apophenia, pareidolia, is why humans see the Man in the Moon or faces in clouds. Apophenia is why we're so prone to believe in conspiracy theories and paranormal experiences. It explains Jung's synchronicity and the gambler's fallacy and the sort of expectancy and confirmation bias that Vegas illusionists still prey on.

When it gets out of hand, doctors consider it a prelude to OCD, autism, even schizophrenia.

Linnea's eidetic apophenia wasn't just biological wiring on the occasional fritz; hers was dialed-up, supercharged, *always on.* She conjured patterns and correlations out of unrelated sensory data, all the time, seeing what others couldn't, seeing the *unseen*, until she couldn't *unsee* it.

Ghosts. Everywhere.

At least until that last case, Jon Parlor III. She's still recovering from the things Parlor did to her, the things he took from her, in his barn in Ruther Glen, Virginia.

If Rio's gift was his easy, social adaptability, a chameleon-like charm, hers was this preternatural deductive logic, a Holmesian leap of inference and connection and insight, that she could neither turn off nor fully explain and that most people wouldn't believe even if she tried. And it *wasn't* charming. At its worst, it made her fierce, intense, prickly.

Some thought she was being more than just difficult; they thought she was flat-out crazy, including the platoon of therapists and clinicians who treated her throughout the years—even before Parlor—who freely prescribed haloperidol or loxapine or thiothixene or electroconvulsive therapy to control her weird ghosts, those phantom connections she made that no one else could see.

Sure, she was likely slowly, inevitably, going insane due to her special gift, her curse.

But she also wasn't wrong, most of the time.

* * *

She sits now in Abby's car, wraps her hands around the wheel, imagining what it's like to be twenty-two again, driving south toward Nashville with the windows rolled down, the rustic smell of tall grass cut low along the highway.

A tiny nick on the windshield from a spinning piece of quartz.

Road dust across the dashboard, a thousand miles worth. A faded handprint, below the rearview mirror.

A car charger but no phone.

Two hair ties in the center console, one green, one blue . . . *green was her favorite color* . . . one quarter, a dime, and three pennies . . . *exact change of a mcdonald's happy meal from a five-dollar bill* . . .

A Fancii Mila compact mirror, glass cracked.

Green lint from an American Eagle sweater, red strands from an L.L.Bean flannel.

Red hair . . . *abby's hair was blonde* . . . caught in the passenger seat headrest.

Two forgotten Dunlop guitar picks in the passenger floorboard . . . *purchased at fanny's house of music* . . . dusty, crushed petals of the plains coreopsis . . . *native to mississippi* . . . an empty vape cartridge . . . *seats still smell like her perfume, ellis brooklyn sun fruit.*

The car smells like *her* . . . *she slept here some nights, out on the road* . . . her perfume and her lotion and her tanned sweat.

Five bottle caps. Three Budweiser, one Corona, the fifth Good Bug . . . *served on draft and by the bottle at the ash street bar* . . . a local Mississippi beer.

Ash and grease marks on the back seat, trash in the floorboards. Pet fur . . . *she'd had both a cat and a dog* . . . a battered paperback horror novel, a receipt from a Brite Bubbles laundromat in Atlanta. A Marlboro cigarette butt . . . *abby didn't smoke, she vaped* . . . crushed limestone, pea gravel, and Blacktrap rock from a hundred parking lots.

Crumpled tinfoil. Crumbs of past meals.

More flower petals. Black-eyed Susan and cosmos.

A tiny, crushed pill . . . *she was prescribed effexor for depression* . . . a torn tissue. A smear of crystalline power.

Another guitar pick . . . *but no guitar or case* . . . this one a heavy tortoise-shell Fender . . . *no luggage* . . . a different gauge than the Dunlops.

All these tiny, ephemeral hints of who Abigail Marie Walden was, where she'd been, the things she'd done and the people whose paths she crossed in the last months of her life.

All gone . . . *just a ghost* . . . just like twenty-two-year-old Abby herself.

* * *

After Linnea goes through the Subaru's trunk, she thanks Terry Lomax for his help, and suggests he keep the car locked up inside, safe, and further untouched, until the true investigators come for it.

"Fine. Okay." He hesitates, twisting his phone in his hand. "I mean, that's it?" He doesn't try to hide his confusion, the questions. He and Rio stood in the corner of the garage while she worked, quietly talking, and she couldn't begin to guess what Rio did or didn't tell him, what he imagined as she sat alone in the car.

"Yeah, that's it," she says, exhaustion settling on her like a heavy, gray blanket. Like a thick fog. She wants to curl up and sleep in a dark room and let the headache building up like a thunderous wave behind her eyes finally crest and break, leaving only a placid, dull calm behind.

It never used to take this much out of her, this special gift of hers, but now that she's older, the mindfulness exercises she's haphazardly adopted, coupled with her current various medications, have reined in the worst of the incessant chatter, dulled the cacophony of flashing images, the ghosts flitting in her peripheral vision. But that unquiet peace has come at a hard cost.

Everything's gotten a lot harder in the aftermath of the Parlor case.

"Take a moment and write down whatever you remember about the day you found the car, and I do mean everything." She gently rubs her eyes—Lomax hasn't stared at her scars, not once—and then motions at Rio it's time for them to go. "You went over that with us before, but you'll have to go over it all again with the Walden investigators. And honestly, it's good practice. You never know what you'll remember, what you're *capable* of remembering, what details you might recall or come up with. You never know what's important . . . until it is."

Lomax thinks about that and then nods before nodding toward the car. "How about you? You come up with something important?"

"No," Linnea says, shaking her head truthfully. "Not a damn thing."

CHAPTER

11

Port Gibson, Mississippi

After Linnea calls Dan and tells him she isn't going to make it home for another day, she tries to sleep for a couple of hours, drawing the hotel curtains as tight as she can, turning the AC up as high as it goes, burying herself under the thin sheets she piles up on the bed.

How many hotels like these? How many unfamiliar parking lots?

She leaves the TV on, but the sound turned down and her eyes shut so the images flicker and dance silently and unseen on the walls all around her. That doesn't mean she isn't seeing images anyway—*faces*—behind her closed eyes.

Ghosts.

Not just Abby Walden, although she's there too, front and center. But dozens and dozens of other women, an all-too familiar choir now, a constant haunting chorus, always the same women because it is *always* women.

On TV, in movies, command centers are all so impossibly high-tech, all polished, gleaming chrome, lit by the nascent light of a million flat-screen monitors, with important-looking people talking in headsets, as numbers and images and DNA strands and clocks and codes and 3D maps scrolled endlessly by. There's an immediate and intense sense of something important *happening*, as if the entire world is focused on the singular problem at hand. And in September 2012, that problem was finding sixteen-year-old Erin Byrne, who disappeared, feared abducted, after visiting the Basilica of St. Mary of the Angels in Olean, New York.

But there was nothing high-tech about young Linnea Wren's first command center, just an old state police post in Olean, showcasing an ancient, noisy Keurig and a stack of yellowed BOLOs for just about everyone but the person who would later prove to be the most viable suspect in Erin Byrne's disappearance. Laptops overworking exposed power strips, heavy, water-stained cardboard boxes scattered here and there, a stack of metal-legged chairs against a wall, and a couple of trashcans drowning in a fast-food take-out bags. Even an abandoned plastic Christmas tree from an old Troop A1 New York State Police post party, leaning in a corner with stray ornaments and tinsel.

And no 3D or computerized map, just a large fold-out piece of paper tacked to one of the walls, a topo map of nearby Allegheny State Park and National Forest in muted greens and browns.

After saying her prayers at St. Mary of the Angels, red-haired Erin Byrne had disappeared so thoroughly into that emptiness, there was nothing to even mark where she'd been . . . until they found the first body.

Just like Abby Walden.

Abby is part of that chorus now, alongside Erin, and two other young women—skeletal remains—Linnea uncovered in shallow graves near Erin in the Allegheny, in what proved to be a dumping ground for her first true serial, Brian Wallace Mershon.

She knows by heart the faces and names of all those women, just like she remembers the faces and names of the monsters who ended their lives.

* * *

When Linnea finally gives up trying to sleep, she calls Senator William Walden at last.

He doesn't cry or yell or curse when she tells him that Abby is dead.

Instead, he just breathes, deep and distant and shuddering, like a death rattle itself. The sort of breath that sounds like his whole soul has fled his body to parts unknown. Heaven, if you believe in that sort of thing, and Linnea doesn't know what she believes. Senator Walden made a fortune buying and selling companies and people before he ventured into politics, is intimately connected to both New York state and national politics, a kingmaker who once razed lesser kingdoms with a phone call. Linnea doubts he has much interest in Heaven either and if he does, likely only because he owns a piece of it.

He's still and silent for so long she thinks he's put down the phone and walked away. But then he asks her to tell him everything . . . orders her to tell him. And she does. And when she's done, he stays silent again for a long time, so she just waits, sitting with him quietly too, almost like she's holding his hand from more than a thousand miles away.

After Linnea arrested Connor Wyeth, a twenty-six-year-old serial in Abilene who murdered four girls and kept their bodies wrapped in blue tarps in a storage shed behind his elderly mother's trailer, she sat with Edith Wyeth and held *her* hands, quietly explaining how her only son—the boy who checked on her each day, bought her groceries, kept her meds straight, paid her bills, drove her to Euclid Baptist on Sundays, occasionally put a vase of wild Indian paintbrush and pink evening primrose by her bed—was going to jail and likely the electric chair for killing and stalking girls still too young to drive a car.

She held that old woman's hands, tracing the blue veins beneath her wrists, all the years gone by written indelibly on her skin. Edith Wyeth didn't cry either, just *breathed* in and out, steady as the ticking grandfather clock down the hall. And when Linnea was done telling her all she could, when Edith was done too, she thanked Linnea for taking the time to explain it to her, as if you could ever truly explain something like that.

She thanked Linnea for not blaming her for Connor's atrocities but also wondered aloud why someone hadn't discovered her son earlier, why someone hadn't stopped him sooner. Now, as Linnea waits for Senator Walden to speak again, she wonders if he's also blaming her for not finding his doomed daughter soon enough.

Finally, he says, "Are you telling me Abby was murdered by some sort of madman, one of these so-called serial killers?"

"Yes. That appears to be right."

"Appears to be . . . or is? I don't want to be *managed*, Ms. Wren, or handled, or mollified. I want fucking *answers*. Clear, specific answers."

"Your daughter is at least the sixth victim of a multistate serial offender, a predator."

"And how did this . . . *man* . . . find Abby? How did they encounter each other? Know each other?"

"I can't answer that. As I understand it, the federal task force heading up this investigation is still in its early stages. They don't know yet. We don't know."

"What *do* you know, then?"

"That there will likely be more victims like Abby. Until he is stopped."

Senator Walden's voice is smooth, cold, and reflective, like glacier ice. A whole mountain of it. "And this task force? Will they stop him?"

"They'll do everything they can to find him."

"That's not what I asked. Will they *stop* him, Ms. Wren?" More ice, dazzling, blindingly cold. "I know your history, and I also know that we are both parents, so you understand my intent here—my *intentions*. But let me put it plain. Will these men move Heaven and earth to stop this monster that killed my daughter and tossed her away like trash?"

"I assure you, they're good, very good."

"I don't want *good*, Ms. Wren. I don't want closure, and I don't want justice. What I want now is . . . *anger*."

Linnea won't argue with Senator Walden because she can't; she's long known the value of anger. "I'm sorry, I didn't want to make this call like this. We wanted to see you in person. But someone from this task force will be reaching out to you, and I wanted you to hear it from me first."

"How many times have you delivered news like this?"

Linnea's free hand finds the scars around her eyes, a tic that's grown more and more worrisome. She touches the delicate skin, traces the scars from her last case, "Over the years, Senator, too many."

Senator Walden goes silent again for another long moment. "I went through many hard years with Abby, coping with her anger, and mine too. The boys, the depression, the drugs. I watched her grow and change in so many ways I never could've imagined, yet she never became more solid or more real to me than that beautiful little girl I once held hands with and once held in my arms. I still saw *her* behind that angry façade, the child I remembered." Linnea knows he's talking as much to himself as he is to her, how he needs to say these things, to hear them out loud. "I couldn't *not* see that one day at Rehoboth when a wave knocked her on her eight-year-old butt, and she came to me both crying and laughing. Or that Christmas in Normandy it seemed to snow for three days straight, and how we watched it together, counting endless flakes. Or the first song she ever wrote. The sound of her voice. I used to tell her she was my sun, moon, and stars, and I don't know how you can love someone more than that." That glacier ice in his voice finally breaks. "I don't know how you ever *stop* loving someone like that."

"Heaven and earth," Linnea says. "They haunt us."

She remembers one of Connor Wyeth's sixteen-year-old victims, Ramona Caldwell. Ramona's favorite color was purple, and she was wearing a purple dress when she was found in that storage shed behind Edith Wyeth's house.

She remembers them all.

"I knew you would understand," Walden says. "Thank you."

"I haven't done anything."

"But you will," Walden says, before quietly clicking off the call. "You will."

After he hangs up, she sits in the silent dark for a long time before throwing her clothes back on and heading down the street to the Ash Street Bar and Grille.

CHAPTER

12

Port Gibson, Mississippi

LINNEA FINDS RIO already there, as if he's read her mind.

He's sitting near the back, although the place isn't that big. A handful of tables, a couple of TVs, a beat-up bar. Lots of wood paneling, dark and closed-in and musty. The sort of place to grab a burger or wings and beers and watch a game. The sort of place mostly empty during the week but near busting at the seams on Friday and Saturday nights, since there weren't a lot of options in Port Gibson.

The sort of place with license plates on the walls and neon beer signs that don't work and pictures of youth football and basketball teams now long grown-up and gone and framed photos of big fish that someone once pulled out of Turkey Falls Creek or Eagle Lake.

Rio's drinking water, picking at a burger. He slides the burger over to Linnea as she sits and when the server walks by, she orders a Good Bug.

"Dan upset?" he asks.

She takes a bite of his burger before sliding it back. "Disappointed. Worried."

"I know. So am I."

"You don't have to say that—any of it."

"Maybe not, but I *need* to."

She takes a sip of the beer when it arrives. It's bright, citrusy, cold. "C'mon, we are *way* past *need to's* and *have to's.*"

"I shouldn't have put you through that with the car."

"You didn't. *I* did. I wanted to. And it's done."

Rio hesitates, rubbing at a name etched on the table. He finally asks, "Is it?"

Another long swallow of beer. It's almost empty, and she already wants another. "I'm sorry," she says. "I got nothing out there." She shrugs off a bunch of other stuff she *could* say, how it didn't feel the same anymore, not after those months recovering at Gracie Square, not after succumbing to her new regimen of meds. She feels like a painter whose hands shake too much now, a chess master who doesn't remember how to play.

My eyes were stitched shut and now I can't see.

So much was taken from her and that most of it all, but she also can't help wondering if that's also the only thing she shouldn't be so fucking angry about.

But if she's bad at lying to Rio, or Dan, she's worse at lying to herself.

"I also spoke to Walden." She cuts Rio off before he can protest. "Look, I'm sorry, I know, we should've done it together. We should've done it in person. But we couldn't wait anymore, and I didn't want him to hear it from Schweiger's task force or Devine or whoever the fuck else. And for the record, it went about as well as you can imagine."

She rubs between her eyes, touches her scars again. They feel hot to her, inflamed.

"The senator won't let this go," she says, "and he doesn't want *us* to let it go, and he was very blunt about both things. He's got the resources and influence to make this loud and messy for everyone else involved in this. He'll likely make it *worse*, until or unless he gets his way."

"I know," Rio says, then lets it go. "I like the kid, Lomax."

"Does he remind you of a young Adan Rio before you got all jaded and cynical?"

"You mean before I met you?" That elicits a thin smile from them both. "No, maybe more like a young Linnea Wren."

"You didn't even know me when I was that young. And I've *always* been jaded and cynical." She signals the waitress for another beer. "You didn't try to sell him on how awesome the FBI is?"

"No, I did not. But he did check up on us. Wanted to know why we're out doing PI work now."

When the second beer arrives, she holds it for a long minute, letting the cold from the pint glass seep through her fingers. "What did you say?" They were once an easy Google search, or at least she was, and a few months back Dan caught the younger of their two daughters reading those old online articles, and it worried him. Between Olivia and Lucy, Lucy has always easily been the most like Linnea. Too much, they both agree, and that worries her too.

"I told him we'd seen our share and done our part." He reaches over and his warm fingers brush her cold ones. When he found her down on Parlor's remote farm in Virginia two years ago, he had to carry her two miles back to the road. As bad shape as she was, he wasn't much better, a busted clavicle, three broken ribs, what they would later learn was a punctured lung, burn marks too on his hands and smoke inhalation after they set that barn on fire.

But he carried her anyway, holding her tight, all the way to the road until he could get help. Never once left her side even in the immediate days after, holding her hand whenever she started screaming, whenever someone else tried to touch her, when they finally pulled the stitches from around her eyes.

His fingers were warm then, so warm.

Adan Rio is still the only person she'll let touch her now other than Dan and the girls.

"You don't mean that," she says. "If you truly thought we were done, you wouldn't have had us meet with your charming friend Devine."

"He's not quite a friend." He sips her beer and makes a face. "And if *you* thought we were done, you wouldn't have gotten within a country mile of here." He gives the Good Bug back to her. "You wouldn't be sitting in this bar, of all places, right now."

She finishes off the beer and raises the empty glass in a weary salute to the also nearly empty Ash Street Bar and Grille. "Not like there are a lot of options around here, now are there?"

"Exactly," he says. "Exactly."

* * *

Later, after she downs a third and final beer and they work their way through his burger, they start back for their motel.

The air is thick and muggy. The few streetlights dim, flickering. Despite the murk and her buzz, it's easy even for Linnea to picture Abby Walden standing out here in front of the bar by her car on a night just like this, swaying with a small buzz too, still smelling of smoke.

What did you see? Who did you see?

Who saw you?

"Hey, who is Harriette Person?" she suddenly asks, too loud, maybe more than just a little drunk, pointing to a much newer building adjacent to the ramshackle Ash Street Bar. Some kind of fancy memorial library, although she has no idea who Harriette Person is or why there's a library in Port Gibson memorializing her.

"Don't know," Rio says, squinting at the sign. "Town's favored daughter?"

"Huh," Linnea replies, taking in the library, the seven large glass windows hidden by blinds that front the second floor, the two doors and four tall windows on the first, covered by posters and hand-drawn signs announcing new releases and library programs. Across the street, there's a square park or green space dotted with metal benches and tables.

In the dark, the park is invisible, little more than small trees swaying in the night breeze.

In a bigger city like New York or even Poughkeepsie, street parking would be at a premium during business hours. You'd viciously fight for a spot and finding an open one is the sort of tiny victory that might put a smile on your face all day. But in tiny Port Gibson, they're probably never full, one reason Abby's lonely Subaru drew Officer Lomax's attention.

Rio now follows her eyes as they sweep the library, the street, the still and silent park. "What are you—" But before he finishes, his phone buzzes, multiple text messages pinging one off another. He glances at the first one, then ignores the rest.

"Who is it?" she pointedly asks.

"Nothing," he lies. "Let's keep walking, get back to the motel. I'll deal with it there."

She crosses her arms, sidesteps so he can't walk around her. In their line of work, they both know no good news ever comes at night.

Nothing, *nothing*, good happens after dark.

"Try that again," she says.

He looks down the silent street, almost like he's enjoying the peace and quiet one last time. "Arkansas," he finally admits. "You were right. It's Arkansas."

CHAPTER 13

Mena, Arkansas

Linnea and Rio drive the rest of the night to Mena, more than six hours away, and get there before dawn.

A dozen swirling police lights are visible just off the Wolf Pen Gap Trailhead, painting a gravel lot and a concrete bunker bright blue and red. The bunker itself little more than two bathrooms and a water-hose hookup, a rough rest stop, a way point, in the Ouchita National Forest.

Two portable POWERMOON balloon lights are already set up, one in the lot, the other nearest the women's restroom, the white globes seeming to hover like eponymous moons or even falling stars over the activity below, illuminating everything in a dire light, chasing eerie, capering patterns out among the thick shortleaf pine, black gum, and cherry.

Devine meets them at the perimeter, guarded tiredly by a handful of Arkansas DPS troopers, sharing cooling coffees from the back of an open flatbed. Handheld radios crackle here and there; voices stay muffled.

Devine doesn't show a badge, and no one askes Linnea and Rio for any ID.

No one says a word, but all eyes follow them as they trail Devine across the lot beneath the pale balloon lights high overhead.

* * *

"Body was already moved," Devine says moments later, breaking the silence as they approach the women's restroom. "Taken over to Hot Springs. There's nothing in Mena, no worthwhile facilities anyway. Task force will set up tomorrow at the University of Arkansas Rich Mountain Community College, for however long they need to be here."

"What do we know about her?" Rio asks.

Devine stops short of the entrance. At his back, inside the restroom, shadows play on the walls, as evidence techs move about. More lights are set up there, a couple of yellow aluminum tripods. Linnea realizes the only light these bunkers ever get is whatever sunlight might filter through the three glassless windows. They're nothing more than concrete Porta Potties, and even in the middle of the day, the brightest day, they'll still be gloomy, dark.

Like boxes—like coffins.

Devine continues, "Kayla Rene McCune, thirty-four."

"That's older," Rio says. "Older than the others."

"Yeah, but she looked young." Devine gestures to a passing tech, a young guy with thick glasses and thicker hair, bundled up beneath a DPS hat. "And a mother of two." The tech returns with a set of gloves and booties for each of them. "Been missing for almost two weeks now. Worked in admissions over at Hendrix College."

"How far away is that?" Linnea slips on the Tyvek shoe covers but hesitates with the black, nitrile gloves. There's something about that smell, the powdery grit on her fingers. A powerful memory, one of the strongest she's experienced since Gracie. It used to take her days to feel like she'd scrubbed herself clean of gloves like these.

"One hundred fifty miles, give or take."

"Family around here?" Rio asks.

"None that they know of yet. Maybe some over in Cabot." Devine snaps on his gloves. "Supervisory Special Agent Schweiger is on his way, he'll have more."

"I didn't hear anything on the news." Linnea knows the kinds of stories that draw the mainstream media like moth to flame, those that ran on continuous chyrons.

"*Single* mother," Devine says. "Black."

They all know the kinds of stories the media often ignore.

"There's no identifiable demographic then," Rio says, finishing with his gloves. "No apparent preference on race, age, ethnicity."

"Got to be something?" Devine asks.

Linnea finally wrestles into her own gloves. It feels like she's wearing slick and shiny snakes on her hands, suffocating her, strangling her.

Again.

"For starters," she says, "mostly women that won't be missed, not right away, or ones that won't draw a lot of media attention, at least not for a while." She takes a deep, centering breath. "What you don't know yet is *how* he knows that about them. The question isn't what connects all these girls to each other—it's what connects each one to *him*."

* * *

Even with the tripod lights, the bathroom interior is deep and dark.

Smells dank, old, medieval.

Shadows coil here, but it's just the Arkansas DPS evidence techs, who stand aside, so she can get a better look.

I don't want a better look, she thinks. *I don't want to see.*

"Jesus," she says. "It's beautiful."

And she knows how that sounds, can imagine all the freshly horrified faces around her. She didn't mean to say it aloud, didn't want it to come out like that, but it's true.

It is beautiful.

A massive lightning tree stretching the entire length of the back wall of the restroom, lacy, ashy tendrils spreading floor to ceiling, rising overhead. Cinders or smoke or blood. Like a gothic painting, an incredibly intricate and impossible mural. Too ornate and delicate for this place, giving it a gravitas it doesn't deserve. Makes the cinder block room feel like an ancient Viking burial chamber, a barrow. And now there's another smell beneath the stink of old, rusted pipes and standing water: something acrid, something harsh.

Burned hair. The miasma of burned hair.

She nearly jumps when Rio puts a hand delicately on her back. "Devine said she was found there." Rio points to the center of the wall, down by the floor, the very middle of the room, right where the fractal patterns of the image began, unfurling like—

"Wings," she whispers. "Wings."

"I thought that too," Devine whispers. "Goddamn wings." And for the first time in their brief acquaintance, even he seems unsure of what to do, what to say next. "Have you ever seen anything like this?"

"No," Linnea says, ripping off the gloves, turning her back on that fiery sigil, the symbol, on the wall. "I don't know if anyone has."

CHAPTER

14
The Storm

Just as he crosses into Oklahoma it starts to rain again.

It's after midnight, not far from the Muscogee (Creek) Nation, but he pulls over as the dark water sheets down, waiting for the first glimmer on the horizon. Out on the prairie, across the Great Plains, storms can be particularly dangerous, but at least you can see the lightning coming for miles and miles.

And he wants to see the lightning, wants to *feel* the lightning again.

Years ago, one of the tallest lightning strikes ever recorded was captured right here in Oklahoma, a rare upward streaming jet sixty times more powerful than a regular bolt, shooting fifty miles into the air, turning the entire ionosphere white and purple, brushing against the fringes of space itself, nearly reaching the stars.

The First Nations people in Oklahoma have their own gods, spirits, and myths surrounding storms and lightning. The Thunder Beings or Thunder Brothers; Thunderbirds; even the troublemaking Thunder Twins, Kapoonis and Enumclaw, who throws fire spears down to earth while his brother rolls great boulders around the sky.

Native American legends tell of a world covered by roiling water, ruined by flood. Days and days of storms, like this one.

He cracks a window, listening to the wind rise and fall, letting the rain fall hard on his face as he stares into the gathering dark for the coming light.

He isn't religious, not in any real way anyone might understand, but he has been searching for a sign, an omen. Not only the wild fury of the lightning itself, the howling of the storm, but *her.* He's been searching for so, so long. He got close once, a rumor, before their trail went cold again, leaving him following only the rain, waiting for the lightning to light the way.

Dead and dreaming for so long.

He's suffered much—all this *waiting.*

He fears he's leaving a trail too, like contrails in the air behind him. But when that furious tension inevitably tightens behind his eyes and the tempest builds to a crescendo in his brain like a low-pressure system, a wild storm front, there's nothing to do but throw fiery spears of his own down to earth, to unleash the fulmination in his mind, the squall that clouds his judgment and his thoughts. It just happens more frequently now, almost whenever there is rain, whenever there is thunder and lightning.

He wasn't always like this and hardly knows what he is now.

No, I am the storm season

Out across the plains, a wide band of sheet lightning flashing sudden and white, flaring inside the pregnant belly of a massive cumulonimbus cloud, rising ominously over the prairie.

There will be a storm at last, storm, glorious storm

He feels blood pulsing in his veins, hammering his heart. Lightning in his hands, on his skin, glowing in his eyes and illuminating a hundred invisible scars he bears from storm seasons past.

I am the storm season

I will take the lightning angel's wings

I am the light and the fury

He lets the thunder roll over him and then drives alone into the black rain.

Lightning Bell

Part II

CHAPTER 15

New Cornelia, Arizona

ANDI ISN'T TERRIBLY surprised when Luke Keats rolls up to her front door just before sunset, but she doesn't know how to feel about it.

Most folks in New Cornelia live far apart for a reason. The desert's vastness, the distance itself, a clear and obvious signal that intimacy is neither welcome nor a priority. Andi has few friends and isn't in the market for more.

But when he gets out of his Jeep, smiling, holding up what looks like a still-cold six-pack of beer, with Chili bounding happily around his legs, she doesn't think it's polite to tell him to get the hell off her land and leave her alone.

Andi isn't even sure she wants to.

* * *

The beer is cold.

He picked it up from the Circle K in Ajo and packed it in a cooler of ice as he and Chili explored the small town.

"Didn't drive up to the mine yet but hope to soon." He tips back his second can. "You don't get a true sense of just how empty the desert is until you see it, experience it." He raises his beer to the desert around them, as Chili and Ruby chase each other beneath the setting sun. For a moment the sky is alight with neon, the candy color of Ruby's M&Ms. "You're not just picking up a phone and ordering a pizza out here."

"No, you're not. Although Leah Garcia does make a mean gluten-free one. She's even got one of those big outdoor pizza ovens."

"I met her. She and her husband Erwin seemed nice. They extended an invitation to their potluck in a few days."

"Staying then?"

"For a bit, yeah. I mean, that was always the plan—unless or until someone says I can't."

"Like I said, it doesn't work that way."

"So, maybe you can tell me how it *does* work?"

Andi shrugs. He hasn't commented on the StrikeAlert strapped to her, but he's discretely eyed it once or twice. Hasn't commented on her long-sleeved T-shirt even in the heat or Ruby's heavy layers either. She can feel a hundred unasked questions hovering between them. She says, "You come out here to get away, to be alone, but this is a tough place to manage by yourself, if that makes any sense. So, we kind of watch out for each other, help each other out, while still being respectful of what makes New Cornelia one of a kind. Everyone here is so unique—Bella sometimes says you don't find New Cornelia, it finds you, and I guess there's some truth to that."

He smiles. "I get that, I do. Being a cop is like being part of a special society too. Its own rules, spoken and unspoken. I appreciate you and the others helping me out so far. Helping me get my bearings, find myself."

Andi spins her still full can in her hand. "Do you miss it, being a cop?"

Luke considers. "I mean, I miss parts of it. I do." He puts his empty can down into the dirt beneath her lawn chair and fishes another out of the cooler where most of the ice has already melted, wiping the dripping can on his T-shirt. "I'll be honest, it didn't end particularly well for me."

Ruby's now trying, again, to get Chili to sit or roll over, without any luck. The pretty dog stares back at her little girl with her own big eyes, oblivious or just stubborn.

"If there's one thing truly special about New Cornelia, one thing that we all have in common, it's that we are pretty accepting, warts and all."

"Everyone's got their secrets, huh?"

"Just our stories," she says. "And they only matter as much as *we* want them to, as we let them. Some share their stories Before New Cornelia—BNC—some don't. Either way it's okay, and neither choice defines you. We meet you where you are, accept you as you are."

"That's good," he says. "I'm good too, I think. Good for now."

"And that's our motto—good for now," she says, and clinks cans with him.

* * *

They sit for another hour as the sun disappears, the sky's colors softening, night creeping up from behind the Little Ajo mountains.

She learns a few more things about him. He's had Chili only a few months, a rescue dog he picked up in New Mexico. He's owned the camper longer than that but still doesn't feel comfortable backing up the twenty-two-foot trailer in tight spots.

He used to be a sports fan, baseball usually, but hasn't watched a game of any kind in over two years. Instead, he's mostly just been out on the road, searching for something—*what*, he doesn't exactly say, although it's clear he still carries a lot of guilt over whatever ended his law enforcement career. Maybe he once thought he could put it all behind him, outrun it, outdistance it, but that's proving harder than he ever imagined.

She tells him there are no miracle cures here.

She paints him a picture of New Cornelia and some of its notable characters—Bella, Waylen, even Stephen—but just the broad strokes. She colors in even less about herself, but again, he doesn't pry, doesn't push. They talk easily and the conversation rambles far and wide and they leave the rest of the beer untouched until the stars start to pinwheel and Chili finally walks over and plops down between them and Ruby does as well, hot and tired and dirty.

"That's my cue, I guess," Andi says, standing, stretching. "Gotta get this one inside and cleaned up for bed."

Ruby says, "Chili too, Momma. Chili's sleepy too!"

Luke stands as well, and this close, almost touching, she realizes she's probably an inch or maybe even two taller than him. His eyes are grayer, darker, than she recalls from their first meeting.

"Chili's got a bed all her own, little lady," Luke says to Ruby. He leans into Andi, whispers, "We'll get on out of your hair—but thank you for this."

"Hey, you brought the beers."

"I know. But the company, I mean. The time. Just sitting out here, talking. I nearly forgot how much I missed that."

Andi helps Ruby to her feet, points her to the trailer door, and gently swats the dusty butt of her jeans to send her running up the small set of stairs. "Oh, you're going to find we do a lot of that around here. Sitting around, talking endlessly. Not much else to do."

"I'm glad then. I look forward to it."

"Me too," she blurts out casually, offhand, before she can stop herself. "But next time the beers are on me."

"I guess that means there'll be a next time." He looks at her, searching her eyes.

"Well, I'd say we're good for now," she says, smiling, starting up the stairs behind Ruby.

CHAPTER 16

New Cornelia, Arizona

ANDI EXPECTS IT to be another struggle to get Ruby a bath and to bed, but the little girl is worn out from her excitement over Chili, and for once she does both without much complaint, too entranced with the dog to even question the appearance of a strange man around their tiny home.

She doesn't even stare at herself in the mirror, at her chest and back, her arms, like she usually does. Andi puts her daughter down with her little green stars glowing softly overhead, and she's asleep in five minutes.

Andi checks all the doors, the cameras. Other nights she's spooked herself with the shadows her cameras reveal, that shifting desert darkness that seems to breathe all on its own, but there's nothing out there tonight.

Luke is gone, but his presence lingers on, a feeling Andi hasn't experienced in a while, in far too long. Not since the Black Light Club, since Ethan in Texas, although that was different . . . that was *bad*, that was desperation.

But Andi's not sure this night with Lucas Keats was a good thing either. After Texas, there wasn't much room in her life for anything or anyone other than Ruby. Sure, Stephen's been a constant, and she's grown closer to Bella, even Waylen. But she's carefully defined and compartmentalized those relationships, or at least tried to. They've survived only on her closely guarded terms.

There's been no men at all since Andi pulled Ruby from their Tyler apartment in the middle of the night. And although Ruby's mostly stopped asking about her father, finally stopped waking up crying over him, he's still a looming presence, a specter that has just as much weight and substance and gravitational pull as if he was still physically here with them.

A few more visits from Luke and there won't be any avoiding *that* question, dog or not.

Either Luke will ask about Ruby's dad, or Ruby will say something about him and some version of what happened, and Andi has no idea what she'll do then. Better to just stop it before it ever gets that far. But for the first time in months—*no, years*—Andi was at ease tonight. She enjoyed talking with Luke, laughing with him. That thing with Ethan had been secretive, furtive, stolen moments, an escape from Max's increasingly dark aura, and in some ways fueled by it. Tonight, she sat out for hours in the open with Luke, beneath the wide stars, the whole world to see.

A small thing, but somehow important.

Meaningful.

It all started with that message board on Mosaic.

Mosaic was once Reddit-lite, briefly popular with those in the wellness and mindfulness community. The future Black Light Club forum migrated there from Facebook, where it had languished for years under the less active banner of the LSSSG—the Lightning Strike Survivor's Support Group. Started by Wynona Parsons, who was struck while walking her dog in Bergfield Park, it wasn't until the LSSSG hosted its inaugural conference/retreat in Wynona's hometown of Tyler, Texas, that the club started to gain some momentum. That first retreat was attended by nine people—including Andi and Max, right after they left Virginia together—but the second had twenty-nine from nearly twenty states. It was Andi who changed the name to the Black Light Club and gave them a purpose and an identity—

All touched by lightning, all aglow with black light.

And all suffering varying degrees of PTSD, struggling with the difficulty of returning to work and resuming their lives. All experiencing lingering medical and emotional issues, rising medical costs, increasingly unsympathetic doctors, and the cruel and persistent requests by insurance companies for "independent medical examinations" only to terminate coverage. All accustomed to still startling at a hot flash of light, cringing at a loud bang or crack.

Andi and the BLC gave voice to their traumas, their fears, their hopes. It gave them an emotional home, one where they could share a plethora of articles and abstracts—

Behavioral consequences of lightning and electrical injury . . .

Electrical injury and lightning injury: a review of their mechanisms and neuropsychological, psychiatric, and neurological sequelae . . .

Life After Shock, Volume 1 . . .

A place where they could trade information about the small number of doctors who wouldn't dismiss them out of hand, or useful meditation techniques, treatments for tinnitus, even the best lightning detectors to carry. Over time, as it got harder to hold on to their old lives, it got easier to reimagine a new life, a permanent one, in Tyler, a true physical support community that extended beyond message board posts and emails and phone calls, something not much different than what Bella built in New Cornelia.

Wynona. Minnie and Billy. Cole. Stephen. Tassa.

Ethan.

Even Max.

Only Max was the outlier, a package deal with Andi. She knew none of them liked Max but knew better than to say anything in front of her. Sure, Max could be a constant heavy presence, a lingering, dark cloud. Not so much loud or abrasive or even cruel, just . . . intrusive, omnipresent. And it only grew worse over time, like a storm gaining strength, but it wasn't always bad.

There are still the good moments she remembers even when it hurts to do so. Max could be tender when he wanted to be, the way he looked after her in that dark year right after she was struck and died, and never doubted for a moment the things she was experiencing and couldn't explain. The way he could make those things seem miraculous instead of terrifying. Stephen and the others often wanted to believe the worst of Max because he hadn't suffered like that, but in the end, Andi knows she and Max often brought out the worst in each other.

The hard thing about Max's emotional abuse is that for so long it wasn't hard at all.

The last time Andi saw Max he had a gun in his hand.

It looked so big, so preposterous, so *ridiculous*, she almost laughed, although it was no laughing matter.

He'd been drinking heavily after being questioned earlier in the day by the Tyler PD about Ethan Charmas's near-murder. Ethan was beaten senseless with a twenty-eight-inch black aluminum bat, his body dumped behind a Brookshire's grocery store on the east side of town. It took more than three hundred stitches to suture his scalp back together, and his face was so bruised he was only conclusively identified by dental records provided by Andi herself, who got them with Stephen's help from his family back in Maine.

They flew out to Texas to retrieve their comatose son and take him home, the second time in his young life he'd almost died, and in many ways, injured far worse than by his lightning strike.

Ethan was twenty-six.

She wonders sometimes how things would've been different if Max had pulled the trigger that night; eyes blazing, gun shaking. Max had accused her of carrying on an affair with Ethan, sleeping with him, and he wasn't wrong. But in the end he didn't shoot either of them, he *couldn't*, and when he finally passed out, she dumped her old phone, took Ruby and never looked back.

She was gone before dawn.

Tassa sent her a handful of frantic emails asking where she was, where she was going, how she could leave them, how she could leave Ethan—it was the last contact she had with anyone in the club other than Stephen, who eventually guided them both to New Cornelia, after he had nowhere else to go either.

When she broke down in that Ruidoso motel and called her old friend Joyce to warn her that Max might come looking for Andi—a risk she wasn't sure she should take but was even less sure she couldn't not take—she had nearly seven years under her belt living with the real Max, his mercurial emotions, stealing glimpses behind a mask he'd tried so hard and so long to cultivate, a mask getting harder and harder for him to hold in place. She never imagined he could be violent, but she'd allowed herself to get too close to Ethan and nearly got him killed, and she lives with that every day.

As she gets ready for bed, Andi pulls off her thin shirt, revealing Tassa's pendant she almost never takes off, and the permanent, blushing lightning scars still arcing across her body, over her chest, around her heart. Ethan was the last man other than Max to see them, *touch* them, but he understood them, knew their significance, in a way few people ever could. Ethan was struck by lightning while bass fishing with his dad on Sebago Lake in Maine when he was nineteen, and he was blown head over heels into the water, suffering a ruptured eardrum and a shattered ankle, neither of which he would ever fully recover from. He discovered the Black Light Club three years and two dozen doctor's visits later, and moved out to Tyler to join the others like Andi, who'd already made their way there.

He was amazed how her lightning tree scars had stayed so prominent, so visible. His own, extending from his left shoulder all the way to his right leg, disappeared forty-eight hours after his dad pulled him from the lake. Just like Tassa's and Wynona's and Stephen's and Minnie's and Billy's and Cole's. Only Andi's stayed etched on her skin.

And not just mine anymore, she thinks.

You're my lightning angel, Max used to say, but that was before Ruby was born, before her affair with Ethan.

Like staring into the sun.

She isn't ashamed of her scars but stopped imagining someone ever seeing them again.

But now here they are, sudden feelings growing within her, taking root deep beneath her barren, wounded skin, like those plants in Stephen's hothouse. Lightning blossoms of a different kind.

Luke was once a *cop*, a whole other consideration, and maybe a serious kind of complication. Given how things ended for her and the club in Texas, she's not sure buddying up with a former cop is a smart thing to do, no matter why he's not on the force anymore. It won't take much to find out about that—Waylen may have already done so—and Stephen certainly will if she wants to put him up to it, but it wouldn't be hard for Luke to find out about *her* either.

No, she won't let herself make a big deal of it, not yet. It was just a few beers, just one night. But tonight, Luke did feel different. Tonight felt like something close to *normal*, and there hasn't been a lot of normal in Andi's life since that day in Virginia, when a bolt from the sky killed her for more than two minutes and immolated all the years after.

And that scares the hell out of her.

CHAPTER

17

New Cornelia, Arizona

STEPHEN IS STILL skeptical, despite what Andi's telling him.

"Waylen checked it out, while I ran Luke around. He got the plates off the camper, ran them. He is who he says he is."

"Maybe," Stephen says. "But that doesn't mean we *know* who he is."

"True," Andi concedes, but she's mostly relieved about who he *isn't*. "And you know what? You sound like Waylen right now."

They both agree Waylen is a blowhard, all bluster. Andi knows Stephen could've run Luke's plates too, just like he's always helped Andi, both in Texas and after. He's still got contacts and friends in the gaming and hacking and phishing community he was part of.

She also knows he's irritated that Waylen's already checking up on Luke, before he has the chance to.

He fires back, "Even Waylen doesn't believe half of what he says. And I only sound like *you*—or the way you used to."

Now it's her turn for her temper to flare up hot and bright. "Don't tell me I'm not careful. That I'm not always—"

"No, that's not what I mean, not what I'm saying, at all." He cuts her off carefully, gently, not wanting to see her upset.

They're outside, the late morning sun burning a bright hole in the sky. Stephen was in the middle of checking the new solar panels he affixed to his greenhouse trailer when she stopped by, and he's still up on a rickety ladder, sweating badly. "It's not even a question of who he is, it's *why* he's here," he says. He spreads his arms wide to the desert and New Cornelia all around them. "There are thousand better places to camp for a week or so, to get away from it all for a while."

"If you're not sick, weird, or crazy. That's what you truly mean."

But she knows he would *never* use those words for her or anyone else, even if he still sometimes thinks all three apply to him. If she'd been the unofficial leader of their little band in Texas—blown together by their own storm winds—he was the peacemaker and conscience. And historian. He's been keeping an eye out for her since they arrived in New Cornelia and is convinced that Max is out there looking for her and Ruby.

"Anyway," Andi continues, "let's give him a chance, and let's try not pry too much. Folks come here so they *don't* have to explain themselves, that's what Bella says. We'll learn enough in time. And you'll meet him soon enough yourself, I'm sure." Andi helps him wrestle the ladder down. "And that dog of his too. Ruby won't pipe down about it—it's all she wants to talk about right now. All she'll probably want to talk about it forever. It's going to be a problem."

"He's got a *dog* too?"

It's clear in Stephen's tone that he doesn't think the dog is the main problem.

"Yeah, a cute one. Too fucking cute." She sighs, rolling her eyes. "But Ruby really did like that book you gave her."

The truth is the book Stephen gave Ruby has already been forgotten with all the excitement over the dog, over this new visitor. Not a lot of exciting or interesting things happen around here, period, which is the way everyone likes it. And likely Stephen most all.

But all he says, "Before you go, let me show you something."

* * *

It's hot here too, just a different kind of heat.

His new plants are still topped by humidity domes, or in the case of the smallest ones, Ziploc bags, the clear plastic slick and opaque with beaded moisture. Banks of bright LEDs hang two feet above the plants in orderly rows on a twelve-hour timed photoperiod, giving the room the archaic glow of an old TV set.

Andi wanders the rows with him, bending down to peek at his burgeoning garden.

"They're beautiful," she says. "I've never seen anything like them. They almost don't look real."

He pulls back a dome, revealing a tiny carnivorous pitcher plant with its soft, wide mouth and delicate wings. It's the color of spilled blood. *Heart's blood.* He tells her that despite its beauty, the sanguinea is one of the easiest Neps to grow, not nearly as rare or temperamental as some of his others, which will be so much harder to nurture and take so much longer.

She smiles. "But look at how much you've done and you're just getting started. It's going to be a jungle in here before long, a real oasis out here in our desert."

"Once I get a couple more of these mature and healthy, I want to give them to you and Ruby."

Andi laughs. "Stephen, I can barely keep either of us healthy. I never serve enough vegetables, let her eat too much candy, too much soda. I still sneak cigarettes when I can. I'd hate to kill off all your hard work in a matter of days, if not hours."

"Oh, they'll do fine in a terrarium once I set it up for you. And I'll come over now and then, check on them myself, tend them. They're survivors."

"Like us, right?" she says. "We've thrived out here in the desert too." She reaches over and pushes his black, messy hair out of his eyes, making sure he sees her smile. "That'll be nice, Stephen. Thank you. I don't know how your beautiful plants will compete with the early Americana secondhand trailer park vibe we've already got going on, but anything to brighten up the place."

"And easier to take care of than a dog," Stephen finally says with a crooked smile.

Andi smiles along with him. "Got to be, right?"

Serious again, Stephen asks, "So, did our new arrival tell you anything about himself at all?"

"Said he's a cop, an ex-cop now, I guess." She kneels to look at the blood-red plant barely the size of a child's beating heart, ruby bright even through the damp plastic. "Doesn't matter though. I'm sure he'll get bored with us way out here and move on soon enough."

CHAPTER 18

Mena, Arkansas

THE UNIVERSITY OF Arkansas Rich Mountain Community College is a nice, modern building fronted by trees, as well as more than thirty law enforcement vehicles, several of them unmarked.

Linnea sits in their Explorer, sipping a coffee Rio found for her, swallowing three Advil. It's been nine hours since they arrived in Mena, more than eighteen hours since Kayla Rene McCune was discovered in a rest stop off Wolf Pen Gap Trailhead in the Ouachita National Forest.

For the time being, Kayla's been transported to the Mena Regional Health System, which services both Western Arkansas and Eastern Oklahoma. Notifications are going out, relatives are being tracked down, decisions are being made soon about where to send Kayla and what to do next and who will make those kinds of decisions going forward for her now motherless children.

Collateral damage—all the lives hurt so bad by what's happened here, slivers of grief and rage and loss flung far and wide, likely for decades. Kayla's two boys, Kareem and Dante, both less than nine years old, now facing years of ongoing trauma and hurt. Linnea knows they'll never recover. Grief is a black hole that way, sucking in all light and life.

A massive lightning tree, stretching the entire length of the back wall of the restroom, lacy, ashy tendrils spreading floor to ceiling, rising overhead.

You forever *live* with death like this. You never fully heal, never get over it, never go a day without one of those old slivers piercing your heart again, again, again.

At best you survive.

Even though you didn't die, you might as well have, because in so many ways, the best part of you—the healthy, sane, not-fucked-up part you—already did.

* * *

Ten minutes into his briefing she already doesn't like FBI Supervisory Special Agent Malcolm Schweiger, and she suspects he doesn't like her either.

Maybe the room is too hot, full of too many people, thick with the sound of cellphones and whispers and heavy breath. Or maybe it's the look on her face, or the way she sits with her arms crossed over her chest. Maybe it's that she gets up and pours the rest of her coffee into the trash before he even finishes.

But that doesn't stop Agent Schweiger from tracking her down in the back of the room, where the various state and local Arkansas police agencies now drawn into Kayla's murder stand in awkward groups, forming and reforming like blood cells. Rio tries to head Schweiger off, but the agent, thin and tall and short-haired and square-shouldered, beats him to the punch.

"I understand you're Linnea Wren," he says, crowding her, extending a hand. "I've heard a lot about you." The way he says it tells Linnea all she needs to know about what Schweiger's heard and the opinions he's formed. But she still takes the offered hand. "I've studied so much of Adan Rio's work," he continues, after their perfunctory shake. "It was a shock when he left us, caught everyone by surprise. He's still something of a legend around BAU-5."

"He should be," Linnea says. "A legend, I mean. He earned it." She doesn't talk about what she earned and how she left BAU-5.

Schweiger not mentioning this either is telling, suggesting he's never fully considered her one of them.

She was never an agent, just a consultant, a contractor.

Schweiger swallows and blinks behind his expensive wire frames. He's in his mid-thirties, and probably looks good, at least a hell of a lot more comfortable, in an equally expensive suit. But he's dressed in jeans and a scuffed leather jacket, a bland ensemble the BAU manual probably suggested would make him appear more down-to-earth and approachable to the local yokels. His introductory briefing was just as bland, bordering on useless, marked by his clear unwillingness to share much of what he and his team know.

He says, "I have to admit, I am surprised to find you and former agent Rio here." He holds a beat, as if expecting her to fill it. "Here, in Arkansas specifically, in the middle of this."

"The middle of your investigation, you mean. Look, we're not here to get in the way. Just a case we were already working."

"Privately."

Now Linnea holds a beat. "Yes. A private investigation. Because that's what we do now . . . what we *both* do now." She searches the room for Rio, even for that son of a bitch Devine. "Look, Devine called *us*—"

Schweiger cuts her off. "Devine doesn't have an official role here."

"And neither do we." She still has no idea who exactly Devine is or what role he has. "But we're happy to give you everything we have about our victim. Then, you know, good luck with"—she gestures at the crowd—"all this."

Schweiger blinks again and then takes a long look around the community college auditorium as if seeing it for the first time. All the cops and investigators waiting for someone—for *him*—to tell them what to do next. They're stealing glances at him and Linnea as the minutes *tick, tick, tick* by.

Somone over by the shitty free coffee laughs, likely nothing to do with Kayla McCune's death, but it's still an ugly, awful, uncaring sound.

"Fuck me," he says so quietly only she can hear. "Fuck *me*."

Linnea still isn't sure she *likes* Agent Schweiger, but she does feel sorry for him.

"Yeah," she says. "That's about right."

* * *

Twenty minutes later, she, Schweiger, and Rio are camped out together in a room for the UA-Rich Mountain Science Club.

The walls are covered in cheery old announcements, pictures of star systems and centrifuges, detailed lists of club activities. Through the thick glass window, they can all count the various LEO vehicles still swarming the parking lot, coming and going, their emergency light bars silently and urgently spinning, although the emergency is long over.

Schweiger has his jacket off and his sleeves rolled up, sitting bolt upright in a chair. He has a dozen brightly colored folders stacked in front of him, some thicker than others, none that he's shared or even opened.

He says, "We've got three discrete but small teams working this back at BAU-5. One focused on the offender mindset, a second working crime scene profiling, and a third supporting the other two, focused solely on data collection and mining. For the first time, we're field deploying a new AI database portal."

He says that proudly, like it's supposed to mean something.

"Okay, so basically a prototype," Linnea says, nonplussed. The idea of predictive policing was gaining traction even before her enforced sabbatical and was as controversial as the inherent value of offender psychology.

Schweiger turns instead to Rio. "No one has ever had access to this sort of tool. Not when you were at the Bureau." He only glances at Linnea. "Not when either of you were working these kinds of serial cases. We can now track and manage the incoming disparate data, all of it. Remember it, make sense of it."

"And to think, all we had was *her*," Rio says, nodding in Linnea's direction.

Unable to ignore Linnea, Schweiger addresses her again. "I'm well-versed in how you feel about any kind of multiagency task force.

All the pitfalls: consistency, redundancy, transparency." He taps the words out on the table between them. "Too much information and too few appropriately trained people to manage it, too much secrecy across too many institutions. I read all your post-operation critiques."

"Yes, too much of everything," she says.

"With new tools at our disposal, we can never have too much of *anything*."

Linnea shrugs. "Task-force-driven investigations are easy for serials to exploit, particularly adept ones that move between jurisdictions. Serialized murder is still like rediscovering fire for most small police departments and sheriff's offices. It gets messy, complicated, and unwieldy, fast."

"Not anymore."

"I hope you're right," Linnea says, and she means it. "And I'm sorry if I offended you in your briefing. I don't want to tell you how to do your job and I'm not interviewing for one. But remember that *lives* are at stake here, not numbers, or data models, or algorithms. So I hope your fancy little computer can also calculate some luck for you, because luck always plays a part. And sometimes you need to make your own."

Schweiger looks at his hands carefully folded in front of him. "Is that what happened with your last case—with Jon Parlor? You just got lucky?"

Linnea and Rio both react as if she's been slapped. Silence hangs in the air between the three of them, until Schweiger finally speaks. "I'm sorry, that wasn't—"

"No, Jon Parlor's luck ran out," Rio says quietly, coolly, for them both. "And frankly, ours did too. All our cases started with grandiose task forces and big ideas, and most ended with . . . just us."

Schweiger bulls forward. "I appreciate your insights, but this isn't magic. Your methodologies have been studied, refined, updated. They are not the only successful way to investigate these crimes."

"It's not *success*," Linnea shoots back. "Not with every victim you need to find and every devastated family you need to speak to. Every fucking killing you fail to stop."

Schweiger listens coolly. "Passionate speech. Yet, for all that, you're not actually offering to help, are you?"

Linnea takes the question literally. "I wouldn't be much help here." She waves at Schweiger's rainbow folders, at the building, at the cars choking the lot. "Probably not at all."

Schweiger takes off his glasses. "But you did go back to look at Abby Walden's car. A significant piece of *my* evidence. Why? What were you looking for? What did you find?"

Crumpled tinfoil . . . crumbs of past meals . . . more flower petals . . . black-eyed Susan and cosmos . . .

But she doesn't tell him that, just shrugs and says, "Not enough."

Schweiger smiles. "As every hour goes by and the reality of what we're up against sets in, as the magnitude of it grows and the worthless tips and opinions roll in and pile up, critical clues *will* get missed, vital moments *will* slip by. So I need good people too. The best." Schweiger stacks his folders one on top of another, leaving Linnea to wonder what he's accomplished in his career to land a case like this, what mountain he thinks he's climbed to now find himself in the far corner of eastern Arkansas, in charge of everything.

"So, if this *were* a job interview," he says, "what would it take to bring you on board again? Formally. Officially." He looks back and forth between Linnea and Rio.

Rio watches her as well.

"I don't really do formal or official anymore," she says. "And I am *not* user-friendly."

Schweiger nods and smiles again. "Oh, I think I already understand that, Ms. Wren. I understand that perfectly."

CHAPTER 19

Ajo, Arizona

ANDI AND LUKE stare down at the huge hole, at the poisonous blue water seemingly glowing at the bottom of it.

They've already walked through the quaint red museum building, looking at the glass cabinets full of artifacts and history from the New Cornelia copper mine, ancient miner's helmets, rusty gear and nameless equipment, polished minerals unearthed from the mine's heart itself—shattuckite and malachite, as shiny as the fulgurite pendant Andi wears around her neck. Walls covered in topo maps, proclamations, and old gray photographs of how Ajo used to look when it was still a thriving town, images of people now long dead and the desert in full flower after rains long gone.

Indian Village, 1947. Mex Town, Ajo. Snow in Ajo.

From the lookout, they can see the mine tailings to the north and west, massive mounds of detritus—ground rock and silica and unusable metals—dotted by smaller slurry ponds, salted with arsenic and other contaminants. The hole below them is nearly half a mile across, almost a thousand feet deep, an ever-tightening coil of stair-stepped rock that always reminds Andi of a mollusk shell, acres of calcinate or aragonite, the vast exposed carapace of a once great but dead creature, exposed now to the sun.

They lean together over a thin railing that seems far too weak, the only thing between them and a precipitous fall.

"The Ajo Historical Society is over that way," she says, "in that area that was once called Indian Village or Indian Town. Those houses are all gone now, but some of the local retirees maintain another museum in what used to be a mission. It's got Anasazi pottery and padre beads. Blacksmith tools. Even an old water wagon from the early 1900s. A lot of it has been donated by families who used to live here, when Ajo was thriving. A real boomtown." She shields her eyes, pointing west. "The scenic loop is out there, a ten-mile drive that'll take you around the town and out into the Sonoran Desert and back. But honestly, you see plenty of desert where we are in New Cornelia."

"What direction is that?"

Andi points again, this time past the tailings, out into the worst of the haze and heat. "That way."

Luke shakes his head, whistles low. "I had no idea there was such history here."

"That's about all there is anymore because there's almost no future. Ajo is slowly dying off, rusting away, shutting down, like the mine itself. Sure, there's still the high school and a few shops, the gas station, that one Mexican restaurant. But in another decade, that'll all be gone too."

"Is that restaurant any good?"

Andi laughs. "No, not really. Better than a Taco Bell, I guess."

"Don't knock The Bell. Out on the road, Chili and I eat plenty of it."

Andi lets her laugh drift down to a smile. "You see all these old pictures around, but it's still hard to believe that families lived here, that whole generations were raised here. There were drive-ins and restaurants and bars, birthdays and weddings and graduations. Last year's graduating senior class only had twenty-two students."

"Did you go?"

"What, the graduation?" Andi fumbles, trying to hide her embarrassment. "Yeah, I did. I also gave a few bucks to the fundraiser they had to fix the football field. A couple of dollars I couldn't spare, honestly, but it helped, I guess. Go Ajo Red Raiders."

Luke studies her for a moment, his own face dusted with sand. "So, once a teacher?"

She goes still, quiet, gripping the rusty railing. Finally says, "Lucky guess?"

Luke shrugs. "No, just the way you talk about it. All the stuff that you know about this place, that you've taken the time to learn."

"So, I *sound* like a teacher."

"That, and the look on your face talking about the students, the school," he says. "Sorry, these old cop instincts are hard to ignore."

"Is this an interrogation now?"

"No, not hardly, no crime here," he says, raising his hands, laughing. "Just friendly curiosity." A pause. "We're becoming friends, right?"

Now it's her turn to shrug, although she softens it with a smile. "Be honest, you're curious about me, about Ruby." Right now, Ruby and Chili are with Waylen. Andi knew she and Luke wouldn't be gone long, but she doesn't like bringing Ruby to the lookout, letting her hop, skip, and jump around all the dangers and pitfalls surrounding the old mine. It's also always been a convenient excuse for not bringing Ruby into Ajo much at all, limiting the questions she might have to answer or the ones Ruby might ask.

"Sure. And that's no crime either, Andi." Luke leans against the rail, facing her, and a part of Andi wants to reach out and pull him back. "I'm not prying. I *won't* pry. I mean, you don't have to tell me a damn thing. But you also don't have to be afraid to."

"Okay, well, I *was* a teacher. High school. English. The only teaching I do now is homeschooling Ruby." She hesitates, then leans against the railing too, their elbows almost touching. She's never turned her back to the mine before, never looked away from that great hole. She quotes, "The seller of lightning rods arrived just before the storm."

"You write that?"

"No, Ray Bradbury. One of his novels. *Something Wicked This Way Comes*."

"Unless there's a Cliff notes version, then I didn't read it."

She laughs. "A great American writer."

"I'm sure you were a great teacher too."

"I don't think so, honestly." She hasn't thought about the classroom, about her six years teaching, in a long time. "I mean, I loved the *idea* of teaching . . . the books and the gauzy autumn afternoons and Friday night football games. I just didn't like all those kids."

Luke starts to say something but then just closes his mouth, leaving his expression awkward and unfinished and her laughing out loud again.

"No, it's true," she says. "I probably would've been happy standing in front of an empty classroom. It was all so much harder than I imagined, more managerial, more political. A few moments of actual teaching was like this thing you might get lucky to steal between all the paperwork and assessments and whatever. *Learning* seemed totally out of the question, some days. You've never felt fury like a mother who's unhappy over her daughter's quiz grade."

"Is that why you left? Got sick of it?"

"I got . . . sick." She picks up a rock, a knuckle of shiny quartz, and turns and tosses it over the rail, where it flickers in the sunlight before disappearing. "Had kind of an accident and didn't heal very well from it. For the longest time, I wasn't even sure I *could* heal. Then along came Ruby, and . . ." And she lets the rest of it drop, unsure of what else to say, what she wants to say, what she dares feel like she can reveal.

"She's a sharp kid."

"As a tack."

Luke faces the mine again, his arms casually looped over the railing. He studies the ground below, that bright blue water, like he's looking for the rock she threw, the arc of its long, final descent. "For someone who claims not to like kids you've done all right by her."

"It's different when it's your own."

"Sure, you'd think, but I don't know . . ." Luke continues to study the painfully blue water. "When I was in uniform, I saw a lot of shitty parents, parents who did the most awful things to their kids. Maybe they were just products of their own shitty childhoods or emotional trauma or abuse or whatever. Or maybe it was generational or hereditary. I'm sure there were all kinds of excuses and reasons. But trust me, it's hard to be a *good* parent, and all too easy to be a horrible one, to just dump your crazy all over this little person you're responsible for. There's no license for the job, no test, no person yelling at you over the poor quiz grade of a bad day. All you've got is the result, the final exam."

"You're talking from experience too."

"No kids for me. Only what I dealt with it out on my callouts. And my own childhood. My dad had a legendary temper, explosive, which got infinitely worse when he drank. Talk about a shit storm." Luke shakes his head. "Anyway, I faced off with a lot of angry people on the job. There's just so much anger out in the world, period. So much hurt too. Maybe a place like this, with so few people, is a little quieter, a little safer, and that's not a bad thing. Maybe it's the *best* thing." He shrugs. "I'm not sure being a cop and a teacher nowadays are much different."

"You're probably right."

Luke fake punches her in the shoulder. "I almost feel sorry for that lightning rod salesman who hurt you, if he ever does show up here."

"I thought you weren't prying."

"Cop instincts, remember," he says, tapping his temple with a smile. Now it's his turn to pick up a piece of something from the ground, a rock or quartz or some other mineral, and hold it to the sun. "You live in the middle of nowhere, avoid most discussions of yourself, your past, or your little girl. And you carry a gun, Andi. I've known Marine snipers that aren't as vigilant and wary as you."

"Is it that obvious?"

"Well, it's certainly not that hard." He opens her hand and puts the chunk of smooth stone in it. It's still warm from the sun, his own skin.

"Funny, very funny." She squeezes the rock. "Okay, my lightning rod salesman—as you called him—was once in the military. Had all these stories, about all these heroic things he did. Told me so many things, most of which weren't true, only to find out the things I most didn't want to believe were the only real parts of him. It wasn't so much that he was physically abusive, but he was controlling, jealous, and by the end, angry. We weren't good for each other or Ruby. And I'm still worried he might do just about anything to get her back. It's a shitty story, a cliché." She hesitates. "But no, he's not the whole reason I'm out here."

Luke raises his eyebrows at the StrikeAlert swinging from her waist. "No, I reckon not. I hope you'll tell me the rest whenever you're ready."

"I haven't been ready or willing to talk about myself in a long, long, time." She puts Luke's stone in her pocket. "That's a sad story for another day."

"Yeah, I've got one of those too. Sad story and all." Luke pushes himself off the railing, away from that great hole in the earth, and extends his hand to her. She hesitates, then takes it. "Another day it is, then," he says, and they walk together back to her truck.

CHAPTER

20

New Cornelia, Arizona

WAYLEN TELLS RUBY he's popping into the camper for just a moment, to get Chili some more of those rawhide treats she likes.

Ruby eyes him with a flinty gaze, as the dog follows a scent trail between Lucas Keats's Wolf Pup camper and Waylen's RV, circling in and out of the ocotillo and the fairy duster and the chain fruit cholla.

"Momma says we don't get into other people's business."

Waylen laughs. "Just hitting Mr. Keats's kitchenette for a sec, little honey. It ain't like it's snooping, he and your mom asked me to look after you two. I won't be but a second. You love giving Chili her treats."

Ruby toes the dirt and sand, nodding. "I like soda too but can't have it so much."

Waylen crosses his arms and stares down at his little interrogator. Andi dresses her like a boy, and she's always in long sleeves, always bundled up too much for his liking. It makes him sweat just to think about it.

"If there's a cold soda in there, want me to snag it for you?"

Ruby considers, before nodding again, a small, sly smile creeping like morning sunlight across her face. "I might like that."

"Okay then, we got ourselves a deal. Treats and a soda. But you gotta toss the can, hide it away, and good."

"I'll play lookout," Ruby says, without a hint of sarcasm, before turning her back to him and chasing after Chili.

I'll play lookout. As if it's the most natural thing in the world for a little girl to say.

"Waylen, I think you just got had by that damn kid," he says out loud to himself, as he pries open the Wolf Pup's door and lets himself inside.

* * *

Standard layout, queen bed to Waylen's right, then dinette with mounted flat-screen TV, fridge, and flush-mount glass cooktop, and down at the other end, a tub and shower combo and what would normally be a set of open bunk beds, although that's been retrofitted with a door and padlock likely for additional storage.

A curl of rough, tawny-colored blankets beneath the dinette table signal the dog's bed, but otherwise the small camper is neat and clean, every surface scrubbed, everything put away.

Nothing out of place, which makes searching it both easier and harder; easier to get done quickly, but harder to hide the evidence that someone's been looking around. And it's just plain weird—what grown man left to his own devices lives like this?

Andi didn't ask Waylen to poke around in here and would probably madder than a hornet if she were to find out about it—and if not, that old battle-ax Bella would be—but he isn't even sure he's doing this for Andi alone, or even mostly for her. It's not like he's got anything personal against the man exactly, but he just doesn't like the vibe coming off him, everything a little too carefully constructed, a little too perfect.

A little too slick.

Every surface scrubbed, everything put away.

Maybe it's just the fact that he was once a cop and Waylen just doesn't trust law enforcement much, fed, state, or local—anyone with a badge.

He tries to make quick work of the search, opening drawers and cupboards, snapping pictures with his phone. Fortunately, it doesn't take long to find not one but two guns, but it usually never does. A Glock semi-auto tucked beneath a small shelf by the bed, and a Colt slipped behind the toilet, both loaded, with a chambered round. Someone out on the road on their own, who owns guns and is familiar with them (say, a former cop) would want them within reach. Someone well-prepared to use them. And even Waylen can't fault the man for that.

He catalogues as fast as he can—several cellphones, three laptops, old paperback books, clothes still carefully folded in their store bags but no receipts. Weirdly, there are no pictures either, no memorabilia of any kind, anywhere, hardly anything that indicates a past life before the man arrived in New Cornelia. All that absence speaks volumes, but Waylen isn't sure yet what it says.

No, there just isn't a whole lot to look through.

And he can't ferret his way through that one padlocked door

Frustrated, Waylen opens the fridge, finds the bag of Lucky Chicken-Wrapped Rawhide Treats that silly dog likes so much, and does a double-take at the lack of anything else. A few leftover beers and neatly stacked bottled water, packaged lunch meat, a loaf of bread.

No sodas. *Shit fire.*

Waylen stands in front of the mostly empty open fridge and lets the cool air wash over him. He isn't sure what he's learned during his little surreptitious search, other than he's just as unsure about the man as he was before. Hell, maybe more so. No one lives this cleanly, this carefully, this *clinically*, unless they have something to hide.

Mr. Slick, all right.

It might even be time to get some help on this, someone who's got more resources than Waylen and even more interest in Andi—and that's Stephen.

Stephen carries a bright torch for Andi; they go way back from before New Cornelia. There's plenty of secrets and shared history between those two.

Waylen tosses one last glance at the padlock on the door, the padlock as new as everything else, almost gleaming. *Damn slick too.* A

Master Lock, likely carbide, or alloy steel or even zinc, with an owner-programmed four-digit code. No keys to lose, no keys for someone to find. More time and tools than Waylen has to get through.

He grabs a second treat for the dog and heads back out to Ruby, hoping like hell he has a spare RC Cola or some candy or something in his own fridge, otherwise he isn't sure what else he has to bribe his little accomplice with.

CHAPTER 21

Mena, Arkansas

Agent Schweiger asks Linnea to meet him again, this time alone, on a grassy swale behind the college.

They sit on a bench beneath the spreading branches of an Osage orange tree. The air is damp and musty, stray clouds the color of campfire smoke collecting in the nearby hills. Schweiger brings a couple of iced teas one of his agents grabbed for him, and Linnea nods politely at the drink and sets it on the bench between them.

"Thanks for taking another moment to talk to me," Schweiger starts. "Just the two of us. I was hoping to . . . well, honestly, I don't know. Maybe clear the air. To start over here."

Linnea nods. "I know this is only your second active serial, but you've handled major cases before. Three kidnappings, two disappearances."

"You've done your homework."

She shrugs. "I left the Bureau, but it didn't leave me. It doesn't. Not entirely. I still have friends." But as Devine pointed out, they're more of Rio's friends than hers.

"What do they say about me?"

She doesn't hesitate. "Too smart by half. A climber. But good, very good. They tested you with the West Mesa Bone Collector case."

Now it's Schweiger's turn to shrug. "I didn't pass."

"No one does. For what it's worth, we looked at it and came up empty too." Almost every new agent assigned to BAU-5 gets assigned to the Bone Collector case, still an open investigation. "They give you West Mesa to teach you humility. Always starting from behind, playing catch-up, picking up stray puzzle pieces you can't put together fast enough. The very definition of a *serial* is that by the time you truly know what you're dealing with, they're *skilled* at killing, at getting away with it, and only getting better. So, bad days get under your skin, and you can't get away from those either. West Mesa isn't about succeeding, it's a test of how you handle failure."

"Did you interview any of our incarcerated serials about West Mesa?" he asked.

"Most of those interviews never prove to be valuable. If psychological gratification is a serial's primary motive, then psychological gamesmanship is as well. They reveal only what they want you to know. Most can't explain their own behaviors and have even less understanding of them. They're not geniuses and they're not insightful. Certainly not credible."

"Jon Parlor was a genius—143 on the Stanford-Binet."

"Parlor was still crazy and a liar."

"That's not what your original profiles said."

Linnea only stares straight ahead. "Is that a question—or an accusation?"

"I'm just curious why you never tried to interview him."

"Because there was nothing more to say." This wasn't something she was getting into for his entertainment or his edification. She wasn't detailing to him what was done to her, how it affected her. All he had to do was look at her scars.

"Is that case what prompted you to leave the Bureau?"

"No," she says, "I wasn't pressured over that. I wanted Parlor dead for what he did to me. I was the one who couldn't let it go."

"That doesn't sound like our BAU-5 training," Schweiger says. "That's not the FBI."

"No, it's not," Linnea agrees. "*That's* why I left the Bureau."

She then pours her untouched tea out into the grass and leaves it at that.

* * *

Schweiger spends another thirty minutes going through the case outline, what they have, what they don't have, what his thinking is.

She asks a couple of questions but otherwise stays silent as the clouds move in on them, threatening rain.

"I can bring you in on this," he tells her. "I *want* to. And the truth is the two of you are already all over this thing, like dirty fingerprints." Linnea knows they're the *only* fingerprints Schweiger's got, since the physical and trace evidence at the locations where they've recovered bodies is still mostly nonexistent. "If I don't bring you in now, what are the chances you're out there running around, getting in the middle of more of my crime scenes?"

Linnea stands. "We can be gone in an hour, Schweiger, and I promise we won't interfere with your investigation, now *or* later."

Schweiger stands too. "Do you want to know what *my* homework says about you?

"Not particularly."

Schweiger smiles, ignores her. "That you've always been a tireless advocate for victims. You took each of your serial cases personally, didn't create any professional distance between yourself and your work. That discipline made you driven, fierce, combative . . . but also very, *very* effective. You were incredibly gifted."

"But?"

"You're also still incredibly traumatized by what happened on your last case."

Linnea studies the coming clouds, the gunmetal sky, wondering how long they have before they roll in over them. She figures at any moment now.

She turns to him. "You have at least seven victims now spread across nearly as many states in what's possibly an escalating pattern, with zero confirmed links between the crime scenes or decedents and an attack MO that seems impossible. Media containment will be next to impossible when a certain United States senator starts making calls, and he will. And your serial presents as particularly bright, law enforcement savvy, and nothing if not highly motivated." She continues to stare at him steadily, without a hint of humor.

Schweiger blinks at her assessment, flashing first irritation, then a smile, more sad than bitter. "As bad as I thought." The rain starts to come down. One drop, then another, each one faster. Schweiger ignores them. "Okay, then, so what do I do?"

"Whatever you have to," Linnea says, not able to smile back. "Whatever it takes."

CHAPTER 22

Mena, Arkansas

LATER RIO COMES to her hotel room with a slim leather case under his arm.

He sits on the edge of her bed and puts the case squarely between them. "I spoke to Schweiger," he says.

"I thought you might. Divide and conquer, right? Did you guys do that whole secret FBI agent handshake thing? The magic password you never shared with me?"

She rubs between her eyes, touches her scars again. They feel hot to her, inflamed. After meeting with Schweiger, she rang Dan, but it went to voicemail, Dan texting her back moments later that he was tied up with the girls and they'd talk when he was free.

"Schweiger wants our help, Lin. Badly. No strings, no preconditions. All access and total freedom of movement."

Linnea's eyes fall again on the case between them. "And that is?" she asks.

"All access."

They sit silently together. "Did he question you about Parlor too?" she asks.

"Not much."

"But enough, I'm sure." What she truly wants is a drink. A strong one or three. "Has he ever tried to interview him?"

"Honestly, I don't know," Rio says. "It's part of the BAU-5 playbook. I imagine if he gets desperate enough on this thing, he will."

"If he gets desperate enough, he'll try anything. We always did." She reaches out for the case, finding it heavier than she thought. "So, what do you want to do now?"

Rio places a hand on her arm, stopping her. "I want you to go home to Dan and the girls. You don't owe anyone anything, including me. Don't let Schweiger pull you into this anymore than Walden."

"But you're going to help him."

"I don't know."

"Oh, I think this says otherwise," she says, holding up the leather case. "Devine, Schweiger, even Walden, all have your number and know what buttons to push. You're a crusader, a real-life action hero. I know it too." She smiles at him to soften her words. "Just like sooner or later, we both knew we were always going to end up right back here."

"It's still not too late," Rio says, looking at the case in her hands, then at her. "Just walk away."

"It was too late the moment I walked into that Arkansas rest stop, the moment I saw those marks on Abby in Mississippi. Maybe I don't owe Walden, or the FBI, but I still owe *them*. Abby, Kayla, all the rest. And I owe it to myself to at least try."

"You already did. Abby's car."

Linnea shakes her head, touching her eyes again, the tiny cicatrices around them hot to the touch. "No, I'm afraid I tried *not* to, and that's a big fucking difference. I'm scared, Rio, almost terrified. Terrified to go back to those places, but terrified if I *can't*."

She unzips the case, revealing a thin, black laptop. A strange color, a glossy, unnatural black that almost looks purple when she turns it around and around in her hands. It bears several bright labels, first TOP SECRET, then PROPERTY OF BAU-5, then LOOKING GLASS—and a tiny cartoon white rabbit, smiling up at her.

She touches the rabbit, as if she might feel fur. "What's this?"

"Schweiger said some of the agents started calling it Alice, you know, like Lewis Carroll's *Alice's Adventures in Wonderland*."

"Ah, the white rabbit, through the looking glass," she says. "Jesus, stupid cop humor."

Rio smiles and stands. "How much time do we have?"

Before he strikes again?

"I'd say five to six weeks on the outside but probably less. I think he's growing impatient."

"You sure?"

"No," she admits. "I'm not sure about anything anymore." She opens the laptop. "But let's see what the new girl Alice here has to say about it."

CHAPTER 23

New Cornelia, Arizona

RUBY ISN'T AFRAID of the dark.

Not like Momma.

Momma worries there are things in the dark she can't see and that's why she keeps the lights and cameras on all the time, why she has so much trouble falling asleep and is tired and crabby a lot because she tries to stay up and watch the dark all night long to protect Ruby, and Ruby loves her fiercely for that, even if she thinks it's silly.

Even if she doesn't understand.

The dark doesn't scare her, not really, and even on those nights when she hears things sneaking around that she can't see or wakes up to those bad dreams again she can't quite unsee, she has her favorite tiny red metal flashlight, which needs new batteries all the time, but she can click it on fast and wave it around her room to make the shadows run away and to prove to herself that there was never anything there at all.

It's also good for reading beneath the covers too, like the new book Mr. Stephen gave her, about living things that can light up the night. She's never seen a fish or frog glow, only her pretty little plastic stars on the ceiling. Only her momma too, once upon a time.

So, when it's late and she's awake and the dark doesn't scare her, she sometimes sneaks out of her bed and moves quietly around the house, peeking out the windows to see the shiny night stars for real. She moves on tippy-toes and sometimes goes to Momma's room and watches her sleep, finally sleep, and although it hasn't happened in a long time, there were those moments when her momma would softly glow beneath her covers too, just like the stars in the sky, like those on her ceiling, like all the creatures in her new book. A *faerie fire*, the new book calls it, and that makes Ruby believe Momma is magical, like a good witch, a fairy queen.

Momma was hurt so badly by the bad rain and all that hurt made her scared not only of the sky but of the dark and strangers and so many things, but if she could only remember her magic, if she could only *glow* again like a fairy queen, she wouldn't be as scared anymore.

Ruby lays in her bed and stares at the ceiling as her plastic stars fade. She thinks about Momma's new friends, Mr. Luke and Chili, the way Chili smells thick and deep and smoky like Momma's clothes sometimes, how warm and soft Chili's fur feels beneath her fingers.

Chili always looks at her like she's got secrets to share, but unlike animals in Ruby's movie cartoons, Chili can't speak. Or won't. Or maybe she only forgot her magic too, like Momma.

She imagines the fun picnic party coming up and seeing Auntie Bella and all their desert friends but no friends her age, no kids to share her new book with or help teach Chili tricks or to talk again.

Chili is stubborn that way. Stubborn even for a silly, beautiful dog.

She only needs her momma . . . but that's not true. She'll need friends of her own someday, other girls, even gross boys. She's getting too big to be babied and looked after all the time, the same way she's outgrowing her hand-me-down sweaters and her shirts and her shoes, outgrowing her tiny bed and this trailer and this whole place. Momma knows this too. Ruby can see it in the way she looks at her, like she has secrets to share just like Chili, the way she sometimes holds Ruby way too tight, *squeezes the stuffing out of her*, as Auntie Bella might say.

The way she cries all quiet when she thinks Ruby isn't looking.

I'm not afraid of the dark, Momma.

Not when she knows her momma can *glow*. Not when she knows that she'll glow soon too.

She's not afraid of a life beyond the desert. She doesn't remember much before New Cornelia, only snatches of Texas, and then all the little motels and hideaway places after that, their lives a heady blur, constant motion, until they got here. But she does remember green trees and a swath of green grass as far as she could see and a Christmas one time with real snow, delicately falling from the sky, soft as Chili's fur. Remembers catching those cool flakes on her tongue, and how sweet they were, like her favorite M&Ms or Auntie Bella's special cookies.

Ruby slips from her bed and pads through the trailer, peering through the thick curtains in the living room, but if there's anything out there, it's too sneaky or too dark for her to spy.

The stars are gone tonight too.

She sneaks her way to her momma's room—sneaking is bad, she knows, she knows, just like she knows that's *exactly* what Mr. Waylen was doing in Mr. Luke's trailer—and finds her curled up in a mess of sheets, arms thrown above her head. Her hair hides her face but not the marks that swirl along her momma's chest, the ones she mostly covers up, like the ones Momma makes her cover too, but that are so beautiful, like Momma herself.

Her magic.

And if Momma's a fairy queen, then that makes Ruby a fairy *princess*, which means she'll have magic too, someday, when she's older.

I'm not afraid of the dark, Momma.

Someday she'll glow enough to light the way for them both.

CHAPTER

24

Mena, Arkansas

"THE VICTIMS." LINNEA ticks off: "Winn Chu. Allison Dufresne. Tonya Wilkins. Faiza Monroe. Skye Lauder."

"Abby Walden," Rio says.

"Kayla McCune," Schweiger concludes.

The three are gathered in the Rich Mountain Community College's cafeteria, where the entire task force met yesterday.

"Three white, three African American, one Asian. There is nearly a fifteen-year age disparity across the group. Allison Dufresne was the first found. And only one, the last, was a mother."

"But we believe the first true victim was the youngest, eighteen-year-old Chu," Schweiger says.

"And I'm not even sure yet age necessarily matters," Linnea adds. "At least not to him." She flips the lustrous black laptop around on the long table between them so the two men can see the screen. She spent the last twelve hours going through the data Schweiger's task force has compiled, querying Alice, sorting through the vast amount of information the AI has access to, what its algorithms can collate, cull, and sort through. It was, *is*, impressive, seemingly light-years ahead of anything she and Rio used only a couple of years ago, leaving her to wonder where it came from, who created it. Wondering too if it was even legal, or just co-opted technology from one or more of those entities the mysterious Devine fronts for.

Alice already represents a vast digital mosaic of lives lost, all at Linnea's fingertips, yet still frustratingly incomplete. But that was always the nature of these cases, always one more clue or vital piece of the puzzle to search for.

"Five of the women appear to have been moved, likely premortem. Maybe they went willingly, but let's assume they didn't." Linnea hammers at Alice's keys. "Most discovered in rest stops, some as many as one hundred fifty miles from their residences or last known location." She can't recall many serials moving a victim that far.

"Only two were found otherwise," Rio says. "Chu and Wilkins."

Schweiger speaks up. "Chu's body was found in an abandoned gas station ten miles from Swarthmore, where she was starting her freshman year. Autopsy confirmed she'd been there at least five days." He doesn't mention the time frame was nailed down by the maturity of bug larvae found beneath the young woman's skin. It was still hot in middle Pennsylvania in September. "Wilkins was discovered on the side of a road just outside of Raleigh, forty-eight hours after her husband reported her missing."

"So, what makes Winn Chu and Tonya Wilkins different?" Linnea looks back and forth between Rio and Schweiger, before gesturing at the laptop. "I asked Alice. Ran everything I could think of."

"So did we, weeks ago," Schweiger says. "Social media. Employment. Schooling. Time of day, season, lunar cycle. Hell, and I do mean this literally, even the pagan calendar. We couldn't find any corollary."

"Neither could I, or at least nothing that jumped out." Linnea spent hours last night scanning through a year of social media posts for the two women, looking for a common face, a common place, a common *thread* that might bind them together. And there are still so many platforms to work through, including some no longer popular; and several going back *years* for them both, for all of them. In theory, Alice's algorithms could look independently for parallels, but Linnea doesn't yet trust leaving the AI to its own devices. Despite

Schweiger's bluster, she's not sure he fully does either. That's why he wants her and Rio to shepherd it, to *teach* it. "So, I reversed the question, asked myself what possibly made the five other girls the same."

Schweiger nods. "And?"

"Not a thing," Linnea concedes. "Nothing. Either we don't have enough or haven't gone deep enough yet. All we have connecting all these victims is . . . him."

"Sure," Schweiger says, annoyance bubbling just beneath his otherwise placid surface. "That's the point, right? That's why we're all here."

"That *and* those flowery burn marks on our women, as well as the rest stops where most were recovered." Linnea spins the laptop around so Schweiger can see the geo-map of the crime scenes she made Alice populate. "These attacks aren't spread out in an array around a central point. We're not looking at a so-called hunting ground here. There's no *locus*, but there still is a pattern though—just *linear*."

"A trucker," Rio says

Linnea points at the blooming graphics on the laptop. "So far, this route isn't consistent with any trucking scenario. I tried matching this against standard profitable routes for Old Dominion, Schneider National, J. B. Hunt, Knight, you name it. Even UPS and FedEx. No luck. It's not conclusive, but it is dispositive."

Rio counters: "A much smaller operator then, picking up what he can, when he can?"

Linnea shakes her head. "Likely would still imply some kind of center point, a home base. But if you cross-reference the days of discovery, probable times of death, plot the distance of each crime scene from each other, calculate his cooling-off period from one victim to the next—and it's getting shorter, by the way—he's been on the move almost constantly from the start. Even if there's an element of randomness to his victim selection, *this*—" Linnea traces the glowing path with her finger "—looks purposeful, premeditated. He's going *somewhere*."

"Finding his victims along the way," Rio concludes.

"Maybe," Linnea concedes.

"Okay," Schweiger says, "so he's opportunistic. But those are incredibly risky chances to take. Sure, his victims are mostly young, but none are transient. They're not hitchhikers or prostitutes or addicts. They're not even particularly high-risk. Not even Abigail Walden." Linnea notices that he's careful how he talks about Abby. "How are they crossing paths?"

Linnea gently taps the laptop. "I don't know. But he seems to be meticulous with crime scene choice, even though he has *three* crime scenes to deal with for each victim—when he meets and apprehends her, when he kills her, then when he disposes of her. That means managing, imprisoning, his victims over some time. Hours, days? No small feat."

Rio says, "He's focused on the process of killing and that takes planning."

"So it's a ritual for him," Schweiger says.

"Right." Linnea nods. "He *stages* most of the bodies, but with little regard for subterfuge. Even his murder MO, which we still can't identify, is spectacular, specialized, identifiable. Ritualistic. And I think that's the key, those impossible, fiery images he leaves behind on his victims' skin." She sits back.

After a moment, Rio says, "And yet, somehow, his victim selection is . . . random."

"Or only *appears* that way. There's still an organizing principle at work. There must be. Otherwise, it's too risky, dangerous, chaotic." Linnea hesitates, says, "Organized chaos."

The three silently stare at the flashing screen between them.

"And still some kind of timetable too," Linnea says, "a plan or even just a destination, even if it's not evident in the data yet. Even if we can't fully see it." She feels her fingers fly unbidden across her eyes, grazing her scars. "And your Alice's data is good, no doubt about it." But as good as it is, Alice lacks perception or insight. *It watches, observes, records, but it doesn't truly see.* "I'm still going to need all the ambient video recordings we have from the rest stops, from all the last known locations of the victims. Security footage, store video surveillance, game cams, dashboard cams. Crosswalks. Ring doorbells.

Anything you can think of. I need it all uploaded, the week prior and the week after."

Schweiger blinks behind his glasses. "That's hundreds, maybe a *thousand* hours of footage. Most of it shitty quality, quite honestly. And Alice already has access to facial recognition software. We know that Faiza Monroe was in an Augusta Target two days prior to her disappearance, shopping for birthday party supplies for her sister." Schweiger spreads his hands, as if to hold something heavy or unwieldy in them. "That's a ton of footfall data from that one store alone—age, gender, ethnicity."

"I still need to see it, Schweiger. *Me.* This is what I do."

Schweiger glances to Rio, who just nods, before looking back to Linnea.

"Okay. I'll get it, get everyone on it." Schweiger stands and stretches. "Organized chaos," he repeats, shaking his head

He hands them each a thick padded envelope, the few items Rio demanded, the non-negotiables he'd insisted on for them both.

"Where do you think he's going?" Schweiger asks.

Linnea turns the envelope over in her hand. It feels heavy to her, even heavier than the Alice AI laptop, where the killer's trail still blooms in bright, radiant graphics on the screen, a kind of lightning tree or flower too—

The Lightning Tree Killer.

LTK.

Once they have a name, there's no going back.

"Home," she says. "I think he's heading home."

C H A P T E R

25

New Cornelia, Arizona

ANDI KNOWS BELLA is going to suffer later, even sitting at a distance.

The smell of the food, the *people*, is already overpowering her.

Bella is one of the last truly sick ones, most of New Cornelia's original founders having died off or killed themselves. Bella once told her that suicides were so common back then it was never questioned, never mourned. For most of them, it was a release, an escape. They had to bury their own dead, because the presence of any outsider would leave the rest of them sick for days.

That's not true for the newer arrivals like Andi or Stephen or Waylen. Like Luke.

The *world* isn't trying to kill them, the way it's been trying to kill Bella for three decades.

But before tonight's potluck, Andi insisted they all take precautions. Leah hasn't washed her hair in three days, and Tabby's been wearing the same clothes for just as long, although in all honesty, that's as much Tabby's way as it is any care for Bella.

There will be no firepits tonight.

They're all cognizant, aware, concerned. And that's all that Bella herself would ever ask, insisting that their tiny, wayward community needed these occasional get-togethers. You could barely even call New Cornelia a community anymore *with* them, and there would be no way to sustain what little they shared without them.

Of course, Bella contributed to the potluck too.

Two saved boxes of her beloved Biscoff cookies.

* * *

For the first half hour, Bella mostly just watches from her wicker seat under the big striped umbrella Erwin set out for her, about fifteen yards from the long picnic tables the others cluster around. Candy-cane–colored lights stretch above the makeshift outdoor patio, stark and bright against the deepening evening sky, and although Erwin's charcoal grill and his outdoor pizza oven are both dead and cold and covered in tarps, Andi suspects Bella can still taste the grill smoke in the air from two days before.

Conversations drift over her like smoke too, like sweet, slow songs on a radio.

They're all here—Tabby, Erwin, and Leah. Stephen and Waylen. Oren. Diego. Andi and Ruby. Luke. Because Luke understands how much the dog's dander might bother Bella, he showed up late, and left Chili back at his camper. But he's stayed close to Andi and Ruby tonight, helping her little girl fill up her plate a couple of times, making sure Andi has a cold beer in hand; the three of them laughing and smiling.

Andi suspects that from afar, they almost look like a family.

She hasn't spoken about it much with Bella, but she's sure the growing closeness between her and the new arrival is evident, and that probably makes Bella happy. Waylen and Stephen have their concerns about Luke, and the two of them have been thick as thieves all night, but so far, they've mostly kept those concerns to themselves. As happy as she is now, Andi feels equally worried for Stephen, who bears his affection for her like a wound, naked and exposed and raw. She always hoped he would understand how their complicated history made any sort of relationship with him out of the question, and why it didn't make them any closer.

Andi wishes she was beyond needing any kind of romantic entanglement at all, that she had no longings like that anymore. As much physical pain as she's suffered, her heart is just as wounded. Her body has betrayed her at times, but so has her heart, and she doesn't totally trust either of them anymore. If she could only be content to sit back at a distance like Bella and watch her friends and her community and keep everything and everyone at arm's length, even her own feelings and passions.

It might not guarantee that she'll never get hurt again, but when the pain inevitably comes, it might make it a little more bearable.

* * *

It's fully dark, thick clouds massing around the mountains, when Andi finally breaks free from the others and walks to Bella with two beers in her hands.

Bella brought her own boiled bottled water resealed into special plastic-free Welly bottles, made from stainless steel and harvested bamboo, so neither of those beers are for her, but Andi carries them like they're presents or offerings. She can feel herself swaying delicately, a dancer placing one foot carefully in front of the other, following a path only she can see.

If she isn't drunk, she's well on her way.

She collapses cross-legged in the dirt ten feet away, her face catching a candy-cane glow. The string lights at her back bounce and bob, sideswiped by a fresh wind blowing from the mountains, a warm breeze colored by a cool, damp undercurrent, like swimming in a summer-sun pond and occasionally feeling the colder, deeper water grazing against your bare legs.

The storm . . . that's what it feels like . . . that's what it smells and tastes like.

The only person more attuned to weather than Andi is Bella, but not tonight. She only laughs as Andi tumbles down in front of her, intent on making sure her beers don't spill.

"I see you're enjoying yourself," Bella says. "So, you *haven't* forgotten how to have fun."

"It's been a while."

"You clearly needed it."

Andi drinks one of her beers. "Seems so."

"And *he* seems nice."

Andi takes another drink and puts the empty beer on its side. "Tonight isn't about him."

"If it isn't, *mija,* maybe it should be." Bella pulls her long hair back and ties it loosely in a bun. "Maybe there's a reason for our dear little Ruby to keep an old woman company tonight—"

"Ugh, no, don't go there." Andi wiggles a free hand at her, then grabs up her other beer. "This *has* been nice, no doubt, but I'm not ready for all . . . that. I don't even know. It's all so complicated."

Bella sighs, looks at the sky. "No, *mija,* right now, it's the least complicated thing of all."

Andi chuckles. "Waylen, Stephen, have been grilling him all night. I'm not sure they like him."

"They care about you, that's all. Like I do. They just care about different things."

Andi laughs before growing serious again. "Are you okay over here? I hate that you can't join in. I'd like you to talk to Luke more, you know, get to know him too." She hesitates, looks closer. "But you look tired."

"No, you mean I look god-awful. But I'm fine. I promise." Bella waves her away. "This has been good for me too. This energy of everyone altogether, even we hermits need that now and again. Just remember, you aren't a hermit."

Andi tosses a glance back toward the hanging lights, where Waylen and Luke stand silhouetted, along with Ruby and Stephen. Her voice catches in her throat. "He's sweet to Ruby, patient with her."

"You know what they say about a man who is good with dogs and kids . . ."

"Yeah." Andi finishes her second beer and climbs unsteadily back to her feet, her dancer's balance—that graceful pirouette from moments before—already a distant memory. She's drunk. "I'm really, really going to regret this tomorrow."

"Don't," Bella admonishes.

Andi laughs, swaying, as if buffeted by the light breeze, or a big hand pulling her back and forth. She stares out into the dark, lost there. There is so much about her Bella doesn't know, but she wonders if Bella knows how it feels to be caught between the things you want and those you're afraid you can never have. When the world spins around you, full of infinite possibilities and unfulfilled aspirations, hopes and fears, and you have no idea whether to hang on tight or just let go, lost in the dark.

"Do you want me to call Luke over?" Bella asks.

But Andi is ignoring her now, suddenly steady, her bleary gaze drawn sharply to the Little Ajo Mountains, to the roiling clouds hanging low. "Is that—" She yanks at the StrikeAlert on her belt, bringing it close to her face, where, as if on cue, it wakes up, comes to life, beeping and humming and furiously blinking again and again.

Oh no . . . no . . . no.

Then they both see it at the same time—

A spear of incandescent light, colored furious orange by all the hanging dust as the storm's sudden downburst sweeps loose silt and clay across the desert floor below it, far away still but inexorably coming for them.

A flash, then another, as the storm gathers its strength, grows ominously closer.

"Oh shit," Andi says. "Oh no."

Bella calls out to her to wait, to hold on, but by then Andi is already running.

CHAPTER

26

Mena, Arkansas

LINNEA STARES AT the gun for a long, long, time.

Standard FBI-issued Glock 17 with a trigger lock, tagged with a six-digit barcode. It was packed deep in the padded envelope Schweiger handed over, along with a fresh set of laminated credentials specially created for her and Rio.

Consulting investigators. Special investigators.

She runs a thumb over the raised, black credential number—5789, the same number she carried before.

Almost every significant and high-profile serial case eventually turns to consultants, she knew. Profilers and psychiatrists, crime scene and forensic experts, psychologists, psychics and mystics and cranks—as time ticks by and the tension ratchets up and desperation set in.

Some are better than others, some only create more work for the already thinly stretched task force, sending time-strapped investigators on useless clue chases. For some it's simply about fifteen minutes of notoriety and exposure, a chance to get close to a horrific event, a dark tourism that specializes in murder locales and crime scenes and sites for mass disasters, a way to touch all that black energy. It's only gotten exponentially worse with the internet, where a flock of armchair sleuths can suddenly and unilaterally appoint themselves crusading investigators, descending like a murder of crows on crime scenes and victim's families, hovering over the dead, turning investigations into real-time reality shows.

It happened with Jon Parlor III.

* * *

Jon Parlor III, the so-called Jupiter Killer, had stalked, abducted, and killed twelve young women in a rural barn in Ruther Glen, Virginia.

Linnea was his thirteenth victim.

She and Rio had been pursuing Parlor for nine months, and she was ambushed in a hotel garage in Williamsburg, Virginia.

Parlor had bought the small plot of land and the wood for the barn five years before his killing spree and spent at least one weekend a month on the property after it was mostly complete, adding his own finishing touches—some revealed in the press, others known only to him and her—including the hidden room beneath the barn that he referred as the *sepulcher*.

He appeared out of the dark in that garage where she was waiting for Rio and wrested her gun from her hand even as she was drawing it. He punched her in the face and rolled her over, shoving her own gun into her mouth, and then beat her unconscious with it and drove her to that barn where he locked her in a sandalwood box, a coffin, before sewing her eyes shut and then murmuring things to her that she didn't want to hear.

Parlor had taught himself ophthalmological surgical techniques, like how to sew eyelids together, from medical videos he watched on the internet. Taught himself how to *remove* eyes—and other organs.

His sutures were so perfect, so delicate, he didn't damage her vision, something some doctors later said was a miracle.

The real miracle was Rio finding her only four days after Parlor took her.

Rio entered that barn alone and without backup and rescued her, nearly killing Parlor and almost dying himself, and even though she was still blind when Rio dragged her out of that place, she took Rio's gun and shot Parlor three times at close range, execution-style, and then Rio burned the barn down with Parlor inside.

Still, Parlor survived, his badly burned body recovered by the responding Carolina County fire department.

The Jupiter Killer case was already a high-profile media sensation even before Parlor kidnapped one of the investigators chasing him and became a truly massive media circus in the months after. And Linnea Wren—Parlor's only known surviving victim—was in the center ring, culminating in a highly debated three-week trial where she provided testimony via closed-circuit TV.

He was sentenced to death not for the three killings and kidnappings that were ultimately proved on the stand, but for the attempted murder of two federal agents.

Since his trial, Jon Parlor III has been incarcerated at United States Penitentiary Florence Administrative Maximum Facility, a federal supermax prison in Fremont County, Colorado, holding the most high-profile, violent prisoners in the country. He's given exactly two short interviews—the first for *Vanity Fair* and the second for the *Psychological Review*. Both netted him an avalanche of fan mail, none of which he's ever been moved to respond to or even acknowledge, and neither interview illuminated his reasons for kidnapping Linnea or what happened when she was rescued. He's also refused to speak with his wife and nineteen-year-old daughter, but they had changed their names and were moved at the FBI's expense through the Secret Service's WITSEC program. And if they don't exist as far as the rest of the world is concerned, they don't exist to Parlor either, despite the fact he had been a husband and a father for more than twenty years.

But he has repeatedly requested to speak one-on-one with Linnea, at least once a week, every single week, since he arrived at ADX Florence.

Before all this, if you'd met him he might appear no different than any high-priced corporate lawyer or college professor or doctor, maybe a little more perceptive, eyes a little livelier and wit a little sharper. He'd likely prove to be a better-than-average friend and colleague, dependable and hard-working—right until the moment people started to go missing.

Before he held her captive, she didn't have a firm grasp on what might motivate a forty-two-year-old husband and father and well-regarded member of the community, a lawyer and adjunct professor and supporter of the Richmond Performing Arts Alliance, to suddenly begin to weave a multiyear tapestry of horror.

But after those four days in that sandalwood box, ninety-six hours of listening to him whisper to her in the dark, she *knew* . . .

She's never tried to interview or interrogate him, has never once appeared in person at one of his hearings or arraignments, has never even looked at him. A hundred agents and prosecutors have read Rio and Linnea's after-action reports, revealing all the tortures Parlor inflicted on her. And although no one's ever had any reason to doubt Rio's account, or what little Linnea has said she remembered, there are still plenty of Parlor "fans" and conspiracy theorists who believe he was falsely accused or wrongfully prosecuted.

Both she and Rio have long contemplated what Parlor might say if he ever talks again.

There are only three people in the whole world who know exactly what happened in that barn in Ruther Glen, and Linnea prays every day that all three will take it to their graves.

* * *

When all is said and done, Linnea made her fame and fortune out of the ghosts of dead women. She never wanted to think about it that way, but during her sessions at Gracie Square, after Parlor, she was counseled to grant herself clemency that her motivations were never selfish, or fame driven. She merely had a unique talent, a calling, and was pursuing it with principles and conviction.

But what if you can't do it anymore? Why are you even here?

Then she truly is no better than a bystander, a gawker at a traffic accident, another dark tourist.

She's already spent hours going through Schweiger's videos, and she not only hasn't found any connections, it feels very much like what the newspapers used to belittlingly call her "psychic hotline" is all fuzzy and choked with static—a cellular call with two bars, a car radio station out in the desert tuned to a distant station. Where she used to be able to focus like this for days, now she needs to take breaks every fifteen or twenty minutes, her eyes hurting, head reeling, palms sweaty. A repeat of her experience in Abby Walden's car back in Mississippi, that gray heavy blanket wrapped all around her, thick and hot and stifling. Suffocating.

That's why two days ago she tossed most of her meds down the motel toilet, in a bid to flush her system clean, like trying to recall an old number that used to be easy to dial.

She finally picks up the gun and uses her thumbprint to turn off the trigger lock. Rio insisted on the guns, on the creds, wanting full coverage for them, full legal scoping by DOJ, and the ability to draw on the Bureau's vast resources and assets if necessary. *Protection*. But the last time she held a gun like this it was wrested from her hand, ripped from her grasp, and shoved into her mouth.

She stares down at the gun for a few moments longer and then re-thumbs the trigger lock and puts both the gun and the credentials back in their thick padded envelope and shoves the whole thing deep into her luggage.

Linnea goes into the bathroom and flushes the rest of her meds, then opens the Alice laptop and calls up the next set of videos.

CHAPTER

27

New Cornelia, Arizona

ANDI KNOWS JUST how ridiculous she looks and sounds, all drunk and panicked, almost falling.

But her drunkenness only fuels her panic, as she races for Ruby and sweeps her daughter up and stumbles toward her truck, where hot lightning already reflects in its windshield, a bright vein pulsing even in the dusty glass, illuminating the night around her, although the storm is still miles away.

Luke tries to steady her, but she tells him she's fine . . . *fine* . . . that she just needs to get Ruby out of the storm, that thunder and lightning scare her, although no rain has fallen yet. She urges him instead to help Bella back to her trailer or to help Erwin get stuff inside.

Stephen suddenly appears at her shoulder, concern scrawled on his face, but she waves him off too, as she stuffs a protesting and soon to be crying Ruby in the truck and pulls out far too fast, hitting the gas, throwing a fantail of dirt in the air.

Her StrikeAlert beeping and glowing, faster, and faster. Louder and louder.

She hasn't seriously panicked over a storm in years . . . *a stupid, stupid storm* . . . and although her intoxication is mostly to blame, it does little to assuage her guilt over how she's let guard down for the first time in such a long time. Each ruddy lightning streamer coiling in the sky sends a new shiver through her, leaving her hands shaking.

She can't keep the old truck straight, but that's okay, there isn't much to hit out here, and she isn't going far. But visibility drops with each passing moment, as the storm overhead collapses on itself, the threatened rain evaporating high in the sky above before it even has a chance to fall to the ground, salting the night with windblown grit.

Now a wall of rushing, rising air behind her, a massive curtain of dark sediment picking up speed, overtaking her. Not a rain storm anymore, a *dust* storm—and wreathed in lightning.

They call them *haboobs* in the Middle East, way over in Africa but here in Arizona as well, where these infamous dust or mud storms are created when a thunderstorm disintegrates, leaving an out-of-control wind train that can hit speeds of more than fifty miles an hour, choking the sky with clouds of sediment more than a mile high.

Like tonight, they come with little or no warning.

Ruby is finally crying too, as the wind rakes the truck, sounding like a thousand nails on a chalkboard the size of the desert sky, a hail of grit and gravel, some as big as cat's eye marbles, ricocheting off the F-150, rattling the windshield and windows.

The Ford slews left, then right, Andi losing her headlights as a shroud of dust twirls itself around them, threatening to entangle them, yank them skyward. Unable to see, unsure of just how far she still needs to go, she feathers the brakes and when that fails to bring the big truck under control, she gives up and slams them hard, throwing her and Ruby into a tighter and tighter spin as the truck's wheels seek purchase in the eddying sand below it.

One of her outdoor camp chairs, those she and Luke were sitting in only a few nights ago, slingshots past the windshield. Her headlights flicker and falter, reflecting off her trailer, a few yards ahead, too close. She begs for her brakes to have mercy, leaning into them with all her weight, until the truck shudders to a stop just before she plows through her own living room.

She's only a few lunging steps, a half-dozen yards, from the trailer, but she doesn't want to drag Ruby out into the blasting sand, so instead crawls into the back with her and holds her tight and strokes her hair. It's stifling with the windows up and the truck dark, and the wind *breathing* around them, sighing heavy, like their truck's been swallowed up by some great monster.

Right after they fled Texas, she and Ruby sometimes slept in their motel room closets, and this feels just like that. The illusion of hiding, of safety.

Ruby asks her if Chili and Mr. Luke and Auntie Bella are going to be okay and she says *of course they are, of course they are.* She apologizes to her baby girl for not paying more attention, for drinking too much and not seeing the storm coming, for not getting them out of harm's way fast enough.

I'm so stupid, bumblebee, so stupid.

It's so black even the StrikeAlert has winked out, but Ruby tells her bravely she's not scared of the dark, she's not scared at all, even as the wind howls and roars, the sand shifting, and slithering around them like a snake's skin, until, just like that, it's over, almost as soon as it's begun.

The truck stops rocking on its tires and the wind dissipates, blowing itself out, as the dust rises higher and higher. And although the occasional stray rock still ping-pongs off the hood, out beyond the haze, Andi thinks she can even see the glimmer of stars.

The dry storm has sandblasted New Cornelia clean, scoured it, leaving sculptured sand eddies everywhere there were right angles before, and flotsam and jetsam—a chair or bent flagpole here, a handful of aluminum cans there—deposited across the scrub.

Otherwise in the sudden storm's wake, it might well not have happened at all.

Andi wonders how the others fared or if Stephen's greenhouse survived.

Exhausted and now harshly sober, Andi pulls off her long-sleeve T-shirt to cover Ruby's head, to protect her eyes and mouth from lingering dust or falling rocks, and eases her out of the truck. She approaches the trailer, waiting for the motion lights to flicker on, but when they don't, it stops her in her tracks.

A power outage?

But that can't be true, because the lights she left burning inside earlier are still glowing in the living room, and Ruby's room too.

A sliver of light spilling from her front door; a sand dune collected in the *open* doorway.

I locked it, I know I locked it, because I always fucking lock it.

She tells Ruby to stay quiet, to get down, and then guides her back to the truck, opening the passenger door and slipping her inside. For reasons she can't easily explain, she isn't wearing a gun tonight, but she still has the S&W under the front seat.

You know why . . . you didn't want it getting in the way, being a big deal, in case Luke touched you . . . in case he slipped an arm around you . . . and you wanted him to.

She turns her attention back to her trailer, the big gun at eye level, scanning for movement, waiting for something or someone to leap at her. She approaches slowly, carefully, almost at a crouch, but before she can circle around to the back of the trailer, she's spotlighted by a harsh white light.

More headlights—

Luke.

He pulls up next to her truck and jumps out and when he sees she has a gun drawn, he draws one of his own.

CHAPTER

28

New Cornelia, Arizona

THEY WORK AS a team, as if they'd done this sort of thing before. Andi goes around the back, and Luke mounts the stairs, kicking his way through the already open door, and behind the thin walls, she can hear him moving through her small home, banging open more doors, checking closets.

It takes five minutes for him to call out to her that it's all clear, that it's fine.

No, it isn't, not at all.

She joins him inside to find evidence of the storm's passage . . . its damage . . . all the sand and silt that corkscrewed through the open front door and piled up in her kitchenette, mounded around her TV stand, dusted her carpet like newly fallen snow.

But she can't convince herself that the storm alone, that rogue wind, turned out her drawers, dumped out both her and Ruby's closets, pulled out the few old boxes she took from Texas from underneath their beds. The storm didn't ruin her security cameras or rip up the cabling or crush and dent her laptop and the large SkyScan lightning detector in the living room.

It looks to all the world like the work of human hands.

She stands in the middle of the wreckage, fighting back tears, tossing her gun on a couch that looks like it's been slashed by knives, as Luke goes to get Ruby out of the truck. He carries her inside and after checking her room a second time, lets her go in and find her favorite things.

He also hands Andi her T-shirt, and that's when she realizes she'd been standing all along in only her sports bra, her arms, her shoulders, naked and exposed, her scars visible.

Luke stares at them but doesn't say anything as she shrugs herself back into her shirt.

After she goes and checks on Ruby herself, she comes back into the living room where Luke is already picking things up off the floor, righting chairs, searching for a broom to tackle the sand. She stops him and holds his hands tight.

"I guess you could say I was struck by lightning twice," she tells him. "The first was just after my twenty-sixth birthday. I was outside school and got caught in a storm, a freak accident, kind of like tonight's. I never saw a cloud in the sky, not a drop of rain. I *died* then, but was resuscitated, brought back to life, bleeding and smoking. Everyone said it was a miracle.

"The second time was not long after that, while I was still recovering, *trying* to recover. I fell in love with the man who saved me, who took care of me. But I was still so scared, so damaged. And I think he was too, in his own way. I can't, won't, blame him for everything that happened between us, but I do blame him for what he took from me."

She takes Luke's hand and places it on her shoulder, lets him feel, touch, the branches of one of her lightning trees there. Only for a heartbeat though, less than a single breath, before pulling his hand away.

"But he also gave me Ruby—*my* miracle—and I'm afraid he doesn't want to let either of us go."

She then folds herself into his arms and cries.

CHAPTER 29

New Cornelia, Arizona

IT TAKES THEM almost three days to clean up Andi's trailer, and even though Luke offers to let her and Ruby sleep in his camper, she refuses.

Instead, he sleeps on her secondhand couch, both their guns hidden between the cushions, close enough for them to lay their hands on them.

He and Waylen go into Ajo and check the few places you can get rooms—the Sonoran Desert Inn, the Marine Motel—and snap pictures of all the cars, trucks, and RVs with out-of-state plates. Luke is reluctant to use his few friends back on the force to run them, but Waylen says he and Stephen will take care of it.

Andi takes Ruby to get ice cream and tries to explain to her what's going on, what's happened. But all Ruby wants to know is if they're leaving again, and Andi tells her she doesn't know yet.

She just doesn't know.

* * *

It's only after most of the heavy lifting is done that Luke finally asks about Max and her scars.

They talk inside the trailer because she can't stand to be out beneath the sky again, but only after Ruby's sleeping. She doesn't want to let her little girl out of her sight, not for one night, not even a few hours, so she keeps Ruby's bedroom door cracked, a lamp sitting on the floor in the hall, where its light spills over her sleeping form, and Chili curled up at the foot of her bed.

There's been no time to order a new security system, or even the money in her dwindling account to pay for one. And although both Luke and Chili have been a near constant, welcome presence, Andi's still never felt more exposed. As much as she's welcomed Luke's help, *needed* it over the last forty-eight hours, she's not eager to revisit Texas or Max or Ethan either. Not for him, not for anyone.

So, instead, she tells him about the lightning.

"I glowed," she says. "For months it seemed, I *glowed*, with this weird, blackish light, almost a deep purple, like one of those UV black light bulbs. Like some part of that lightning was still *inside* me, trying to escape."

He shakes his head. "Is that even possible?"

She shrugs. "I don't know. Probably isn't. But I saw it. And Ruby saw it too, swears she still remembers it."

"It sounds—"

Her laugh is bitter, resigned. "What? Weird? Awful?"

"No," Luke answers. "Beautiful. Miraculous."

She looks at her hands. "People used to say that all the time. How it was a miracle I survived. How *I* was such a miracle." She sighs. "You ever hear of a thing called a lightning bell? Franklin bells, after Benjamin Franklin?" Luke shakes his head. "He was enthralled by lightning too, one of the first people to truly study the phenomenon. With just a lightning rod and some metal bells, he made a lot of discoveries about the nature of electricity itself, current and conductivity, all because of his silly little contraption. When negatively charged storm clouds reacted with the similarly charged rod and bells, their clanging warned him of coming tempests."

"Like an early storm chaser," Luke says.

"Exactly. We've been studying lightning for more than two hundred years. Have been fascinated by it, terrified of it, for far longer.

Worshipped it, weaved it into our gods and legends, our myths, all to explain it and understand it. Yet we still know so little." She slowly, reluctantly, pulls up her sleeves, revealing her taut skin, the lightning trees blossoming there. "Lichtenberg figures like these are supposed to go away after a day or so, but mine didn't. They never have. They're like tattoos now, inking me forever. A constant reminder of what happened. Another fucking miracle."

Luke stares at the branching fractals on her skin, moving close, turning his head to get a better look at them, almost reaching for them, until she slips her sleeves down again. She says, "I suffered a lot of weird symptoms after I was struck, a lot of things my doctors didn't believe or refused to diagnose. Things they couldn't explain . . . or even begin to understand. I'm not alone in that. Many lightning strike survivors struggle with ongoing clinical issues, chronic issues. Too often we've lumped in with those experiencing long COVID, or myalgic encephalomyelitis, or some other poorly defined environmental illness, like Bella. We're told it's all in our heads."

"Is it?"

"Yes and no. Maybe?" She peeks down the hall toward Ruby, her eyes drawn to the small figure like iron filings to a magnet. "I knew Stephen even before New Cornelia. He's a lightning strike survivor too, like me. Before he was struck, his IQ was a little over a hundred, right around average. Now there's probably not even a scale for the things he can do, the talents he has, no way to describe the world as he now sees it. I think the lightning *rewired* him body and soul." She doesn't like sharing Stephen's secrets and has no right to, but needs Luke to understand, since she knows where this is going. "Whatever happened to him, to *us*, can't be reduced to a clinical diagnosis or a checklist of physical symptoms. These scars on my skin aren't in my head, they're tangible and real and I can touch them every day, even if no one can explain them. Stephen's music and his math, my scars, the way every clock I touch can't keep time. It's like . . . we're lightning bells too. We caught hold of . . . *something*, and it still sparks inside us."

"The lightning still trying to fight its way free."

"Yes. We captured it—and it remade us."

Luke scoops up her hand, holds it. "I knew you were different, special."

Not just me, she thinks, not bothering to hide the bitter look on her face. "Sure, that's what Max used to say. He was there, saw it all."

"I'm sorry, I didn't mean it like that. Not like *him*." Luke squeezes her hand, to signal he's sorry. "Did Stephen know him too?"

Andi nods. "Yes. He was in Texas along with some other lightning survivors. A club, a support group for people like us. The Black Light Club." She holds up her fulgurite pendant. "All we wanted was to understand what was happening to us, to cope with it. A place where we didn't have to explain or justify or defend ourselves, over and over again. That's how it started."

"But?"

"Max resented that he didn't share our connection. I think he would've gladly suffered to have that spark too." She hesitates. "I'm not proud of it, but I got close to someone in Texas, another young man named Ethan, another lightning strike survivor like me. Someone attacked Ethan, put him in a coma."

"Jesus, where is Ethan now?"

"His family took him back east. I haven't seen him or Max since Texas." What she doesn't want to admit to Luke is she's *never* reached out to see how or if Ethan recovered. She ran out on him, on Max, all of them, to protect herself and Ruby.

Luke takes in the trailer, most of the evidence of the intrusion swept away, but it still lingers in the air, like that smell of rain before a storm. "And that's who came here and did all this? Max. Your lightning rod salesman?"

She imagines a shadowy figure going through her things, that shadow waiting for her, here in the dark, "I think so, yes. Who else? Stephen knows that someone's been searching for me, asking around the survivor support community about trying to find me. Max still wants me, and more importantly, Ruby."

"So, what do we do about this Max?"

"I was already contemplating leaving, now I'm not sure how I can't."

Luke smiles. "Fine, good, then we go, tomorrow."

She squeezes his hand. "Not *we*. Just Ruby and me."

Luke looks hurt. "No, that's foolish and unsafe. If this guy found you now, he can find you again. Better to face him with a partner." Luke searches her eyes. "A friend."

"I appreciate that, I do. But I can't ask that. I *won't*."

"I was a cop, Andi. Taking risks, helping people, that was my job, my responsibility."

"And we're neither. Look, I've been running for a while. I've had some good practice." *It's what I do*, she thinks, *how I cope*. "You have no idea what Max is capable of. I'm not sure I do either. This," she says, waving at the room, "might only be the beginning."

Luke nods in the way people do when they're listening but not truly hearing. It's clear to her that his mind's already made up, eyes suddenly darker, harder, a look Andi's never seen.

You've known him for a few weeks, remember there's a thousand looks behind those eyes you've never seen.

Luke says, "He has no idea what I'm capable of either." He stands abruptly and goes to her front door, throwing it wide to the night desert. She flinches at all that darkness, all that sky, the wheel of stars framed by her door, like staring at Ruby's ceiling.

Luke keeps his back to her as he speaks. "My partner and I were called to a disturbance, shots fired at an abandoned apartment complex, and we got separated almost from the jump. Stupid, right? Too much testosterone, both of us hoping to see some action, make the collar, be the hero. It happened so fast, and there I was, racing up a set of stairs, taking them two at a time, when I started taking rounds from an open door above me." Luke mimes like he's ducking, as if something is falling on him. "And I just . . . reacted. Returned fire, center mass, just kept firing until the threat was stopped. I couldn't see anything, basically didn't even look, didn't properly check my background, as we'd been taught to do. I was on instinct, autopilot, and I was so fucking scared. I ended up shooting my partner, Matt Monroe, thirty-one years old and a new father only two months earlier."

Luke is still staring out into the desert but seeing something else. "I critically wounded him, but he survived, barely, launching a subsequent six-month long internal affairs and shooting panel review. The evidence for my unseen shooter was unfortunately not very conclusive, we never found the guy, but it was enough, I guess, to clear me. They kept telling me how lucky I was . . . how it was a *miracle* Matt didn't die." Luke turns around and looks at her knowingly, before continuing, "Settlements were proposed, but it was still a mess, and no matter what, I knew I was guilty. So, I quietly left the department in the wake of it all. I just didn't know what else to do."

"I'm so sorry," she says, as she stands and goes to him.

"I'd only drawn my gun twice before that night I shot my partner and my friend. I wasn't even sure I *could* pull the trigger, the most fundamental question every cop has got to ask themselves. But at that moment, I did what I had to do, what I was *trained* to do. And as bad as it was, I know can do it again." He finally turns back to her. "I promise I won't let this man, I won't let *anyone*, hurt you or Ruby. He'll have to come through me first."

"He might," she says, as he pulls her close.

"Or die trying," Luke says, and then he holds her tight, so tight she almost can't breathe, and she lets him.

CHAPTER 30

Mena, Arkansas

WHILE LINNEA SPENDS three or four hours at a stretch going through videos a few seconds at a time, Rio reviews each coroner or ME's report, crime scene reports from local police response, and those generated by BAU-5's evidence collection teams. Then they get together in her motel room and sit in front of the hot glow of Alice's screen, eating local takeout, using a speech-to-text module to lob their questions at Alice. It's eerily like having a conversation with a real person, another investigator, one who never hesitates, never avers, never doubts.

The AI algorithm chugging mercilessly, unflaggingly away, filtering their data with each query she and Rio throw at it.

Alice finds the first possible connection. It takes only two days.

Linnea finds the next one.

The link is deep in the social media scrub, a one-year-old online post and marketplace search by the first victim—the youngest—Winn Chu.

The keywords are *book, jewelry, fulgurite.*

The link is with Kayla McCune, their oldest victim.

* * *

"Okay," Rio says, "walk me through it again."

Linnea taps away at Alice. "Fall of 2024, less than a year before she's discovered in that abandoned gas station near Swarthmore, Winn reads a book called *Your Heart Is a Star*, a popular YA fantasy romance novel. My girls read it too." She recalls them passing the book back and forth between them, one of the few things they shared without fighting over. "Monsters in love, that kind of thing. It was going to become this bigtime TV series."

"Did it?"

"Apparently not, but it had a wildly zealous following for a while, lots of fanfic, costumes, TikToks, that sort of thing. One of the characters wore a recognizable pendant, called the Tears of Dural, and Alice has found a record of Winn searching online for a similar piece, a replica or reproduction. Probably hoping to get one of her own."

"She and thousands of other fans," Rio says, looking at the screen. "And McCune?"

"She responded to Winn via a public-facing online exchange about a storefront on a personal online craft marketplace specializing in just that kind of jewelry. The two also shared a handful of direct messages in the days after. We don't have those messages yet, they're encrypted, and the platform they used is notoriously uncooperative even in the face of a warrant or court order, but we'll get them. Eventually."

"Yet no record of either woman actually *buying* jewelry from the site," Rio says, his eyes reflecting the scroll of data across Alice's screen. "Nothing in the metadata. And as far we know Kayla McCune didn't run that storefront or any other."

"No, but we do have this."

Linnea calls up another photo from Kayla's social media collage, this one an Instagram post from three weeks before she disappeared, Kayla standing with a group of people from the doctor's office where she worked as a physician's assistant, celebrating a birthday party of some sort. A massive white Costco cake with brightly colored frosting flowers. Tired-looking balloons.

Linnea asks Alice to tighten a red digital circle around Kayla's neck, highlighting—

Jewelry—a pendant—a silver chain tipped with a polished shard of rock or mineral, a crystal blown through with tiny bubbles that look almost like crystallized tears.

She then pulls up a photo from Wolf Pen Gap trailhead, the bathroom where Kayla was found—her body splayed against the wall, those dark burn marks like black angel wings against the concrete. It's still a striking, disconcerting image, but she focuses only on Kayla's throat, calling up a second photo from Kayla's later autopsy, as well as a log of all the items recovered from her body.

No pendant anywhere. Gone.

"The pendant is made out of fulgurite," Linnea says, "often called fossilized or petrified lightning. The one Kayla's wearing appears to be sintered sand, created when lightning strikes a beach or out in the desert."

"Never heard of it. It's . . . pretty."

"It can be. You can find it worldwide, yet it's still relatively rare." The screen scrolls between them. "There are two kinds, rock and sand fulgurite, both formed by lightning. Basically, natural glass, but strongly magnetic if you heat it up. It comes in all sizes and shapes depending on the lightning itself and the surface it strikes. Some people believe it has metaphysical properties, purification, whatever."

Linnea scans the various fulgurite picture Alice flashes for them, each one changing with Linnea's words, like the AI itself is listening. They roll by endlessly. "Here's a piece from Florida, almost sixteen feet long." She points to another grainy image. "This one is branching, fractal." Almost exactly like Kayla's diaphanous black wings, like Rio's World Tree, like the electric flowers on Abby.

It was never lost on Linnea that the burns on the victims resemble *real* lightning strike injuries—those Lichtenberg-like figures she first photographed on Abby—but she was too quick to decide they were the natural postmortem scarring of whatever unknown ECD or weapon their serial was using to incapacitate the women. She knows now the bizarre, beautiful markings themselves hold a meaning—a message—all their own for him.

Spectacular, specialized, identifiable . . . ritualistic.

LTK. The Lightning Tree Killer.

Right there in front of them, a significant pattern, a connection, a fiery etching on each young woman's skin, for the whole world to see.

But you didn't see it fast enough, Linnea, not the way used to. Maybe you didn't want to. Maybe you still can't.

A blind spot that didn't exist before.

Rio clearly sees it too now and is probably thinking the same thing. "Okay, let's say those lightning markings matter, they're a specific signature. But that still brings us back to the jewelry, or lack thereof." Rio's meticulously catalogued all their collected evidence; he knows it as well as she does. "Winn Chu didn't have anything like that on her."

"Possibly another signature though . . . a trophy, a souvenir?" Linnea scrolls back to the one photo they have of Kayla wearing the mysterious missing pendant. "We're going to need Schweiger's team to revisit Winn's family, see if she ever owned something like it, or a piece still hidden away in a jewelry box."

They're going to have to check all their photos and victim files again, go back over all the crime scenes, for any hint of the fulgurite jewelry. Have Alice run an image match across every photo and video they've collected. Linnea needs to know for certain if its presence—or absence—is meaningful. "Winn *was* looking into it, though, maybe a gift she wanted for someone special. Or a memento that an admirer offered to get for her."

She lets that idea hang there. One possibility is that LTK has been using dating or hookup apps to find victims. They've confirmed that a few Lightning Tree victims did use dating apps, at one time or another, but so far neither Alice nor Linnea have found any commonalities. "But this unique fulgurite jewelry was featured in that book, and that book was important to Winn."

Book. Jewelry. Fulgurite.

Lichtenberg figures.

Something about *books* specifically nags at Linnea though, almost like one of her old familiar ghosts finally . . . *finally* . . . whispering in her ear, a ghostly image she can't quite recall. *Or it's just the meds getting out of my system.* Like the jewelry search, they'll need to resort all the collected intelligence and evidence they have, visit with all the families and friends a second or third or fourth time to see if any of the others—including Abby—ever had a copy of that YA book, tucked away in a bookshelf, checked out of a library. Linnea will need to read it beginning to end, although she finds it hard to imagine she'll find what she's looking for between its covers.

But . . . *a wildly zealous following*—is there any chance they were all members of some sort of book group or fan site?

Fulgurite. Jewelry. Book.

Some kind of . . . fan club?

"Hey, what about that website specifically, the storefront?" Linnea asks out loud.

Rio pulls up what they have again. "Registered to username StormCrow20, sold fulgurite jewelry exclusively, pendants, rings, polished pieces. Vials of the stuff. It appears to have shipped from Oklahoma, or did, it's mostly shuttered now. Three hundred reviews, the last one ten months ago. NFI—no further information."

But there's something there, there must be. Linnea queries Alice on all available databases on the owner or username StormCrow20 and then waits until the screen blossoms in colorful roses, geospatial blooms, a flower field of data. She can almost sense it, *see it* now, a glimmering connection, a fractal pattern as tenuous and brief as lightning itself, linking the women for a bright, blazing, horrible moment.

No, forever.

Fulgurite. Jewelry. Book.

Lichtenberg figures and lightning.

The World Tree.

Club?

She starts running down a series of search phrases out loud, one after another, discarding some, refining others, watching the data resize and reshape at her command, as she has a one-way conversation with Alice.

Feels Rio lean in close, shoulder to shoulder.

Some are searches she's already conducted but not in this exact sequence, not in this specific order, reminding Linnea that language is a kind of pattern too, and although Schweiger's AI has infinite patience and almost limitless data, it still has limits. It can't reason on its own, it can't extrapolate without direction, it isn't proactive or emotionally vested. And while it doesn't get distracted, it isn't terribly creative either.

Fulgurite. Jewelry. Book.

No . . . no . . .

Book. Jewelry. Fulgurite.

Lichtenberg figures. Lightning.

StormCrow20 and jewelry and fulgurite and Lichtenberg figures and lightning . . .

StormCrow20 and fulgurite and Lichtenberg figures and lightning *strike* . . .

StormCrow20 and Lichtenberg figures and lightning strike *victims* . . .

Lichtenberg figures and lightning strike *survivors* . . .

And there it is.

CHAPTER 31

New Cornelia, Arizona

Andi wakes before Luke and slips out of her hot bed and tangled sheets, standing naked and exposed in the predawn dark. Only Chili sees her, lifting her large head from the floor as Andi gently steps around her, and although she starts to rise as if she's going to follow her, Andi stops her with a stroke of her thick fur, a gentle pat on her flanks.

There are no mirrors in here, and it's too dark for Andi's reflection in the small, curtained windows. Standing in the black, Andi is blessedly, mercifully, invisible.

I glowed—like some part of that lightning was still inside me, trying to escape.

But there's no glow now, not anymore, and less reason than ever to believe there ever was. All these years gone by, it's still hard to know what was real or just lingering trauma, what was wishful thinking on her part or just Max's own dark fantasies, spun out of his lies and insinuations.

Andi slips on a T-shirt and shorts and running shoes and moves like a wraith through her trailer. Although she mostly feels safe with both Luke and Chili here, she still checks it from top to bottom—once, twice—then stands over Ruby, watching her sleep. Andi hasn't spent a night with a man since Texas, hasn't shared a bed with someone other than Ruby in as long. It was a strange sensation to feel a different kind of weight there last night, pulling her to one side. The weight of hopes, expectations, fears. A different breath too, sharing hers. Luke was patient, easygoing, and gentle. Gave her as much space as the small bed and trailer could allow, even offered to sleep out on the couch—again—but she let him stay. Wanted him to.

But it still felt weird to wake up this morning and have him there, so close she could all but hear his heartbeat beating through his naked skin. For someone who's feared the open sky for so many years, these last few in Arizona she's grown to appreciate the vastness of it all, the infinite sky. The problem with living inside four walls and your own head for so long is that your world can become just as cramped and tight and confined as a single-wide trailer, leaving no room for anything or anyone else.

She kisses Ruby on the forehead and goes back to her room and although the forecast calls for high clouds and sun and heat, she still slips on her StrikeAlert, barely holding on to its latest charge. She also zippers the SIG into her fanny pack and settles it on her waist within easy reach.

She takes one last look at Luke tangled in the sheets in her bed—*their bed . . . at least for the one night*—and then quietly leaves him that way.

* * *

She used to run all the time in Virginia, before she died.

Then she didn't run for years, too afraid to be out beneath the sky. She only started up again when she moved here, and even then, at first, only on bright, blazing days far too hot for nearly anything else to be outside.

Running in the cool of the morning is dangerous because of the snakes, but she keeps her eyes sharp. They aren't even the main reason she brought her gun this morning, only one of them.

She starts slow, pacing herself, angling toward the solar farm. The sun is a fiery mote to her left, like a lit match, the end of a cigarette. Dawn in the desert always starts small, a mere flicker, before bursting wide across the sky in bright fireworks, smearing the sky in chromatic color.

She runs in the predawn dark, feeling the hard ground in her knees, hammering her tight joints. It isn't hot yet, but she's already sweating before she's gone a mile, and the panels of the solar farm remain black hulks in the middle distance, waiting for the sun like her.

She can't tell from her trailer, but the ground rises slightly here, a gentle curl, like a knuckle on a closed fist. It fights for her breath, punches her, and winds her, and she must slow down, even considers walking, before pushing through, ever upward, higher, and higher.

She once was afraid all the stored energy in the solar farm might set off her lightning detector, but that's never happened in all the times she's been up here. The farm has a rusty odor all its own, electric and metallic, and it hums with current. She gives it a wide berth and moves on, past saguaros and cat's claw, through creosote and ocotillo and apricot mallow.

Ajo spreads to her right, the few buildings dark, and then she's suddenly cresting the road to the mine itself, passing the mine tailings, racing to the top to beat the sunrise.

She isn't alone when she reaches the lookout.

The gleaming eyes of three coyotes greet her by the lookout fence where she and Luke stood only days before. They watch her without fear or concern, two tans and a larger gray, all mottled and skinny and feral, sitting on their haunches as if waiting for the sun too.

She stops, breathing hard and heavy. She's never heard of coyotes going after humans, but their presence and behavior are so unusual she keeps her hand by the gun in her pack just in case. As they stare at each other, the gray starts howling—singing—and the other two join in. An echoing chorus of yips and barks, a crooning that makes the three canids sound like a dozen, like a hundred, like they are everywhere all around her. Amplified and echoed by the steep walls of the open mine below them, their wild song seems to carry forever across the desert, all the way to the mountains and beyond.

The sky truly lightens with the rising sun, chasing the shadows away, and with them the coyotes. Suddenly gone silent, the trio slip past the fence line and then disappear into the last of the night the sun hasn't reached, leaving Andi alone again.

She stands that way for a while until the sun itself reaches her face and she can feel its warmth on her skin.

* * *

Later, she walks back down a lot slower than she ran up to the mine, turning over in her head how best to break it to everyone that she and Ruby are leaving.

Bella will understand. She's seen so many people come and go from New Cornelia and has been vocal about Andi doing the same, even if this isn't how either of them ever contemplated Andi departing. She wonders if her friend will say anything about Luke, how the three of them will be leaving, all together.

All these years *not* trusting, yet here she is, seemingly about to run off again with a man she's only just met. She contemplated it with Ethan, and it nearly killed him. She did it with Max, and it nearly killed her. But it was different then. It's different *now.* And so is she. She must be.

She's still twenty minutes from the trailer when she spies a tight cloud of dust moving toward her, a small car bouncing across the desert. She knows it immediately—Stephen's old Corolla—the one he keeps parked behind his twin trailers, covered by a tarp most of the time. He rarely leaves New Cornelia and drives even less.

Seeing the car on the move sparks fresh panic, like the night of the haboob. She can only imagine one reason Stephen might be careening out into the desert like this.

Oh no . . . no . . . no.

She starts jogging toward it, then runs full-tilt, and then gets hit in the face with dirt and grit before it comes to a stop.

No . . . no.

"What is it?" She yells into Stephen's open window, panic rising around her like the rising heat of the morning. He's pale and already scared too, which scares her even more.

"We tried calling, but you didn't have your phone."

No, she doesn't; she left it behind and chose to bring the gun instead.

No . . . no . . . no.

Luke told her it would all be fine, just one night, and then they'd be gone for good. She wanted to believe that so damn bad.

"Max?" she asks. "Ruby? Luke? What the hell's happened?"

"No, not that," Stephen says, shaking his head. "It's Bella."

CHAPTER

32

New Cornelia, Arizona

BELLA IS BREATHING out blood.

Each breath, in and out, leaves a bright crimson stain on her lips, a rosebud at the corner of her mouth. But at least she's still breathing.

By the time Andi and Stephen get there, Erwin and Waylen are already with her. She doesn't keep a phone of her own, other than the one Andi got for her that's stored in the box outside her trailer, just for an emergency like this or one with Ruby. Bella must have made it this far, dialed Erwin, and then collapsed barefoot in the scrub next to the makeshift shower.

She looks so small and frail, lying in the dirt, with dust in her hair, on her face, on her hands.

"This is bad," Waylen says at least twice. "This is bad."

"I have no idea *what* this is," Erwin adds. "No idea what she reacted to."

At least she wasn't attacked or assaulted, which was Andi's fear on the ride over. "It doesn't matter, we have to get her to the hospital."

Erwin blinks. "She wouldn't want that, Andi, and you know that."

Andi does and also knows what a hard proposition it'll be. Ajo's original hospital has long been shut down and shuttered, now little more than a rambling, wind-scoured shell on a hill above the town plaza. There's a hospital in Casa Grande, a hundred-mile drive, and a tribal hospital in Sells, seventy miles away. There's also the Desert Senita Community Health Clinic in Ajo, surprisingly robust and servicing Ajo's mostly elderly population, but if Bella is as bad as she looks, she'll need an airlift to Casa Grande or even Tucson, anyway.

"I'm taking her to the health clinic *now*," Andi says, making it clear she isn't going to argue about it. She turns to Stephen. "You and Erwin go to my place, grab up my phone, wallet. Bring Ruby. And tell Luke I've left. I'll call him later."

"Let me go with you," Stephen says. "You shouldn't do this alone."

"No, really, please just get Ruby and meet me at the wash just west of here. Mile marker eight." She knows that Stephen and Erwin can get what she needs from her trailer and make a straight line out of New Cornelia and meet her enroute to Desert Senita in Ajo. "Give me your keys, I'm taking your car." Even before she finishes, a look passes over Stephen's face, as if he wants to say more, but Andi says to Waylen, "Help me get her up now, okay? Gentle."

Andi kneels beside Bella, whose eyes are fluttering now, reminding Andi of butterfly wings, the tiny, gossamer-like pygmy-blues that flit around the desert, twinkling with their light-reflecting scales. "We're going to get you some help."

Bella coughs blood, whispers, "*Mija* . . ."

Andi wipes tears out of both their eyes and lifts her up.

CHAPTER

33
The Storm

HE LAYS AWAKE because he doesn't like to sleep, doesn't like to close his eyes.

He doesn't like the things he sees behind them, these things he's done.

When he lays quietly like this he can feel his heart beat. Each beat generates a spark in the cardiac muscle, a tiny jolt. Each blood cell a tiny electrode. No one thinks of it this way, but we're all animated by lightning. We all live in a storm of our own creation.

There is no escape, it rains every day somewhere. Some who have been struck by lightning fear it forever, but he welcomes it, worships it, wants it.

I am the storm season

A part of him is ashamed of what he's become now, what he is becoming, but he has no more control over himself now than lightning itself. There's only one who can teach him.

Her.

I am the storm season
I will take the lightning angel's wings
I am the light and the fury

He is chaos, a god in the making, leaving death and destruction in his wake.

The sacrifices so far have kept him aloft, but she will truly raise him up, she will light the way, and he will ride her wings all the way to the stars and beyond.

He gets up and walks outside where the southwest stars shine, where the towering sky is clear and infinite for now, but not for long.

I am the storm season

And he has arrived.

Storm Season

Part III

CHAPTER

34

Mena, Arkansas

LINNEA KNOWS THAT Dan can tell in the first few minutes of their call that she is off her meds.

It isn't so much what she says or even doesn't say, it's that sixth sense born of having lived and slept with someone for nearly two decades, having made a family and life with them. Maybe Dan's intuition or insight isn't all-consuming like hers, maybe he can't use it to solve crimes or save lives, but it's just as powerful and poignant in its own way.

It kept them together, held her together, when the whole world was falling apart.

It's late. She can tell he's in bed, failing to read the latest draft of a student's story, failing to sleep. He sounds tired, sleepless too, like her. It's quiet in his background, quiet enough that he sounds close, giving her the illusion he's there next to her in bed, the way they used to talk in the dark when the kids were asleep, holding hands, his breath on her shoulder, on her face. When she first got involved in her serial cases, she used to stow her duty issue weapon in a gun safe in their closet. Later she began leaving it openly in on her nightstand, protected by a trigger lock but still within reach.

Some nights they'd lay together, and she could see it reflected in moonlight or streetlight, the heavy weapon pointed toward the window, like some sort of totem or ward, as if she were afraid something from the night outside might try to crawl in and get them.

There's not been a gun in the house since Rio pulled her out of Parlor's barn.

Tonight, she asks mostly about the girls, and he fills her in on the last few days. Their daughters are capable of texting her on their own, and often do, but rarely confide in her about anything serious or weighty anymore. Since Dan has always been home the most, the parent who didn't spend several months in a psychiatric hospital, the girls tend to want him to carry their heavier burdens, relying on him to decide what and when to share with their mother and how. They are dimly aware of his drinking history but it's nothing on par with Linnea's trauma from her captivity and torture. They've intuited or sensed—in that nonjudgmental way only kids can—that their mom is still fragile and feel just as much responsibility to protect her now as she does them.

It's been hard on us, me, and the girls. I never knew how hard it would be.

In that way, they aren't much different than children who've suffered through a divorce, carrying the guilt and shame, wearing the scars from it, even though she and Dan have been married forever. No different than how during the bad days after her rescue and her long recovery, he probably felt like he'd been divorced too—or worse, left a widower. Like a part of his wife died during the last case.

After they talk about Olivia's upcoming soccer tournament this weekend, a spring event in New Haven, she asks him about his writing, something she hasn't done in months.

"Before I left you said you had a new idea, a glimmer of something?"

"Yeah, I tried a couple of pages."

"And?"

"It's silly, Lin. Stupid."

"Want to tell me about it?"

"No, not so much. It's late for both of us." He likely knows she's just trying to avoid talking about whatever's going on in Arkansas.

She used to do that all the time, whenever she was out of town and deep in an investigation, consumed by a case, crowding everything else out of her life for those ghosts in her head, giving them center stage, so she could see clearly whatever they were trying to show her. Hear them. Leaving the rest of the world mostly a distraction, including her family. Maybe that was the only way to embrace that gift of hers, to shield the rest of them from all the things she was exposed to, but she knows now it also left her cold, unapproachable, unreachable, and she wouldn't warm up again until she came home.

She asks, "Do you remember that book the girls read, that fantasy book, *Your Heart Is a Star*?"

"What, the series? Silly stuff, but wildly successful, the sort of lightning in the bottle success that every writer dreams about."

She knows that it's just the sort of success Dan's always dreamed about. "What was it about? What was the point?"

"Oh, Lin, it didn't have a point. A theme, I guess, about being true to yourself, how fleeting love, and life, can be. Loss, the sort of loss that speaks to us most loudly, most poignantly when we're young, when every loss feels like your heart is about to explode. Why all the interest?"

"I don't know, it just came up."

"Came up in the case?"

"Something like that."

"Think it's important?"

She's quiet on her end for a while, wondering if he's staring up at the ceiling, the way she is. "No, I don't think so, probably not the book itself, not the story. But it is a piece of the puzzle."

He probably suspects she doesn't truly need his input on the book. Knows her well enough to know that if it truly is some clue, some piece of evidence for whatever the hell is going on down in Arkansas, she's probably already pored over it two or three times already, filed it away in that *memory palace* of hers, as he once called it, a mnemonic device people have used for centuries to remember and retain things. Linnea's never described her eidetic skills that way to him or anyone else, but he's always told her he imagines her memory palace as a labyrinthine castle of infinite doors, holding everyone else's memories too.

She says, "Keep at your own story, okay? I'd like to read it when I get back."

"Any idea when that'll be?"

"No . . . not yet."

"Sure, okay. Girls miss you. We all do. Hope you're okay."

She laughs. "Oh, I'm not." She laughs more, but quieter. "I'm just kidding, Dan. I'm fine."

He forces a quiet laugh too. "Want to talk about it? Do you need to talk about it? Should we bring in someone else?"

"No, nothing like that."

"What would Rio say if I asked him? Where is he with this thing?"

"He's with me, Dan. We're together on this. We're good."

"You want me to say anything else to the girls?"

"Just tell them I love them."

"They know that."

She knew that, but wanted him to do it anyway. She says, "You too then."

"I know that too. Same, babe, same." He hesitates, then adds, "Hey, be careful." But he says it too fast, too stressed, too loud, as if he's admonishing himself, rather than her. "I mean, I saw something about tornados down in Arkansas. Big storms."

"Oh, I'm not going to be Arkansas anymore," she admits, just before she hangs up. "We leave for Oklahoma in the morning."

CHAPTER 35

Okmulgee, Oklahoma

LINNEA AND RIO cross into Oklahoma near Fort Smith, Arkansas, following I-40 to Checotah, before turning north onto Highway 62, near Henryetta.

They grab a hotel in Okmulgee, the capital of the Muscogee Creek Nation, what used to be called one of the Southeastern Five Civilized Tribes or now the Five Tribes of Oklahoma—Cherokee, Choctaw, Chickasaw, Seminole, and Muscogee (formerly the Creek). The Muscogee Creek Nation, or MCN, is the fourth-largest Indian tribe in the United States and maintains one of only thirty-eight tribal colleges in the country, the College of the Muscogee Nation.

On the drive over from Mena, Rio pulled everything he could about the college, including its staff and current enrollment, just under than two hundred students.

The modern campus sprawls over a thirty-seven-acre campus just outside of Okmulgee, and the person they're looking for keeps an apartment nearby. That person of interest is a few years older than most of the other tribal students, taking courses at the college on Contemporary Myskoke Life, Introduction to Natural Resources, and Preservation of Cultural and Historical Sites. Sparse social media posts show a lot of time spent walking the sandy shores of nearby Lake Eufaula, as recently as a month ago.

No criminal record, a small digital footprint, and the Bazaar portal hasn't been updated in six months. The last sale was in that same time span to a woman in Charleston, South Carolina. It's clear now that fulgurite for the site's jewelry has been sourced all around the United States, but plenty of it has been recovered right here in Oklahoma.

The person they're looking for was supposedly raised in nearby Okfuskee County, one of the top counties in the state for lightning strikes—StormCrow20.

When they knock on the apartment, Linnea still doesn't quite know what to expect. They have a license picture, but the large, heavily tattooed man who opens the door is too old, even if his angular and angry face shares the same history, same contours, same dark eyes.

There's also clearly a gun tucked beneath his colorful superhero T-shirt, so Rio holds up the borrowed FBI credentials way up high, says, "Easy, friend, easy there," while flashing his own gun from beneath his coat.

Just as things appear to start to slip sideways, a younger woman appears behind the man and stares hard at Rio's creds. She takes them from him and looks at them closely before returning them, before looking Linnea up and down. She isn't unattractive, but her face is all sharp corners and right angles like the old man's, the colorful spikes of one of her tattoos visible at her neck and shoulder, another jutting from the frayed collar of her T-shirt. Her hair is shaved military short on one side, but hangs dark and long on the other, strands of it carefully plaited. She smells like smoke, like ash, and a large, bright piece of fulgurite swings from her neck, larger than any pendant Linnea saw cataloged on the site.

Linnea is somewhat surprised she's still alive.

"StormCrow20?" Linnea asks. "Tassa Linscott?"

Tassa says something to the old man in what Linnea presumes is native Muscogee, and he quietly retreats into the darkened apartment behind her, but not far. He hangs there in the gloom, a brooding presence.

"That's my dad," Tassa says. "He's not part of this. He won't know anything about it."

"About what?" Rio asks, slipping the credentials back into his jeans, hiding his gun again too. "Do you know why we're here?"

"Sure," Tassa says. "I'm guessing it's about what happened back in Texas."

Linnea shoots Rio a glance. "Texas?"

Tassa nods, knocking a fresh cigarette out of a crumpled soft pack of Marlboros. "Back in Tyler, a few years ago. You're here about the Black Light Club."

CHAPTER

36

Okmulgee, Oklahoma

Tassa Linscott sits on the ratty apartment complex playground swing, her arms draped over the rusty chains. She's been chasing cigarettes for an hour, one after another after another, listening to them talk about their case, and talking about the Black Light Club.

Her father watches them from the porch of their shared apartment, smoking too.

Linnea and Rio sit opposite Tassa on a beat-up bench. It isn't conducive to taking any kind of notes, and they don't, but even before they knocked on the door, Rio hit record on his phone. FBI credentials or not, Oklahoma is a one-party consent state.

Linnea can't take her eyes off the fulgurite around Tassa's neck. Although it's overcast outside, Oklahoma sky the color of cinderblock, the rock still shines, pearlescent, almost like frozen lunar light, a full moon's teardrop, or a petrified piece of cresting sea wave. It's hard to imagine the celestial forces, the unearthly *power*, that turned common dirt and sand into that delicate, ethereal shape.

"I was struck when I was fourteen, out by Lake Eufaula. I was walking on the shore, on the sand. It was raining a bit before, I remember that. But not much after. It blew my sandals off." Tassa pulls on her latest cigarette, pointing with it at water they can't see. "They found them floating in the shallows, not far from where my dad pulled me off the beach. The bolt went through me, into the sand below, and created this." She swings the fulgurite around her neck, letting it tick back and forth like a metronome. "That's when I first learned what lightning could do, what it could truly do, although I didn't start making the jewelry until later, you know, when the whole school thing didn't pan out the first time."

"That was your site on Bazaar?" Rio asks.

"Yeah, but again, that came a bit later. I wasn't much of a student before I was struck, even less afterwards. Had this constant kind of ringing in my ears, this weird sound I couldn't escape, almost like ocean waves, and I've never even been to the beach. Not a real beach anyway. Just that shitty lake."

"You still deal with it now?" Linnea asks. "The sounds?"

"Oh, I deal with it." Tassa pats something unseen in her pocket, leaving Linnea to guess what kind of drug it might be. "Anyway, back then, they"—she points her cigarette up to the porch, to her dad eyeing them from a cloud of his own cigarette smoke—"put a lot of stock in this idea that I was touched by lightning. That I was chosen. All those Native American signs and portents and omens and shit. But not me, I was young and angry, hurt and confused. I didn't want to be special that way. I didn't even want to be Myskoke if that makes any sense. I understand better now. Appreciate it more now." She flips her cigarette into the dirt, steps on it with a heavy boot. "The club, Andi and all the others, helped me with that."

"Andi?" Linnea asks.

Tassa nods. "Audrey, Audrey Ellis, although we all called her Andi."

"You were nineteen when you left Oklahoma, went to Texas," Rio says.

"Barely that, and my mom raised hell, worried like you wouldn't believe, but there's no way she could stop me. She thought I was running off to shack up with some pervert I'd met online. Never had the heart to tell her there's plenty of those right around here. She's gone now. But we got right in the end." She smiles at Rio, and it's so small and sad, Linnea can see beyond the tattoos and rough edges, the tough talk and cigarette smoke, to the girl Tassa Linscott once was. "Anyway, our little club wasn't like that. Just people like me, kind of a makeshift family, who'd experienced something they couldn't deal with, stuff they didn't *want* to deal with, even if it wasn't related to what had happened to us."

Linnea asks, "And everyone in this club were lightning strike survivors?"

"In the club? I mean, yeah, I guess. Well, except for Max Conroy, Andi's plus-one. They'd come from somewhere back in Virginia, where Andi was struck. Max was like her boyfriend, but it was more fucked up than that. He'd been there the day she was hit. She fucking *died*, heart stopped, and he did some sort of CPR to resuscitate her. That was his story anyway. He never stopped talking about it. She used to say she wouldn't have survived without him. We all thought she wasn't going to survive *with* him."

"And this is Max Conroy and Audrey Ellis?" Rio asks.

"Yeah, but it all blew up after Ethan was attacked." Tassa looks skyward, remembering. "Stevie, Stephen Chao, knew more about that situation than I did. He was tight with Andi. I mean, we all wanted to be, in our own ways." There's something winsome, lost, in her voice. "All I know is Max was a big-time suspect for nearly killing Ethan, rightfully so, and everything went to shit after that, so we all went our separate ways. I guess we knew it could never be the same. I knew it couldn't." Tassa fishes for another cigarette but doesn't immediately light it, just twirls it in her fingers. "I grew up a lot when I was out in Texas, and although I'd love to say I came back fully healed, put back together, that's not true. Hell, I might've even been worse off for a bit. It took me a while to find my footing. Funny that I finally found it back here, with my people, my culture, my true family. Like I said, I got right with them, atoned, I guess. That's the word, right? And got right with me too. Things are okay now. I'm in school doing what I need to do. I'm older, wiser."

She finally flicks her lighter over the Marlboro, letting the flame dance in the wind, until the cigarette burns cherry, before clicking the lighter off. "Look, I'm willing to spend a few minutes here answering your questions, but when I walk back inside, we are done. *Done.* Understand? I know you said this is all about some missing girls and I appreciate that, I'm sad about it, I am, but I'm not going to dredge up all this old shit."

"We understand," Rio says. "We do. Just a few more questions, and we're done too."

"You said that Max was difficult, jealous." Linnea keeps her eyes on Tassa's fulgurite. "Was he ever jealous of you?"

Tassa blinks. "I mean, not at first. He was clingy, kind of annoying, but for a long time, most of the time, he wasn't so bad. He could be decent, could be funny. He was not a dumb guy, not at all, and he loved her, that much was clear. They loved each other. He was just kind of on the outside, looking in. And it only got weirder after Ruby was born. Sure, I'm not going to lie, I was attracted to Andi. I loved her, maybe we all did. But she never thought about me that way though. I was more like a daughter. And she had one of those already."

"With Max?" Linnea asks.

"Well, yes. Although Andi and Ethan were sneaking around for a while, and I figured they were going to run off together with Ruby. We all figured that's what prompted Max to, you know . . ." Tassa spins a loose, crazy circle around her head.

"So you think he attacked Ethan?" Rio asks.

"Sure, one hundred percent. Max had a temper, was jealous. He put Ethan in a fucking coma although no one could prove it, and then ghosted Texas soon as I did—just about the time everyone else up and left too."

Linnea asks, "Andi?"

"Before that, faster than any of us. Gone while Ethan's family was taking him back east. I thought that was cold, her not sticking around for him." Tassa blows smoke. "But Andi was a runner, and in some ways, we all were, I guess. That's how we ended up in Texas in the first place, running from our problems from somewhere else."

"Where she'd go?" Rio asks.

More smoke. "No idea. I did try to reach out to her, and Stevie did too, but . . ." Tassa shrugs. "I was totally on my own, so I drifted back here, got my shit together, kept my head down. I didn't want to be associated with what happened in Texas, didn't want to answer more questions, and still don't." She looks pointedly again at Rio. "Kept making my jewelry, off and on, just to keep myself afloat. It wasn't much, but better than flipping burgers."

"StormCrow20," Linnea says.

"Yeah. The day I was struck." She pulls up a sleeve, where a date is tattooed on her forearm—*March 20.* "But I copped some of my dad's info when I set up that site, so I wouldn't draw too much attention."

"What kind of attention?" Rio asks.

"*This* kind," Tassa says with a heavy shrug. "Or, you know, the kind a lot of women get out in the world, a world where girls go missing all the time. The internet is like a million pairs of eyes staring at you, sizing you up. Some guy in Toledo jerking off to you while his wife's at work, sending you pictures of his tiny dick you don't want to see. And those are the tame ones." She rolls her eyes. "But yeah, someone looking for Andi or Max, someone looking for me, someone hoping to spin up some story about the old club. It happened now and again."

"You still get much of that?" Rio continues. "Attention? Or people searching out the club?"

"I *never* made a big deal about my past, but people found out anyway, digging up stuff about the Black Light Club. We were well known in the survivor community, because we *made* a community, all our own. A haven for people like us. The whole thing was kind of cool, neat, weird, for a while. But I guess there's still plenty of people suffering out there the way we did."

Linnea appreciates what it's like to struggle with something you don't understand, can't explain, and that no one else believes in. "Do you remember a woman named Kayla McCune buying a pendant from your site? Or messaging you? How about Winn Chu?"

"No, I really don't, but I'll give you access to whatever records I still have, whatever there is."

"What about something more recent?" Rio stands and nods up at Tassa's dad on the porch balcony, still watching them below. "Someone reaching out to you online, or asking around about you on campus?"

Tassa breathes out more smoke. "Am I in danger?"

"Do you think you are?" Rio asks, his eyes on her.

Tassa bounces a weary glance between Rio and Linnea. "Fuck me, I get it now, you think this person might be coming after *me*—maybe already even tried. You thought you might find me dead."

"We didn't know what to expect," Linnea says, truthfully. "We're trying to understand, that's all."

"Yeah, well." Tassa sighs. "Look, sure, I still get weird emails, messages, but I delete that shit right away, don't even read it. You can search through all that too, I guess, if you think that'll help. As for my dad . . ." Tassa looks up at him, smiles and waves. "He's old school, been super protective, ever since I came back home, ever since my mom died. He's got dementia though, sits inside that apartment all day, goes crazy in his head watching all the bad shit on the news, or sits out on that balcony and watches the world go to hell out here. So, he sees things, hears things, remembers things, which may or may not have happened or may not be true. Forgets things too and talks about people I don't know. He's still fighting old fights, and he was nothing if not a fighter. *Hadcho*, kind of means *so brave as to be crazy*. That's mostly my dad now." She says it with pride, admiration. "If someone's been around, he's the last one worth questioning about it."

Linnea thinks there's more to it than that, but senses Tassa's not going to let them talk to her father, and pushing to do so might do more harm than good. A quick nod and glance from Rio means he agrees.

Instead, Rio tuns his attention to the sky, gray and growing shinier by the moment, a wet light effusing behind the clouds. "Looks like rain. Doesn't that make you nervous? It would me."

Tassa flicks ash. "Astraphobia. Fear of thunder, fear of lightning. There was a time when I couldn't stand to be outside, couldn't even stand to be near a window if there was a cloud overhead. Now?" She flicks more ash, says something in Myskoke. "Fuck it."

Rio laughs and Tassa does too. "For my people, the whole world was once covered by water," she says. "Water all around, until the Master of Breath blew the waves away. Mankind was formed from the wet clay left behind. In a way, we were all born in a storm. So, no, I don't fear them anymore." She holds up her fulgurite. "This is the first piece I made, from the sand beneath my smoking body. It's like a part of me is now fused with that sand, the clay, the earth. I didn't die like Andi did, but I was reborn that day too. We all kind of were. It just took me a long, long time to understand that."

Linnea walks over and says, "May I?"

Tassa slips the chain from around her neck and hands it to her. Linnea holds it up, looking through the jewel-like mineral. "It's beautiful."

"And it's *me*," Tassa says, as she takes it back.

Rio asks, "Did you make any of those for the other members of the club?"

"Yes, everyone. Other than my own, I always thought Andi's was one of the prettiest I ever did."

"Max?" Linnea asks. "Max too?"

A look passes over Tassa's face. "Fuck no. Why would I? He wasn't one of us."

Rio flashes Linnea a look too, one she hopes Tassa doesn't catch.

"Anything else you can tell us about Max, about Andi?" Linnea asks.

Tassa rubs a thumb over her fulgurite, lost in thought. Linnea isn't sure if she's remembering or regretting or both.

"Look, I think in some ways, Andi was the most traumatized of all of us. Like, she lost the most when she was struck. Not only did she *die*, really die, which is all kinds of fucked up when you think about it, but she also suffered all that same shit afterward that we all did, the pain, and the fear, and the medical stuff that no one believes. Then she got joined at the hip with Max and got herself knocked up." Tassa breathes in, breathes out. "The rest of us had issues before we were struck. Billy had a king-sized drug problem, Ethan was cut off from his rich family, Minnie had like three kids with three guys, one in jail, and didn't have custody of any of them. Stevie Chao was just . . . odd. Getting lit up gave us a purpose—a *reason*. It gave us Texas and the club and for a while made us special. Wynona used to say our shared tragedies galvanized us. But it was different for Andi. She'd had a stable life, a big-time future ahead of her, only to have it all burned up in the blink of an eye." Tassa snaps her fingers. "It really did a number on her. Yet she took care of us and looked after us and was the strongest of us all, I guess." Tassa stands now, looping the chain back around her neck, letting the playground swing rock gently behind her. "She gave us our name, the Black Light Club, because she said we all held an inner glow, a black light, a dark star. But it was more than that. The story going around was she literally *glowed* after she was struck, like a lightbulb or something."

"Did you ever see that?" Linnea asks, incredulously. "Light like that?"

Tassa shakes her head. "No, I never did. I heard it from others, and some even claimed it happened to them too. But Max swore on it and so did Ethan. Ethan one time told me that when they were lying in bed together, it was like lying next to a fallen star. How all her scars would just . . . *glow*."

"Her *scars*?" Linnea asks, trying not to throw a look at Rio. "What about them? Were they unusual too?"

Tassa nods. "Oh yeah, I guess I didn't make that clear. Most of those emails and messages I've gotten over the last couple of years weren't about me. They were about Andi and the stories about her scars."

"What about them?" Rio asks.

"They never went away. Her lightning scars never disappeared . . . they even kept growing."

CHAPTER 37

Tucson, Arizona

BELLA IS AIRLIFTED from Desert Senita to St. Joseph's Hospital in Tucson.

Andi drives behind her, pushing Stephen's small car to its limits—Ruby curled up worriedly behind her—arriving a few hours later under a clear, cerulean sky.

It takes almost as long for Andi to get anyone to talk with her, since she isn't a relative.

Finally, a young, tired-looking doctor whose name is stitched in cursive on his scrubs—*Dennon*—grabs them both a Styrofoam cup of coffee and finds a quiet corner to talk in the endless maze of white hospital walls.

Ruby's out of earshot but watches them from a hard plastic chair the color of sea foam.

"You brought Ms. Francis in?"

Andi blinks. "Wow, I'm not sure I even knew that was her last name." The doctor's eyelashes are impossibly long, almost like a girl's, shading brown eyes. He can't be more than thirty and looks like he hasn't slept more than two hours in the last two days.

He asks, "And you know Ms. Francis how?"

"I'm kind of a neighbor of hers, we live out near Ajo." Andi isn't sure how much more to say, how much this Dr. Dennon truly needs to know to care for Bella. "We've been friends for a couple of years." She gestures to Ruby. "She looks after my daughter sometimes."

Dennon flickers a smile at Ruby, who doesn't return it. "Does she have children of her own? Any family nearby?"

"I . . . I . . . don't know. She doesn't talk a lot about that, about her past, I mean. Just, stories, you know?"

Now it's Dennon's turn to blink so slowly she can almost count each lash. "That kind of information will be helpful going forward. We're going to need—"

She cuts him off. "No, I understand that. I do. But Bella . . . Ms. Francis . . . has lived out near Ajo a long time, alone, by choice. She has strong ideas about modern medicine, the modern world. She's convinced plastics, electronics, and phosphorescent lights are poisons, deadly to her."

"And you brought her here anyway?" He motions with his coffee to all the light and sound around them, the acrid smell of solvents and the static hum of unseen machines, the very nature of a modern hospital.

"I didn't know what else to do."

Dennon dumps his untouched coffee in the trash. "Well, Ms.—" He leaves it open-ended, waiting for her to supply something, anything.

"Andi. Andi's fine."

"Okay, Andi. This presents a whole host of problems, ethically and legally. Problems better suited for Ms. Francis's family, whatever family she's empowered to make these kinds of decisions." He looks over to Ruby again, who stares back defiantly, like she's challenging Dennon, daring him not to help them. "But given the unique situation we're in, I'm going to break protocol here. Your friend Bella is dying, and it's got nothing to do with lightbulbs or cellphones or whatever. She has cancer, truly advanced stage four pancreatic cancer."

"Oh . . ." It comes out like a long sigh.

Dennon appears even more tired and sad. "I'm sorry."

Andi looks wildly around the long white halls, as if there's someone else coming along to take in this news, to deal with it. But they're all eerily empty, and it almost seems that she and Dennon and Ruby are the only three people in the whole hospital. "Okay, so what happens now? I mean, like, how do we treat her?"

"No, I'm sorry, I guess I wasn't clear. We don't treat this, not at this point. We're only looking at palliative care now, ways to keep her comfortable, lucid, and in as little pain as possible, for the next month or so—maybe even less. Hospice if that's an option."

"There's nothing like that, not in New Cornelia. There's just . . . me." She fights tears, looks over Ruby. "Just us."

Dennon seems to understand. "Okay, then, let's get Ms. Francis awake, and maybe she'll be willing to talk about some family, some relatives, somewhere."

"I don't know. I just don't. I'm her friend, that's all."

Dennon rubs his tired eyes. "She's going to need friends too, Andi. For as little time as she has left."

* * *

When Bella's eyes finally flutter open, she doesn't seem surprised that she's in the hospital.

Irritated, but not surprised, not even when Andi relays Dennon's prognosis.

"Oh, I suspected, *mija*. I always knew."

"You knew you had fucking *cancer*?"

Bella smooths out the sheets, seeming to inch away from the beeping machines hooked up to her. She won't even look at them. Her voice is like sandpaper, like her throat is still coated with Sonoran Desert dust, although her face is scrubbed and clear from where she fell in the dirt outside her trailer. "No, that I was *dying*. From the moment we're born, we're all dying—"

"Don't give me that new age shit, Bella. Not now."

Bella gifts her a thin, weary smile. "It's okay, *mija*. The doctors here will give it their little names because they need to call it something, need to classify it and diagnose it. But I know what this is. I've always known." And maybe she does. Now that Bella is away from her beloved New Cornelia, it's unavoidable just how sick she's gotten. So thin, her skin yellow and diaphanous, like the flimsy paper of a phone book, the whites of her green eyes as moon-pale and ghostly as the belly of a deep-sea fish. All her beautiful gray hair wispy as ashes. It's almost like the desert sun and air had cast some kind of sorcery over Bella, making her seem healthier than she ever truly was, an incantation that's dispelled under the harsh lights of the hospital.

Maybe it was only wishful thinking that ever let them overlook that she was dying.

Bella blows a weak kiss to Ruby, who is asleep on a chair that pulls out into an overnight couch. Andi has no idea what strings Dennon pulled to get this room for them, or how much it might cost, or how long they'll have access to it. Bella says, "I guess I gave our sweet Ruby a scare."

"You gave all of us an awful scare, you crazy old woman."

Bella laughs. "Such excitement."

"There's nothing exciting about this. This is serious, Bella. *Ms. Francis.* The doctors here are going to want to talk to you about your family, about arrangements—"

"There are no arrangements to make, *mija*, other than to get me home."

"Bella, we can't take care of you there."

"No one needs to take care of me. I'm not one of Stephen's little plants to tend and feed and water. Besides, I've been taking care of myself a long, long, time."

Andi struggles with what to say, how to convince her otherwise. Something in her eyes must have betrayed her thoughts, because Bella says, "And I still expect you and Ruby and that young man to get on your way. Sooner the better."

"He's not that young. And you know I'm not. We can't, obviously, not now—"

"You absolutely can."

"Wait, how did you even know we were planning to leave?"

"Because it's the *smart* thing." Bella coughs and it's clear even those few words exhaust her. She reaches for Andi's hand, searching. Although her fingers are too weak to twine into Andi's, she lets Andi hold hers. "And after what's happened at your trailer, leaving is the *right* thing."

"It's *running*, Bella. Running again. Like always. And I can't run out on you like this."

"Stay or go, it doesn't change what happens to me."

"No, but it changes . . . me . . . I think. Changes *us.* Me and Ruby both. She'd never forgive me, even if I could forgive myself."

"That sweet little girl doesn't need to sit around and watch an old woman die."

"No, but we can help a dear friend enjoy whatever time she has left."

Bella slips her hand free and weakly clutches the sheets. For the first time, Bella appears scared. "There will be nothing enjoyable about this, *mija*. Nothing at all. The best part will be when it's over, and the sooner the better."

Bella's eyes flicker to Andi's shoulder, and Andi turns to see Luke standing at the door behind her, concern on his face. He's wearing a creased baseball hat and the same jeans and shirt from last night, so he must've come directly here. He doesn't come in, just stands there, patient and waiting. Bella smiles at him and he smiles back.

Andi smiles too.

"Well, until that happens," Andi says, "let's do the best we can." She stands. "You're going to have to hang out here a couple of days, no matter what. So, let's make a list of everything you want, anything at all. Anything you can think of. Those cookies you love, a bottle of your favorite vodka. Whatever. I'll get it for you." She looks over to both Ruby and Luke. "*We'll* get it for you."

"And then?" Bella asks.

"And then I'll bring you home."

CHAPTER

38

Amarillo, Texas

THERE'S THIS IMAGE Linnea can't shake, of Abby Walden lit by lightning.

Hair fiery and smoking, her skin flaking black ash. A fresh lightning tree blooming red across her skin, across her arms and chest and face, as the lightning itself opens great neon wings behind her, crackling and flaming and far too bright to look at.

The inherent power is almost impossible to fathom.

She can't comprehend it; she can barely even look at it. But she stares it down all the same as her own eyes burn and smoke in their sockets and that bolt thrums across her own skin, boiling her own blood.

Feels her bones blacken and crack beneath her skin as her lightning tree erupts.

Look, Linnea. Look, goddammit, don't ever look away again.

And then those electric wings carry Abby aloft, carry her heavenward, as the lightning burns her alive. Rising higher and higher into the night sky, until she is one more star there.

Burning bright.

* * *

Linnea and Rio are west of Amarillo when Schweiger calls and demands a full update.

He suddenly left Arkansas just before they did and flew to D.C., and she reminds herself that he doesn't work for them, that it's technically the other way around, and if anything, it's their job to check with *him*.

Rio said as much after they left Tassa Linscott in Okmulgee.

So now they're pulled over on I-40 at the Cadillac Ranch, ten Cadillacs buried hood-deep in a cow pasture, their exposed surfaces brightly painted and graffitied. She's seen the art installation featured in movies and on TV, but in person it looks even weirder, wildly out of place. They remind her of Rio's tattoos, but unlike his, these are exposed for all the world to see.

Rio has Alice open on the dash and Schweiger on cellphone speaker, although Andi's mostly been content to stare out the open window and let Rio do the talking for them both. She still smells Tassa's cigarettes; neither the distance nor the hours in the car seem to have dissipated that lingering smoke.

Hair fiery and smoking, her skin flaking black ash.

"After we met with Tassa Linscott," Rio says, "after she provided better context, we recorrelated our victims, looking for a specific connection that might've escaped us the first time. Not an obvious trait, not age or occupation or even access. We went deeper into their individual histories, their medical backgrounds. I think we finally have something." He pauses, looks over to Linnea. "Lightning strike *survivors*, Schweiger. Three of our victims were struck by lightning and survived."

Silence settles on the other end, before Schweiger finally breaks it. "Winn Chu, Faiza Monroe, and Kayla McCune?" Although it isn't a question, just a recitation of what Rio's just emailed him.

"Yes. Chu when she was thirteen, Monroe when she was twenty, and McCune when she was eighteen."

"How did we fucking miss that? How is it possible we didn't find this earlier?"

"Chu was a minor at the time, and other than her medical records, her family never talked about it. The other two occurred before the widespread adoption of social media. So, no GoFundMe campaigns, nothing like that to latch on to. McCune was even going by her maiden name back then. We did find a short article in her local paper, and I'm sending it over to you now, but you'll see it didn't even name her, as most of these kinds of stories don't, particularly if the victim survives and the family doesn't want publicity. Same was true for Monroe."

"Still . . ." Schweiger says, clearly disappointed and frustrated.

"Still, I think we would've got there, eventually, even if we hadn't pointed it in the right direction. Most people aren't excited to advertise a trauma like that, and not everyone wants to reopen old scars." Rio looks again at Linnea. "But we got it now."

"And we did have it, we just didn't know it, didn't see it at first," Linnea finally chimes in. "A recorded comment from Kayla's mother when she was interviewed by your agents." She recites it now from memory. "*How much bad luck is one good girl gonna get*? At the time, the interviewing agents thought it had to do with Kayla's dad dying young, her being a divorced single mother, her youngest son's learning disability, or the fact that her older boy was already racking up some juvenile run-ins." *Grief is a black hole that way, sucking in all light and life.* "But Kayla's mother was also talking about how her baby girl was struck by lightning after she snuck out of the house to drink with some friends in Cabot City Park, and then was so scared she might get whipped for it she tried to hide it from her parents for two days."

Rio says, "Hid it for the rest of her life."

"Those agents didn't follow up with the right questions then," Schweiger says bitterly. "Didn't push in the right direction."

"It was one comment, Schweiger," Rio says. "Easy to miss."

Just one comment out of hundreds of hours of audio and video recordings and other data and intelligence, and even more every day with each new victim.

"That's how it works," Linnea adds. "Picking up pieces here and there, finding the ones that fit, hopefully in time to be useful, but sometimes still too late." She wonders if she would've picked it out faster before her recovery, although she's glad the meds are finally working their way out of her system, even if she doesn't physically feel a whole lot better. But it does mean her long-dormant brain is kicking into overdrive, fired up now by weird dreams, and startling images—

A fresh lightning tree blooming red across her skin.

"Given how hard it was for us," Schweiger says, "even with all our resources, then how the hell is LTK identifying and finding these women?"

"Likely, through the club," Linnea says. "This Black Light Club thing, an online support group for people like Winn and Faiza and Kayla. It's defunct, but we believe at some point they all reached out to the club or crossed paths with someone associated with it."

"Like Linscott?"

"Yes," Rio says. "We're already going back through the club's orphaned pages, all the dead links, that sort of thing."

Linnea adds, "We hope we'll be able to retrieve something, and Tassa gave us access to all her records, such as they are, from her online jewelry sales." She doesn't tell Schweiger that she's using Alice to dig up all Tassa's deleted emails and messages, or that she herself has asked for a compilation of all ambient surveillance videos from Tassa's school, the apartment complex, and any gas stations or quick marts in a three-mile radius of both. She and Rio still have a sense that Tassa might've gotten a lot closer to the LTK than she ever realized.

"Okay, so LTK has a real lightning fetish," Schweiger says. "That explains the Taser, this device he's used to incapacitate them, and some of our victims. But what about our others? You two were looking into Abby Walden for *weeks*. She was never struck by lightning."

And right before her, those electric wings carry Abby aloft, carry her heavenward, as the lightning burns her alive.

"No," Linnea agrees. "She wasn't." Nor is there any indication she ever read *Your Heart Is a Star* or owned a piece of fulgurite jewelry. "So we're matrixing *all* the disappearances with local weather forecasts, indexing for rain, and thunderstorms specifically. Even tornados. A significant storm might be a precipitating event for him, figuratively and literally, a signal or trigger he can't ignore."

"His ritual," Schweiger says. "So maybe the others were only a prelude before the main event, like practice, or preparation. Or he's purposely altering his victim profile, hiding his real intention, obscuring his endgame. Like you said, organized chaos."

"Like a storm," Rio says.

"I still think we have to focus on the club," Linnea says. "The club itself is important, and maybe that's the locus we've been missing."

"Was LTK a member?" Schweiger asks. "A lightning strike survivor too?

"Possibly," Linnea admits. "Or . . . someone who *wanted* to be."

Rio says, "We've already got lines on most of the old Texas Black Light Club members. Ethan Charmas. Minerva Ruiz. Cole Parham. William Tucker. And even a list of those who never moved to Tyler."

But some, like Stephen Chao and Andi and Ruby Ellis, were proving far harder to find, even with all their resources. Linnea knows Rio's called in Devine for some specialized help. She doesn't know if Schweiger knows that.

"A week ago, you suggested LTK was going home," Schweiger says. "This club was mostly based in Texas, right? So is that where you're headed now?"

"No," Linnea counters, before Rio can answer. "There's someone with ties to the club we want to put eyes on first, want to talk to if we can."

"A person of interest?"

"Just an avenue of inquiry," Rio says. "It's still early."

"I don't think you understand," Schweiger says. "It's already too late. I guess you two haven't been paying attention to the news these last twelve hours."

Of course they haven't, their collective heads buried deep in the sand of the case, like the Cadillacs in front of them.

"What?" Linnea asks. "What's happened?"

"LTK. It's out. *He's* out. Someone on the task force or back in Arkansas tipped off the press. They've leaked our case, all the details, all our work. You and your involvement." The fury in Schweiger's voice is palpable. "That's why I'm here in D.C., answering questions I don't have answers to. The whole fucking world knows about him now."

CHAPTER

39

Las Cruces, New Mexico

He was arrested last year in—of all places—Truth or Consequences, New Mexico.

The charge was burglary, and he spent nearly sixty days in jail because of it, and while incarcerated, the Tyler PD paid him a visit, as did Army CID investigators.

Max Conroy was a popular man.

When Linnea spoke with the lieutenant leading the open assault case out of Texas, he told her they were convinced that Conroy was their attacker but didn't have the evidence, then or now. Army CID politely but firmly declined to divulge their interest in Conroy, but after another call to Devine, he promised them he'd have it in a day or so.

When Conroy's jail stint ended, he submarined for a while, before public utility records had him resurfacing six months ago in Las Cruces, renting a tiny place on the southeast side of the city.

They have his current booking photo from T or C, and he isn't bad looking, although he was more open, more *accessible*, in his teacher's photo from his stint at W. T. Dupont. At least in the latter, he was smiling, even if the smile didn't quite touch his blue eyes, a few degrees colder than the rest of his face.

They also have Audrey "Andi" Ellis's W. T. Dupont teacher's photo, and back then, she was extremely pretty, with a mess of dark curly hair and a bright smile that was all teeth. She looked like your favorite sorority sister, the sparkly, cute friend in a rom-com. The sort of friend Linnea's never truly had, not in college nor in the department.

Tassa shared a handful of Black Light Club pictures from Tyler too, and the progression over time in Andi is both easy and hard to see. The hair shorter, the smile slowly disappearing. She *darkens* throughout those pictures, like something was passing over the sun, shadowing her. Conroy is in them as well, always with a heavy arm around her, always in her space, occluding her.

They don't have anything more recent, no photos of Andi yet after she left Texas. It's as if she and another of the BLC crew, Stephen Chao, dropped off the face of the earth simultaneously, a coincidence not lost on her or Rio, meaning she knows it's not a coincidence at all. Alice has been working away on it, sifting, sorting, making connections, connecting Andi and Stephen to each other, connecting them to the few surviving members of the club. Ephemeral connections across time and space. Devine's been doing the same, in his own way.

It's only a matter of time before they find Andi and Stephen, but time as always is the one thing they don't have, particularly after the press leak debacle.

The last tangible hint they have of Andi is a single call she made to an old friend, Joyce Castro, a teacher from her W. T. Dupont days, who was with her the day she was struck by lightning. Andi called Joyce to tell her that Conroy might come around looking for Andi—called Joyce specifically to *warn* her, after seven years of silence.

That call would've been in the first weeks after Ethan Charmas was put in a coma in Texas.

Joyce relayed that Andi seemed scared, truly frightened about what Max might be willing to do to get her and Ruby back. But the call didn't last long, the connection not very good, and they got cut off midsentence, washed out by some sort of distortion or static. Joyce said it reminded her of that day in September all over again, and she ran down the weird symptoms Andi said she suffered after she was struck—the lights in her apartment constantly flickering, phones forever humming and ears always ringing, clocks never keeping time right anymore. Joyce admitted she didn't truly believe all that stuff back then, no one did, but hearing the fear in Andi's voice, that scratchy white noise on the phone, brought it all back.

There was one more thing Joyce remembered clearly from that call, far more surprising than even the sound of Andi's long-lost voice. It was the sound of a little girl on the line with her—

Momma . . . Momma . . . Momma.

Ruby Ellis.

That was three years ago, so based on what Tassa told them, Ruby should be about six or seven or so now.

There's a version of this where they can make the LTK timeline work around Conroy's incarceration in Truth or Consequences. And he ticks off more than a few BAU-5 profile boxes: *Educated. Attractive. Orderly. Cunning. Controlled. Controlling.* But they have no registered vehicles for him, no known employment, and no idea how he's been making his money or surviving. Rio suspects it might prove something to do with military fraud or theft, whatever the army was so keenly interested in, but they just don't know yet.

A full serial profile is still being put together for him, a historical and family background workup, but even with what little they do have it's apparent that Max Conroy's adult life has been a collection of convenient masks he's hid behind.

Military hero. Charismatic teacher. Devoted boyfriend. Loving father.

That doesn't make him a killer though.

At this point in a case, Linnea usually has *that* feeling, her intuition, gut instinct, a lodestar pulsing brightly in her head, leading her forward, signaling *this is him . . . this is the one.* She sees it all unveiled. But even without her meds, there's still no glimmer here, no pull, nothing.

Just . . . silence . . . just awful darkness.

Sitting now outside Conroy's little rental in Las Cruces, she has no idea if he's their killer or not. And while Conroy is a mystery she's yet to fully unravel, Andi Ellis is equally enigmatic.

A woman struck by lightning and dead for more than two minutes, whose whole life was defined in a thunderclap, a bolt out of the sky. Conroy may or may not be LTK, but either way, Linnea is starting to wonder whether it's Andi Ellis who holds the true secret to all these women's deaths. But until they find her, they only have him.

Linnea touches a fulgurite pendant Tassa gifted her, a surprise that touched her in ways she still can't put words to.

A new lodestar, hanging above her heart.

* * *

They watch for another hour before deciding to approach.

Rio has run the plates on the one car parked outside the yellow house, a subcompact Mazda, but it doesn't come back to Conroy. The utilities are in the name of the home's owner, paid for by the owner, and included in Conroy's $650 a month rent. He has a Boost cellular, and with Alice's help they've determined that he's also been using the Burner app to create additional virtual numbers for calling and texts. A thousand-meter ping trace puts the associated phone in the vicinity of this house right now, or at least the vicinity of the nearest cell tower, but that doesn't put it in Conroy's hand.

The phone hasn't moved in two days.

Rio's already scouted the place three times, clocking side streets, alleys, ways in and out and around. The postage stamp backyard is knee-high in dead weeds, the few windows blocked by dirty miniblinds. There's a liquor store and a taco place a street over.

Clearly they should just keep waiting, watching, and let Schweiger put a full surveillance team on Conroy for however long it takes to get enough probable cause for at least a document search warrant. Rio's already made those arguments but to no avail. Linnea doesn't want to wait, not after their case was blown wide in the media. Not when there's nothing preventing them from just walking right up to the door and knocking.

"You ready?" Rio finally concedes, opening his coat to reveal the gun Schweiger gave him holstered the way he always used to carry his duty weapon. The moment brings back electric flashes, so many sudden memories, they surprise her with their intensity, but she still can't put a gun in her own hand. "Okay," he says, understanding. "I'll go up, see who's home. You hang back."

"I'm not fucking hanging back."

He looks ready to argue again but does not. "Then blade off to my left, behind me." Rio points to the front door, where there's a window to the right that he will use his own body to shield her from. "No cameras that I can see."

If Conroy *is* LTK, if he's seen the news and knows the extent of the manhunt after him, then who knows what they might be walking into.

"I don't want you to take another bullet for me," she says.

Rio smiles, opens his car door, says, "Trust me, I don't want either of us to catch one." He hesitates, the empty silence between them heavy and full of so much. "Okay, so together."

"Okay, let's do it," she says, opening her own door. "Let's just get it done."

He hesitates a moment more, and then gets out. They walk up slowly, Rio focusing on the visible window, Linnea glancing up and down the empty street. She fixates on Conroy's likely car, not recalling it from any of the ambient surveillance footage she's reviewed via Alice. The Mazda is bland, unremarkable, wouldn't look out of place in a Target or Walmart lot—the perfect nondescript car—but it nags at her all the same, like worrying at a hangnail.

Still doesn't fit her mind's eye image.

Has his own wheels, something nondescript, roomy. Also has a credible reason to be on the move so much for such long distances. Regional sales, maybe? Truck driver?"

She looks up and down the street again. Maybe there's another vehicle?

Most discovered in rest stops, some as many as one hundred fifty miles from either their residences or last known location . . .

A truck or an RV.

A trailer?

At least the old rental house is horror movie perfect—sand-blown paint, dark windows—giving off an "abandon all hope" vibe loud and clear.

"Still no movement," Rio says. She sees him breathe, center himself. This is what he's always been so good at, a natural hunter. "Just going to knock on three."

"Got it," she says. And although she told herself the whole walk up here that she was going to stand right at his side, shoulder to shoulder, no space between them, she finds herself hanging back, shifting behind him, just a bit.

Stop it, goddammit, just stop it.

But as Rio knocks on the door, the last thing she hears him say is "Oh shit."

CHAPTER

40

Tucson, Arizona

ANDI IS SURPRISED when Stephen shows up at the hospital.

Not that he wouldn't be concerned about Bella—everyone in New Cornelia is, even if they don't know the full extent of her diagnosis—or unwilling to make the trip to see her, it's just she can tell almost immediately the trip doesn't have anything to do with Bella at all.

He came here to talk to *her*.

He's brought Ruby another book, a whole bag of them, and as she looks through them, Andi finds her and Stephen a couple of those sea foam–colored chairs and buys them both a cup of coffee, but he ignores the coffee and barely looks her in the eye.

When she tells him that Bella is dying, truly dying, he fights back tears.

He tells her there's been no signs of Max down in New Cornelia, no further clues regarding her intruder's identity or whereabouts, although Stephen's spent the past several days checking everything around his own small compound, finding no obvious signs of disturbance. But she also knows he doesn't have the same security system as she does. Doesn't have anyone looking out for him, the way Andi has both him and now Luke. But he isn't totally vulnerable either. He still has online contacts in the lightning strike survivor community they were both once invested in, and even more in the gaming and computer hacking circles he used to frequent, the same ones he leaned on to help forge new backgrounds for her and Ruby after they fled Texas and to monitor the ongoing progress of the Black Light Club police investigation in Tyler. Keeping tabs on Max's movements and whereabouts whenever he could, a digital finger on Max's electric pulse.

He now admits that he's been using those contacts to do a little sleuthing on Luke Keats.

"You've been doing *what*?" Andi fights to keep her voice low. "I asked you to leave him alone."

Stephen looks stricken, as if she's truly slapped him, but forges ahead anyway. "At least I didn't sneak into his trailer, the way Waylen—"

She cuts him off with a furious glare. "Are you really telling me Waylen broke into Luke's trailer? Have you lost your mind? Both of you?'

"I know, Andi, I'm sorry. I was worried about you, we both were."

Again, she tries everything she can to tamp down her anger, knowing that he means well, that he's always meant well. Remembering how she found him after one of his dark spells in Texas, seeking to escape the Matrix in his head by taking razors to his wrists. She'd pressed her hands to his ruined veins, trying to squeeze them shut, trying to keep his blood inside him, only to have him tell her, *You don't have to do that, please don't do that. I'm so sorry, it's such a mess.* And how she'd scolded him between her tears, *How dare you, how dare you do this? After everything you've survived, you don't get to do this to yourself or me.*

He had touched her face then, leaving his blood there, a crimson flower beneath her left eye that ran down her face along with her unclaimed tears. Told her he thought he loved her, but she only shook her head, said, *You're just delirious, dying, lost too much blood* and then smiled and knelt close over him, kissing his forehead, telling him *And I know a thing or two about dying.*

She can't be mad at Stephen for caring about her so much when he's cared so little for himself.

He goes on, chastened. "Luke's record as a police officer was okay, Andi. Nothing outstanding, zero commendations and citations and only one formal citizen complaint—stalking and harassment—that was apparently settled." He searches her face for a reaction to that, then glances over at Ruby, who's still engrossed in one of the books he brought her, or seemingly so. Ruby's been tense and anxious ever since the storm, and although Andi's never thought of her as a clingy child, she's been more so the last few days. Always orbiting Andi, always one eye on her. "The other thing was a shooting incident involving Luke and a partner, resulting in the partner's serious injury and an internal affair inquiry and a shooting board review which apparently cleared him of any wrongdoing, although the details were ultimately papered over with a settlement agreement."

"I *know* all this, Stephen. Luke already told me." He never mentioned the harassment claim, but there's a lot she hasn't told him either. And she's too tired to get into all this with Stephen. "I appreciate what you're trying to do, really I do, but I'm exhausted and I need to see to Bella. We can talk about all this when I get back to New Cornelia."

"Back to Luke, you mean."

She can hear the acid in his voice.

"Back *home*, Stephen." It surprises her how adamant she is, how strong that word sounds to her ears, how heavy it sits in her mouth.

Stephen hesitates, then leans in close. "I *know* where Max is. Or rather, I *did* know."

That hits her in the gut, takes her breath away. Now she's the one who feels like she's been slapped.

"He didn't break into your trailer," Stephen continues. "He couldn't."

Andi knows Stephen was never convinced, and maybe deep down, a part of her wasn't either. Despite the brutality of Ethan's assault, trashing Andi's trailer feels too overt, too obvious, even for Max.

But she pins Stephen with a hard-edged stare. "You said he was looking for me, you said—"

"Yes, I—"

And now she understands with a certain brutal clarity why they're having this conversation here and now, away from New Cornelia, without Luke around. A conversation Stephen probably wanted to have with her this morning before they found Bella sick, before things started to spin out of control.

It hits harder than she imagined, leaving her blinking.

"Oh, Stephen, you *wanted* me to think that, didn't you? All this time you've wanted me to be scared because you needed me to need you."

Stephen starts crying again, sad, heavy, desperate tears. "No, it wasn't like that . . ."

She bores into him. "Now you're afraid if I really do believe Max has found me in New Cornelia, then I'll be off again, but this time I might not give you a chance to join me."

He rubs at his face, anger in his own eyes. "You're going to leave with *Luke* now."

As angry as she is too, some part of her sympathizes, some part of her even now understands—

How dare you, how dare you do this? After everything you've survived, you don't get to do this to yourself or me.

"Did *you* trash my trailer, Stephen? Was it you?"

He shakes his head. "No. *No.* And I wasn't lying, Max *was* looking for you, trying to reach you, but—"

But before he can finish, Luke appears, down the hall, watching them both.

CHAPTER 41

Las Cruces, New Mexico

THE STENCH WOULD be stronger if he hadn't been dead for at least a day and the AC wasn't running full blast.

Linnea doesn't need an ME's report to know the cause of death, those familiar ashy black wings, the spreading fractal patterns, a massive lightning tree growing out of the corner of the small house.

It's difficult to be sure, but it sure looks like Max Conroy struggled until the very end.

* * *

Rio calls Schweiger, but as they wait for the FBI evidence team, they do a quick search on their own.

Although the front door had swung wide open at Rio's first knock, that cloying, awful smell hitting them both in the face, they still don't want to disturb the scene, at least no more than it already has been. Max Conroy's killer was clearly searching for something, that much evident from the visibly tossed drawers and overturned furniture, everything covered in a fine, ashy soot, the gritty remnants of Conroy's hair and skin.

Linnea finds a lone picture of Conroy and Andi Ellis together. The woman in that photo doesn't look much different than the ones they already have, but if eyes could be haunted, hers certainly are.

Linnea wonders if that's how people look at pictures of *her* and her scarred eyes.

In the photo, Andi is wearing a fulgurite pendant, larger than the one Linnea herself now wears. It was captured in the flash in the old picture, holding it close to Andi's heart.

"It's *her*," Linnea says. "LTK's looking for Andi Ellis."

"We haven't found her yet," Rio says, "so he likely hasn't either."

"He's closer though, if he learned something from Conroy." Linnea stares at the black fractals stretching along the wall, unable to imagine what Conroy would've known that she and Rio and Devine won't soon uncover. Uncertain what LTK achieved by killing him. Still, she can feel the precious minutes ticking down in her head, in time with her own beating heart. "This is somehow about *her*. Maybe it's always been about her."

"We still have a line on Stephen Chao as well as others from the club," Rio says. "LTK could be any one of them."

"Or none of them." Her fingers brush her eyelids. "I just thought we were getting somewhere here."

"We did . . . we *are*," Rio says.

Linnea nods as she stands in the ashy living room. "But there was no storm yesterday or the day before, I already checked. And Conroy doesn't fit the profile of any of the other victims—he wasn't even a lightning strike survivor."

"He was part of the Black Light Club."

"No, that was his whole deal, his whole growing frustration in Texas. He wasn't a member, he *wasn't* special, not like Andi."

"So why kill him?"

"Exactly," she agrees. "Why waste the time to track him down and kill him?"

Rio kneels next to Conroy's body, examining it, his dark eyes studying the man's scorched features. "He knew *something*—either something about Andi Ellis or LTK."

"Or both," she says. "Knew where to find her . . . how to reach her. Maybe he's been communicating with her."

"Threatening her?" Rio asks.

"Or warning her," Linnea says. "We are still talking about the man's daughter. Whatever he may have done in the past, whatever happened between him and Andi Ellis, Max Conroy is a victim now too." She moves to the door, Conroy's ash spinning in the air around her, her stomach suddenly churning. "I don't feel so great, let's get out of here."

CHAPTER

42

Tucson, Arizona

"I NEED TO STAY here a few days, just be here with Bella," Andi tells Luke. "I don't want to leave her."

Andi doesn't say *I don't want her to die while I'm gone.*

"You don't have to," Luke says. "I'll take Ruby back to New Cornelia, look after her."

"I can't ask you do to that. I won't."

"You're not asking, Andi. I'm offering."

They're standing just outside Bella's room, where Ruby now huddles close with the older woman, talking to her. Bella's touching Ruby's face, her hair. She might even be singing to her, smiling over her.

Stephen all but fled the hospital when Luke arrived, and although Luke asked her what that was all about, she didn't want to get into what Stephen told her, although she's still shaken by it. It puts her now in a difficult spot with Ruby, since she doesn't feel like she can trust Stephen or rely on him now.

"She can still go to Waylen's," Andi continues. "She can—"

"It's fine," he cuts her off gently. "Ruby can stay with Chili and me. Easy." He brushes a hand over hers and looks like he might reach for her fulgurite pendant, brush his fingers against that too, but doesn't.

"No, you can stay at my place," she says. "It'll be easier for Ruby."

He studies her face. "What about your lightning rod salesman, Max?"

Andi shakes her head. "I'm not so sure that's a problem anymore."

Luke glances down the hallway where they both last saw Stephen. "Okay, fine. If you're good with it, I am. You'll be back in a couple of days then. And we'll be there waiting for you."

She continues watching her little girl, wondering when Ruby started looking so tall, so gangly, so mature. It's like it happened overnight, ever since that night of the sandstorm.

He follows her gaze and pulls her close. Whispers deep into her hair, "Trust me, I've got this."

"I hope so," she says against his chest. She doesn't want to argue with him about taking Ruby back home. And for right now, New Cornelia is still home.

She pulls back and fishes her phone out of her pocket. "I'm going to text you a list of things Bella wants that you and Ruby can get here in Tucson. I'll get whatever else we need before we leave town."

Luke nods, waits as the list comes through. When it does, he reads it to himself, smiles. "Biscoff cookies?" he asks.

"Yeah, the biggest fucking box you can get. All of them."

"Will do."

She kisses his cheek, trying to pull herself together before corralling Ruby for the ride back to New Cornelia. "Thanks for racing up here, for everything." He'd even brought her a backpack with extra jeans and long-sleeved T-shirts. "Tell Stephen and Waylen—" But she doesn't know what to tell either of them anymore.

She waves at Ruby to let her know it's time to go.

"Just tell them I'll be home soon."

* * *

She kneels next to Ruby, tells her it's going to be okay, and that Mr. Luke is going to take her home until she can get Aunt Bella out of the hospital.

Ruby nods, but won't look at her, won't look at Luke standing a few feet away to give them this moment.

"Just a few days, Ruby Tuesday," she says. "I need you to be super strong and take care of Chili and Mr. Luke for us. For me." Andi kisses the top of her head. "I need you to take care of yourself too."

"I will," Ruby answers stoutly, and this is where Andi still finds her special little girl to be such a mystery. She truly has no idea what goes on behind those blue eyes of hers, what she thinks about when she looks at herself in the mirror, or even all that's happened over the last few weeks—Luke and Chili, the storm, the wrecked trailer, now Bella.

She's got to be terrified, Andi thinks. *I know I am.*

"Okay, how about this," Andi says. She pulls the lightning detector from her waist and belts it to Ruby beneath her secondhand shirt. "You hold on to that for me, okay?" She slips off her fulgurite pendant and drapes it over Ruby's neck as well. It's been so long since she's taken it off it immediately feels weird for its weight to be absent. "And this too, until I get back. If you start to miss me or Auntie Bella, you touch it, you think about us. Make a wish on it."

"Is it fairy queen magic, Momma?" Ruby asks, marveling at the treasure she now wears. Andi isn't sure exactly what Ruby's talking about, but if Ruby wants to believe in magic, who is Andi to tell her different? After all Andi's experiences and all the things she herself can't explain, magic is as good an explanation as any.

"Yes, it's magic, bumblebee. All the magic you'll ever need."

CHAPTER

43

New Cornelia, Arizona

Despite bolting from the hospital in Tucson, Stephen waits around outside Andi's trailer until Luke and Ruby finally return.

After he visits Ruby and Luke lets him get her settled in bed with Chili curled up beside her, he joins Luke outside again, where Luke is already cracking a beer and falling into one of Andi's chairs, watching dusk settle and the sky darken and deepen. This time of year, the first constellations to appear will be Cassiopia, Cepheus, Draco—the last representing Ladon, the great dragon from mythology that guarded over the golden apples in the garden of Hesperides.

The apples granted immortality to whoever ate them. But Ladon was defeated by the hero Heracles and his poisoned arrows, and Ladon only found immortality in the stars, forever coiled around the North Pole on star maps.

Luke doesn't offer Stephen a beer but motions for him to join him. "Thanks for helping with Ruby in there," he says. "She was clearly glad to see you, more than you were glad to see me. And more than Andi was glad to see *you* earlier. So, I guess that means we need to have a talk."

Stephen hesitates, hangs back, before finally sitting down.

"Look, I'm sorry for your friend Bella," Luke continues. "I truly am. It's going to be tough when she passes." He studies the horizon, where Draco's stars are soon set to appear. "And it's going to be tough too when we leave, me, Andi, Ruby, because you and Andi have been friends for such a long time . . . far longer than New Cornelia."

"I don't know what you mean."

Luke shakes his head. "Yes, you do. Andi told me how you and her go way back. All the way back to Texas, and everything that happened there. Your *club*." Luke stares at his beer. "I know about all of it."

"I don't think Andi would tell you all those things . . . share those things about us."

Luke ignores him. "You've been a good friend to her, looked after her. But Andi and Ruby need more stability, more safety, more security now."

"You?"

Luke drinks his beer, letting his silence answer for him.

Stephen's hands coil and tighten in his lap even as he fights to still them. "You've only been here a few weeks—she doesn't truly know you . . . *can't* know you." Stephen stops himself, as Luke fixes him with a stare, an expression more curious than threatened. But Stephen feels the sudden heat in the air between, a kind of friction.

Luke says, "And you think you do?" He turns the can in his hand, and his hands are strong and veined, larger than Stephen's. "What is it you think you know about me?"

"I don't mean that. I don't know . . . I just . . ."

Luke nods, then returns to his beer. "Hey, it's okay, relax. You *like* her, I get that. And you're worried about her. We both are. That's why we're both here for her." Luke polishes off the beer and drops the can in the dirt, crushing it with his hiking boot, before raising his shirt to reveal a black gun in his waistband. It looks massive even for his hands. "That's why we're not going to let anything happen to her, right?" Luke nods toward the desert, toward the newly crowned dark. "Now, is there anything you want to tell me about this Max guy?

Anything at all? Something I need to know, or Andi needs to know. Something you've been holding back from her?"

Stephen hesitates, recalls Waylen describing Luke's camper, its smooth, empty surfaces. That tiny, locked room, with all its mysteries and secrets. "You know as well as I do that Max Conroy didn't wreck Andi's trailer."

Luke stares at him, the gun still exposed. "Why, because you think I did it? Or because *you* did, to spook Andi, to worm your way back into her life? All because you're jealous of me." He sighs. "It's been a long day for all of us, and I'm not going to argue." Luke stands. "What I am going to do is circle about, take another good, hard look, and make sure there's no one dangerous lurking around." He taps the gun. *Tap. Tap. Tap.* Then smiles. "Want to come help me?"

Stephen studies the pistol, the way Luke's hand casually rests on the knurled grip, the way it looks so natural there. Even after all the computer and video games he's played, the heroes he's pretended to be, Stephen's never considered himself brave. He's never even been in a fistfight.

"Isn't that what happened to your partner?" Stephen asks. "I mean, he was helping you, right? Then you got separated, or you left him, the specifics are unclear, and in all the confusion, you shot him. Twice." Stephen knows the public story Luke told, probably the only one he told Andi. But he also knows that Luke's partner, Matthew Arnold Monroe, had filed a complaint about Luke three months *before* the shooting—a complaint that was never fully unsealed, like the settlement that ended Luke's police career. "Seems helping you is kind of dangerous too."

Luke's face doesn't betray anything. "Is that what you think?"

Stephen looks out to the surrounding desert, now fully cloaked in the shadows of dusk, all the saguaros standing at crooked, old-man angles, a descending gloom that extended forever, on and on. It was still too early for bats and owls and coyotes, for most of those things that hunted in the dark. But not all of them. He says, "I don't think Max is the real threat out here at all, and neither do you."

Luke smiles a final time, then moves his shirt to cover the gun again.

"I do appreciate you helping with Ruby tonight. It's easy to forget how hard all this might be on that little girl." Luke pulls a set of keys from his pocket and tosses them to Stephen, who fumbles them before catching them in his lap. "Why don't you get on home? Take Andi's truck, since she hightailed it in your car."

Stephen clutches the keys, slick in his hand from his own sweating palms.

"Don't worry about tomorrow, or the day after," Luke says. "We'll call on you if we need you. But honestly, I think I got it from here."

And then he goes inside Andi's trailer.

* * *

After Stephen gets back to his own place, after he sits motionless beneath his tiny lights for more than an hour, he wanders out to his greenhouse to check his plants.

The terrarium he's been putting together for Ruby is still where he left it, partially filled with the peat moss and sand mixture the delicate nepenthes will need. All he can do now is run his hands through it, let it slip through his fingers. He stands in the middle of the beautiful, hot, fecund green he's nurtured and given life to, and contemplates calling Andi right now, trying to talk to her again, but he knows he's lost his chance.

He did nothing to protect Andi from Max, nothing to stop what happened to Ethan, and has stood by these last weeks and let Luke insinuate himself into Andi and Ruby's life until it was too late. Andi always told him how smart he was, marveled at his ability to master arts and hobbies and games, but the real world and all its messy complications still confounds him, all the confusing and painful interactions between living and breathing people.

He's forever a bystander, a distant observer.

A constellation in the sky.

* * *

He doesn't know what time it is when the sound wakes him.

He fell asleep in a chair in his greenhouse, damp now with his own sweat, the misters still going strong. They hiss and hum, the ceiling fans turning, all set against the *tick tick ticking* of the timers.

Like that *tap tap tapping* of Luke's fingers on the gun.

The plants around him gently move, swaying, as if swept through by a great hand.

He isn't sure what he heard, what roused him, but it seemed to come from outside, just beyond the wall at the far end of the greenhouse. Near where he parked Andi's truck.

He struggles standing, his body crooked from the uncomfortable chair, careful not to make a sound of his own in case there's someone outside. The greenhouse air, always thick and fetid, fructuous, has a different odor now, something spikier, a hint of rot, of eggs gone bad. He breathes deep, tasting it.

In the mostly dark, the pitcher plants look like open mouths, tasting the dirty air too.

That smell . . .

The smell of propane.

Six 250-gallon propane cans stored to run his 12,000-watt Westinghouse generator.

A tricky job getting it all wired up properly, requiring constant maintenance, and although he searched for rock or sand damage after the massive haboob, it's possible he missed something.

Also, an easy target, if someone wanted to hurt him.

He was happy when Andi found him in Texas bleeding to death from the lateral razor cuts in his wrist, how she alone pulled him back from the brink. He'd been searching for a magical light, a way to escape his own head, and there she was, glowing for him.

He's so glad she isn't here now.

He runs for the door, any door, grabbing at plants as he goes, trying to carry as many as he can.

When the greenhouse goes up, it explodes skyward like a great dragon unfolding, massive black and red wings unfurling, as the fireball rolls into the desert night sky.

Draco. Ladon. The guardian of Hesperides.

He runs toward light, any light, looking for an escape, and just like that day he was struck by lightning, everything in him suddenly ignites and his entire body thrums with impossible energy and he's blown off his feet.

The secondary explosion rumbles and rolls through the main trailer half a heartbeat after the first, superheating the metal hundreds of degrees, and sending debris spinning sixty yards in every direction, trailing smoke, and embers.

Flowers on fire, falling from the heavens.

CHAPTER

44

Steins, New Mexico

JUST OUTSIDE OF Lordsburg, heading toward Arizona, Linnea's stomach finally gives out on her.

A combination of lack of sleep, shitty food on the road, adjusting to the meds sweating out of her body. It's past midnight and Rio is behind the wheel and she's reviewing a surveillance video from that liquor store near Conroy's house, as well as their property list from Abby Walden's car, when she tells him she needs him to pull over, to get some air.

They are on a dark stretch of nothing between New Mexico and Arizona, the sky black and salted with stars. They passed a brightly lit Flying J fifty miles back, but all they have now is a flyspeck rural rest stop—little more than crushed gravel and a loose arrangement of buildings—but Linnea tells Rio it's enough. When he pulls over, she sits for several minutes, contemplating just how far she can get before she hurls up her guts, although she already feels a little better with the sudden lack of forward motion, the deep quiet and the stillness.

"How're you doing?" Rio asks, offering her a water bottle from the cooler they keep stowed in the back, an old surveillance habit that won't die easily.

"How do I look?" she asks, before raising her hand, stopping him before he can answer. "Yeah, that's what I thought. I'll be okay, just needed a breather." She takes the offered still-chilly bottle and presses it to her forehead, where it feels good, like a cool and steady hand pushing the hair out of her face, and it makes her think of Dan.

"Nothing?" Rio asks, gesturing at Alice, and she only shakes her head no.

For the last hundred miles, she's been alternating videos from the liquor store in Las Cruces, the Target in Augusta, and retail locations in both Oklahoma within three miles of Tassa Linscott's apartment and Port Gibsson, Mississippi, where Abby's car was found. She's also been reviewing that evidence list from Abby's car, and she's at least started perusing the file of recovered emails and messages from Tassa Linscott's StormCrow20 account. Also, she's all but confirmed that Max Conroy *was* trying to track Andi Ellis down and had been for at least the last nine or ten months, not long the first LTK murder.

He knew something . . . he was trying to warn her.

Similarly, Devine's got a digital lead on Stephen Chao in Arizona—something to do with exotic mail-order plants—and promised them something more concrete before morning. Chao's been operating under at least two aliases, but the very specific nature of the exotics he's been ordering are like faint tracks in the snow—or in this case, footprints in the desert sand—a trail far easier to follow than Andi Ellis herself.

Devine's confirmed Chao was in southern Arizona as recently as three months ago, so maybe she's there too. They *are* making progress.

And they're getting closer to LTK too. That tableau at Conroy's house was proof of that, more than tying up a loose end, or revenge. It was also a message, a warning.

We're close. I know it, I finally feel it . . . and LTK feels it too.

Rio finishes off his own water, tossing the empty bottle in the back. A car pulls past them, briefly illuminating him, and then a boxier camper, fanning them both with even more light. In its pale wash, Linnea can see just how tired Rio looks too. He's been mostly silent since they left Las Cruces, but now says, "Remember that first thing we worked, the Saint's Rosary killings?"

It takes a while for Linnea to open her eyes, to find her voice again, to recall so long ago, when all the cases were still new and exciting, and she was still so strong and sure of herself. "Thirty-five-year-old welder. Florida."

"You picked his face out of two videos more than a *year* apart. Gas station video from the second victim, and about thirty-five seconds of cellphone footage shot at a music festival where he grabbed his fourth."

"His last," she says.

"His last," Rio emphasizes. "That ID wasn't all we had, but it was enough. They electrocuted him after eight years on death row."

"Florida State Prison in Radford, same place they electrocuted Bundy in '89."

"Yes. And his last words were *God have mercy on her.*"

She smiles grimly. "Everyone gets religion in the end."

Rio continues, "That moment when you seemingly picked his face out of the air, when you saw it, saw *him*, seemed like a miracle to me then, and it still does now, even after all these years. I know you've always felt the weight of that, this unique ability you've felt a responsibility to use, that *not* using was somehow selfish or cowardly." He turns to her. "I know you think you've carried that alone."

But it was Rio alone who carried her out of Parlor's barn while bleeding near to death, even though she was begging him to let her go. Rio has shouldered more than his share too. They worked on a dozen serial cases together before Parlor, when BAU-5 heard about her reputation as a local cop and brought her in as a consultant. He was her first federal partner, her only FBI partner. The only partner who ever truly wanted to keep working with her.

Rio points at Alice in her lap. "But now with all these computers and algorithms, with the right questions and enough data and videos and time, it doesn't need to fall *all* on you anymore."

"You sound like Schweiger."

Rio smiles. "And maybe he isn't wrong. Look, I understand why you needed to try this, why you felt like you had to do this, to prove something—"

"We're getting close, you said so yourself."

"Maybe too close." He hesitates. "What you've proved though is that you still have a lot to share, a wealth of experience and insight. All invaluable. I know BAU-5 approached you about teaching, and I think it's time you consider it."

She scoffs. "A fucking classroom. A desk and PowerPoints." She shakes her head. "And you?"

"I'm no teacher, Lin. You know that. Besides, everything I know, I learned from you."

She knows that's not true, far from it, but understands why he's saying all this. The thing with Conroy's murder in New Mexico has spooked him. He's finally accepting just how adept, motivated, and particularly dangerous this serial is, and he doesn't want her anywhere near it anymore. Doesn't want her exposed and vulnerable again. They probably dodged a bullet at Conroy's shack; a couple of days earlier, maybe only a handful of hours earlier, who knows what could've happened or who they might've run into.

Rio says, "You don't need to be out here, Lin, not like this. No more sleepless nights on the road or cold hours in a car. You can go *home* to your family and know that you're not sacrificing anything by doing so."

She sits silent, stone-faced, Alice clutched in her lap. She knows he's not saying these things to hurt her, but they hurt all the same. "Well, fuck you too."

Rio laughs, puts a hand on her shoulder. "Okay, do you want to talk about our last case then? *Really* talk about it?"

She fights tears. "No, you promised me—"

"And now I want you to promise *me*," he says. "I've never asked anything of you, not like this, but I am now. Go home. I'll keep sending you what we have, you'll still have access to Alice and BAU-5, whatever you want. But promise me you're done *here*. Promise me."

She wants to argue, to fight with him, but she can't find the words.

"I'm sorry for dragging you into this," he says. "It was selfish." He settles back, stares out the windshield into the dark. "But I missed this too. I missed *you*."

"I know," she whispers, still fighting tears.

Rio nods, breathing deep like he's finally cleared the air. "I'm going to hit the head," he says, opening the door. "After that, we'll find a hotel, both grab some sleep. I'll call Schweiger, work with him and the team on Stephen Chao and the Arizona angle, and then we'll get you on a plane home."

"What about Andi Ellis?" she asks. "What about *Abby*?"

"We can still save Ellis. As for Abby . . ." Rio lets the rest hang there for a long moment. "We've done all we can, like always." He zips up his coat, and then eyes the sky above them. "Fuck me, I think it's going to rain."

* * *

She sits in the dark, waiting for Rio to return.

Alice lays open before her and through her drying tears she idly scrolls through all the videos, all the photos from the crime scenes, all the lost connections and missed moments.

She's back in Abby's car now—

That tiny nick on the windshield from a spinning piece of quartz.

Two hair ties in the center console, one green, one blue . . . *green was her favorite color* . . . one quarter, a dime, and three pennies . . . *exact change of a mcdonald's happy meal from a five-dollar bill.*

She's in the Target in Augusta now, looking toward the parking lot—

Faiza Monroe's old Ford . . . *already had an appointment to get the tires rotated* . . . unopened mail sitting on the passenger seat . . . *her sister's birthday gift still missing* . . . some kind of oblong SUV or truck, parked three rows back, near the far edge of the lot . . . *green or blue . . . something dark.*

She's at the Circle K two miles from Tassa Linscott's apartment—

Ten gas pumps . . . *only eight working* . . . thick raindrops on the store's surveillance camera lens . . . *three days of rain* . . . an empty lot adjacent . . . *no, not completely empty* . . . a shape, a blur, a ghost of a truck or van . . . *something dark.*

She's back in Abby's car—

Fancii Mila compact mirror, glass cracked.

Red hair . . . *abby's hair was blonde* . . . caught in the passenger seat headrest.

Ash and grease marks on the back seat, trash in the floorboards. Pet fur . . . *she once had both a cat and dog* . . . a battered paperback horror novel . . . *not your heart is a star but* . . . *but* . . . a library book she never returned . . . *who is harriette person* . . . *memorial library* . . . seven large glass windows hidden by blinds . . . *because it was night.*

But Abby was there *earlier* that day.

Now she's in Las Cruces, at Milo's liquor store, west of Conroy's—

A Las Cruces PD cruiser.

Two kids on bikes.

That boxy truck or van again . . . *green or blue* . . . *something dark* . . . more hint or blur than shape . . . *but something hunched, black.*

She's at the Ash Street Bar and Grill—

Curbside parking here . . . *as well as across the street, where there's also a square park or green space dotted with metal benches and tables* . . . enough parking for other cars . . . *even though it was daytime.*

Because Port Gibson is so goddamn small.

Ash Street Bar and Grill.

Fulgurite. Jewelry. Book.

No . . .

Book. Jewelry. Fulgurite.

No, not a book, but books . . . the library.

Harriette Person Memorial Library.

Linnea sits up, her hands tugging on the fulgurite pendant Tassa gave her, all of Alice's windowed screens flashing past her, the ghosts in her head now colorful and clear and strident.

The library . . .

A dark SUV or even truck, something green, blue, black.

Maybe it was raining that day, the sky dark . . . because he hides in the dark, in the storms.

It was storming that day, Linnea. You don't have to check. You know it.

She *sees* it, sees it all . . .

And she glances up just in time to see Rio talking to someone up by the bathroom, but she can't tell if it's part of the couple they saw earlier, or someone else. The figure is tall, their back to Linnea, their faces hidden. Their hands too. There's so little light, and with heavy raindrops now patterning the windshield, everything is distant and blurry, a shadow against shadows.

Soft. Muted. Dark.

Dangerous.

Because he hides in the dark, Linnea, in the storms.

The gun Schweiger gave her is in the bag, all the way in the back. Too far too reach, and she's too late to realize she might need it.

A surprising bright light plays against the backdrop of the restrooms, a brutal white camera-flash that quickly rolls over Rio like a sudden summer storm.

Summer *lightning.*

CHAPTER

45
The Storm

LASHING OUT WAS foolish, one of the few true mistakes he knows he's made.

But with the final storm clouds gathering, knowing he's so close, knowing it's almost over, he had no other choice.

He felt the rain on his face, tasted the temperature dropping, smelled the raw musty exhalation of the coming storm's lungs, and when that urge overcomes him he knows what he must do.

What he can't stop himself from doing anymore, even if he wanted to.

I am the storm season

She is within reach, finally within his grasp, and he will not allow anyone or anything to keep her from him.

Tlaloc. Raijin. Zeus. Shango. Perun. Indra.

Kapoonis and Enumclaw.

All these gods of storms and flood, thunder and lightning. Ancient cultures everywhere made sacrifices to worship and appease these deities, and he will soon join their pantheon.

She was marked for *him*, to show him the sign, to light his way.

I will take the lightning angel's wings

The sacrifices in his honor have already begun, even if no one knows his name yet.

He listens for the rumble of thunder and makes ready for the deluge that will mark his ascension.

That will drown them all.

Deluge

Part IV

CHAPTER 46

Tucson, Arizona

ADAN RIO DOESN'T remember much about what happened in Jon Parlor's barn in Virginia.

More specifically, he never *tries* to recall much about that night. It's not only that he promised Linnea they'd never talk about it, or that he lied three times under oath about the exact sequence of events that transpired inside that barn, or that he *didn't* lie about how she tried to kill a man, execution style, in front of him.

There's something about pain, about *dying*, about feeling your own heart slow and your soul, the *teyolia* bound to your heart, fleeing for the next world—Mictlan, Tlalocan, or the Sky of the Sun—that's both hard to forget and impossible to relive.

He's been hurt before, in combat. His heart has been hurt too. But nothing like that.

This is what he does remember—

An old barn draped in darkness and oddly crooked stairs down to the room below the hay.

Names and other words written on the walls all around it that he later washed off, before deciding to burn the whole fucking thing down.

Then a long walk up to the road, and the sound of crickets. It was so hot that night, that whole week, and he was sticky with sweat and blood, and he held Linnea as tight as he could, even though she kept slipping from his arms.

The sound of crickets or cicadas he still hears when it gets too quiet sometimes.

How light she felt in his arms, as if she'd lost fifty pounds. It was like carrying a ghost, and he kept talking to her, so she wouldn't touch her eyes . . . so she wouldn't pull at the thread.

So she wouldn't know how bad it was.

It started to rain on them, as he was holding Linnea close to him, faltering those last few steps under her weight.

It started raining—just like in those moments before he was attacked in Steins, New Mexico.

Adan Rio doesn't remember much about Ruther Glen, Virginia, then or Steins now, but he does remember the pain.

* * *

Rio's in the Banner University Medical Center in Tucson, Arizona, close to Davis-Monthan Airforce Base, home of the 355th Wing, A-10 Thunderbolt and OA-10 forward air controllers, platforms he's familiar with from his time in uniform.

For the past day and a half, whenever he's awake, he's been watching their familiar silhouettes make patterns in the skies outside his window.

Last time he was in Tucson was to train at the base's aircraft boneyard, the largest in the world, more than four thousand planes reflecting the history of American aviation and warfare. He was practicing tactical plane assaults using one of the boneyard's decommissioned Boeing passenger jets, and remembers standing on the wing in late afternoon, the heat like a furnace, looking out over the sweltering Arizona desert.

He wishes he could remember more about that rest stop in New Mexico, or at least the face of the man who assaulted him, and whatever it was he said to Rio just before he hit him with fifty thousand volts, somewhere north of three microcoulombs, more than enough to short circuit every synapse in his body, and to cause the ugly memory loss he's still struggling with. While he was down his assailant also beat him with something heavy and sharp, and then stabbed him. He's got three cracked ribs, a busted shoulder, and two missing teeth to show for the fight he lost and doesn't even remember.

Eighty stitches hold together a three-inch-deep incision beneath his ribcage.

When he first came to wrapped head to toe in tubing in this bed, he called out for Linnea, *yelled* for her, until Schweiger put a hand on his bandaged shoulder and told him Linnea was fine—*she's fine, Rio, she's okay*—but that he should be dead. That most anyone else *would* be.

That was thirty-six hours ago, and he still hasn't seen Linnea in person.

And he still can't recall much of anything important, nothing worthwhile about his assailant, about LTK, nor even the last thing he said to Linnea in their Explorer before he went up to the rest stop. All he has are reminders, his myriad wounds, including the now fading lightning tree scar on his ribcage, delicate and rosy, reaching . . . *growing* . . . toward his heart.

No, I remember rain.

He should be dead, just like that night in Virginia.

He has an ancient Aztec poem his mother once told him tattooed in blue along his ribcage, a constant reminder of death itself, how fleeting life is—

Oh, only for so short a while you have loaned us to each other, because we take form in your act of drawing us, and we take life in your painting us, and we breathe in your singing us

But only for so short a while have you loaned us to each other

Because even a drawing cut in obsidian fades, and the green feathers, the crown feathers, of the Quetzal bird lose their color, and even the sounds of the waterfall die out in the dry season

So, we too, because only for a short while have you loaned us to each other

And yet, Rio has survived, again and again. Fallujah. Wanat. Horn of Africa. That meth lab in London, Kentucky.

Riviera Beach, Florida. Salem, Oregon. Ruther Glen, Virginia

Steins, New Mexico.

"You look like hell, by the way," Schweiger says from the doorway, where two other FBI agents and a uniformed deputy from the Pima County Sheriff's Office stand guard.

Rio's survived it all, and all he's got to show for it are the scars he carries on behalf of those who didn't. He's not afraid of dying anymore.

"It was pretty much a ghost town, that place you and Linnea stopped at," Schweiger continues. "Used to be a mining town, like back in the forties. But water had to be brought in by rail, and when the line shut down those deliveries, so did the town. Everyone got a free rail pass to move somewhere else, and most did, leaving behind their homes, even their possessions. A lot of the buildings burned later, but a couple started doing some renovations and even ran ghost town tours for a while, until the husband was murdered in 2011. Shot five times, still unsolved. A ton of bad history there and now you're part of it too."

Rio doesn't care about the story, the history. Schweiger is stalling.

"Tell me where we're at with the case," Rio says, his own voice sounding distant, unused. "Tell me what happened in New Mexico. And tell me where the fuck Linnea is."

Schweiger nods at the agents at the door, who quietly shut it behind him. He pulls up a chair next to Rio's bed and takes off his glasses and slips them into his pocket. "We have a fair amount of developments to go over, if you feel up to it."

Rio feels like throwing Schweiger out of his chair, and probably would, if he still wasn't in so much pain.

I always remember the pain.

Schweiger says, "I want you to know that Linnea was here with you at the beginning, constantly, but you were so doped up you likely don't remember that. She got pulled away, had to deal with something, but at her request, we've been giving her updates every hour."

"The case?" Rio asks. "LTK?"

Schweiger checks his phone and puts it away again.

"Home."

CHAPTER 47

New Paltz, New York

THERE ARE SO many memories of Linnea's career everywhere around their house, it's inescapable.

Old clothes and cuffs and cuff keys. A chipped mug. Challenge coins. Photos and news clippings tucked here and there. Linnea never purposefully brought her work home with her, she never intended to, it just followed her here anyway, barging into their lives, elbowing its way in, taking up residence.

After the FBI agent who picked her up from her redeye flight brings her to the house, even Dan notices she's carrying new official credentials.

A new oiled gun as well.

The new pendant around her neck.

She tells Dan something seriously had happened to Rio out in New Mexico, and that she only has three hours on the ground, maybe less, and she knows that he's wondering why she even bothered to come at all.

Two reasons, but only one matters now—

She promised Rio.

* * *

They retreat to his basement office to talk privately, something they haven't done in a long time, mostly so they don't wake up the girls.

She collapses into the chair at his desk, while he leans against his shelved books.

She sits silently for a moment, shuffling some of their daughter's school papers left forgotten on his desk—reports he'd helped them with, quizzes they did well on and were proud of. She doesn't remember any of them, doesn't remember Dan even mentioning them. Some were before her stay at Gracie Square, some after.

She says, "God, I'm a shitty mom."

"No, you're *conflicted*." He finds one of the spare stools they keep down here from a mismatched set from their kitchen and drags it over to his desk and perches next to her. "And fortunately, you're a pretty good wife." He smiles at her. "So tell me about Rio."

She does, haltingly. Lots of stops and starts. How Rio was attacked by the serial they've been chasing at some remote rest stop in New Mexico and how she saw it all unfold in front of her, fifty yards away in a shadowy rainstorm. How she was paralyzed and useless and terrified and how by the time she finally could move, his attacker was gone.

How she almost watched Rio die and still can't explain why she walked away, unscathed.

"Luckily," she says, "Schweiger had some sort of tracking transmitter in the laptop we were carrying, as well as the cred folios he gave us. He got a team to us and probably saved Rio's life, while I didn't do a damn thing." Schweiger was furious that they hadn't stayed with evidence collection team at Conroy's home, that they were running off on their own again, until she reminded him that's exactly what he'd agreed to.

"Don't blame yourself."

"Of course I do. He's recovering in a hospital in Tucson, Dan."

"He'll understand."

"Sure, he always does. That's twice now he's been put in the hospital because of me. I'm tired of the people I care about having to *understand* all the time." She looks at him steadily. "It apparently takes a lot of understanding to deal with me."

"Don't I know it," he agrees, and there's that smile again, another tiny moment she can hold on to, even as she touches the new pendant against her throat. At least she's not touching those damn scars.

He says, "And it isn't a competition to see who gets more stitches." He hesitates. "But this must be close to over now though, right? That's why you're here, that's why you're home."

She touches Tassa Linscott's pendant again. "We *were* so fucking close, Dan. But no, it's not over. Not yet. There's something I need to do."

"So, you didn't really come back east to see me and the girls either."

"No."

She knows it hurts him, but she sees no reason to lie to him, and other than not telling him all the details of her old cases, particularly her last case, she never has.

But all Dan says is "There's no way the man you've been chasing got out of that rest stop without leaving evidence, a trail for the FBI to follow. He made a mistake, attacking Rio."

"He took a calculated gamble. I'm not sure why."

"He saw his crimes splashed all over the news. Saw *your* face, knew what he was up against."

She laughs bitterly.

Dan says, "You always say you can't truly understand their motives."

"No, but their *actions*? Those are usually predictable."

Dan shrugs. "Lin, you're brilliant. You truly are. But don't give yourself that power. No one can perfectly predict the future, not even you. And anyone who claims otherwise is lying."

"We've been working with this new algorithm, this AI crime analysis thing that the FBI developed. It's . . . impressive. Supposed to put me out of a job."

"You were out of a job," he reminds her. "So, what is it, a magic crystal ball then?"

"A fancy laptop, but yeah, something like that, I guess."

"Did it warn you that you and Rio were about to get attacked?"

Linnea stacks her daughters' papers in neat piles. "No."

"If your Magic 8-Ball didn't see it coming, then how the hell could you?"

She sits silently again for a long time, squaring off the stack of papers, making them perfect. "*This* close, Dan. I finally *saw* it . . . the vehicle he's in, how he's been—"

"Then *go*," Dan says, standing. "Go find him." He pulls her out of her chair and pulls her close, and she can feel his beard on his face, his arms around her. "Just promise me that next time you're face to face with him you'll do whatever you have to make sure he doesn't hurt you or Rio or anyone else again. That's all I ask. Do whatever you got to do . . . and then come home."

She hopes he doesn't feel her tears, and then hopes he does.

"You want me to wake the girls," he asks, "even for just a moment?"

"No. I'll see them when I get back. When it's done. I *promise*."

"Okay, good." He kisses her temple. "Where to now?"

But instead of answering him, she just draws him closer.

CHAPTER 48

New Cornelia, Arizona

RUBY KNOWS IT'S wrong to spy on people.

Knows better than to be *sneaky*, even though her momma showed her how to hide deep down in the closet or underneath the bed. Showed her all the best ways to make herself small and almost invisible.

But she also knows what anger sounds like, and what fear sounds like too. And although she's not sure exactly what's going on right now, she hears both in Mr. Luke's voice as he walks around outside their trailer and argues with Momma on his phone.

They're not fighting about Auntie Bella, still sick over in the big white hospital in the city, but about Momma's friend, Mr. Stephen. And since Mr. Luke went outside to argue with Momma over it, that means it's something he doesn't want Ruby to hear.

Momma would say *it's none of your business, bumblebee.*

But Mr. Stephen, with his flowers and his books and the twinkly lights in his trailer, is her friend too, and in a way that Ruby can't explain yet but still feels deep inside, a tug at her heart that threatens tears—*and she hates crying*—whatever's happened to him is kind of her business too, and she doesn't want to wait until Mr. Luke, or Momma, gets around to telling her the truth, if they ever do.

It's also wrong to lie, and Ruby figures in a long list of bad things you're one hundred percent not supposed to do, lying might even be worse than spying or sneaking.

At least spying and sneaking are fun, a game, like when she sometimes sneaks into Momma's room at night. That's what her momma used to call it when she first showed Ruby how to hide, how to disappear, after they left Daddy behind in Texas.

We're gonna play a game now, bumblebee, it's gonna be so fun.

* * *

As she slips out the trailer's back door, she leaves Chili inside with her favorite treats and one of Ruby's old stuffies, a little nappy-furred dragon, knowing the dog will get bored soon and start looking for her and barking. She's got only a few minutes, so she crouches alongside the trailer (keeping a sharp eye out for snakes the way Mr. Waylen and Auntie Bella taught her) and then belly crawls as fast as she can out to the edge nearest to Mr. Luke.

She finds his shadow in the sand, getting small and then big again like a fairy tale giant as he moves around, and she shrinks back small and tight against the warm, rusty metal, hoping he doesn't see her own.

We're gonna play a game now, bumblebee.

She doesn't fully understand everything he's talking to Momma about, but she listens close, scrunching up her nose to concentrate, following the words as best she can, sounding them out in her head, even if she doesn't know them all—

An explosion . . . a fire . . .

Stephen Chao . . .

"The propane tanks, Andi. All those propane tanks near his trailer. His greenhouse or whatever that thing was. They went up. All of them. Some kind of accident."

Mr. Luke stares out at the blue sky, his back to her. Only a few feet away.

"I don't know," he says, answering a question Ruby can't hear. "But there will be an arson investigation. He was driving *your* truck. I let him take it back to his place last night."

Mr. Luke waits as her momma talks more, and Ruby wonders if she's now crying.

"I just don't think you should come back here, that's all," Mr. Luke says, and there's that anger in his voice again, just a little bit. "I'll load Ruby up now, and we'll come for you. Then we're gone for good."

She covers her mouth when she hears her own name so loud and clear, desperate not to make a sound. It's weird to hear someone talk about you when you're not there, when you're not supposed to be listening, and for a moment, Ruby *does* feel guilty. She feels *bad*. Here she is, crawled up in the dirt and dust, scared of snakes, hearing things she's not supposed to. But she *really* wants to know what's going on and she *does* want to see Auntie Bella but not at that big, creepy hospital, not with all those machines and the bright lights and awful noises. She knows Auntie Bella doesn't want that either, and Momma promised her and Ruby she'd bring her back here, back home, where she belongs.

Mr. Luke knows all that too, so Ruby doesn't understand why he's trying to do it all differently now, and still doesn't understand what's just happened to her friend Mr. Stephen.

"I know you promised her," Mr. Luke says. "I know what you said and what she wants. That's just not a good idea anymore. It isn't."

Ruby still can't hear her momma, has no idea what she's saying way over there in the city, in the hospital with Auntie Bella, but she can guess. Like she can always guess when Momma's sad, like she easily guesses when it's going to rain before it does or can guess the very moment Chili is about to pad into her room even before she appears.

Mr. Luke says, "There will be *questions*, Andi. Cops. Everything. And they're going to talk to everyone, including you, eventually."

Ruby doesn't have to hear Momma for real to know that Mr. Luke isn't happy with whatever she's saying.

"Fine," he tells her momma, as he continues to stare at the sky, and she wonders what he sees up there, what he's looking at. There are no stars, no clouds, nothing. Just endless, empty blue. Boring. If Ruby looks too hard, she's afraid she'll get lost there. "I'll deal with it then. I'll deal with all of it." He pulls the phone from his ear and Ruby worries he's about to turn around and see her, to catch her, so she swallows hard and shrinks back, small as she can, but he doesn't move, just clutches the phone, squeezing it tight in one of his big hands until the knuckles turn white, and then he goes back to talking to her momma. "It was quick, Andi. He likely didn't feel a thing. Probably never even knew what happened and maybe we never will either. Still no body yet. All that heat and fire, maybe nothing to recover."

Ruby covers her mouth again, swallowing a cry, because she finally understands what's happened, even if she still doesn't know all the words. Her and Momma's friend Mr. Stephen is *dead*. He got all burned up. No more twinkly lights, no more flowers, no more book gifts. Never again.

Dead is a word she knows well and knows exactly what it means.

She also knows now why Mr. Luke wants to go to her momma in the city and not have her come back here. Why he's trying to take them away for good. He and Momma are still worried that Daddy or whoever tore up their trailer and then hurt . . . killed . . . Mr. Stephen.

Mr. Luke is scared that what happened to Mr. Stephen could happen to them too.

But Ruby isn't scared of Daddy. Although it's been so long since she's seen him—and even if it might anger Momma to know this, she still misses him sometimes—he would *never* hurt Ruby. He told her too many times how much he loved her, how *special* she was, how she was his bright and shining angel, and she believed him then and still does now.

They don't need to be afraid of Daddy.

But that doesn't mean there's not something else out in the desert, out in the dark, something she *is* afraid of.

Something that will find them, wherever they go, no matter what they do.

Ruby tugs at the necklace Momma gave her, the lightning one, the *magic* one, and makes a wish for Momma to come home.

CHAPTER

49

Tucson, Arizona

After her call with Luke, Andi wakes up dreaming about Stephen.

Not that he came to her in this dream, necessarily. Not like a ghost or apparition or even a premonition. But he was trying to say something to her, tell her something important, even though his mouth was on fire. And now he'll never get to tell her what was so important because he was blown all to hell in a freak accident or something much worse, and Luke feels it's too dangerous for her to return, even though Ruby's there with him, and Andi has no idea how much danger *they* are in.

She told Luke to take Ruby back to New Cornelia, she told him not to worry about Max.

He told her he'd keep them all safe.

Now she's not sure either of them were right.

She wakes up in Bella's room dreaming about Stephen finding Bella staring at her, and although Andi's not sure if it's still part of her dream, or if Bella is even awake or alert herself, Bella leans forward and whispers, *I could swear you were glowing, mija.*

Glowing like a star.

* * *

Dr. Dennon tells her it was only the pain meds talking.

Bella is on a potent cocktail of benzodiazepines, opiates, and antipsychotics, a palliative sedation to ease her respiratory issues, her pain, her anxiety. A mixture they'll increase over time, and a mixture Andi is going to have to be comfortable administering all on her own when she takes Bella home.

She wants to go today, now, something Dennon strenuously disagrees with.

"I understand, Andi. But we're better able to manage her care here. Or, better yet, as I've mentioned already, there are any number of hospices I can recommend." He's brought another coffee for her, which she reluctantly takes. "I know you mean well, it's just . . ." He's not afraid to look her in the eye, and she wonders—even at his seemingly young age—just how many hard conversations like this he's already been through. "I don't think you truly appreciate the responsibility you're asking for, and it's only more problematic because Ms. Francis is unwilling to give us much information about any true family."

"I told you. I *warned* you. You ignored me."

"One thing I can't ignore is *you're* not next of kin."

"She's old enough to make her own decisions, and I think she's made those abundantly clear."

Dennon clears his throat. "She's in tremendous pain and despite her admirable bravado, she's terribly afraid. She's dying, Andi. We don't like our patients to make those kinds of decisions on their own, under those circumstances. I know I don't."

"But she's not on her own. I've been here the whole time." She finally sips the coffee, a kind of peace offering. "I appreciate that I wouldn't have been able to do that without you. I'm not blind to what you've done for me and for her. I'm just asking you to turn a blind eye a little bit longer."

Dennon says, "What about your daughter?"

"What about her?"

"Do you truly want her to see what's going to happen? Because she's going to watch Ms. Francis's progression up close, day by day, and it will only get progressively worse. This isn't going to get better. At this stage there are no miracles, none I've seen. It could take days, or weeks, but either way, both you and your daughter are going to have a front row seat to that woman dying, painfully, and although you might think you know how you're going to handle it, I suspect you have no idea how that little girl will."

"We'll be fine."

Dennon nods, clearly unconvinced. "There's one last thing then," he says, "and it's non-negotiable."

"Okay," she says warily.

"I need to know who you truly are. A full name, a *real* name."

"Why?"

He steps closer, leans in, so no one else can overhear them. "I have no idea what your situation is, and part of me doesn't care. You seem decent and kind and more importantly you clearly care about Ms. Francis. So it doesn't matter if you're on the run for fraud, or wanted for murder, or just struggling with addiction. But I do need to *know*. I'm not letting you walk out of here with that woman in tow if you're not going to be able to see her care through, if you're just as likely to get hauled off or run off in the middle of her dying."

"I'm not *on* anything. I'm not out to steal her meds. And I'm not going to abandon her. I'm not sure you get to decide all that anyway. If Bella, if *Ms. Francis*, wants to go, then she goes. You're just a doctor, an opinion in a white coat. And I can always get a second one of those."

Even Dennon smiles at that. "Maybe. But you might be surprised at the amount of red tape I can tie all those opinions up in, like a big red bow. I have a lot of latitude and authority as the physician of record attending a dying patient whose faculties are diminished."

Andi wants to punch him. "Why are you making this hard?"

"Because I need to feel good about it. I need to look at myself in the mirror tonight or the night after. And because as silly as it sounds, I took an oath. I have a responsibility to do the right thing, the best thing, for my patient. Just like you want to do the best thing for your friend. So we can either work together on this, or we can make it very hard on each other."

And as angry as Andi wants to be with Dr. Dennon, she appreciates the impossible bind she's put him in, the way the situation looks to him from the outside, his fears of elder abuse and fraud and who knows what else. She knows how *she* looks to him, a desperate, difficult, and evasive woman with a lot to hide. She knows he'll run her name to make sure she's not some wanted fugitive or killer. But she also knows he's right. She can either work with him, or he can make sure she never walks out of this hospital with Bella.

"All right," she says. "You show me everything I need to take care of her, get me all the scrips and whatever else, and I'll tell you whatever you want to know about me."

He doesn't smile like he's won an argument, but he does look relieved. "Good, thank you."

She extends a hand. "My name is Audrey Ellis, and my daughter is Ruby."

CHAPTER 50

Port Gibson, Mississippi

LINNEA FIGURES OFFICER Terry Lomax has been weirded out ever since he met her and Rio.

He read all about them after he granted them access to Abby Walden's car, the same one an FBI evidence collection team later searched and photographed, then transported on the back of a trailer to Quantico, Virginia.

Read all about the serial killer and kidnapping cases they once solved, until Linnea became a case, a victim, herself. Lomax probably figured something like that would fuck up just about anyone, probably for a good long time, and it was probably evident in the few hours he spent with her that she was still fairly fucked up.

Maybe he thought she was crazy, but she's thankful he seemingly also didn't forget what she told him—

Take a moment and write down whatever you remember about the day you found the car, and I do mean everything, you never know what you'll remember, what you're capable of remembering, what detail you might recall or come up with. You never know what's important . . . until it is.

He took to heart the words of someone who knew as well as anyone and made copious notes for himself after their first visit.

So he doesn't seem surprised when she calls him from her FBI flight out of New York and asks him a whole list of questions about Port Gibson's Harriette Person Memorial Library.

Seems even less surprised when she tells him she'll be on the ground in four hours.

* * *

After she lands, she has Lomax review all his notes with her and all the photos they both made of Abby Walden's Subaru.

They then drive over to the Ash Street Bar and Grill and sit out in the heat on the benches in the park across the street. She has him jot down even more impressions about the morning he found Abby's car, as she takes photos of the spot from different directions, different angles, trying to get him to not only remember what he saw but also to help them both imagine what Abby herself might have seen when she walked to her car from the bar that night.

That's when he realizes two things:

One, it was raining a lot in the week surrounding that night, because the streets were still slick, still dark and damp. He even remembers the water drops on the windshield of Abby's empty car.

Two, that car wasn't parked in front of the bar, as he first reported, but the *library.*

* * *

Lomax introduces Linnea to DeeDee Carter, who he's known most of his life.

They went to grade school and high school together, but then he went off to play starting small forward for Ole Miss and she had her own plans to pursue nursing at Alcorn State, but as far Linnea can tell, nothing came out of those big plans for either of them, so they both ended up right back here in Port Gibson.

Now they're all standing together at the library's front desk where DeeDee works, bright sunlight leaving squares on the pale carpeted floor around them,

She's pretty, with long purple braids, one of which she thoughtfully twirls as she looks at a picture of Abby Walden on Linnea's phone. "Oh no, Ms. Wren," she says, "I don't remember her, that was weeks ago."

"You don't remember a pretty white girl?" Lomax asks.

DeeDee smiles and pulls at her braid. "She's not that pretty."

Linnea smiles too, appreciating the fact Lomax is doing a fair imitation of Rio.

He's going to be a very good cop someday.

She thumbs past the photo, finding one the FBI took from inside Abby's car. "How about this book? Maybe she comes in, looks around, checks it out." She doesn't say *maybe to get out of the rain*. Instead, she points to a table to the right of the big front window, where the library has a permanent stack of books for sale. "Maybe buys one of those?"

Because she didn't want to drive in the rain. Because she was tired or bored or hot.

Because of a thousand reasons that I'll never know.

But she wanders in here and buys an old paperback, and then wanders next door to the bar to read it, to wait out the storm.

"May I?" DeeDee uses her fingers to enlarge the rumpled book jacket image on Linnea's phone, pursing her lips as she thinks, before nodding at the piled books. "Those are our real old titles, some donated by folks from around here. Kind of a fundraiser thing we do. Fifty cents to three dollars each." Despite her purple-tinted glasses, she leans close to get a better look at the paperback captured on her phone, the one Linnea spied in Abby's car. An old horror novel, *Call the Dark*. DeeDee makes a face, horror clearly not her thing, but she shifts over to a computer and starts typing. "Yeah, that could be one of ours. We had three on our shelves at one point, and it looks like we sold one. But we wouldn't have any record of that, just, you know, whatever she paid up front here. Probably not much."

"No, probably not." She takes one last look at the grainy phone image, before swiping it closed. "How about another book, *Your Heart Is a Star*?"

"Oh, I read that." DeeDee types some more. "Crazy popular. Lots of copies, but they're all shelved now."

Lomax asks, "You remember some guy in here coming around that time too, buying some books, checking 'em out?"

DeeDee twirls a braid again. "You mean checking *her* out."

"Something like that," Linnea says.

"No, but my hours are . . . weird. All over the place." She looks to Lomax. She's probably seen him in his uniform a dozen times, but Linnea can tell she's looking at the uniform, at Officer Terry Lomax, with new eyes. "Are you investigating that girl that got killed up the way, the one whose car you found?"

"Sort of," Lomax answers. He gestures at Linnea. "She's doing the investigation, with the FBI and everything.

"Wow, just like TV," DeeDee says. "That girl's been in the news . . . a whole bunch of other girls too."

Lomax nods. "No one's been up in here gossiping about strangers wandering all around the library?"

DeeDee laughs. "You make it sound like we're a bunch of old hens, cackling and carrying on all day. This here is work."

"Sure, just shoulder to shoulder in here." Lomax laughs too, raising his eyebrows toward the empty stacks, the quiet, sun-drenched vestibules. "Gotta beat the book nerds off with a stick."

Linnea can't disagree. The nicest, newest, least-used building in Port Gibson, so new she can almost imagine the smell of fresh ink and fresh paint. Fancy and modern too, with six computers for public use, all currently sitting idle, all the latest conveniences.

Computers and—

"Cameras," Linnea says. In a stroke of inordinately bad luck, there are no cameras outside, she already knows that, but—"How about cameras *inside* here?" She points to a dark fisheye on the far wall, facing the door and sunlit windows at her back.

DeeDee follows her gaze. "Yeah, I mean we have a few. I don't know how far the video goes back or how to access it." She makes another face and fiddles with her glasses. "Honestly, Ms. Wren, I'm not even sure those things are plugged in or whatever. Not all the time."

"But we can check, right?"

She hesitates. "Sure, we can do that."

"Okay," Lomax says. "How about it then, and while we do, you can tell me all about how things have been going since you got back.

How *you've* been." He leans over, whispering, as if it wasn't just the three of them in the whole building. "And if we get anything useful off those cameras, anything at all that helps Ms. Wren, we're celebrating with dinner over at Maxey's."

DeeDee regards him seriously from behind her tinted glasses. "Are you talking like a *date*, Officer Lomax?"

He glances over at Linnea and then turns back to DeeDee Carter, shining her up with as nice a smile as he can. "One hundred percent."

CHAPTER 51

Tucson, Arizona

RIO REMEMBERS THE first time he met Linnea.

He'd been with the FBI for only three years when he suddenly found himself in the Critical Incident Response Group's Investigative and Operations Support Section, Behavioral Analysis Unit 5, not because of any specific investigative expertise he had, or big case he'd cracked, but because he was awaiting permanent transfer over to CIRG's Tactical Section Hostage Rescue Team and was conducting counterterrorism training in the interim with BAU-1.

His prior Black Label Classification security clearance and his extensive strategic and tactical background were a perfect fit for Hostage Rescue; he was also trilingual—English, Spanish, and German—an expert marksman, and both easygoing and easy to get along with.

Everyone liked him.

Everyone except Linnea Wren.

She was already something of an urban legend by the time they crossed paths at the BAU—a local New York homicide detective who'd made a reputation by assisting other state and local departments across the country with missing persons and murders. Her techniques were unusual, unorthodox, and difficult to replicate, but in most cases successful. She'd attended some FBI-sponsored training herself a few years prior and had been on the Bureau's radar ever since, when someone in D.C. decided to bring her into the fold as a semipermanent consultant to the BAU, although not without controversy.

The problem was she didn't like teams, or task forces, or apparently *people*, and she really didn't like Rio when they met for the first time when he picked her up from Ronald Reagan Airport.

It was humid that day, the kind of Virginia day that sticks to you, the kind of day he'd experienced a hundred times in South American jungles. She looked washed-out and exhausted after the trip from Poughkeepsie, and he made the mistake of asking—casually, professionally—if she wanted him to run her by her accommodations first before heading down to BAU's home base in Quantico.

She didn't.

"I'm sorry, Agent Rio, I appreciate the polite way you're telling me I look like shit, but I'd rather just get to work, if that's okay with you."

He laughed, and she didn't appreciate that any better. "I gather you find this amusing," she said, "and I assume you drew the short straw to come up here and hold my hand. I know there is a significant contingent of your fellow agents who think my presence here is an unserious distraction at best, or a threat to their so-called field work at worst."

"You do have a reputation, Detective Wren," Rio had said. "But look, I'm new to CIRG too, and I'm not even assigned to BAU-5. I'm training with BAU-1 and just offered to help, no straws involved. I don't know enough to make a judgment about you or anyone else. Today I'm just a driver."

She looked at him long and hard, a look he'd eventually grow accustomed to in the ensuing years, although few ever did. He later learned it was her sizing him up, *seeing* him for the first time, trying to figure out his background and past. "Have you ever even worked a homicide case, Agent Rio?"

"No," he admitted. "I have not."

"Then what is your specialty? What is it that you do?"

Unwilling to wilt under her gaze, he answered with a question of his own. "They told me you've been a cop for fifteen years. Have you ever drawn your weapon in the line of duty and fired it at a living suspect?"

That stopped her, those hard eyes of hers blinking, blinking. "No."

"*That's* my specialty, Detective Wren." And before she could ask anything else, he added, "But if you think so little of their work, why come here and work with them at all?"

"Because I have a special talent almost no one else has, and if I can help even one person, *save* just one person, then it's worth it."

"Well, on that we agree. But . . . there goes your reputation."

"What do you mean?"

He smiled, said, "They told me you were a cold, uncaring bitch. Guess they got the uncaring part wrong."

She didn't say anything during the rest of the drive down to Quantico. Neither did he.

But a week later she asked to meet him for lunch, where she told him about her first serial victim, a young woman named Erin Byrne, and the man who killed her, Brian Wallace Mershon.

Two weeks later, he asked to transfer to BAU-5 to partner with Linnea Wren.

* * *

"I'm sorry," Linnea tells Rio when he opens his eyes. "Sorrier than you know."

He checks the window, trying to gauge the sun, the time, how long he's been out again, how long she might've been sitting there next to his bed. He loses these hours, drifting in and out, as the setting sun plays across his bed and the floor. Schweiger last came to him yesterday or maybe the day before. They talked about Linnea and the Lightning Tree Killer.

"Don't be—you needed to go home."

"You fucking made me *promise*, remember?"

No, he doesn't, but he's glad she listened to him.

"That's where you should still be." He struggles to sit upright.

"I am sorry about leaving you here, but that's not all. I meant Steins too . . . I didn't . . . I didn't do enough. I was paralyzed with fear. I didn't do *anything*." She reaches out and grabs his hand, squeezing it tight, making him wince. "But I'm never going to leave you alone."

She then leans over and kisses his forehead, quick, fleeting, cool to the touch. She looks both tired and rested, yet somehow rejuvenated too, despite the flights back and forth across the country. Going home has helped her, even as Rio wonders just how much it resolved for her.

She continues. "We're clearly too fucked up for anyone else to work with."

He smiles. "True." He brushes her hair back, notices Tassa Linscott's fulgurite pendant still swinging from her neck. "How's Dan?"

"Somewhat angry with me, and he has every right to be—but he understands. He's worried about you too and glad you're okay. I'll deal with it when we get back. When we *both* get back."

He tries to raise his arms; they weigh heavy on him, like they're encased in cement. "I'm not going anywhere fast."

"Three oxycodones, three shots of tequila, and you'll be right as rain."

Rain reminds him of Steins, of thunder and lightning . . . *of blood and pain . . . and he always remembers the pain*. "I talked to Schweiger about the case. Lin, he said there's been developments."

"I haven't been just gallivanting back and forth across the country. I've been working too." She pulls the Alice laptop out of her shoulder bag. "We did good."

And now he sees it, that old light in her eyes, that *glow*, the certainty that the puzzle is finally coming together, that the end, whatever it might be, is finally in sight. And although maybe he should feel guilty about that, he also feels a sense of relief—that she's *back*, that her vision, her gift, her curse, is working for her again.

She says, "We've been on the right track from the start."

"I knew we were getting close."

"Yes," she says, laying the laptop across his knees and flipping it open. "And you're not going to believe just how close we are now."

CHAPTER 52

Ajo, Arizona

WAYLEN *KNOWS* THAT Luke Keats killed Stephen Chao.

As sure as he knows there is no way on God's green earth that weird, scatterbrained, but also very smart, very precise young man somehow just blew himself up.

No, he doesn't buy *that* for a second. No faulty propane tank or battery spark, no loose line. No mysterious phantom from Andi's past.

Everything went to shit after Luke Keats arrived. Andi's place got all torn up, then Bella got sick, then Stephen's trailer went up in flames.

Without a doubt, whatever the hell is going on, it's been smiling Mr. Slick all along.

Only now Waylen's got to figure out how to prove that, not only to Andi, but maybe to the authorities as well. But if he's heard it once, he's heard it a thousand times: it's not what you believe, not what you *know*, it's only what you can prove.

Proof matters in a courtroom if things were ever to get that far.

Proof, as they say, is a son of a bitch.

* * *

Without Andi around to get him some beer and whiskey, Waylen drives his truck over to Ajo's lone stop-and-rob to see what might be cheap or on sale on the shelves between the motor oil, the expired ramen, and the beef jerky. Not his favorite Malloye's, but he does find some airplane-sized bottles of Jack Daniels and a cold sixer of Budweiser in the leaking freezer. He plans to settle in, drink up some courage, and then decide whether to confront Mr. Slick himself—who's been sallying back and forth between his Wolf Pup and Andi's trailer on the other side of New Cornelia—or drop some anonymous but highly specific emails to the Arizona Department of Public Safety.

He's just walking out of Circle K at dusk when he finds a man, a *stranger*, waiting for him by his truck, tall and square-shouldered. Hair short and gray. Leaning casually back against the hood of Waylen's Silverado with his arms crossed, watching Waylen from behind mirrored aviators, although it's near dark.

There are two guns in Waylen's truck, neither registered, plus the permitted holstered Ruger revolver at his side and the Glock in the small of his back, but he can't put his hands on either of those fast, since his arms are loaded with the beer and whiskey he just bought. And he probably couldn't drop it all fast enough anyway, if the stranger intended to shoot him. He could run, just bolt, but the stranger against his truck doesn't look like the sort of man Waylen could outrun, not even years ago, when he was a leaner, fitter, different man himself.

The man raises his hands to show they're empty, a clear indication that he *is* armed, and asks, "Are you Waylen Ray Burrows?"

He sounds like he's from the Northeast, maybe Boston.

"Who wants to know?" Waylen fires back. He's stopped walking, leaving them about fifteen feet apart, and Waylen can feel the beers sweating through the thin plastic bag.

"Relax, Mr. Burrows," the stranger says, hands still raised. "Take a deep breath, pardner. Better yet if you want to drink one of those beers to calm yourself down, go right ahead. I wouldn't mind one myself." He eyes Waylen's holstered Ruger. "But go easy now. Nice and slow. Don't want you to hurt yourself. Put the bag down and keep your hands where I can see them."

"I've done nothing wrong. I'm not breaking any laws. You need a warrant for this."

The man pushes himself off the truck but doesn't approach. "Waylen, I don't need a warrant to talk to you, and right now that's all we're doing, just talking. Just shooting the shit. Right out here in the open where everyone can see us. Both of us."

But the street looks empty, just the two of them.

Waylen's hands start to shake, sweat running down his face.

"People are going to miss me," Waylen says, and knows how weak that sounds. How pathetic. "I've got plans for this."

The man takes two steps forward. "Oh, no doubt. I've read all about your little plans. All your secret forum postings, all those hidey-holes you and your friends go down to chat about overthrowing the government, kidnapping the president. Insurrections and aliens. Bigfoot and conspiracies. It's always wheels within wheels with you folks." Two more steps. "But here's the thing, Waylen, something I want you to remember long after we're done here." Two more steps. "You never hear the bullet that gets you. *Never.*" A few final steps and now he's only an arm's length away but still hasn't reached for a gun or a Taser or a poisoned dart. "So, if I truly cared about that cult Kool-Aid shit you've been drinking, we wouldn't be having this conversation at all."

Waylen steadies himself, slowly setting the bag down on the warm concrete, even as the man reaches in and pulls out two beers. He tosses the first to Waylen and loudly cracks the other for himself.

"Who are you?" Waylen asks shakily. "What the hell do you want with me?"

The man swallows half the can in one swig and closes his eyes and smiles, like it's the best damn beer he's ever had in his life. "Call me Devine, and I don't want *you* at all. I just want to talk a bit about someone I think you know. *Two* someones."

"You're not taking me away?"

The man called Devine smiles, but there's no warmth, no sincerity. It might be the most horrible smile Waylen has ever seen. "Oh, not today, Waylen. Not so long as you tell me everything you know about Stephen Chao and Audrey Ann Ellis."

"*Andi*?"

Devine, still smiling that awful smile, doesn't blink. "Sure."

Waylen pops the beer Devine gave him and drinks the whole can in two gulps, thankful to hold on to something to steady his hands.

And right now, it truly is the best damn beer he's ever had.

He's got no idea who this Devine is or who he represents, or why he's here, but if Waylen's got information this man wants, something this man needs that only Waylen knows, then for the first time in a long time, he's glad to be talking to someone in authority, someone with some real power, someone who's willing to listen to him.

That smile told Waylen everything he needed to know.

Waylen grabs another beer, says, "Then I reckon you want to hear about Lucas Keats too."

CHAPTER 53

Tucson, Arizona

THE PIECES ARE all on the figurative table in front of them, now they just need to fit them together.

Tassa Linscott. Max Conroy. Stephen Chao. Audrey Ann Ellis. Ruby Ellis.

The Black Light Club.

They won't all fit, they never do, but Linnea knows she's got enough.

She sees it . . .

"Okay," she starts, "Tassa, Stephen Chao, and Andi Ellis are all lightning strike survivors, all part of a former survivors' group in Texas. One big happy family."

"Until one of their members is brutally attacked," Schweiger says.

"Mr. Ethan Charmas," Rio says. "He was put into a coma by Max Conroy, Andi's boyfriend."

"And more importantly, the father of her child, Ruby," Linnea continues. "Also, the textbook definition of a controlling asshole. Jealous. Narcissistic. Charmas's assault likely stemmed from a relationship, either real or imagined, Conroy suspected Andi was having with him. That one act shattered the club, sending everyone into the wind. Conroy's been looking for Andi and his daughter ever since."

Rio says, "Admittedly, he *was* a good profile for our serial, so good we ran him down, only to find him already dead in New Mexico, in pretty much the same manner as our seven victims."

"Offed by LTK. But why?" Schweiger asks.

"Because LTK has been looking for Andi too," Linnea says, "and Conroy, to his credit, was apparently trying to warn her. We got the inquiries he was making, the emails he was sending out. We spoke with Tassa Linscott and saw the emails she was receiving too. There's still a whole loose community of lightning strike survivors out there, and it was becoming increasingly common knowledge among them that *someone* was running around out there with a fetish for lightning strike survivors generally and Andi specifically."

"Why her?" Schweiger presses.

"Because she was well known in that community. Unique. Special. What we might now call an influencer. There were rumors about her, stories." Linnea prods Alice to spin up a new set of images, dozens and dozens, a panoply of lightning strike survivors revealing their Lichtenberg figures, their lightning trees. "Andi's scars, her trees, *glowed*, and supposedly *never* went away. They marked her, forever."

"And now that's *his* mark too, part of LTK's ritual," Rio adds.

Schweiger looks at the images, looks like he's going to reach out and touch them. "Okay, what about the other members of this club?"

"We've cleared Tassa Linscott," Rio says. "Wynona Parsons is dead and has been a while, long before all this. Minnie Ruiz lives with her sister in Redding, California, where she works at a Black Bear Diner. Cole Parham and his partner live in Midland, Texas, and so far, both have refused to talk with us. Billy Tucker was a habitual drug user who fell off the map after the club disbanded, but we're still looking. And according to Ethan's family—their lawyer, specifically—he's still in a coma under the very, very expensive private home care they pay for. Your task force is doubling back on everyone, but there are dozens if not a hundred others who were also loosely affiliated with the club online at one time or another."

"But only one Andi Ellis," Linnea says, "and only one LTK."

"And if he's as close to finding her as we all believe," Schweigert starts, "then his attack on you at Steins seems—"

"Foolish?" Rio interjects.

Schweiger continues, "Risky and shortsighted, at best."

"Well, he is fucking crazy," Linnea says. "But also very determined, cunning, and ruthless. And with the media leaks, knows we're close enough to compromise everything he's been working up to. He must've decided taking a swing at us was worth the risk, hoping to buy him the last bit of time he needs."

Schweiger doesn't seem convinced. "But also giving us a proactive timeframe around his travels, along with the license plate readers and Border Patrol checkpoint on I-10 between New Mexico and Arizona, as well as that young couple who were with you at Steins around the same time."

"Yes, all those other rest stops *like* Steins," Linnea says. "We've suspected all along he was in a truck or trailer, something with some heft and size, some range, and more importantly, some privacy, to move his victims such long distances. After I reviewed all the ambient surveillance videos again, including what we got off that I-10 LPR, now accounting for the hours around the attack on Rio, I've narrowed it down to three dozen possibles."

Linnea clicks through them, one at a time. Image after image after image.

It's possible Linnea *saw* LTK's vehicle at Steins, or out on the highway, stalking them, even if she barely remembers it now, only a reflection, a hint, a *ghost*.

"Even better," she says, "I checked back in with Officer Lomax in Port Gibson, and we were able to pull video from inside that library near where we found Abby's car. I went through all those videos too, and with Alice's help, I got these."

Even more images. A litany of them.

A collage of time and place, of the past. Seconds here, a blurry snapshot there.

Finally—

A face . . .

A dark-haired man in five frames out of . . . what?

Hundreds? Thousands?

Linnea continues, "LTK found Abby in that library. Was it a chance meeting? Did he follow her there? Was it just raining that day?" She stares at the mysterious figure on her screen. "We may never truly know, but my bet is he finds most of his victims in libraries and bookstores, quiet places where it's easy to approach them—even those he isn't stalking specifically because they're lightning strike survivors, those he's already identified through the club or others associated with it. It's possible he's been using the public computers in libraries to send emails, locate former club members, keep tabs on the case, whatever. I'm having Alice grind away on it now, a massive grid search around the areas where we believe he kidnapped them." She looks at the image one last time. "I think he likes quiet places . . . when it's not storming."

"A place like New Cornelia, Arizona," Rio says. "New Cornelia is about one hundred and fifty miles from here, a tight-knit border community, off the grid, way off the grid. The handful of folks who live there all claim to have unique medical issues or problems, not dissimilar from the lingering issues some lightning strike survivors say they struggle with."

"Insular and remote as hell," Linnea adds, "and the perfect place to hide." She pauses, studying the topo map of New Cornelia she's brought up for all three of them to see. "Perfect also because there's not much rain." She looks to Schweiger. "No rain, no storms, no *lightning*."

Rio says, "We digitally tracked Stephen Chao down to New Cornelia, where he was receiving exotic plant shipments. He was also conducting internet searches on Conroy and likely in contact with him as well. More than that, he was running background checks on a man named Lucas Keats, a former Missouri cop, who doesn't seem to be a lightning strike survivor. But we just don't have much other info on him yet."

Schweiger's silence poses the same question Linnea and Rio have already asked themselves—

Is Keats LTK?

"Concurrently," Linnea adds, "Devine has run down a super-secret government watch list target, a conspiracy theorist named Waylen Burrows, who's in New Cornelia too, who's *also* been orchestrating some heavy-handed poking around on Conroy and Keats online, as recently as a week ago. Divine's having a little face-to-face chat with him." She checks the time on her phone. "Probably talking to him right now."

Schweiger says, "You two brought Devine back into this?"

Linnea ignores him. "The only important question is why are two strangers at the ass-end of Arizona looking under rocks for what was once the prime suspect in our case? Or for that matter, this new unknown, Lucas Keats? What are the odds?" She taps the laptop. "Alice here will tell you they're fucking astronomical."

"Our best guess," Rio says, "is they were doing those searches on *behalf* of Andi Ellis."

"Ellis is alive and well and hiding out in New Cornelia," Schweiger says. "She's been down there this whole time."

Linnea adds, "And that's where LTK is going—if he's not already there. Like I said, *close*."

"Then we need to get down there too, ASAP." Schweiger pulls out his phone. "Get to Ellis, get to Chao."

"Unfortunately, Stephen Chao's already dead," Rio says.

"And Andi's not in New Cornelia right now," Linnea adds.

"What?" Schweiger asks, his phone still hanging in the air. "Then *where*?"

"She's right here in Tucson," Linnea says, shutting down Alice. "Less than ten miles away."

CHAPTER 54

New Cornelia, Arizona

JUST AFTER SUNDOWN, it starts to rain.

Chili hears it before Ruby, the dog's ears first picking up the sighing wind, then the soft patter of fresh drops on the trailer's roof.

Ruby tries to count them—*plink, plonk, plink, plonk*. She sets aside the Kuo book, the one Mr. Stephen gave her as a present. She's been thinking about him all day and when she can't stop thinking about him, she sometimes can't stop big tears from welling up in her eyes, but at the sound of the rain, she heads into the living room with Chili trailing behind her. Mr. Luke is sitting on the couch, tapping away on his phone.

"Hey, Ruby, what do you need? A glass of water?"

"It's *raining*," she says.

Mr. Luke gives her that *I'm not so sure look* she knows all too well from Momma, like when Ruby tells her about the saguaro monster outside her window or that time she saw a big gray wolf sleeping in the shade by their truck. It's the look all adults give kids when they don't want to believe them but don't want to call them liars either. Being a liar is *bad*, like being sneaky, like spying. But Mr. Luke does stop clacking on his phone and politely pretends to listen, titling his head all funny, exaggerating the effort.

He winks and smiles at her, and she's not sure she likes that and she's not sure why.

He says, "Well, heck, you might be right. Real rain too, not like that dust storm a while back." He rubs his jaw, where he looks like he's growing a beard. Mr. Stephen tried to grow a beard once and all it did was make her and Momma laugh. "Can't imagine it'll amount to much."

"Momma lets me sit with her when it rains. I get to sleep in her bed too. Whatever I want."

Mr. Luke puts his phone away. He's already complained how nothing electronic seems to work all that well around their trailer. "You and your mom really don't like storms, do you?"

"Momma gets scared. But I don't. I help her. I hold her hand, so she won't cry."

He smiles again, and this smile she does like. If the first one was kind of silly and fake, like the smiles painted on the dolls she doesn't play with anymore, this one is real, from the heart.

"That's a good thing to do. And that's what I'm doing too. Helping you and your mom while she's with Bella."

"When are they coming home?"

"Hard to say. Your mom and I have been talking about it though. Soon. Real soon."

Ruby knows a lie when she hears it, and although Mr. Luke isn't lying all the way, he's lying a little bit.

He points at the necklace Momma gave her. "Your mom always wears that, right?"

Ruby touches it, holds it up. "It's magic and now it's mine."

Mr. Luke laughs. "I bet it is. We could all use magic, right?" He rubs his face again like he's trying to make yawns go away. "Hop over here and let me take a look at it."

She approaches and climbs onto the couch. She holds the necklace up again, and he doesn't grab it from her or anything, just kind of stares at it. She can feel his breath on her hair, on her face. He's kind of looking at her all over now, looking at her neck, her exposed shoulder. He says, "Hey, did you hurt yourself?" Then, lower. "Did someone hurt *you*?"

"No," she says, "I'm just magic too, like Momma. A fairy princess."

But before Mr. Luke can say anything else, Chili growls. Low, deep, almost like faraway thunder, but one hundred percent a *real* growl. An angry growl. It startles Ruby because she's never heard Chili make that kind of noise.

It startles Mr. Luke too.

The rain doesn't scare her, but whatever Chili's worried about does.

Mr. Luke slides off the couch and kneels next to Chili. "Hey, girl, what's got you all riled up? You afraid of the storm too?" But Ruby notices Mr. Luke isn't trying to touch Chili; her ears are flat, her fur all rumpled and spiky along her back like a hand has ruffled through it, like when Ruby's own hair gets all staticky when she's been hiding under her covers.

Chili growls again and takes a careful, crouched step toward the door.

Ruby follows Mr. Luke's eyes, trying to decide if *he* is scared or not. He only looks at her and whispers, "Go to your room, okay? Just wait there until I call for you."

Then a loud noise shatters the trailer's quiet, sending Chili into a wild, barking fit. It's Momma's lightning machine, the one she always wears, but Ruby's wearing it now, just like her magic necklace, since she left her momma at the hospital.

The one that warns them when lightning is coming.

And it's coming.

CHAPTER

55

Tucson, Arizona

THE COUPLE APPROACHES Andi at nightfall, just as she's returning to the hospital from picking up a few more things to take back to New Cornelia, a few items that Dr. Dennon suggested.

He gave her his cell number and made her promise to call if there were any issues, or if she had a change of heart, or later decided to bring Bella back to Tucson to one of the hospices he'd already contacted. So she's deep in thought about all those things, honestly not paying attention, when the pair cut her off before she can duck back out to the parking lot or find another way into the hospital.

The woman is taller than her, hawkish face, hair pulled back in a tight ponytail, shot through with gray streaks she clearly makes no effort to hide, and offset by only the barest hint of makeup. She reminds Andi of how Bella might've looked years ago, the sort of look that people would consider pretty, if she put any effort into it.

Her companion is dark-haired, dark-eyed. Younger, but it's tough to tell because he's been in some sort of fight and clearly got the worst of it. Badly bruised and lacerated face, and he's carrying himself awkwardly, like each step is broken glass, the walk of someone who's still fighting broken bones or ribs. Both are in jeans and bland dark jackets, and if they're not cops, they're trying hard to pretend they aren't.

"Audrey Ellis?" The woman asks. "Andi?"

"I'm sorry, you have the wrong person," Andi answers, trying to move past them without breaking stride, even as she frantically ticks off what her options are, what choices she's got. Her best guess is they've tracked her down over Stephen's death, like Luke warned her.

But she stops when she sees the pendant around the woman's neck, a shiny piece of green and white fulgurite, and she knows whose hands crafted it. "Oh," she says. "Oh no."

The woman clocks Andi's stare and touches the pendant. "Yes, you know it, it's one of Tassa Linscott's."

"Is . . . is she okay?"

"She's fine, Andi. She's back home and doing well. And I think she'd want you to know that."

"Is this about Stephen, about what happened to him?"

"Stephen Chao? Partially yes, but we're mostly here about you. We're hoping you can help us—that we can help each other."

"Max?" Andi asks.

"Max Conroy is dead too," the man says. "Recently killed in New Mexico."

Killed? Andi doesn't know how to respond to that, what to make of it. If she imagined the news would bring her joy or relief, she doesn't feel either. She doesn't even believe it. "No, he's here in Arizona. He killed Stephen."

"No, we don't think so, but we do want to talk about Max and Stephen, about New Cornelia," the woman says, "about everything that's happened there. I'm afraid we just don't have a lot of time."

"Why is that?"

The woman blinks, and although the light out here isn't great, Andi can pick out scars around her eyes, scars that might look like unflattering crow's feet in different light.

"Let's go inside," the woman says, "or somewhere else quiet. We need to show you some things."

Andi doesn't like the tension in the woman's voice. Doesn't like the tension in the air.

Doesn't like those scars around her eyes.

"I'm here with my friend, a *dying* friend. She has terminal cancer and I'm going to take her home tomorrow. We can talk there."

"We'll make arrangements," the woman says flatly.

"I *am* the arrangements," Andi fires back. "There's no one else."

The man says, "Ms. Ellis, we've spoken with Dr. Kyle Dennon. That's how we found you. He made us aware of the situation, and we are sorry about your friend. But I can't stress this enough. We are on a clock here. We need your cooperation. And you are going to want ours."

He's so calm, so reasonable and persuasive and reassuring in a way his partner isn't. But nothing he's saying right now is putting her at ease.

She won't look at the woman's eyes but can't help staring at the fulgurite pendant around her neck.

Andi's scared and mad now. "I want to know who you people are, what the fuck is going on, and I want to know right now."

The woman says, without a hint of warmth, "So do we."

* * *

But they already know everything about her.

They know all about the Black Light Club, about Texas and Max, and they've somehow pieced together how she and Stephen have been staying mostly off the grid in New Cornelia. The woman, Linnea Wren, and the man, Adan Rio, are private investigators or cops or FBI agents—it's a little unclear despite the badges and credentials they flashed her. Whoever they are, they've been looking for her for a couple of days, and some kind of killer too, for far longer than that.

"So, he's killing people who've been struck by lightning?"

"Yes," the woman, Linnea, says. "Some of his victims are lightning survivors, although others appear to have been merely opportunistic . . . strategic." Linnea looks to Rio, something unsaid passing between them. "He seems to have fixated on this idea of lightning, and more importantly, you."

"*Me*? Why me?"

"Probably for the same reason Max Conroy did," Linnea said. "He's decided you're special, magical, unique. Honestly, we don't fully understand, and he might not either."

Andi thinks Linnea Wren sounds very, very tired.

Linnea goes on: "It's possible he's someone you met previously, or someone who tried to contact you through the club, or someone who just heard about you and then made up all these other stories in his head. I promise you that we're already running down every single lead. But whatever his reasons, this man has been working his way to Arizona, methodically tracking you down."

"To *kill* me?"

"Killing is not the sole purpose," Linnea says, "merely part of the process, his ritual."

"Fuck me," Andi says.

Linnea smiles, but it doesn't last long. "And there's this, Andi." Linnea opens the laptop she's been carrying, and flicks through some images, arraying them on the screen in a tableau. "Please take a deep breath."

Andi ignores that warning and immediately wishes she hadn't. It might've kept her from crying out at the harsh pictures, the horrible sight.

The women, all the victims.

All the lightning trees that both scar and adorn their bodies.

"Oh my God," Andi says.

No, that's impossible. This is impossible.

Linnea wipes away the images, replacing them with new ones. "We think we have a pretty good idea of the kind of vehicle he's been moving around the country in, and a partial composite of his face. We're using the most advanced crime analytics and modeling in the world to refine that. In another day, maybe another ten hours, we'll likely have a name to put with that face."

Andi stares at the shadowy figure in Linnea Wren's still frames. It's so hard to make sense of it, the man could be anyone, everyone. "But you don't you have that much time," she says, as the realization hits her like that bolt all those years ago. "Oh no. No. No. No. *Luke.* You think it's Luke."

"Lucas Keats," Linnea says, "has a . . . complicated history. But as much as we might've thought or even hoped he was LTK, that's impossible now."

"LTK?"

"The Lightning Tree Killer," Linnea replies.

Despite her growing horror, Andi walks them through the last few weeks, the party at Leah and Erwin's, the dust storm, the mine. Her trailer. All the places Luke was with her, and how that proves he couldn't be anywhere else. "That's good, right? Luke isn't your LTK. He's safe. Ruby's safe."

Another unsteady flicker between those two.

"When's the last time you spoke with Lucas Keats?" Rio asks.

"A few hours ago," she says. "I think. We talked earlier, argued over me coming back to New Cornelia, after what happened to Stephen. We texted some back and forth." She works it over in her head; she was tied up with Dennon, then visited Bella, then went to the store. She's been so wrapped up in Bella's care, she doesn't know exactly when she last spoke to him.

She doesn't know when she last talked to Ruby either.

But she does know *why* they waited until just now to tell her what they'd been working up to from the very moment they approached her.

They wanted her calm. They wanted her collected.

They wanted to extract anything that might help them before she lost her mind.

"Your daughter, Andi," Linnea says. "Ruby's gone."

CHAPTER 56

New Cornelia, Arizona

When the monster came through their door and Mr. Luke jumped at him, Ruby's whole world went white.

There was a horrible sound, buzzing, like those big ole bug zappers Mr. Erwin keeps outside his place, the kind of zappers that glow Crayon Vivid Violet for a moment (one of Ruby's favorite shades) when they sizzle a moth or what Mr. Erwin calls a *no-see-um.* But if that's what it was, it was the largest zapper in the whole world, because it filled their trailer with a purple and white light that arced and flashed and sizzled all over the place.

The floors. The walls. The windows.

She couldn't escape it, and neither could Mr. Luke, who disappeared into that hot light and just like that was gone.

The monster barged through the door wearing lightning that made Ruby's hair stand on end, all staticky like Chili's fur, and then Chili leaped at it too, barking and barking and barking, and the trailer smelled the way the desert does sometimes in the mornings when the sky's all fuzzy and gray and then the room got so hot, so fast, and all Ruby wanted to do was curl up and scream for Momma.

But after the monster called out *her* name, Ruby did more than that. She ran.

* * *

She's out in the desert now, running in the dark, clouds rumbling overhead and rain pattering on her face.

The same rain Mr. Luke wasn't so sure about back in the trailer, like she's not sure if he's even okay or not.

She's worried, very worried, that he's *not* okay, that he got all burned up just like Mr. Stephen. But her momma talked to her about this, about what to do if they ever got separated from the trailer or from each other. They even practiced it. *I need you to take care of yourself, all the ways you know how.* So all she needs to do is calm down and remember everything Momma said about how to find her way to that place in the dark even if everything looks both different and the same in the dark.

I'm not afraid of the dark, Momma.

No, she's not scared of all this inky blackness, even though she doesn't have her phone that barely ever works anyway or her favorite red flashlight. Even though there's no faerie fire to light her way, and the pretty necklace Momma gave her isn't glowing either. No magic at all out here, just the warm wind and the heavy clouds overhead hiding her stars and drops of rain collecting in her hair.

Just her.

She stops, squints, and tries to figure out where she is, where to go next, telling herself if she does start to get scared, she'll remember that snow from that one time. Or she'll finally find her own magic and glow like Momma or turn the rain overhead into big, cool flakes of snow instead, and then her momma will know she's okay and won't be afraid to find her because the sky will be full of soft snow and not rain and thunder and lightning.

That's when she hears something moving fast and low toward her, and she doesn't know if it's the lightning monster or that gray wolf she saw that one time (that Momma never believed in) or just a coyote or some other kind of monster that grabs little girls in the dark and steals them away to the mine (that Momma told her never to go to).

Ruby starts running again but doesn't get far when the fast and low moving thing in the dark catches her, knocks her down, and rolls with her in the sand.

A familiar, musty smell of her old clothes hits her too—and stinky ole smoke.

She screams thinking the lightning monster's caught her, that it's going to pull her up into the sky with it, way up into the clouds, where they'll follow the storm far away from here and she'll never see her momma again. It called out her name at the trailer, called out *Ruby, Ruby,* and that means it knows who she is, and if it knows who she is, that means it knows everything about her.

But it's only Chili, pretty, wonderful Chili, snuffling at her and licking her face and she can't hold the dog tight enough even as she squirms against her. Chili's *hurt.* That's the smell all over Ruby—Chili's singed and torn fur—and she's favoring one of her paws, which hangs ugly, and there's a cut on her head leaking blood everywhere. But she's alive and she found her way to Ruby and although for a moment, just a moment, Ruby truly feared the dark, she doesn't now, and she won't be afraid again.

She kisses Chili's bloody head, hugs her to her, and tells her it's going to be all right, that her momma will come for them both. They just need to stay okay long enough. Just need to find their way to the place Momma told her to wait for her if she ever had to run away.

But if the lightning monster knows her name, it knows that too.

But where?

Mr. Stephen is gone.

Mr. Luke is gone.

Auntie Bella is far away in Tucson.

Mr. Erwin with his bug zappers is far away too, and so is Mr. Waylen, and she's not sure she could even find her way to those places, not even in the daylight.

She squeezes Chili tighter and asks her, *Where do we go*? But all Chili does is pant heavy and lick and whine because she's hurt, hurt bad, and she doesn't talk like magic animals, so even if Chili knew what to do, she doesn't know how to tell Ruby.

Ruby doesn't want to cry, doesn't like that she's crying, but at least the rain will wash away her tears.

She's never felt rain like this, never really been out in a storm—Momma always told her *no*—and despite everything, it amazes her. She likes the way it rolls down her face, squirms its way beneath her clothes. Outside rain feels so different than being in a tub or shower or even a swimming pool. It feels real, it feels *alive.* Like the way Chili's fur feels beneath her fingers.

Somewhere far away, but not *too* far, the sky flashes white, as the storm bears down on them.

She's got to go, to keep moving. She doesn't have any magic right now, but she's got Chili, and the rain to hide her, and she can still be as sneaky, smart, and careful as she's ever been.

It's okay to be sneaky, to lie, to disobey, so you don't get hurt.

She's got the rain to hide her.

Ruby makes up her mind, and kissing Chili again, heads toward the lightning.

CHAPTER 57

Ajo, Arizona

RIO STILL DREAMS sometimes about his ex-wife, Miranda.

It broke apart for them in all the ways you'd expect, the constant grind of his military deployments wearing down her resolve, his post-combat struggles wearing down his desire to reassure her.

She had a miscarriage just before she left him, before he joined the FBI, and the last thing she said was that she was glad they didn't have a child together, when they couldn't even take care of each other.

But in his dreams, Miranda did have the baby, a little girl they named Yaretzi, in honor of his mother, meaning *You will always be loved*, and both Miranda and Yari are happy and healthy, although he's nowhere to be found.

No matter how often he has these dreams, he's never in them. He sees everything as if from high above, this life he could've had, how things might've been, if things had only been different. It doesn't make him sad or angry, just grateful for the dreams at all, grateful that he can dream of something so beautiful, even if it doesn't include him.

He has the name *Yaretzi* tattooed next to his mother's name, *Xochil*, both surrounded by brightly colored double-bladed marigolds and dahlias, a bouquet of flowers near his heart.

* * *

As Linnea would say, it's already a logistical nightmare.

Rio and the rest of their small team have commandeered the Ajo Historical Society, located in what was once the St. Catherine's Indian Mission, white stucco buildings with red clay tile roofs topped by crosses. The old mission is filled with artifacts from Ajo's history, as well as both ancient and current maps that Schweiger's already pulled off the walls and spread out on whatever tables he could find.

The mission's parking lot was just big enough to set down the HH-60 Jolly Green that Schweiger borrowed from Davis-Monthan AFB. He and Schweiger, along with Linnea and Andi Ellis plus two FBI agents out of Tucson, made the flight in little over a frantic hour—battling winds and a low cloud ceiling—and got on the ground just before the storm blew over them in earnest.

Devine, who's already been here all day, made calls to Border Patrol's BORSTAR tactical unit, and rounded up some local help who know the lay of the land—Waylen Burrows, the conspiracy theorist from New Cornelia, and Erwin Garcia, also from the town. But the area they're working in is so remote, the weather and the late hour stymying travel and coordination, that it's going to take a while before either Devine or Schweiger can get a full state, local, and federal response out here. And maybe a lot longer, if the storm keeps up.

Ruby Ellis has been missing for more than three hours.

Devine found Lucas Keats barely clinging to life out at the Ellis trailer, and Ruby's abandoned and uncharged cellphone in her bedroom, and they have no idea if she's in the hands of the Lightning Tree Killer or not.

No idea if she's still alive.

The circling storm doesn't give them much hope, but Rio knows Linnea won't tell Andi that.

She won't want to accept it either.

* * *

"Okay," Rio says, "there's limited highway egress out of here." He taps at the maps arrayed in front of him. "North to Gila Bend, south through the Organ Pipe National Park, which takes you down to Lukeville and Sonoyta, basically the border, or back east through the Tohono O'odham rez to Tucson."

Schweiger nods. "I ran the probabilities through Alice. She likes east to Tucson—but only within the margin of error."

Meaning the AI likes *all* of them, even accounting for weather.

"There are a hundred farm roads, back roads, trails, you name it, cut all through this area," Erwin Garcia adds, surveying the maps with a practiced eye. "That's a needle in a sand dune."

Linnea now summons up three images on Alice.

"Okay, how many can truly handle this sort of vehicle?" She shows the group the three most likely—all camper vans—all similar size and shape, out on the road or at a rest stop, out in the dark, all about the same.

"After Andi's trailer was trashed, we looked for strange trucks and campers around here," Waylen says, waving at Ajo beyond the walls. "Didn't find anything like that, or much else, truth be told."

"So, he's parked it offroad somewhere, out on one of those backroads," Devine says.

"Could be." Waylen points at the pictures on the screen. "I like the last two, the Terrain or Solis. Say, the Solis, definitely. That one's built for tough terrain, off-the-grid. That's the one I'd have."

"If he was already on the freeway," Devine notes, "the TECs lookouts and LPR cameras would've picked him up. They will if he rabbits."

Rio shakes his head. "Still so much damn territory to cover."

Too much, with so few of them.

"Yeah, but no one's moving around in this weather," Erwin says. "If you haven't been in a real storm like this in the desert, you don't have any idea what you're dealing with. There will be flash flooding in the washes, roaring water everywhere, in a matter of minutes. The desert comes alive, and then it turns into a swamp."

Linnea shuts Alice down and looks up. "He *wants* this storm, it's important to him. So, he's not moving around, and he's not running, not anymore. He's exactly where he wants to be."

"With my daughter," Andi says, who's otherwise been silently standing apart from them. She approaches, furious. "He has *my* little girl out there, and you're standing around here talking about the goddamn weather. Talking so calm like this is a fucking science experiment."

Rio sympathizes—and they shouldn't be having this kind of conversation in front of her, with her daughter out there, and normally they wouldn't. But they don't have a choice. They're running out of both time and choices.

"We're going to find her," Linnea tells Andi. "We are."

Don't make promises like that. Please, please, don't do that . . . we don't make promises we can't keep.

"How?" Andi asks, angry, tearful. Furious. "How are *we* going to find her?"

Rio turns to her, "With your help." He then turns to all of them, ignoring Schweiger's suddenly stony stare. "With all of your help."

CHAPTER 58

Ajo, Arizona

"YOU ARE OFFICIALLY out of your fucking mind," Schweiger tells him. "Out of your goddamn mind. And I thought Linnea Wren was the crazy one."

They've stepped away from the others, standing in something that might've once been a closet or a confessional. It smells of sand and age, time ticked by. Rio flirted briefly with Catholicism in his early twenties—he's briefly flirted with a lot of creeds and beliefs—and is surprised at the catechisms he still remembers, the prayers he still knows, that seem to echo from the dark corners and recesses of this old building.

"No," Schweiger says. "No."

"Those two locals know the area, so we split into teams. Me, Devine, and Burrows. You, Linnea, and Ellis. Your two agents pair up with Garcia. We cover as much ground as we can, at least all three primary directions, and whatever in between."

Schweiger shakes his head. "Devine doesn't have any legal standing here. And you—you can barely stand at all."

"That's why I'm keeping you arm's length from Devine. You'll still have plausible deniability. And me? I'll be fine."

Schweiger laughs angrily. "I don't know if you've taken a good long look at that Ellis woman, but every rumble of thunder, every flash of light, she practically breaks into a cold sweat. She's far from fine. We've got no phone pings, no air coverage, no surveillance platforms. Even if we somehow find LTK in this mess, we're barely equipped to deal with him. At best, the arrest gets tossed anyway on any number of legal and ethical grounds. Worse, we get one of these so-called posse members of yours hurt. Or *killed*. This isn't the Old West, Rio. No, we're not ready, strategically or tactically."

"It's not ideal. But we just make it work."

Rio can see the struggle play out on Schweiger's face, a battle over what they need to do versus what makes the most sense, what he'll have to answer for later, all the reports he'll have to write and the second-guessing he'll inevitably face. But there's still a little girl out there, even if Schweiger already thinks it's too late. And that's what this is all *truly* about—he thinks they've already lost her.

He thinks *he* has lost.

"We don't know if she's dead or alive," Rio reminds him, presses him. "We don't even know for certain that LTK has her. Devine said the scene at the trailer was inconclusive and we haven't gotten much out of Lucas Keats." If he took as bad a jolt from LTK as Rio did, then they won't get much out of him for a while, until it's too late. "There's a version of this where that girl is out there in the dark, in the desert, *alive*, but alone."

"Do you believe that version?"

"What I believe doesn't come close to mattering."

Schweiger's clearly not convinced. "This is how it all went down for you before, isn't it? Trying to be a hero. No backup, no protocol, no plan. And look how that turned out for you and Linnea."

"She's alive, and so am I."

Schweiger takes off his glasses, rubbing angrily at the rain-spotted lenses. He looks young without them, a kid struggling with a test. But this isn't theory or history. It's real.

Rio tells him, "Despite what you think, despite that storm overhead, Andi Ellis is not going to just sit idly on her hands here, waiting for us to make up our minds, waiting for a *plan*. She's a mother and that's her daughter out there, so unless you're ready to tell her that little girl is a lost cause, not worth the risk, you might as well let us get her ready and get whatever help we can from her. Because we'll need her. We're going to need all of them."

Schweiger slips his glasses back on and looks out through the doorway where the others stand waiting, waiting for *him* to make the call, at least for the moment, until they start taking matters into their own hands.

When he looks back to Rio, Rio knows the argument is over.

"Okay," Schweiger says. "I want us all mobile in five."

CHAPTER 59

Ajo, Arizona

"I HATE THE RAIN too," the woman Linnea tells Andi. "Long as I can remember. So many nights out in the rain, searching. Hoping." She leans against a wall, both hearing the rain fall on the other side. "Everything even smells different after a storm."

"It's called *petrichor*," Andi says. "The smell of rain itself. I once told my friend Bella that every raindrop is like a tiny thunderstorm—each one holding a lightning spark. She used to say it was just the desert coming alive."

"I like that thought, but I still don't like the rain." Linnea listens to it fall a little longer. "I want to say I'm sorry. Normally, you wouldn't be here like this."

"And this is normal for you?" Andi says.

"That's my point, I guess. I've worked a lot of serial cases." Leaving Andi to wonder just how many that could possibly be, how someone could turn this into a *job*, making a living out of so much death. "And there's nothing normal about any of them." Linnea walks over and picks up a museum brochure, glancing at it, before tossing it aside. "But it's easy to forget that, to lose sight of the forest for the trees, when you can't even find the forest."

"Will Luke live?"

Andi hasn't been able to see him or even speak to him; the Border Patrol transported him to Casa Grande even before she arrived with this woman and the others, and no one has bothered to update her on his condition.

But Linnea shrugs—doesn't even try to sugarcoat it, and in some ways, Andi appreciates that more. "Devine said he was hurt bad, but he put up a hell of a fight. That's something. We're lucky we got to him in time. Your daughter was lucky he was there."

Andi fights her tears. "And that's what this is . . . luck."

"Sometimes that's *all* it is." Linnea listens to the rain. "You know, we truly aren't so different."

"I doubt that."

"You've been . . . marked, special. From the moment you were struck by that lightning bolt. And I've always had a special gift too, for these kinds of cases."

"That's no fucking gift."

"Exactly," Linnea says. "I have a couple of daughters who've suffered for years because of me and this special thing I do. Because I've always believed it was important that I was special, maybe even more important than being a mother. Because I thought I was running around saving the world. Now I'm not so sure. But I don't know that I want to give up being special either."

"Then we're not alike at all. I never wanted this for me. I never wanted this for Ruby."

Linnea smiles, and when she does, it almost makes the scars around her eyes disappear. "Then you've been a better mother than me. You've always protected Ruby, first and foremost. I know that. I can see that."

Andi shakes her head. "You still don't know a thing about me."

"I know you've been strong, so strong, for you both. And I know I'm going to need you to be strong now too, strong as you've ever been. I need you to hold onto your anger, to the pain of losing her, because that pain will give you strength. But I also need to know *everything* about Ruby to help me find her. Because when we find her, I want you to be the first thing she sees. Trust me, you're going to be the first thing she wants to see."

Andi lets Linnea's words wash over her, lets the hurt, angry tears finally flow. "Do you believe she's still alive?"

"In most cases, no, but this isn't like most cases. This isn't *normal.* So I think she might be. It's very possible. It happened to me."

"What do you mean?"

"I was taken by a serial, Andi. One I was chasing, like the one who's stolen your daughter. Whatever else my abductor wanted, killing me wasn't the first thing, not even the main thing. He wanted me *alive*, as long as possible. He needed a special kind of witness and did something awful so I could never unsee the things he wanted to show me. And I think the monster who has Ruby now isn't so different. We may not understand, may never fully understand why he's doing these things any more than he does, but I also suspect this was never truly about you anyway. This has always been about *her.*"

Andi tenses, she doesn't like where this is going. "I don't know what you're talking about."

"Ruby." Linnea pushes off the wall and moves close to Andi. "I've now read hundreds of messages and emails and internet posts Tassa Linscott collected over the last two years about you and the Black Light Club, even some of Max Conroy's emails, and no doubt we'll discover that LTK is behind one or more of them. But if you really look close enough, a pattern emerges, a theme becomes abundantly clear. One theme again and again, Andi. You, and your daughter." Linnea puts a gentle hand on her shoulder. "This monster knows you . . . and he knows Ruby."

Andi wipes at her tears. She doesn't much like this woman with the scars around her eyes, and can't imagine she'll *ever* like her, but she doesn't need to. She needs this woman's help, and she might be the only person in the world who can.

This woman will do whatever it takes to bring Ruby back safe.

"I tried so hard to protect her," she tells Linnea. "Tried so hard to hide the truth."

But she pulls out her phone, the battery almost dead, like always. Just like Ruby's phone, like nearly every damn electronic device around them both.

"Ruby's always been special too," Andi confesses, as she finds those secret photos she's never shown Stephen or Bella or almost anyone else.

Photo after photo, seven of them.

Ruby at birth.

Then a single sequential shot of Ruby every year thereafter, the same pose, same harsh revealing light, revealing *everything.*

Only two other people in the world have seen these pictures.

But now she holds her phone out to Linnea and says through tears, "There's something you need to see."

CHAPTER

60 The Storm

HE HAD HER.

Almost had her when he burst through the door, his suffering almost at an end.

I am the storm season

But the man and dog slowed him down, fought him, and then he momentarily lost the lightning, before losing her altogether, when she ran into the dark.

Now it's getting hard for him to concentrate or to even think, the high-pressure system howling behind his eyes, crushing his brain. The storm overhead leaves him feeling so small, so infinitesimal, when he wants to feel infinite.

I am the storm season

Lightning flashes furiously above the barren desert and each pulse animates his heart, the way he imagines the girl finally feels it now too, as the seasons grow longer and she grows older, growing into her gift—her lightning trees and electric wings.

Each storm strengthens her, each season *empowers* her. But she's not infinite either, not yet. Right now, she's alone and caught in the storm, like him.

A scared little girl, lost in the rain.

He thinks he hears her scream out there in the dark, and that damn dog barking.

She can't go far, won't go far, not without her mother.

I am the storm season

I will take the lightning angel's wings

I am the light and the fury

CHAPTER

61

Ajo, Arizona

Rio admires Waylen's attitude and hopes he lives through all this, as Waylen stares him and Devine down and tells them both to go fuck themselves.

"I only want to go with Andi," Waylen says.

Devine smiles grimly, glances at Rio, then shrugs. "Fine, then don't go at all."

Waylen pushes. "Think you two can find your way around on your own?"

"No," Rio concedes. "But trust me, we'll try, with or without you. We want your help. We need it. But we're not negotiating."

"You gonna give me back my pistols?"

Rio says, "Yes. In fact, I was wondering if you might have a few more out there at your RV?"

"Registered?" Waylen asks.

Rio answers for them all. "Loaded."

Now it's Waylen turns to smile big. "Oh, yeah, I got just the thing."

CHAPTER

62

Ajo, Arizona

JUST BEFORE THEY head out, Andi stands in the doorway, safe from the rain, one last time.

She can't remember when she last willingly walked into a storm such as this, can't remember the last time she felt real rain on her face. It must've happened once or twice after that day in Virginia, but she's not sure.

Ruby's never been out in the rain.

When they flew back here from Tucson, Andi was trapped in the belly of that loud helicopter, barely able to talk or even think, wrapped in silence because of the rotors and the rumbling thunder all around, cocooned from the elements by inches of steel.

Safe.

But out in the desert there won't be anything to protect her at all. Just the wind, the rain, all that lightning.

She watches the forked bolts chase their tails across the black sky and tries not to shake.

Please let me do this, please let be as strong as that woman thinks I am.

She hasn't had a moment to process all her grief either, Stephen's death or Luke's injuries. Abandoning Bella back in Tucson, and

Ruby's disappearance. It's all too much and her heart might break if she lets it, but despite the anguish and the panic stampeding through her like a thousand black horses, she'll drown out there in that fucking storm before she lets that happen.

Instead, it's only her reverie that is broken by Rio and Linnea.

Rio approaches quietly, says, "Andi, we've split up into teams, to cover as much ground as possible. But we're just grid searching here, effective, methodical, yet slow. We don't know for sure that the man we're looking for is still in New Cornelia, what vehicle he may or may not be in, or even what landmarks or routes he might be familiar with. But Linnea told me that you game-planned scenarios if Max Conroy turned up or if you and Ruby ever got separated. So, if Ruby did get out of that trailer, got away, or later escaped, where might she go?"

Andi's not sure if he's doing this just to give her a small dose of hope, to distract her, or to merely make her feel like an important part of what's going on, but she appreciates it.

"There is a place," she says, "not far from our trailer."

Rio nods. "Waylen Burrows also mentioned that you know how to handle yourself." He doesn't need to explain to her what that means.

"Yes."

"Good," Rio replies, unholstering his gun and handing it to her. He also doesn't need to tell her it's already loaded, but she press checks it anyway before slipping it beneath her shirt.

Andi thought she caught a glimpse of something like angel wings tattooed on Rio's wrist.

Linnea hasn't said anything this whole time, not since Andi showed her Ruby's pictures, just watching it all unfold now with those wounded eyes of hers.

Something unspoken passes between Rio and Linnea, a fleeting glimpse, that Andi barely catches, but it's there all the same—

They're praying . . . they're praying.

Rio says to Andi, "Let's go find your little girl."

CHAPTER

63

Ajo, Arizona

THE SOLAR FARM's black panels suddenly loom large in the truck's lights, somehow both bigger and more sinister in the storm.

"There's a way to pass through up just a little bit more," Andi tells Agent Schweiger, who's driving, with Linnea in the back. They're all straining to make shapes out of the dark between the rain and wind, the lightning flashes. "You don't want to drive into those panels."

"Or that mine I saw on the map," Agent Schweiger adds. He's spoken to her only through gritted teeth, and although she doesn't understand the clearly tense dynamic between Rio and Linnea and this FBI agent, she suspects her presence here is one source of it. She wonders how much worse it'd be if Agent Schweiger knew Rio had armed her. "I'll circle around as much as I can. If your daughter's there, she should see the lights, she'll come to us," he says next.

"No, I don't think so," Andi says. "She won't until she sees me. *Me.*"

"Then let's make sure she does," Linnea says. "We get out, search every inch until we're satisfied."

Agent Schweiger says, "That's going to take time, Linnea."

But Linnea opens her door before Agent Schweiger even stops the truck, and she motions at Andi to do the same. "We'll be fast."

Schweiger grinds his teeth harder but doesn't protest. With the rain whipping through the open doors, Andi asks him the same question she put to Linnea, "How many people have you ever recovered alive, Agent Schweiger?"

He clenches the steering wheel as hard as he's been clenching his teeth, his eyes focused on his headlights, disappearing into the gloom. "You've shown yourself to be very resourceful, Andi. I assume your daughter learned that from you and is equally resourceful."

"That wasn't the question, and that's not an answer."

He nods. "I know."

"Listen, I hear something," Linnea cuts in. She cocks her head into the rain, and for a moment, it looks to Andi like the rain has washed away her scars "Does that sound like . . . *barking*?"

* * *

Of course, Andi forgot about Chili.

That silly, sweet dog.

All the stress, the grief, the fear. She didn't think to mention Luke's dog to anyone, and they didn't know enough to ask her about it. With all their attention on Ruby, no one had the opportunity to check her trailer or Luke's camper for signs of a pet.

If Chili's here, she'll be with Ruby . . . she must be.

She runs through the dark with Linnea and Agent Schweiger at her heels, ignoring the cutting rain in her face and her pounding heart, the flashing lightning overhead turning the whole world black and white, or even the agent's now drawn gun. He's ordering her to stop, slow down, but she ignores that too, ignores everything but the sound of that faint barking over the rumbling thunder.

Runs as fast as she can, because she's a runner, and always has been.

She runs headlong into the storm for her daughter.

CHAPTER 64

New Cornelia, Arizona

THEY'RE TWO MILES away from Waylen Burrows' trailer, loaded with enough guns to invade a small country, when Waylen spies something and tells them to *turn, turn, turn.*

Rio does.

Down a small road already turned to grasping, sticky clay.

The man Garcia back at the mission wasn't exaggerating—the desert's come alive, crisscrossed by small rivers that didn't exist a few hours ago, fat and swollen with rainwater, coiling like snakes. But Waylen's Silverado, strong enough to pull his massive RV, powers through it, throwing up wet sand like the prow of a ship cutting through waves, bright headlights fizzed with falling rain.

Lights that now reveal a camper van in a mess of aloe, ocotillo, and agave.

Devine starts, "Is that—"

"One of ours? New Cornelia?" Waylen finishes for him. "Nope. Not a chance. That wasn't here a week ago. Hell, that wasn't here *yesterday.*"

Without a word, Rio cuts all the lights and veers sharply right, angling through some prickly pear. If someone was looking out the van's window right at that moment, they should've already lost the Silverado's position.

"*Damn*," Waylen says, like he just won a scratch-off. "That's a Solis, just like I guessed."

"How many people fit in that thing?" Rio asks.

"Sleeps four," Waylen answers.

Devine asks Rio, "Think our guy's alone?"

The number of serial pairs across the decades was minimal, less than ten percent of all of them. Rio knows LTK's most likely alone, unless he has that little girl in there with him.

"Assume he isn't," Rio says.

"Okay. Man, it's deep-sea dark out here," Devine says, checking the load on the AR-15 he took from Waylen's makeshift armory. "Can't see shit, but hopefully they can't either."

"You move right, stay low," Rio says. "I'll go left."

"Meet at the front or the back?" Devine asks.

Rio considers their options, none of them good. The camper van is a black hole, no lights at all. In the rain, in the dark, it's all but invisible, except for the sporadic flashes of lightning, growing distant by the second.

The storm is growing stronger and Rio's not sure if that's a good thing or not.

"Front," he says. "You sweep the truck cab. I'll post at the door, test it. If it's locked, join me, and I'll breach."

"How?" Devine asks.

"Dynamically," Rio answers, shouldering the long gun he took from Waylen's RV. "But remember, there might be a little girl in there."

"Hey, what about me?" Waylen asks.

"Stay here," Rio orders. "If anyone comes back that doesn't look like either of us," he points to himself and to Devine, "shoot them."

"Until they stop moving," Devine adds.

"Yes," Rio says, "until the threat is clear. Until they're fucking *dead*."

CHAPTER

65

New Cornelia, Arizona

Andi finds Chili first, battered but alive, lying on her side beneath one of the solar panels.

But no Ruby.

No, no, no, no.

When the others finally catch up, she's cradling the dog. "Luke's dog, Chili," she tells them, struggling to get the words out in the wind. "She and Ruby were inseparable whenever Luke was around."

Linnea kneels and gently runs her hands over the wet, wounded animal. "She's hurt bad. Her fur's burnt, scorched, like Keats back at the trailer. Like all the others."

"LTK," Agent Schweiger says, breathing hard, standing over them, using a small flashlight to probe the rainswept darkness covering the solar farm. He's still got his gun up, tracking after the light.

"I found this too," Andi tells Linnea over the wind. "Wrapped around Chili's neck."

Andi's own fulgurite necklace.

"She thought it was magic," she tells Linnea, "maybe she left it for Chili to help her, to protect her."

Linnea grabs her hand, squeezes it. "Which means she was here, Andi. She was *here*, and very much alive."

"But now where?" Agent Schweiger asks over the wind. "Where the hell is she?"

CHAPTER

66

New Cornelia, Arizona

RIO LEARNED LATER Jon Parlor's barn in Ruther Glen was a reproduction of a Dutch barn, one of the oldest types of barns in America, and one of the rarest. Broad gabled roof, cathedral interior, mortised and tenoned and pegged beams, massive wooden columns, all space for a threshing room floor.

A pentice over the front door to protect against the weather.

And a hidden room where he found Linnea.

But he didn't know all that the night he approached it. Didn't know if she was inside, or even alive. All he knew was that he was going in there, going straight through the gates of Hell after her, if he had to.

And in some ways, he did.

* * *

The rain cuts like thorns on his skin.

Bites him like dark bats on the wing.

The storm may be receding, heading off west, but it still bears unimaginable force and power. Rio can barely see Devine, who sweeps the muzzle of the AR-15 across the windshield and driver's side window of the Solis camper van, before shaking his head and moving back to join him in a crouch. To the extent they can see anything at all, they're using silent hand signals, the same ones special forces operators have employed forever. Same ones he and Devine used together in another darkened desert, years ago, where they rescued two Marines from a downed helicopter near the Somali Sea.

Clenched fist. Fingers spread. A cutting motion, left to right.

This is the part of their old job that he could never fully explain even to Linnea, could never quite put into words at all, a part of himself he tried to lock up and hide until it was needed, a need that made him feel most alive, most useful. He always felt she was the real investigator, after all, the brains, the intellect, with that gift of hers and an unerring sense of right and wrong. She was the embodiment of law and order, of justice.

He was always . . . *vengeance.*

He knows she never felt that way, never treated him as anything other than her equal, but if he ended up being her shield, protecting her from the worst of the things they had to face, he was also her sword, always ready to draw blood.

He killed his first man when he was thirteen years old.

That's one of several reasons Rio made sure he and Schweiger weren't paired up. He dry-chewed two oxycodones in the back of the helicopter, and it's only pure adrenaline and the fading numbness of those pain meds that are keeping him upright and conscious now. But this is what he was born to do. First with the military, then with the FBI. It's who he is, who he's *always* been.

Like all the serials he's tracked—a killer too.

He puts his hand on the sliding panel door, as if he might feel something through it. Movement. Breathing. A heartbeat. It's cold to his touch, foreign. He pushes against it gently, and then slowly tests the handle.

It gives—and even over the storm, Rio hears an audible *click,* and then the panel door suddenly slides back on its own and Rio pushes inside, falls inside, Devine right on his six, the man's muzzle practically in his ribs.

The interior is just as dark, but there's an immediate smell. Pungent. Strong. Undeniable.

Blood.

Blood.

CHAPTER 67

Ajo, Arizona

It was a little more than a week ago that Andi was up here with Luke, staring out over that great hole in the ground, but it feels like forever now.

Before Bella's party and the haboob. Before Andi's trailer was trashed. Before Bella lay dying in the hospital. Before Stephen died and Luke was attacked.

Before Ruby was gone.

It was barely forty-eight hours ago that she was up here alone and found those three coyotes waiting for the sun to rise, that eerie shared moment, her last moment of peace before all hell broke loose. Now she's here again, the tail end of the rain tumbling down and all the thunder and lightning rolling overhead, her recovered fulgurite pendant wrapped around her hand—she can't, *won't*, let it go—as Agent Schweiger slowly pulls them into the overlook, headlights illuminating the empty lot.

She grips it tighter and tighter until that fraught bit of frozen lighting cuts her skin and draws blood. She focuses on that pain, uses it, just like Linnea Wren told her to.

Linnea understands pain, understands what it means to hurt, to *be* hurt, and if she and Andi find the man who took her daughter, Andi is going to hurt him too.

Badly.

She still doesn't know why she decided to bring them here, of all places, after warning Ruby again and again never to approach the mine. But maybe that's all she has now, an instinct, a premonition, a mother's intuition.

The one place her little girl is *not* supposed to be. The one place Ruby will think her momma will come looking for her.

They're just about to get out of the truck and approach the small red museum when Agent Schweiger's phone goes off. Cell reception has been shaky, at best, the whole time, but he's nevertheless been trying to reach the other teams consistently since the solar farm, angrily dialing and redialing, sending unread messages. Excited or relieved, he holds the phone up high now, trying to maximize the thready signal, and although Andi can't hear the call, her body clenches tight like a fist, both hoping and dreading and praying too that it's news about Ruby.

"They found the goddamn van," Agent Schweiger says aloud. "One of our probables." He glances at Linnea, who's in the back seat with Chili, a blanket thrown over the wounded dog. Linnea doesn't react. "A probable ID too." Andi hears something that almost sounds like victory in Agent Schweiger's voice, the thrill of the race almost won, only to watch his face go pale even in the dark. "It's . . . not good."

"Is it Ruby? Is it my little girl?"

"It's—" He regains his composure. "I'm sorry, Andi, we don't know. They don't know exactly *what* they have yet, but, son of a bitch, we know who he is now. At least we got that. His name is—"

"I already know who it is," Andi says. "I *know*. Now."

She's had her suspicions ever since she showed Linnea her daughter's photos.

But Andi doesn't care anymore because standing in the headlights is Ruby herself.

* * *

She appears out of the darkness tentatively, like she's not sure she believes the truck is real.

That Andi herself is real.

At this distance Andi can't tell if she's hurt or if she's alone; she's soddened and dirty as Chili—*please don't let that all be blood, please don't let that all be her blood*—and almost unrecognizable, but it's her little girl.

She almost glows in the glare thrown by the headlights.

Andi abandons the truck, and this time she draws the gun Rio gave her.

When she reaches Ruby, she throws her arms around her, pulling her close. She drinks her in and swallows her up. She's soaked through and through, shaking uncontrollably, but she still *smells* like Ruby, even in the rain. Now that Andi's holding her close, it's easy in the harsh headlights to smear away the mud or sand from her face and check her for bruises or cuts, to see how hurt she is, even though it's nearly impossible to see anything else. Andi laughs. Cries. "Oh, Ruby, oh, bumblebee. I'm so sorry, baby. So sorry."

Ruby says, "Momma, Momma, no, the monster—"

Then the StrikeAlert lightning detector still clipped to Ruby's waist goes off, just as something appears from behind the museum—a man, Ruby's monster—its hands, its whole body aglow. Or just something shining bright *in* his hands, some kind of device or contraption or gun, sparking and arcing, momentarily too incandescent to look at.

Like staring into the sun.

Andi pulls Ruby behind her, fumbling to raise the unfamiliar gun, to get a clean shot, but not before she takes the full brunt of the electric shock. The familiar current courses over her, around her, through her.

It hurts so fucking much—but not as much as the fear of losing her daughter.

Andi *shines.*

She *burns* . . .

. . . a black light, a black burning light like a dark, dying sun inside her heart.

Andi screams "*Ethan*, please, no!"

And for the second time in her life, Andi Ellis is struck dead by lightning.

CHAPTER 68

Ajo, Arizona

When LTK attacked Rio at Steins, Linnea barely had time to react.

It happened so fast, so surprisingly, and she suddenly felt so afraid again, so *helpless*—just like when Jon Parlor grabbed her. She never had a chance then.

She does now.

She bails out of the truck a heartbeat after Andi, gun drawn. Schweiger might be yelling at her, after her, but she doesn't hear him. She doesn't even bother to try.

Andi Ellis disappears in a flash of static and lightning, even brighter than the headlights, as Ruby Ellis falls to the wet ground, mostly shielded and hopefully saved by her mother.

Their attacker is all lit up, wreathed in electricity, ablaze in all his glory.

His hands glow white-hot, and Linnea can't imagine how he's not electrocuting himself in all the rain. But she moves forward anyway in a fast crouch, low and to his left, bearing down on him, aiming center mass, aiming for somewhere deep inside that bright, black-tinged corona, close to where his heart should be, just as Rio practiced with her again and again. But then, just like that, all that sparkling light around him flares out, replaced instead by a sudden darkness so deep, so impenetrable, she can't see a thing.

She loses her shot, too afraid she'll go wide or low, hit Andi or Ruby. Her hands are shaking, and despite all her time on a patrol beat and in Homicide and even when she was detailed to the FBI, she's never once fired her gun at another living person other than Jon Parlor. This is when Rio is supposed to appear at the last moment, to save her like he did before, to save Andi and Ruby.

Her night vision is squirrelly, everything the color of TV static, even with the truck headlights still gleaming behind her. But she thinks LTK is tracking away from her, back to her left, so she starts in that direction after him, hoping to cut him off, even as something hot and fast and furious buzzes past her ear, an angry insect, and she realizes almost too late it's a bullet.

Then another, and then another.

Another.

The truck windshield blasts out, as do the headlights, and then it *really* gets dark.

She's all but blind again, truly blind, but gets lower, still dodging unseen rounds, still moving forward, running up to the small red building, toward the mine, toward LTK.

Schweiger must be running now too. She hears shoes hitting the wet pavement, a staccato drumbeat following her, his voice calling out *Police, police, drop it, drop it.* Or maybe that's her voice, but either way, he doesn't have a better shot than her because he's not shooting at anything, although his gun is equipped with a laser sight and that bright red pencil beam swings wildly back and forth in front of her, as if Schweiger's signing his name in big cursive letters in the night sky. It helps her focus, helps her find her target. Schweiger calls out for her again, but she keeps moving and prays he keeps up.

There, there, *right up ahead*, right in front of her, she finally *sees*—

Something.

She barrels toward it until the ground gives way and she falls toward the mine.

CHAPTER

69

Ajo, Arizona

Rio and the others were already mobile and on their way back to Ajo by the time he finally got hold of Schweiger and told him what they found.

Close enough now to hear the rapid report of gunshots and shattering glass as they roll up to the mine lookout, Waylen directing the way.

Rio's out of the truck even before Devine brings it to a full stop, scanning over his long gun, running as fast as his wounds from Steins will allow, covering the last thirty yards on foot, where he hopes to find Schweiger, Andi, and Linnea.

Just like back at the camper van, Devine cuts the headlights so they're not backlit, leaving them in dark. But with the storm finally spent, the clouds overhead are little more than gossamer streamers, unraveled threads, and Rio can spot stars between them, so many stars, too many to count. He's only ever seen stars like that glowing in the skies over Pakistan, over Africa, whirling endlessly over the deck of a Navy destroyer at night in the South Pacific.

But that's not the only thing shining up here.

On the ground not far from a small red building there's a purplish glimmer, something faint, liminal, no more than candlelight, but visible all the same.

Mother, daughter, together.

Andi and Ruby Ellis.

Both . . . *shimmering* . . . wrapped in a gentle purple nimbus of their own making.

It's not real. Whatever he's seeing isn't possible, just a trick of the light, a trick of the night. He saw things in Parlor's bloody barn he didn't believe either, but the glowing little girl looks right up at him and says, "Please help my momma, please."

She's holding a gun in her hand.

And even that isn't about to stop Rio from running past the girl, to find Linnea, until Devine calls out to him, "I got Linnea and Schweiger, you help those two."

Rio hesitates, hearing echoes of the poem his mother told him . . .

Oh, only for so short a while you have loaned us to each other, because we take form in your act of drawing us, and we take life in your painting us, and we breathe in your singing us

But only for so short a while have you loaned us to each other

Because even a drawing cut in obsidian fades, and the green feathers, the crown feathers, of the Quetzal bird lose their color, and even the sounds of the waterfall die out in the dry season

So, we too, because only for a short while have you loaned us to each other

And then lays down his gun and gently takes the one from Ruby's hands, and kneels beside Andi to give her CPR, fighting to bring her back to life.

He holds his own breath, so he doesn't blow out the tender dark light around her.

CHAPTER

70

Ajo, Arizona

LINNEA DOESN'T DROP all the way into the trackless mine below, plunging only fifteen feet down to a canted shelf of loose rock and scree before tumbling to stop against a high-lipped ledge. But the fall does knock the wind out of her.

Knocks her gun free too—and it disappears into that huge hole.

She's struggling to stand again, to get her bearings back and her breath too, when LTK suddenly looms over her. Down here in the open mine's dark mouth it's still hard to tell much about him, still can't get a good look at his face, but he's wearing several thick layers of dark clothes, the outermost jacket rubbery and damp, reminiscent of wet tire tread, and he's got something heavy in his hands.

Something heavy *on* his hands, coils and wires wrapped all around his wrist and fingers, like weird gloves.

He's babbling now, about storms and rains and angels with lightning wings, but after all these years, she knows it's all gibberish, all nonsense. She can't, won't, let this man's demons possess her. She's got enough of her own.

Those weird makeshift implements of his spark with current, like the starter in her and Dan's gas fireplace, and she knows in another moment his hands are going to glow, electrify, *burn*, and he'll put those burning hands around her neck.

A red pencil beam plays over LTK's chest, searching, seeking. Schweiger fires from above and LTK ducks, dodges—although she's not sure Schweiger hit him, it's the tiny opening she needs.

She goes after LTK, clawing at him, pushing and shoving. She goes for his eyes, raking until she feels something soft and tender and irreplaceable give.

She smells something earthy and pungent—

The smell of rain itself . . . every raindrop is like a tiny thunderstorm . . . each one holding a lightning spark.

Everything washed clean—*alive*, and Linnea desperately wants to live.

LTK screams then, high, and horrible and inhuman, pinwheeling away from her, toward that rocky lip. He desperately grabs at her again, maybe hoping to drag her down with him or that she'll stop his fall, pull him back from that fatal precipice, but with his hands white-hot and blurry with homemade lightning, she doesn't think twice about it.

She kicks him away from her.

Sees him spiral over the edge, wreathed in his own white light.

He glows all the way down, fainter and fainter like a falling star, bouncing off ledges and jutting rocks until he hits the blue-black water far below.

* * *

Schweiger and Devine wordlessly help her clamber back up to the overlook, where she finds Rio and the rest of them, waiting.

Rio is kneeling next to Andi Ellis, who is sitting upright, coughing, and crying, her daughter clutched to her close.

The rain is gone for good and the world smells alive.

Rio goes to Linnea, pulls her to him. "I'm sorry I didn't get here fast enough."

"No, no, I'm okay. I'm good. You got here just in time."

He looks over to the yawning mine pit. "What happened down there?" he asks.

"It's over," is all she says. Then asks him, "What about up here?"

He looks back to Andi and Ruby Ellis, still holding each other tight, and whispers to her, "It's just beginning."

CHAPTER

71
The Storm

IN THE END, there are no lighting angel wings.

Nothing to hold him aloft, nothing to raise him up.

The rain does not rescue him, and the lightning only blinds and burns . . . again.

He falls out of the storm, out of the sky.

And keeps falling forever . . .

After the Rain

LINNEA AND ANDI sit outside together on a mesquite-shaded bench in front of a low-slung adobe building. It's sunny, hot, and pretty. The sky so smooth and clear and blue you can see for miles.

Both wear dark sunglasses.

Linnea carries Alice with her, closed on her lap. She says, "I have everything here if you want to see it. Everything we've uncovered, everything we know now."

Andi rubs a hand over the head of the bandaged dog at her feet. Chili's tucked in beneath her legs, seeking the shade as much as she can. Linnea knows the dog will never run again, but knows it will be cherished and cared for every day of its life. Andi asks, "What do I *need* to know?"

"Without an actual trial, not much. Even had he lived, the evidence inside his camper van was . . . overwhelming."

They found Abby Walden's beloved Taylor acoustic guitar inside that van, among other things.

"Waylen told me it was horrible."

"Let's call it definitive," Linnea says. "Ethan Charmas, as you already know."

Andi pats Chili again. "I knew him. I loved him, for a while."

Linnea says, "And he knew Ruby."

Andi shakes her head. "I thought he was in a coma or dead." She looks at Linnea. "I guess I didn't think enough about him at all. I was selfish, scared. I took Ruby and ran."

"His family wasn't truthful with us, or at least not fully. He came out of his coma more than a year ago—changed, again, like after he was first struck by lightning. They had money and resources, and he used both to disappear, to find you. I was able to track his cross-country movements and social media and internet searches, searches about the Black Light Club specifically, other lightning strike survivors generally, as well as the materials and plans and purchases he made to build that device of his, a supercharged, super-sized Taser."

"Is that what that was? Or just what you're calling it?"

"That's all my report says. We didn't recover it when he fell down the New Cornelia mine."

"You saw it though."

Linnea nods. "I saw . . . something . . . and that's all that matters."

Andi sighs. "So he was really looking for me and Ruby this whole time?"

"Yes. We've fit the puzzle together, mostly. But there are gaps, pieces still missing. There always are."

"That's normal," Andi says, with a bitter smile.

"Yes, normal." Linnea taps Alice. "But it's all here, his whole story, if you want to read it. Only if you want to know, want to understand."

"That's what you do, right? You find these horrible monsters and put them in jail or kill them, all while trying to figure out why they are the way are and why they do the things they do, and then all that crazy shit lives rent-free in your head."

"Something like that." She shrugs.

"No thanks, then," Andi says. "But does knowing, understanding, ever make it any easier? Make it better?"

"I used to think so, but now . . ." Linnea trails off. "Sometimes it seems there are so many Ethans out there, the world full of desperate wanderers unconnected from anything other than their own obsessions or grievances, strangers even to themselves. In your case, he got obsessed with Ruby—with *her* Lichtenberg figures, the 'lightning trees' she was supposedly born with and that never stopped growing." Linnea pauses, looks at Andi. "Only three people would have known about Ruby's lightning trees or had seen them. You, Max, and Ethan Charmas. Assuming it's even true."

Andi stays very still, sunlight playing off her sunglasses. "But that's impossible, right? No one can be *born* with those."

"Impossible," Linnea agrees. "Anyway, I never saw any marks like that on Ruby, and neither did Rio or Schweiger. And that's also in my report."

"Thank you," Andi says.

"But I do have one question."

"What's that?"

"Is Ruby really Max's daughter—or Ethan's?"

But just then, Ruby herself comes bounding out of the adobe building, leading Luke by the hand. Her hair is cut differently, and it's clear Andi is letting her grow it out, letting her grow into the young girl she already is.

Andi's fulgurite pendant swings from her neck.

Luke's arm is still in a sling, his face still bruised and scarred, some of which Linnea knows he'll carry for the rest of his life.

Like her. Like Andi.

Welcome to the club.

Andi speaks quietly, abruptly, voicing thoughts it was clear that she didn't want to have in her head, didn't want to have to live with. "Do you think Luke broke into my trailer to blame it on Max? Did he kill Stephen, make it look like some kind of accident? Did Ethan?"

Linnea looks at her. "I saw the arson report, Andi. Those tanks had a faulty connector, took a beating from the earlier haboob. I think you can put your mind to rest there. And as for your trailer? Sure, it's possible Ethan did an earlier foray, hunting for you and Ruby. But . . . you also know better than anyone—storms do funny things, impossible things." Linnea lets slip a knowing smile, and gives Luke a small wave. "Again, we never have all the pieces, never understand it all. But it's okay to believe Luke is simply a good guy who cares about you and your daughter very much. He saved Ruby, after all."

Now it's Linnea's turn to reach down and pet Chili. "His dog most certainly did." She gives the dog one final pat on the head. "And sometimes, Andi, in this work that I do, saving just one person is all we can hope for. One person is *enough*."

Ruby runs up with Luke in tow. "Momma, Auntie Bella is awake, asking for you."

Andi says, "I need to go. Thanks for this, for making the time."

"It's okay, I wanted to. I needed to." Linnea stands. "How is your friend Bella?"

"Hanging on, it's truly day by day now. She hates it here at this hospice, wants to be back out in that damn desert, but this is a good place. Quiet. Safe." Andi offers her a Biscoff cookie from a box she's been sitting with. "Casa de Luz—House of Light."

Linnea takes a cookie. "Saw on the news that it might rain later."

"Really?" Andi looks over to Ruby, to Luke. Smiles at them both. "I hadn't heard."

Linnea smiles too. "Good." And although Andi doesn't ask for it, she reaches out and hugs her and says to her, "When my partner first saw those Lichtenberg figures, he said they reminded him of something called Yggdrasil, the World Tree. It connects everything and everyone, the entire world."

Andi whispers to her, "Do you believe that?"

"I don't know. But it's a nice thought, I guess. Now I've got a plane to catch."

Andi holds her tight for a few more heartbeats, neither woman ready to let go, connected now and forever. "Heading home?"

But Linnea only smiles, hiding the scars around her eyes.

* * *

Dan watches from their kitchen window, as Lin and the girls circle the yard, talking.

Lin's been showing them that new necklace she came home with, some kind of mineral.

Now they're stopping at an old honey locust where they all once carved their initials, and with Lucy in particular, they look so much alike out there, same hair, same eyes. She and Lin even stand the same way, as Lucy runs her hands over the gnarled trunk, tracing her own letters.

It's surprising how much she's grown over the last year, even over the last month since Lin got home, getting almost as tall as her older sister and now Lin herself.

With their backs to him, both wrapped in similar hoodies, it's tough to tell them apart.

"I'm sorry to interrupt," Rio says from over his shoulder. "I'm sure it can wait."

Dan turns to see Rio there with a dark laptop bag and a thick padded envelope holding what he guesses are the early case files and witness statements and Linnea's new FBI credentials and badge. Probably a gun too. He knows Agent Schweiger called her yesterday, and although she didn't say anything to Dan, he knows she spoke briefly with Rio too, late last night.

She's not back on her full meds, but she is taking better care of herself. She's been good with the girls and with Dan. It's been a welcome respite for them all. But Dan's seen the media reports and he knows what's going on, even though Lin's been avoiding the news since she returned from out west.

They found three bodies in Wrangell-St. Elias National Park and Preserve, in Alaska.

But Rio's patient, decent, he'll stand there all day if he needs to.

I'm sure it can wait.

Dan only says, "No, I'm sure it can't—I'll go get her."

And then he heads outside to get his wife.

Acknowledgments

WITH THIS BOOK, lightning has now struck seven times . . .

As always, I need to thank my family and friends, as well as Michelle Richter at Fuse, Holly Frederick (and her team) at Curtis Brown, and everyone at Crooked Lane—specifically Sara Henry—who helped shape this book into the version you now hold. At times it felt like storm wrangling, but I'm proud of our work.

Books come from very different places, and while I can't always trace how a story falls into place for me, I can point to two disparate articles that sparked the idea that became *The Lightning Tree.* The first is "Allergic to Life: the Arizona Residents Sensitive to the Whole World," by Mae Ryan, from the *Guardian*. I first touched on the concept of electrosensitivity (electromagnet hypersensitivity) in my novel *Call the Dark* but knew I wanted to explore it further in New Cornelia, my fictionalized take on Snowflake. Fortunately, I had another real Arizona community to model New Cornelia on, and that was Ajo—my wife's historic hometown and a place I came to truly appreciate after she showed it to me through her eyes. I hope I've done it justice. The second article was "Inside the Hidden Society of Lightning Strike Survivors," by James Walker, also in the *Guardian*. This piece was one of several that afforded me insights into this little-known world, and if you're curious to learn more, I urge you to check out the website for Lightning Strike and Electrical Shock Survivors International (lightning-strike.org).

So, two articles five years apart led me to my own story about a mysterious lightning strike survivor and the scars—both physical and emotional—that still mark her. Hopefully, I've treated this fascinating phenomenon with dignity and respect, while also educating and entertaining.

Finally, this is my first published book after retiring from carrying a badge and gun for thirty years. I can now say I'm a "full-time author" and spend my days dreaming up stories like this one.

Thanks to all of you for helping make those kinds of dreams a reality.

See you next time . . . and stay out of the rain . . .

JTS